"HOW CAN YOU CLAIM TO KNOW ME?" HE DEMANDED. "WE'VE NEVER MET BEFORE."

"Of course we have not met," said the prisoner. "I have traveled far from my homeland, across the breadth of the Great Sea, following the vision of the Dreamer. I saw the vision with my own eyes. You possess the Words of Making."

"Your Dreamer is wrong. I've never heard of the Words of Making."

The prisoner made a scoffing sound. "The Dreamers are never wrong."

Gerin took a calming breath and drew magic into himself. The power filled him with warmth and vitality, made him temporarily forget his weariness. "Do not move," he said to the prisoner.

He was going to test the truth of the man's words . . .

D0824084

By David Forbes

The Osserian Saga

Book Two
THE WORDS OF MAKING

Book One
THE AMBER WIZARD

DAVID FORBES

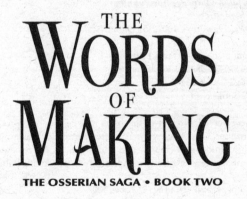

THE WORDS OF MAKING

THE OSSERIAN SAGA · BOOK TWO

An Imprint of HarperCollinsPublishers

This is a work of fiction. Names, characters, places, and incidents are products of the author's imagination or are used fictitiously and are not to be construed as real. Any resemblance to actual events, locales, organizations, or persons, living or dead, is entirely coincidental.

EOS
An Imprint of HarperCollins*Publishers*
10 East 53rd Street
New York, New York 10022-5299

Copyright © 2007 by David Forbes
ISBN: 978-0-06-082032-9
ISBN-10: 0-06-082032-2
www.eosbooks.com

First Eos paperback printing: October 2007

HarperCollins® and Eos® are registered trademarks of HarperCollins Publishers.

Printed in the U. S. A.

10 9 8 7 6 5 4 3 2 1

This one is for my mom.

Acknowledgments

I want to thank my agent, Matt Bialer, for his tireless work in making these books the best they could be. Trust me on this, it's wonderful for a writer to have an agent who really "gets" what he is trying to do. There were a number of suggested changes I originally balked at, thinking "Are you nuts? There's no way I can do that!" But, alas and dammit, after considering them I realized he was right and that they made the books better. I believe in the end I ended up making every single change he sent my way. So thanks, Matt!

My editor at HarperCollins, Diana Gill, deserves a load of thanks for helping me trim the fat from this volume and avoid, as much as possible, the problems and pitfalls that creep into second novels in large fantasy series. Those pitfalls that may remain (I will leave it to you to find them!) are entirely my fault.

Patrick St-Denis at Pat's Fantasy Hotlist (http://www.fantasyhotlist.blogspot.com), provided the first-ever review of *The Amber Wizard* and was kind enough to read the initial draft of *The Words of Making*. His comments are much appreciated and helped to improve what you hold in your hands.

A note for my mom, who was aghast at the number of horses

Acknowledgments

killed during the siege of Agdenor in the first volume: No animals, real or imaginary, were harmed in the making of this book. (I will remain silent on the matter of trees.)

And a final thank you to Lari Reed for her helpful and humorous comments about acknowledgments, for being cute, and (last but certainly not least) liking *Star Trek*!

THE
WORDS
OF
MAKING

Sontel

Girding Mountains

*Arlosan
Uplands*

Horon

*Kaldas
Highlands*

Farad

Soharel River

Ferondril R.

The Long Sea

Url-Azgish
(ruins)

Heart River

Irinil

Igrin Hills

Pellur

HELCAREA

Kirosi River

*Plains
of
Drommon*

Moriteri

Neiyes   *Mt. Kail*

Graymantle Mountains

*Nirovai
Deep*

Kalemnon

ELLOHAR

Withered Hills

Avelnur

Serel

*Gap of
Ellohar*

Redho

HUNZAR

Mendan Mountains

DOREL

Rhosa

Mespa

Samaro River

Tumlaren R.

*Gap of
Ellohar*

Ghesevaras

Sunde

Scale in miles

0   100   200   300

NEDDAR

David Forbes

OSSERIA

*Fourteenth Century
of the Common Age*

Uplands
of Eithos

Cape
Igaz

Hazi

Brendis
Bay

Tieren's Fence

MALAGAR

Bay of
Tassair

Theril River

Lingul

Faranwood

Darron

Failian River

KERYA

Muros

Maurelian Sea

Roumael River

Hallas
Bay

Strait of Sechel

HARLAD

Londros

Cape
Veilas

Marcarax

Saros R.

Brindal
Haro

Athram

Hanadi

Tappan R.

Landwall Mountains

TAGEREA

Pomman R.

Brangaran

Valesh Peninsula

ARMENOS

THRENDELLEN

Taldos

Turen

Winding R.

Trothmar

Gedsengard
Isle

Gulf
of
Gedsuel

Urkein

Candago R.

Cressan

Ailethon

Neldemarien

Almaris

The Seawall

Pelklar
Islands

Agdenor

KHEDESH

Tan
Orech

Edonia

Azren R.

Halir
Barellen

Lormenien

Orech R.

Tolthean

Indis R.

Istameth

Khedesh's March

Haranwaith

Orleth

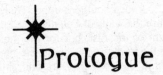

Prologue

March 22, Year 1306 of the Common Age

Lightning fractured the ink-black sky while a howling wind drove sheets of rain against the windows of Nellemar Atreyano's private chamber in the summit of the Seilheth Tower. Two hours earlier he'd had one of the servants pull back the heavy velvet drapes so he could watch the storm's approach from the west. The storm had slammed into Gedsengard Isle like a hammer a short time later, a fury of wind and rain, thunder and lightning, and raging sea. *Something has angered Paérendras,* he thought, slouched in a cushioned high-backed chair that faced the tall windows. It had been a long time since the sea god of Khedesh had shown such rage and wroth, and Nellemar was not one to miss the displays.

So much rain struck the rattling panes of glass that he could see nothing beyond the windows but flickering, ghostly smears of illumination as lightning licked across the sky—each flash followed by a room-shaking crack of thunder. The smoldering, dwindling light of the fire in the hearth cast only a sullen red glow, but he made no move to stoke the flames—he was warm enough, and more light would only make it harder to see outside.

The lightning flashes grew less frequent, and the rain lessened enough so that he could once again peer beyond the glass. If he leaned forward and strained his eyes, he could just make out the rim of Barresh Harbor far below Castle Cressan, and the wavering yellow light of the Fist upon Harrow's Rock beyond the harbor's southern edge. There were a few lights visible within the walls of Palendrell, even dimmer than the guide light of the Fist, but for the most part the town that encircled the harbor was completely black, its people shut safely behind the locked doors and shuttered windows of their stone houses.

Nellemar stretched and yawned. It was getting late, and it seemed the worst of the storm was passing. There would be little else for him to see, even perched as he was more than a thousand feet above the quays and piers of Palendrell, though he knew the dawn would reveal capsized boats, battered piers, broken masts, and splintered spars in the wake of the vicious storm.

He began the long spiraling descent through the Seilheth Tower, whose foundations lay in the bedrock at the top of the cliff that frowned down upon the harbor. The castle itself was built upon three separate shelves of rock cut into the cliff face, one above the other like the tiers of a layered cake. High walls with drum towers completely enclosed the buildings on each tier, as much to protect the castle inhabitants from accidental falls as to defend against invaders.

The circular wall of the stair had been lined with dark brick after being cut from the bedrock, and an iron handrail bolted through the brick into the hard stone behind it. Nellemar carried a lantern in one hand and gripped the rail with the other. The stair was steep and long, and he knew that a fall here could easily break his neck.

He allowed his mind to wander a little as he made his way down. He would be sailing for Almaris soon, for his niece Claressa's wedding to Baris Toresh of Tolthean. As the younger brother of King Abran, it was his duty to be present at the marriage of a princess of the realm. He was also Grand Admiral of the naval fleet of Khedesh and Warden of the Seas, charged with protecting the trade routes of the Gulf of Gedsuel from pirates and corsairs.

Nellemar at last reached the door at the end of the stairs, which he unlocked with a brass key. The stairs emptied onto a narrow gallery whose arcaded front overlooked the Twilight Hall. The largest room in the castle, the council chamber of the keep stretched eighty feet from end to end, with thirty-foot-high ceilings from which three chandeliers, hammered into the shape of sea anemones, dangled on chains. Set into the western wall were tall windows that gave a breathtaking view of the harbor and town below. On days when the skies were clear, the setting sun ignited a line of reflected fire on the waters of the gulf that pointed toward the heart of Barresh Harbor like the Harpoon of Paérendras. The eastern wall of the room was hewn from the rock of the cliff itself and had been left rough and unfinished.

He followed a curved staircase down from the gallery and crossed the hall to the windows for one last look outside. Lightning flashed and grumbled in the distance, connecting clouds and sea with jagged lances of luminance.

He'd been master of this rocky, windswept island for eighteen years, and in all that time had never failed to stop whatever he was doing to sit and look at the fury and majesty of Paérendras, the god of the sea and those who sailed upon it; and when the storms passed, he always prayed to the god and asked forgiveness for whatever offense had called his wrath upon them.

Nellemar now spoke his prayer quietly in the hall, and was about to turn away from the glass when something in the distance caught his eye.

There was a ship near the Fist, floundering in the sea as great waves crashed down upon its listing hull.

He placed his free hand against the cold glass, trying to make out details of the distant ship. The floundering vessel was a three-master with her sails furled and two banks of oars along her hull. It was enormous—far larger than any vessel in the harbor, including his flagship, the *Rising Dawn*.

His breath fogged the glass as another great wave slammed down upon the ship from the larboard side. The mainmast snapped as the ship rolled over, its deck now partially submerged. He could imagine the sound of taut ropes breaking and whipping madly about as the mast and spars tumbled into the cold, churning sea.

A door opened somewhere behind him and urgent footfalls rushed into the room. "My lord, there is a vessel—"

"Yes, I see it." Nellemar did not turn from the glass to face Tronus Foskail, the castellan of the castle. "Do we know whose it is?"

"No, my lord. It is a design I do not recognize."

Another huge wave crashed into the ship's keel, which had risen out of the water as its deck rolled into the sea. The force of the wave pushed the helpless ship closer to land, snapping another mast in the process.

The ship was near to Harrow's Rock and the light tower of the Fist that sat upon it. In calmer weather the light of the Fist guided vessels to the harbor at night and warned them away from the sheer-sided spire of black rock upon which it sat, but Nellemar could see that the partially capsized ship could no longer maneuver and would soon be driven to its destruction.

He turned from the window and faced Tronus. The old castellan clutched the open neck of his sleeping robe with his free hand and waited for the lord of the castle to issue his command.

"Assemble a company of soldiers," said Nellemar as he crossed the floor of the hall. "I'm going to see if there are any survivors."

Nellemar and twenty-five guards were soon descending the cobblestone road that wound its way from the lowest level of the castle to the narrow strip of land that separated the base of the cliff from the wall enclosing Palendrell. When they were about halfway down the road, one of the men stopped and pointed toward the sea. "My lord, look."

Nellemar glanced up—you did not descend this road in the dead of night after a fierce storm without watching where you put your feet—as another wave crashed into the keel, driving the ship across the submerged boulders that ringed

Harrow's Rock like a skirt. The wind had subsided and the rain had stopped, which allowed him to hear the distant retorts of the hull splintering. Two more waves converged on the vessel; the thudding impacts sent sprays of water high into the air.

The ship, now resting uneasily on the rocky shoals, had capsized completely, its deck having vanished beneath dark foamy water, lost from view. The last two masts had snapped off and were smashed to bits beneath the crushing weight. Another wave struck the vessel, then another, the ship surging forward, colliding with the sheer-sided base of Harrow's Rock with a roar as deep as a thunderclap. The side of the hull cracked further, pressed against the granite spike of rock with no way to relieve the stresses placed upon it. The inexorable push of the storm-swollen waves continued to pound the ship until the hull collapsed with a sudden, gut-felt boom.

The keel snapped and the ship broke into two parts. The stern and bow, now forcibly separated by the intervening bulk of Harrow's Rock, rolled across the shoals and disintegrated. Whatever cargo it had carried, and whatever crew manned it, were lost.

Nellemar clenched his jaw. "We'll still head down to see if any survivors make it ashore."

"My lord," said the ranking lieutenant, Olander Soron, "I think I see a longboat there, heading toward the beach."

The guard pointed at a black smudge against the dark water. It was difficult to see, and without the dim light provided by the Fist would have been impossible to make out at all. But Nellemar saw that the man was right—there was something in the water that looked like a boat, moving toward the beach to the south of the harbor.

His men reached the base of the cliff, where the road joined a causeway that crossed over the stretch of treacherous scree-covered land between the cliff and the town's wall. The causeway ended at the Salmon Gate, with a relief of its namesake fish set in the keystone above the arch.

The lieutenant thumped the heel of his hand against the

closed gate. "Open in the name of the duke!" he bellowed.

An eye-slit in the postern door slid open, then quickly closed. Nellemar heard the distinctive sound of metal bolts grinding back from their mortises as the door was unlocked. The postern swung open a moment later to reveal two men in hooded cloaks holding lanterns aloft. They stepped aside as Nellemar's men pushed their way past.

"My lord, I take it you are here about the ship," said one of the door wardens, a sallow-faced man with a mangy, sodden beard.

"Yes. We saw a longboat headed for the beach. Alert the Harbor Watch and have them look out for any survivors who may find their way here."

"I believe Harbormaster Pallan has already done that, but I'll relay your command to him, my lord."

Nellemar and his men set off through the rain-soaked streets toward the gate in the southern wall. The houses and buildings they passed were built of stone, three or four stories high, with narrow alleys between them that led to small enclosed courtyards. The roofs were sharply peaked and made mostly from red tile, though other colors were scattered about like patches sewn onto a vast red blanket. There was little timber on Gedsengard; its main exports were wool from the sheep that grazed on the highlands in the center of the isle, and a particularly fine white marble drawn from the mines and quarries along the island's eastern and southern reaches. What wood they had, both native to the island and brought in from the mainland, was used mostly for shipbuilding and repair.

The men made a turn and suddenly had a wide view of the harbor. Nellemar could see ships bobbing against their moorings as the storm swells washed through. The *Rising Dawn* was a dark silhouette on the far edge of the harbor, and he wondered what damage they would find when his men inspected her in the morning.

Men of the Harbor Watch were moving along the piers, carrying lanterns and calling out to one another as they scrutinized the choppy waters for signs of survivors. Harbormaster Pallan was a capable man; Nellemar did not doubt that the waterfront would be adequately safeguarded. He had no idea if the ship had been friend or foe, though he felt a foreboding in his heart that its intentions were hostile to Khedesh. He knew he had no reason to feel that way—there had been no indication on the ship itself of any ill intent, no corsair flags or other obvious signs of piracy—but that did not make the feeling go away.

They turned down another, wider road that ended a hundred feet ahead at the Gate of the Fisher King, a creature of legend said to dwell in the underwater caves that dotted the island's shores. A bas relief image of the king—part man and part fish, with squidlike tentacles for arms and a flowing beard of seaweed—stared down from the face of the gate.

Two more door wardens opened the postern so Nellemar and his men could leave. "Keep a close watch," he admonished the wardens. "We know nothing about the men coming ashore. Be ready to sound the alarm if they are our enemies."

"Yes, my lord."

Beyond the postern, the road made a gradual ramplike descent into the coarse sands of the beach, which lay beyond the rocky foundations upon which the walls had been built. The cliffs that girded the town curved in a half-moon shape that blocked the beach toward the south, where the stone intersected the sea.

Nellemar and his men trudged over cold wet sand. By the light of the Fist, they could faintly see the boat, which was rocking in the surf as several dark shapes dragged it from the water. The stone tower rose a hundred and fifty feet above the flattened top of Harrow's Rock, which itself spiked upward more than two hundred feet from the pounding surf. The summit of the Fist had been carved in the shape of a clenched hand, the light-housing in which the fire burned a glass-walled chamber shaped like a ring upon the Fist's giant forefinger.

"Be ready," Nellemar said as they neared the boat. His legs, already tired from the long descent from the Seilheth

Tower and the march through town, began to burn with fatigue as his boots pushed through the soggy, heavy sand.

"Hail!" he called out. "We saw your ship flounder. We've
come to escort you back to the town. Are any of you injured?"

A few paces farther, one of the guards ahead of Nellemar hissed and drew his sword from its scabbard. Nellemar
raised his head to get a clearer view of the longboat.

Surrounding the boat were monsters.

"What in the name of the deep *are* they?" asked Lieutenant Soron.

"I have no idea," said Nellemar. "Weapons." He drew his
sword, and his guards readied their own weapons. None
of them had bows, however; an oversight he now regretted
deeply.

Two men clambered out of the boat. One was obviously
injured, and would have collapsed without the support of his
companion.

A steady wind blew across the beach and tore a ragged
hole in the dark clouds, through which the cold light of the
moon shone, frosting the beach with silvery light. It gave
Nellemar and his men a much better look at the things that
had come out of the longboat.

They were tall and thin, with lean ropy muscles pulled taut
over long limbs. Their legs had two knees. The upper bent
back like a man's, while the lower bent forward and tapered
to an ankle just above widely splayed toes. This gave them a
strange, bobbing gait as they moved toward Nellemar and his
men. With each step they took, their heads thrust forward on
long, sinuous necks. Their eyes were black pools set beneath
bony ridges. Their chins tapered down to a sharp point, as did
the tops of their heads, which curved back over long skulls
to a bony peak resembling a scimitar blade. Thin, quill-like
spikes flared backward from the hinge of their jaws; Nellemar wondered if the tips were poisoned, like the spines of
certain fish.

One turned, and he saw a short, thick tail protruding from
the base of its back. The tail did not look flexible enough to
be used as a whiplike weapon, and it had no barb or spike

on its tip. *Probably helps them balance better,* he thought, gauging them with a soldier's eye. The creatures wore hauberks of mail with bits of plate at the chest and shoulders, and carried swords and pikes as weapons.

"Come no closer!" he shouted. "Lay down your weapons! You have invaded the sovereignty of Khedesh and will be shown no mercy if you do not immediately disarm and submit to my authority!"

The uninjured man lowered his companion to the sand, then straightened. He wore billowing pants of silk or some similar material tucked into calf-high boots. Instead of a cloak, he wore a knee-length coat of heavy brocaded wool with a high, stiff collar. His black and curly hair fell to his shoulders. The whiskers of his beard tapered to twin points below his chin like the prongs of a fork. A palm-sized medallion hung from a chain around his neck, and he wore several jeweled gold rings upon each hand. He did not carry a sword, only a short knife with a curved blade that dangled from his belt.

"Your threats mean nothing to me," he called out, speaking with a heavy accent that Nellemar did not recognize.

"Fail to heed me," Nellemar replied, "and you'll soon find your head spiked upon my walls."

The man snarled. *"Dothraq tan'shour luhj!"*

At this, the creatures threw back their heads and emitted a throaty, cawing sound, then propelled themselves toward the Khedeshians, kicking up plumes of sand from their long-nailed toes. They crouched so low as they ran that their torsos were almost parallel with the beach.

Nellemar's men spread out as they approached. Five of the guards arrayed themselves in front of Nellemar, standing shoulder-to-shoulder, their weapons held ready. Once again, Nellemar wished that they had bows.

One soldier hurled a dagger at the creature bearing down on him. The throw was deliberately low, aimed at the thing's exposed leg below the hauberk. Its crouched gait and the length of the hauberk made for a small target area, but the guard had aimed true and thrown well. The dagger's blade sank into the tough reddish skin just above the forward-bending knee, slipping between the bones. Blood sprayed out of the back of the leg where the tip of the dagger burst through. The thing shrieked and dropped its pike as its injured leg reflexively folded up toward its body. It lost its balance and slammed hard into the beach. The pike flew from its hands and stuck point first into the sand like a bannerless flagpole.

As the creature writhed on the ground, clawing at its leg to pull out the knife, the soldier stepped forward and severed its head.

Then the rest of the creatures were upon them. One soldier went down instantly with a pike through his chest and out his back. A second later another lost his sword arm below the elbow. As the man screamed and clutched at his severed limb, the creature brought its weapon about in a vicious swing and decapitated him.

Though Nellemar's men outnumbered their enemy more than two to one, the creatures' speed and longer reach was proving difficult for the Khedeshians to overcome. One of Nellemar's guards hacked through the leg of a creature from behind while it was engaged with another man, who then drove his sword up through its jaw and out the top of its head as it staggered. But other men were not faring so well, and Nellemar feared that despite their greater numbers, the fight could easily go against them.

"With me!" he said to the men protecting him as he dashed off.

Nellemar kept his gaze fixed on the boat and the two men near it. Once he skirted past the area of fighting, he charged the longboat with all the strength he had left in his legs. They felt dead and leaden as they churned in the wet sand, slowing his pace to what seemed a crawl—but he pressed on, forcing himself to move for the sake of his men.

The uninjured man at the longboat saw him approaching and shouted a command toward the creatures. Several of them turned, and two paid for the distraction with Khedeshian swords in their necks. Another backed away from the man it was fighting, spun about and dashed off to intercept Nellemar before he could reach the boat.

One of the Khedeshians picked up a pike that had been dropped by a creature and hurled it at the back of the thing racing toward the longboat. The pike was too heavy and unwieldy to make an effective spear, but it landed at an angle between the legs of the creature, which tripped over it and went down hard in the sand. The soldier ran at the thing and drove his sword down through its back before it could get up. The creature shuddered and twitched, then let out a ghastly shriek before it died.

Nellemar and his men were nearing the longboat when the uninjured foreigner whipped the knife from his belt with a quick, fluid motion and hurled it at them. The soldier running in front of Nellemar—his name, Rullo Astis, flashed through his mind—could not react quickly enough, and the knife caught him in the throat. Nellemar saw the point break through the back of his neck like the nose of an animal peeking out of its burrow. The soldier went suddenly rigid, then toppled forward and lay still.

The man at the longboat closed his eyes and held a clenched fist to his temple, while his other hand gripped the medallion hanging from his neck.

Later, Nellemar would reflect on that medallion, but at the moment, his mind went blank as he felt his blood chill, as if he'd been dropped into the frigid waters of the sea. The sensation took his breath away, his run faltering and his legs buckling beneath him. The men with him were affected as well, stumbling and clutching their hearts.

Nellemar forced himself to draw a deep breath when the corpse of Rullo Astis twitched and pushed itself up on its hands. The sight so shocked him that he could only stare, gape-mouthed, as the dead man rose to his feet.

His men shouted in dismay, and Nellemar turned to see the other dead Khedeshians also rising. One corpse had no head, which lay on the sand at its feet while it grasped awkwardly for a knife in its belt. Another corpse, whose left leg had been chopped off below the knee, dragged itself across the beach toward one of the living men. The corpse's face was devoid of any expression, its mouth hanging open stupidly, like the maw of a fish.

The sight stirred something in Nellemar, who snapped his own mouth shut and raised his sword. Some of his men, clearly unnerved, thrust their hands toward the corpses and made the sign to ward off evil.

Astis had turned to face him. Nellemar could see a dim green glow in the corpse's eyes, like moonlight shining through a film of sickness and disease. The knife hilt still protruded from his throat.

Behind him, one of the Khedeshian soldiers shrieked as a corpse drove its sword down through the top of his skull.

"Destroy the bodies!" shouted Nellemar. "Our brothers are dead! Their corpses are being used as weapons against us!"

He swung his blade two-handed and took off Astis's head, cutting through the neck just below the knife that had killed him. The head flew through the air and rolled across the sand. Nellemar was horrified to see that its eyes were still blinking and looking about.

Astis's body did not fall. Its hands groped blindly for Nellemar's throat, and he kicked it in the chest and sent it sprawling.

Meanwhile, he was aware that his men were fighting back. Several of the corpses had been hacked to pieces, which nevertheless continued to twitch with whatever foul power coursed through them. He noticed that the bodies of the dead monsters had not risen and wondered why that was so.

Thinking that the uninjured man at the longboat was working this foul magic, Nellemar charged toward him. The man did not try to flee, nor even take note of him. He seemed in a trance, his eyes rolling upward behind slit lids that revealed only bloodshot whites.

Nellemar raised his arms and smashed the pommel of his sword into the man's head just below his left ear. The man collapsed in a heap, and at the same time the corpses dropped like marionettes whose strings had been cut. The sepulchral light fled their eyes; the severed limbs ceased their twitching.

However, three of the monsters, though wounded, were

still alive. The soldiers, enraged by what they'd been forced to do to their dead friends, surrounded and quickly killed them, swarming over the bodies in their rage and hacking the creatures to bits.

When the carnage was over, a weary Nellemar turned to Lieutenant Soron. "Bind him," he said, gesturing to the foreigner he had struck, "and see if his companion still lives. We're taking them back to the castle."

It was a long, grueling trudge back to the castle. Harbormaster Pallan met them inside the Gate of the Fisher King and told them that no other survivors from the ship had been seen, though drowned bodies of men and ghastly creatures had begun to wash ashore. "I've never seen their like, my lord," said Pallan with a shake of his balding head.

"Nor have I, but be glad the ones you found were all drowned."

The injured foreigner died before they reached the castle—something heavy had crushed the back of his skull.

The other foreigner did not regain consciousness. Nellemar ordered that he be taken to the dungeons and kept in an isolated cell, then commanded that Tomares Rill, his Master, meet him in his salon.

Nellemar's wife, Omara, appeared in the corridor outside his salon in her nightdress and slippers, a heavy robe pulled tightly around her.

"I heard about the ship," she said. "Is it true that there were monsters aboard it? And that one of the men somehow raised the dead?"

He nodded, almost too tired to speak. It was an effort just to keep standing. *She has a network of ears and eyes that rivals the spymaster of the realm,* he thought, amazed—though after all this time, he knew he should not have been surprised at how quickly information found its way to her, even in the dead of night.

Omara was the daughter of Sedifren Houday, baron of Claitovel and the most powerful noble of Lormenien, who fancied himself nearly a king in his own right and lorded over his vassals as if he were indeed their sovereign ruler. Houday's arrogance was surpassed only by his ambition. Baron Houday had an enviable network of spies throughout the kingdom that he allowed his daughter to use. Nellemar was not supposed to be aware of this, but he had his own sources of information that his wife knew nothing about, some of whom kept watch on *her* and those she communicated with. Over the years, she had cultivated spies of her own—in addition to her father's, here on Gedsengard and elsewhere—who whispered to her in secret all that they saw or heard or read.

"I must see to this matter," he told her. "Go back to bed, Omara." He moved past her, toward the door to the salon, but she put her hand on his arm to stop him.

Her face twisted into an expression of loathing, a startling— and disturbing—transformation. It lasted only an instant before it vanished, like detritus swallowed by the sea. "Magic of some kind. Only something as *vile* as magic could—"

He pushed past her and opened the door. "I will speak to you in the morning. Good night."

He half expected her to barge into the salon and rant about magic's corruptive influence and how Prince Gerin, Nellemar's nephew and heir to his brother Abran's throne, should have been censured in the harshest terms possible after the Neddari War, in which a spirit unwittingly released by Gerin had goaded the Neddari into a conflict with Khedesh that killed thousands.

Omara could no longer speak about Gerin without erupting into a profound, violent rage. "He should never be allowed to sit upon the throne. No wizard should *ever* be king." She spat the words as if they were the harshest kind of curse. "And if your brother will not willingly do what is best for the kingdom and name Therain as his heir, then he should be forced to by the Assembly of Lords."

He made it a point not to argue with her when she was like this. Nellemar knew that his brothers Abran and Bennjan thought him weak for it, but that was not it at all. He simply did not bother wasting his breath on matters of no consequence. Omara despised her nephew's wizardry for reasons not entirely clear to him. Certainly the fact that Gerin would rule for hundreds of years was part of it, leaving no hope that any of Omara's children might, through some twist of fortune, rise to the Sapphire Throne—for he knew that her heart's desire, and that of her father, was to found a new Atreyano dynasty from their line. Nellemar did not believe that Gerin's wizardry would alter the chances that one of his sons would come to the throne, but he knew Omara did not see it that way.

However, that did not adequately explain the depth of her hatred for Gerin's powers. It had occurred to Nellemar that she herself might not know the true reason; maybe it just *was*, the way he hated cats and celery, for instance. Trying to convince him not to hate them was pointless—and anyone who tried to do so would just be wasting their time. Which was why he did not argue with Omara over things he considered of little consequence. What did it matter if she hated Gerin's wizardry? Especially when there was no hope of convincing her to change her views. The same reasoning kept him from trying to alter his brothers' opinions of him. They believed what they believed, and trying to change that was as futile as trying to talk the sun into not rising.

Nellemar sank wearily into the chair behind his desk, folded his hands across his chest, closed his eyes and lowered his head. He would just rest a little until Master Rill arrived . . .

He startled and came awake at a sharp rap on the door. He had no idea how long he had been asleep. Even if it had been hours, it was not nearly long enough. For a few seconds his body refused to move, ignoring his mind's command to lift his head and open his eyes. He tried again, willing his fingers to unlock and his hands to separate. They did not obey immediately, but after a second knock and the muffled words "My lord, are you in there?" coming through the heavy wood, he was able to stir and flutter his eyes open.

Straightening in the chair, Nellemar called out, "Come in!"

He propped his elbows on his writing table and rubbed his bleary eyes as Tomares Rill crossed the darkened room and bowed to him. Rill was a short, gaunt man with a hawklike nose, pockmarked cheeks, and a predilection for wearing high-necked white shirts beneath the large-sleeved robes of blue and gold that signified his membership in the Guild of Grael Physicians. The Graels were one of the orders located in the capital city of Almaris whose members were sent to the noble houses that could afford their services—paid in the form of a stipend to the member and a fellowship fee to the order itself—and that used them as teachers, counselors, healers, spymasters, and anything else the Graels' unique training and talents could provide.

Nellemar pushed back his chair and stood. He felt just as tired as before, if not more so, but could not rest just yet. "You will accompany me to the dungeons and assist in the interrogation of the prisoner," he told Tomares.

They left the salon and shortly reached a spiral stairway that descended to the lower levels of the castle. Before descending, Nellemar turned to Tomares and showed him the medallion and several other items that had been found on the prisoner.

"What do you make of these?" he asked.

Tomares examined a small statue carved from some dark, finely grained wood. No larger than a forefinger and sanded smooth and lacquered, it depicted a robed and hooded man holding a staff close by his side. Within the hood's cowl, the lower half of his face was covered by a veil.

Then he looked at the rings the man had worn—bands of gold inlaid with emeralds and rubies—some silver coins stamped with an unknown woman's face in profile, and a small leather-bound book written in a foreign tongue. An image of a hooded and veiled man similar to the small wooden statue had been embossed onto the book's cover.

"I do not know what to make of these," said Tomares as he paged through the book, shaking his head. "I don't recognize these characters. The language is utterly strange." He held up the silver. "These are obviously currency, yet of no kingdom in Osseria."

"What about the medallion? He was touching it very deliberately when he raised the bodies of the dead. Is it a device of magic?"

Tomares turned the medallion over several times, peering at it closely. He ran his finger around the decorative edge in which runic characters had been inscribed. On one side was a raised image of a mountain with rays shining from its summit; on the other, again the image of the hooded and veiled man holding his staff.

"I cannot say, my lord. It may have magical properties, but I have no means of detecting them. It may contain power of its own that this man draws upon. Or it may act as a doorway for him to obtain magic from some other source. It may have no magical use at all, and is merely an affectation he is attached to. A charm from his wife or king, perhaps. This is a question better suited to your nephew or the wizard training him. I'm sorry I cannot be more enlightening."

They proceeded to descend the spiral stair. At the bottom, they followed a narrow corridor to a heavy iron door flanked by two armed guards. Beyond the door, a short passage ended in a low-ceilinged staircase that descended to the dungeons themselves. Doors of black iron lined both sides of the corridor that stretched ahead of them for forty feet before ending abruptly in the raw bedrock of the cliff.

The gloom of the cells seemed to swallow the light of Nellemar's lamp as he and Tomares walked the length of the passage to the guards waiting at its end. Torches flickered and danced upon the wall.

"My lord," said Lieutenant Soron with a bow of his head.

"Is the prisoner awake?"

"He is, my lord."

The prisoner sat upon a narrow wooden bench bolted to the wall opposite the cell door. The bench also served as a bed, and was the only thing in the room other than a chamber pot. The man's long wool coat had been removed, exposing a scarlet shirt with intricate gold embroidery rising up the forearms like stylized flames. His hands were manacled together by a six-inch iron bar, which in turn was connected to the wall by a heavy chain.

Despite his predicament, he stared at Nellemar with a mingled expression of haughty arrogance and contempt. There was no fear or worry in his eyes. Then he grinned, a savage look exposing white teeth within the dark cloud of his beard. His skin was sun-darkened and weather-beaten, leathery like an old hide.

There was something about the shape of his face that was utterly foreign to Nellemar. He'd seen many peoples from all across Osseria: the Threndish with their narrow faces and heavy-lidded eyes; the thick, blunt-featured folk of Armenos and Tagerea; the dark-haired, pale-skinned people of Colanos and Harlad and Kerya, whose eyes had a peculiar almond shape that gave them an ethereal, otherworldly air; the thin-lipped, delicate features of the proud Helcareans; and others.

But this man looked like no one he'd ever before seen. There was nothing *obviously* dissimilar about him—the differences were subtle, almost below the threshold of Nellemar's awareness. The low hairline, thick bushy eyebrows, hooked nose, enormous dark eyes, high prominent cheekbones . . . none by themselves out of the ordinary. It was the unique combination of these features that was so strange, a mingling of various traits that Nellemar, to his shock and dismay, recognized for what they were.

Signs that this man had not come from Osseria.

"If he tries to make a spell, cut off one of his hands," Nellemar said to Soron. The lieutenant nodded, his hand tightening on his sword.

"I saw you raise and animate the bodies of my dead soldiers," Nellemar said to the prisoner. "Tell me how you did it."

The man leaned back against the bare stone wall and let his hands drop to his lap with a clanking of chains. "I defended myself using the Mysteries of Bariq the Wise."

Nellemar took the medallion from Tomares and held it up. "What is this? Is this how you use these Mysteries of yours? Is it magic?"

"I do not know the word 'magic,' so I cannot answer you. What you are defiling in your heathen hand is the Mark of

Bariq the Wise, the Veiled Power whose servant I am. You took his statue from me as well, and his holy book. The Mark is a symbol of my station, nothing more."

"How did you animate the bodies of my men? And why didn't your monsters rise as well?"

The man let out a snort of derision. "Your ignorance is deeper than I would have thought possible. A child of the Harridan knows more than you about the Mysteries of Bariq. I am surprised you know enough to put your boots on the proper feet. Perhaps your servants do that for you, yes?" He laughed contemptuously. "One of the powers granted to me as an Adept and Loremaster is that of *tar-fet*, new life that can be granted to the recent dead. I send a piece of my spirit into the dead flesh so it will do my bidding. But *tar-fet* is reserved for human flesh alone—it cannot be sullied in the body of a murdrendi, which has no soul."

"Who are you?" said Nellemar. "Where are you from, and why are you here?"

"My name is Vethiq aril Tolsadri, Voice of the Exalted, Adept of Bariq the Wise, Loremaster of the Mysteries, and First of the *Kaashal*. The country of my fathers is Aleith'aqtar, which in your tongue means Land of the Obedient. It lies far across the Great Sea, which my ship the *Kaashal* crossed before being dashed to bits in that accursed, Harridan-sent storm."

I was right! thought Nellemar. *He is not from Osseria. His face does not lie.*

"My lord, that is not possible," said Lieutenant Soron. "No ship has ever sailed across the Maurelian Sea. It is endless."

"You are as wrong as you are uncouth," the prisoner said. "Ships from your lands have indeed reached our shores without sinking in the perils of the crossing. They were taken, their crews assigned to the appropriate Power. It is a long, difficult voyage, but the sea is not endless. I have crossed it, as have others before me. How do you think I learned your heathen tongue? Our coming here has long been prepared. We know you do not worship the Powers, or even know of their existence, though that will change."

"Is that why you're here?" asked Nellemar. "To teach us to worship these Powers of yours?"

"No, that is not why we have come. But the Havalqa—for that is the name of my people, the Steadfast—bring the light of the Powers wherever they go, so that all people may find their proper place in the order of the world."

"I ask again, why have you come?"

"Answer the duke, or you will know pain such as you have never felt," said Lieutenant Soron.

"I do not fear your torture; you have less power over me than you believe, young whelp. But I will answer your questions. There is no harm in you knowing because there is nothing you can do to stop what is to come." Tolsadri shifted on the bench and straightened a little. Soron tensed at being called "young whelp," but kept his anger in check.

"We come because our sacred Dreamers have said the Great Enemy of the Powers will arise here, one who will threaten all of the world with his dark might. They have told the Exalted that the means to defeat him also lies in these heathen lands. My ship was but the first of a great fleet that will conquer your kingdoms in the name of the Powers. Make peace with whatever false gods you worship. Once the fleet reaches these shores, your way of life will end."

1

Three books floated above the table in the work chamber in Blackstone Keep, held aloft by a levitation spell Gerin had been practicing for the past hour. In his previous attempts, he'd moved the books no more than a foot or two before the spell collapsed upon itself. Sweat glistened on his forehead as he fought to keep the stack level; if the top two books slid off the lower one—which was the only one he was actually levitating, having slipped the spell's power beneath it like an invisible platter—they would fall to the table before he could create additional spells to hold them up.

Gods above me, this is hard!

Gerin gestured with his hand, and the books began to move toward him, wobbling through the air. He was seated at one end of the table; Hollin had placed the books at the other end. His task was to lift them and bring them to him across the table's length, a distance of about fifteen feet. The table itself was cluttered with all manner of objects: magefire lamps of varying heights and designs; stacks of books and scrolls; a flagon of water and two pewter mugs; a vase of withered flowers; loose pieces of paper and parchment; three maps of different areas of Khedesh; a half-eaten wheel of cheese; the remains of a loaf of black bread; a scattering of pens and inkwells; blotting cloths; and a small bust of Venegreh, the founder of Hethnost, the fortress where most of the few hundred wizards left in Osseria now lived.

His original plan had been to levitate the books above the height of the tallest objects on the table and bring them to him in a straight line, but to his great annoyance he discovered that the higher he tried to lift them, the more unstable they became. He'd dropped the stack six times before finally giving up on that course of action. He would have to navigate them through the treacherous obstacles on the tabletop from a height of less than ten inches.

The floating stack dipped and trembled as it threaded its way slowly across the table, like a drunken man walking in an overly careful manner. Gerin used his right hand to help him direct the books, pointing the way with his forefinger, though his hand movement had no real effect on his power—it simply helped him better envision the path the stack had to follow.

He managed to maneuver them about a third of the table's length before he lost control and the books fell upon the wheel of cheese.

"This is ridiculous," he said. "The spell just isn't stable enough to do what you want me to do."

"I doubted you'd be able to succeed," said Hollin. "Levitation spells are terribly difficult, and are rarely used. They're more for theory and practice. They have little practical application because of their limitations."

"Then why bother to have me learn them?"

Hollin folded his arms and gave Gerin a look.

"Oh, all right," said Gerin. He started counting off reasons on his fingers. "It helps me learn to concentrate; I should know as many spells as I can; it's always possible that spells that are hard for less powerful wizards will be easy for me. Is that enough, or should I continue?"

He was annoyed that levitation was so difficult as to be impractical. Yesterday, when Hollin told him that levitation would be the topic of study for today, he had gone to bed dreaming up all kinds of uses for such spells: hurling tens or hundreds of arrows at an enemy at one time without the need for bows, or the range limits that came with them—who knew how far a magically flung arrow could fly? Flinging knives or darts at multiple attackers; smashing a battering ram through an enemy's gate without the need to risk soldiers to man the ram; moving matériel and troops across rivers or gullies without the need for bridges or boats; even levitating *himself* to simulate flight in some fashion, though he deduced there must be some reason a wizard could not levitate himself, since he'd never seen or heard of such a thing being done.

He found out quickly enough that he had been right about that: Hollin told him at the start of their lesson that a wizard's magic could not be used to levitate the *source* of the magic, therefore a wizard could not levitate himself. As Hollin showed him some of the more basic levitation spells and answered his questions, the crown prince realized that his dream of using levitation as a weapon in warfare was impossible.

They'd talked about the theories of levitation and studied different spells for several hours before Gerin made his first attempt with the books. Because of other matters that needed Gerin's attention, they were unable to start until late in the day, the sun already setting, casting long rectangles of dusty light across the beamed ceiling.

"We're finished with this for now," said Hollin. "These spells are apparently as hard for you to invoke as they are for any other wizard."

When Hollin left, Gerin spent some time reading a volume of Atalari history sent to him by the Master Archivist of the Varsae Sandrova, the great library at Hethnost. He came across a passage describing the power-imbued armor the Atalari had worn into battle that shimmered with a rainbow iridescence. The description hit him powerfully, for he had seen that armor once in a vision atop the massive cliff called the Sundering.

The Atalari were the ancestors of wizards, beings of magic who had long ago ruled the northlands of Osseria and shunned contact with races who had no magic of their own. He had seen the Atalari during the height of their powers in a terrifying vision shown to him and his sister Reshel by a long-dead spirit named Teluko, once a prince of his people, the Eletheros. The vision had shown the final slaughter of the Eletheros at the hands of Atalari warriors; old men, women, and children had been mercilessly killed before Gerin's eyes. He still dreamed of a young boy and girl who fled in terror of the invaders swarming through their city, killing and raping and burning everything in their path. The boy had been murdered with a spear through his chest; the girl had jumped screaming from the cliff rather than face her brother's fate. The magnitude of what he'd seen—the extinction of an entire people, wiped from the face of the world because of an enemy's mindless hatred—still shocked and disturbed him. That slaughter had driven Teluko's older brother, Asankaru, a spirit who had assumed the guise of a Neddari god, to madness.

There was a knock at the door. Master Baelish Aslon entered, the old teacher of the castle, holding a small sealed scroll in a trembling hand. "This arrived a short time ago, my lord," he said as he shuffled across the room. "A message from your father."

Gerin stood and took the scroll from him. "Your tremors are getting worse, Master."

Aslon shrugged. "I am old, my lord. My body fails, and there is nothing to be done. Hollin tells me there is no spell of healing that can reverse the effects of aging." He smiled, exposing worn yellowed teeth. The old man was completely blind in his left eye, its pupil as white as milk. "At least I still have my wits about me. Or so they tell me. I suppose if they failed me I would not even know it. One small mercy, at least."

"Thank you, Master. Would you care to sit?"

"Oh, no, thank you, my lord. I have to get back to that whelp Tomma. He shows great promise, but I have to keep at him or I find him napping at all hours of the day instead of doing his chores. He's a bright young lad, though. I will send him to the Chapter House of Laonn soon to finish his training and take his vows."

Gerin broke the seal on the scroll and opened it. The mes-

sage had been written by one of his father's scribes—he recognized the narrow slanted scrawl of Tendrik Havenos—but
the words were unmistakably his father's; brief and cool, as
if he were communicating with an minor lord rather than his
son and heir. *Will he ever forgive me?* Gerin wondered as his
jaw clenched.

He read the message, his scowl deepening, then tossed it
onto the table in disgust.

"I take it the news is not good?" asked Hollin.

Gerin looked up to find that the wizard had returned to
the chamber. He gestured toward the message. "See for
yourself. The royal archivists have had no luck finding any
reference to the Chamber of the Moon and feel they've exhausted every possibility. My father has commanded them to
stop unless we can provide him with further 'illuminating'
information."

Hollin picked up the note and read it quickly. "This is not
terribly surprising. I know you think he's still angry with
you—"

"He *is* still angry with me."

"—but it doesn't mean that everything he does is a rebuke.
The archivists have made a long search without success. It's
prudent to have them stop until we can point them in some
other direction. I'm also disappointed that they haven't found
anything. I thought our best hope to learn more about the
Chamber of the Moon would be found in Almaris. Maybe it
still is. But we need to find something else for the archivists
to look for. Another name for it, a hint as to how Naragenth
hid it. Something more than just the name."

"Then the search is doomed. How in the name of the gods
can *we* find out more about it? That's what we want *them* to
do! If we could unearth more information, we wouldn't need
them."

Hollin sighed. "I know, it is a quandary. The archivists at
Hethnost are still searching. Perhaps they'll find something
that will help."

Gerin nodded but did not feel confident. For a year and a
half they'd been looking for knowledge about the Chamber

of the Moon. While training at Hethnost—and unknowingly under the compulsion of a Neddari sorcerer—Gerin had stolen forbidden black magic and used it to summon the spirit of Naragenth, once the king of Khedesh, and the only other amber wizard to have existed before the discovery of his own amber powers. Naragenth had lived eighteen hundred years ago, in a time when wizards were far more numerous and jealous of their power and status. He'd managed to gather the greatest wizards of his age in a conclave in which all of their knowledge was placed in a single location: the Varsae Estrikavis.

The Wars of Unification had begun soon after, plunging all of Osseria into a conflict that resulted in the birth of the Helcarean Empire. Naragenth and the other wizards had been killed during the war, and with them died the knowledge of how to find the library. Wizards had searched for it without success ever since.

Gerin had used the forbidden spells to summon Naragenth's spirit from the grave to ask him directly where he'd hidden the library. The spell—a difficult magic created by a long dead outlaw group of murderous wizards called the Baryashin Order—had never before been used, but Gerin managed to make it work. The ghost of Naragenth had appeared before him, and Gerin convinced him that he was indeed dead and no further purpose could be served by keeping the location of the library secret.

"The Varsae Estrikavis was hidden where no man could find it, in the Chamber of the Moon," the spirit had said.

"Where is the Chamber of the Moon?" said Gerin. *"I've never heard of it, not in all the accounts I've read of your library."*

"Of course you have never heard of it. The Chamber of the Moon was a great secret, and one of my greatest creations. It is not in Osseria. It can only be reached by—"

And then something had gone wrong with the spell, disrupting its power and returning Naragenth to the world of the dead before he could reveal his secret. Later, they learned that the spell had caused a catastrophic imbalance between the worlds of the living and the dead, so attempting to summon Naragenth a second time was not possible.

Naragenth's assertion that the Chamber of the Moon was "not in Osseria" had led Gerin to wonder if it had been hidden on one of the islands off the coast of Khedesh to better safeguard its contents. His uncle Nellemar controlled Gedsengard Isle, the largest of these islands, and after the end of the Neddari War, Gerin asked him to search for any evidence that Naragenth had hidden his library there. It did not take Nellemar long to explore and send him a message that he could find no trace that the old king had ever visited the island or built a secret library there.

There was another knock at the door. A servant entered and told them that Gerin's younger brother, Prince Therain, had just arrived at the castle.

Therain, the lord and master of Castle Agdenor, had borne the initial assault of the Neddari when they'd invaded Khedesh. They met him in the entry hall of the keep. Donael Rundgar, the hulking captain of Therain's personal guard, stood behind him with his arms crossed, searching the large room with his eyes, as if expecting assassins to emerge from the shadows. Rundgar was fiercely dedicated to Therain, to the point where anyone he did not know personally and intimately—including Gerin—was considered a potential threat. Gerin would not have been able to stand a man like that around him, but apparently the arrangement worked well enough for his brother.

"How was your journey?" Gerin asked as Therain shrugged off his cloak.

His brother made a dismissive gesture. "The same as always: dull. Hello, Hollin."

"Hello, Therain. You seem well."

"Good as ever. Have you been able to teach Gerin anything since I was here last? We both know how thick-headed and stubborn he is. Skull made of wood, kind of like this table."

"One or two things might have sunken in."

"I *was* going to ask if you wanted to join me and Balandrick for a trip into Padesh tomorrow to sample some ale," said

Gerin. "But if all you're going to do is insult me, your older and wiser brother, not to mention your lord and prince . . ." He stroked his chin thoughtfully. "That might be reason enough to toss you in the dungeons for a day or two. Treasonous insults directed toward a royal personage."

"I'm a royal personage, too."

"I outrank you."

"All right, all right, I recant. You're the most brilliant crown prince ever. A genius. A luminary among luminaries. A true—"

"Enough already. I think I like it better when you're acting like Claressa."

Therain scowled. "Now *that* was low."

Gerin, Therain, Balandrick, and four of Gerin's guards rode out of the castle the next day at the sounding of the noon bells. They followed the winding road down Ireon's Hill, then turned toward the town of Padesh. The road cut straight across an open field of grass before plunging into a small woods that cupped the southeastern edge of the town. The Padesh Road was well-traveled by merchants and farmers, who made sure the hard-packed dirt was kept clear and passable. There were a few scattered travelers on the road behind them, but for the most part they were alone.

The trees abruptly ended a few hundred feet from the town's ivy-covered wall. The road continued through the rocky field that separated the woods and the town, ending at one of the town's two gates. The single unmarked door in the wall was open and guarded by a lone watchman dozing on a stool. Men and women—some on foot, some on horseback, some driving wagons or hauling carts behind them—made their way into town, most heading for the market at the heart of Padesh. Only a few were heading out, a clutch of farmers lucky enough to have already sold their goods and eager to be on their way home.

A group of women emerged from the gate, lugging a two-wheeled cart. Gerin felt the blood drain from his face and reined his horse, Ranno, to a halt. Beside him, Balandrick muttered a curse.

"Are those women what I think they are?" asked Therain.

"Yes, my lord," said Balandrick through clenched teeth. "The Daughters of Reshel."

There were six women with the cart, all wearing drab gray robes with hoods pulled low over their faces. The cart itself had sides of slatted wood about a foot high. On the bed lay a body wrapped in linens, its hands folded across its chest. An old man followed behind the cart, leaning heavily on the arm of a younger man whom Gerin took to be his son.

"We have them at Agdenor as well," said Therain. "Their robes are brown, though, and they wear them with a red sash."

"I still don't know what to think of them," said Balandrick. His voice was anguished, and there was a pained, pinched look around his eyes. Balandrick had loved Reshel, Gerin's youngest sister; secretly at first, but later she had loved him as well. Despite the differences in their stations, they had even briefly contemplated marriage before her death atop the Sundering. "I've only seen them a few times, and it always makes me feel . . ." He shook his head, unable or unwilling to speak what was in his heart.

Therain reached out and squeezed Balandrick's shoulder. "They sprouted up like mushrooms after a long rain. Two groups were already working in the countryside around Agdenor when some women in the castle petitioned me for permission to join the order. Gods above me, I didn't even know there *was* an order until they showed up."

"What did you tell them?" Gerin asked. None of the Daughters of Reshel in his own duchy had asked his leave to become part of this budding order.

"I questioned them about what they planned to do, what their vows were, if they were serious about it, that kind of thing. And then said yes. I didn't think it would be a good idea to refuse women who wanted to pledge themselves to our sister. What does Father think about it?"

"I don't know," said Gerin. "We haven't spoken about them, and I haven't brought it up. Though I'm sure he's aware of them."

The women turned the cart onto a rutted path that swerved

off the main road and down a long rocky embankment toward the town's graveyard. The lichway was bordered with spirit posts—wooden poles on either side of the path carved with prayers to ward off evil spirits and hung with garlands of flowers.

"I doubt he approves," said Therain.

Gerin was momentarily overcome by guilt. The sight of the women sent a flood of memories rushing through him. He had failed his little sister, whom he had sworn to his father to keep from harm.

"Come on," said Gerin, spurring Ranno forward. "I'm thirsty."

He found himself stealing glances at the women as he approached the town. Balan was right: it was hard to know what to think of them. The Daughters of Reshel had first appeared a few months after Reshel's death. He had heard about them from Balandrick, who in turn learned of them from some of his men who'd been patrolling the Naevost Road and come across a group of the women taking a body to its grave.

Reshel Atreyano, Gerin's youngest sister, had sacrificed herself atop the Sundering to provide him the magic he needed to return the spirit Asankaru to the world of the dead. Had that not been accomplished, the imbalance between the worlds of the living and the dead might well have destroyed all life in Osseria. Many hundreds of people had died simply because the world of the dead had intersected *this* world, an occurrence that by its very nature was lethal to any living thing.

Reshel had killed herself so her people might live. Word of her sacrifice spread rapidly through the kingdom. Nobles and commoners alike whispered in awe of the royal daughter's courage and selflessness. The High Priest of the Temple in Almaris quickly declared her to be a saint of her people, naming February 19—the date of her death—as Saint Reshel's Day.

Since that day, Gerin had wondered if he could have done the same thing. Could he have made that ultimate sacrifice? He'd been prepared to die, but at Asankaru's hands, not his own.

The Daughters took vows to help the sick and prepare the bodies of the dead for burial. Their duties were similar to those of the Brothers of Twilight, though the Brothers were sworn to Bellon, while the Daughters had allegiance to no god that he was aware of. Gerin had been astounded when he learned of their existence. That his little sister—shy, quiet Reshel, a lover of books and learning—could inspire such devotion seemed inconceivable. He had yet to speak to any of the Daughters; the few times he'd seen them he shied away, reluctant to disturb them as they went about their solemn tasks. Perhaps he should change that, he thought as they passed into Padesh. Ask them why they dedicated their lives to this cause, and what about his sister's life so captivated them.

He realized that much, if not all, of the devotion of the Daughters came not from Reshel's life but from her death. And that was what disturbed and troubled him.

Part of him was pleased that she was being honored in such a way, that her sacrifice had gained an even greater meaning than it already had. But other aspects of the Daughters were not as pleasant. On the first anniversary of Reshel's death six of the Daughters in various parts of Khedesh had killed themselves by slitting their throats, the method Reshel had used to end her life. He had no desire to have his sister honored by a suicide cult, and was shocked and appalled. In fact, most of the Daughters served honorably and had been equally horrified by the suicides. He was told that since then, they did what they could to make sure that women who wanted to join were not doing so out of a misplaced desire to end their own lives and ascribe meaning to their deaths by linking them to Reshel's.

"When are we leaving for Almaris?" asked Therain. The men and women thronging Herren Street—the main avenue that ran from east to west through town—stopped to gawk at the royal brothers in their silk and linen finery passing by on horseback, surrounded by their well-armed and well-armored guards.

"A few days. I've been tarrying just to annoy her, but we'll need to be leaving soon or Claressa will be in real danger of missing her own wedding."

Therain laughed. "Can't have that, can we? If she doesn't get married, she'll be staying with you at Ailethon. Maybe forever."

Most of the houses and shops in Padesh were built of wood, two or three stories high, with thick thatch roofs. A few of the larger buildings, like the Shrine of Menpha and the mayor's house, were made of mortared fieldstone. The market lay at the center of town, where Herren Street and Padlet Street—the main north-south avenue—crossed one another.

Gerin was heading for the Red Vine, a tavern along Padlet Street just off the marketplace, a hard-packed dirt square filled with wagons, carts, stalls, and ladders from which merchants and farmers sold everything from bread, fruit, vegetables, cheese, and wine to rolls of wool, burlap, linen, and leather. Jugglers and acrobats tumbled in small open spaces crowded with onlookers; women stood upon stall roofs and ladders, their arms laden with bracelets and other baubles and trinkets. A pall of dust and smoke hung above the square, heavy with eye-watering smells, both good and bad.

"I feel nothing but pity for the man she's going to marry," said Therain. "Baris Toresh has no idea what he's in for."

"I met him when we were in Almaris for Father's coronation," said Gerin. "He melts into the scenery."

Therain whistled and shook his head. "She will eat him alive. Don't get me wrong, I love my dear twin sister with all my heart, but the thought of being married to someone like her is almost too much to bear."

"We could warn him, my lords," said Balandrick. "Help him make an escape. Give him some food and a map. It would be the decent thing to do."

"Or a mercy killing," said Therain. "Put the poor bastard out of his misery. He'd thank us for it if he knew Claressa the way we do."

"No, that would lead us back to Claressa staying with me, and we can't have that," said Gerin. "Poor Baris will just have to fend for himself."

Near the edge of the square, in the shadow of one of the taller houses, was a small wooden platform raised a few feet above the dirt. A man stood upon it, addressing a growing crowd of onlookers. There was nothing remarkable about the man's appearance. He was of average height and build, a little lean, perhaps, but certainly not starving. He wore a homespun tunic of brown wool over leggings and spoke passionately, moving back and forth across the creaking wood, his eyes darting across the crowd with a piercing gaze, his arms waving and jabbing to emphasize his words. His accent marked him as a man from the northern coastal regions of Khedesh.

"The One God is returning from His long absence to ensure that we follow the Chosen Path He has revealed to His servant the Prophet," said the man. His voice boomed from the platform, drawing more and more people to him. "Follow the Prophet! Hear his words! Open your eyes and your ears and your heart to him and he will teach you *dalar-aelom,* the Way of the Faith.

"Why should you follow the Prophet? Because there is a darkness coming! Heed my words! The One God returns now for a reason. The timing is no accident, no random chance. His Adversary is about to return, and if we do not all look to the One God for guidance, every corner of our world will fall under the shadow of His Enemy."

The Adversary! Gerin was stunned by the man's words. Before he'd become a wizard, he had felt a powerful divine presence in his rooms at Ailethon, and it touched him in an indescribable way. It spoke his name and said, *Your time is coming.*

A second visitation had occurred on the road to Hethnost. Gerin had seen a man that no one else had, sitting by the side of the road. The man claimed to be a messenger of the Maker and warned him that the Maker's Adversary was returning after a long absence from the world.

The messenger had also said, *Even a prophet may not fully understand what he is shown. Be mindful of what you are told.*

Now, in the marketplace square, Gerin called out to the man, "What is your name?" The crowd, seeing noblemen surrounded by guards and sensing trouble, melted away.

The man looked startled to have been spoken to. When he saw Gerin and realized he'd been addressed by someone of noble birth, he straightened and bowed his head. "My name, my lord, is Viros Tennor."

"And who is this Prophet?"

"The Prophet of the One God is Aunphar el'Turya, my lord. I am but one of his heralds, sent to proclaim his message."

"Your audience appears to have fled. I would hear more about this One God of yours."

Tennor did not hesitate. "Yes, my lord. I would be honored. I will tell you all that I can."

2

Therain shot Gerin a nasty look that Tennor could not see. His younger brother obviously didn't think talking to a stranger who was more than likely a religious fanatic would make for much fun, but Gerin didn't care. He considered this too important to ignore. He had to know more about this Prophet and what he was teaching.

Gerin felt the convergence of powerful forces at work. Not magic, at least in any capacity that he could grasp. It was not something he could fully describe, even to himself, but was convinced that this seemingly chance meeting with Viros Tennor had not been chance at all. He felt a vague sense of manipulation, as if he were a pawn being shuffled across a board he could not see, toward goals he did not understand. The old indignation that he'd felt after the first appearance of the divine entity kindled within him.

Tennor's eyes widened when Gerin revealed his name. "My lord, again I am honored. I only hope I may do justice to the words of the Prophet."

"So, tell me," said Gerin, "who is this Prophet?"

"As I said, my lord, his name is Aunphar el'Turya. He—"

"I heard you the first time. I remember his name. I want to know who he *is*. Why does he believe what he does?"

Tennor swallowed audibly. "Of course, my lord. I apologize.

"The Prophet was once a priest of the Temple in Almaris,

a man of great distinction and honor. But he had an encounter with the One God Himself, who commanded him to be His Prophet and prepare the world for the coming of the Adversary."

"Is this One God of yours Telros?" asked Balandrick.

"No. The One God is not a part of the pantheon of Khedesh."

"I don't see why we need another god," said Balandrick.

"The One God is the father of *all* other gods, whether of Khedesh or Threndellen or Helcarea. It is He who created the world and all things contained within it, including our gods and the gods of other lands."

"What is the name of this One God?" asked Therain.

"He has not yet revealed it. When His herald spoke to the Prophet, he called the One God the Maker, but in a later dream the Prophet saw a vision of light in which the One God spoke to him and proclaimed Himself to be One God above all other gods and men."

The herald, thought Gerin, shocked again by Tennor's account. He wondered if that could be the same messenger who had appeared to him. He had asked the being who claimed to be a messenger of the Maker what the Maker's name was and was told that it was not for him or any man to know. "Did this herald have a name?" he asked.

"Not that was given to the Prophet."

"Where can I find the Prophet?" Gerin asked. "I'll be in Almaris soon for my sister's wedding."

Tennor looked surprised. "My lord? You wish to speak with him?"

"Yes. Is that a problem?"

"No, my lord, of course not. The Prophet's home is in Arghest, at the end of the Street of Poplars."

"Do you know your letters? I would like you to write a letter of introduction to the Prophet if you are capable."

"Yes, my lord, I can write. A person of your station needs no letter from me in order to see the Prophet, but I will be pleased to write one for you. I have no paper here. I can—"

"That is no matter." Gerin tossed him a silver dera, told

him to purchase what he needed and then bring the finished letter to Ailethon.

"I will do as you ask, my lord."

"See that you do. Good day, Viros Tennor."

They left him and continued toward the Red Vine. Therain made a sound of disgust. "There are emissaries of the Prophet everywhere around Agdenor. They're like cockroaches scurrying about. But *everyone* seems to be listening to them! I don't understand why people think we need another god."

"This has something to do with those visits you had," said Balandrick. "You saw something on the road to Hethnost that no one else did. Something divine."

"You don't think this One God of his is what appeared to you, do you?" said Therain.

"I don't know. What the messenger of the Maker said to me and what the herald of the One God said to this Prophet are almost identical. I'm going to see the Prophet when we get to Almaris and hear what he has to say. Maybe he can help me understand exactly *why* this being appeared to me and what it wants."

They reached the inn and changed the subject to more mundane things. Their father had hinted that Therain would be betrothed to Laysa Oldann not long after Claressa's wedding—an announcement might even be made while they were in Almaris. They pointedly avoided discussing when Gerin might wed, and whom. He and his father had clashed about it several times over the past few years.

Gerin had met only a fraction of the eligible noblewomen the kingdom had to offer—none of whom particularly appealed to him, or offered the kind of strategic union his father desired—which was why Abran, in the bustling royal court of Almaris, felt better able to make the choice for him. But Gerin chafed at that thought. Meanwhile, it was becoming a scandal that the heir to the throne was still unwed at twenty-four years of age.

And then there was his wizardry. Gerin feared how it would affect his marriage, worried that the long life of a wizard would doom any union almost before it began—he would live for centuries, after all, and his wife and children would not. How could anyone endure such a marriage? How could he watch his children grow old and die while he looked no different than he did today? He knew that other wizards had married Gendalos—the "short-lived," a term given to nonwizards in ages past—but he also knew that those unions often ended in sadness and regret.

He'd spoken to no one of this secret dread. Not to Hollin or his father, Balandrick or Therain. He knew that Hollin would understand, but the others would just scoff and think him a ninny-hammered fool. And even Hollin would tell him there was nothing to be done. As the crown prince he *had* to marry; it was a duty he might delay but could not refuse. Since there were no female wizards among the nobility of Khedesh, it was all but certain he would marry a Gendalos.

Marry her and leave her behind. Even if she lived to a grand old age, he would still face centuries of life after her death. The thought left him awash in a profound sadness for reasons he could not fully articulate. He'd not yet even met the woman he wanted to marry, but a part of him was already gloomy about her death, already grieving. He shook his head. *Maybe I am a ninny-hammered fool,* he thought.

They left the inn a few hours later and made their way back to the castle. "Do you still have pilgrims coming to visit her tomb?" asked Therain as they neared the foot of Ireon's Hill.

Therain did not have to explain what he meant; Gerin knew quite well. Not long after Reshel was laid to rest in the Atreyano crypt that lay beneath the castle, pilgrims had arrived to pay their respects to the fallen royal daughter. At first Gerin had agreed to allow small groups to visit the tomb, under close supervision by the castle guards. But over time, more and more pilgrims arrived; some even managed to chip away small pieces of the marble to take as keepsakes and mementos. At that point he'd cut off access to the castle for all pilgrims. He would not tolerate such ghoulish vandalism, and he worried that allowing so many outsiders into the castle would grow into a security problem.

"They still come, yes," he said. "We built a monument for her on the northwestern foot of the hill, by the pond. Any pilgrim who comes to the castle is directed there."

The monument was a white-marble statue of Reshel, her hands folded, her eyes downcast and sorrowful. It stood upon a pedestal upon which had been inscribed the words that also graced her crypt: RESHEL ATREYANO, BELOVED DAUGHTER, WHO DIED THAT HER PEOPLE MIGHT LIVE.

Much later that night, Gerin lay in his bed, weary but unable to sleep. The words of Viros Tennor spun through his head. Once more he felt as if he were being drawn into a confluence of forces too large for him to see or understand, that his meeting with Tennor had been not chance but part of a scheme designed to set him upon one particular path and no other. He feared that every decision he made would send him further down that blind road. It felt much like the compulsion of the Neddari, which had driven him inexorably to the fateful release of Asankaru. What Tennor had told him reduced his choices, limited his options: he *had* to see the Prophet now. He could not visit Almaris without speaking to the only other man who'd had an encounter similar to his own. Mysterious events had been dormant in his mind, nearly forgotten for two years, and now he might finally find some answers about them.

But would he like the answers he found? Or would they just make everything worse?

3

They left for Almaris late in the morning two days later, a massive caravan of soldiers, servants, wagons, cattle, sheep, and horses. Claressa rode between Gerin and Therain near the head of the caravan, looking every part the princess—head held high, a silver circlet in her hair, clothing immaculate, calfskin gloves spotless, riding cloak draped down her back and across the haunches of her chestnut mare, Thela. It seemed she was posing for a portrait rather than clomping down Ireon's Hill toward the Padesh Road.

Give her a few days of travel, thought Gerin. *She'll look as worn as the rest of us.* He knew, though, that his sister had an uncanny way of retaining her regal, dignified bearing even in the worst of circumstances. There was something undeniably majestic about Claressa. Even if she were thrown head first into a peat bog, she would find some way to emerge in a distinguished and stately manner. Many people found her cold, haughty, aloof, and arrogant—Balandrick, truth be told, could barely stand to be in her presence—and she was indeed all of those things at times, as Gerin well knew. But she was also smart and strong-willed, perhaps the strongest willed of all the Atreyano children. And that was saying a lot. He wondered if her marriage would soften some of her hard edges, or harden them into permanence.

"Nervous?" Therain asked her.

"About getting married? Goodness, no. I'm looking forward

to it. A new life, a new place to live . . ." She threw a long glance over her shoulder, up the hill at Ailethon's high walls. "But I'm sad to be leaving. It's strange to think that I may never come back again. I've lived in this place my entire life."

"I'm sure you'll adjust," said Therain.

"Of course I will. I'm certainly not the first woman to leave her home for marriage. Women adapt, as easily as men. More easily with some things."

Therain rolled his eyes. "I was just trying to help."

Gerin once more felt a deep wave of pity for Baris Toresh, Claressa's husband-to-be. But in his heart he realized it would be strange for him not to have Claressa around. One by one his family had left Ailethon—and him—behind: first his father, off to Almaris to become king; then Therain, sent to take control of Agdenor from a troublesome lord only months before the Neddari invasion sent all of their lives reeling; Reshel dying atop the Sundering; and now Claressa. *There's no one left to leave me,* he thought. Balandrick would remain as the captain of the castle guard as long as he lived—Gerin had no doubt of that. In his way, Balandrick was as loyal to him as Donael Rundgar was to Therain. But Balandrick was not family; he was a servant and a friend—the closest friend he had ever had—yet it was not the same thing as a family of one's own. He wondered how keenly he would miss that in the weeks and months to come.

The caravan crossed the Kilnathé River on the Leidhegar Bridge and entered Ossland. King Olam's Road was wide and paved, the result of Helca's massive road-building efforts in the early years of his empire. There had been a road linking Ailethon to Almaris before the Helcareans conquered Khedesh, but according to the histories, it was little more than twin ruts in the dirt. Helca's roads were designed to allow his armies to move quickly, without getting bogged down in mud. It was a testament to the prowess of his engineers that so many of his roads were still used throughout Osseria.

After seventeen days of leisurely travel they reached the Whispering Wood, a small but dense forest that sprouted

from the flatlands a few miles west of the city. Beyond the
abrupt eastern edge of the woods began the Ardanne Plain,
a verdant stretch of low grassland reaching all the way to
the Almarean Plateau. In the distance, Gerin could just
make out the highest towers of the Temple of Telros and
the Tirthaig—the royal palace from which he would one
day rule—poking above the horizon, shining brightly in
the westering sunlight like spear points just pulled from a
hot forge. A steady wind blowing from the east carried the
salty tang of the sea.

As the plain neared the coast it swept upward into the
rocky promontory of the Almarean Plateau, from which
two long headlands projected eastward. They bent slightly
toward one another at their tips, like a forefinger and thumb
coming together. The deep-water harbor formed by the
headlands was called the Cleave, whose mouth opened to
the Gulf of Gedsuel. Almaris was built upon the plateau,
just north of the mouth of the Samaro River.

At the juncture of the plain and plateau was Nyvene's
Wall, which also went by the more popular name of Traitor's Fence. It was more scaffolding than wall: wooden poles
sunken deep into the soil, with cross beams hammered between them, so that the entire structure looked like some
nightmarish tangle of mast and spar rising a dozen feet
into the air. But these beams held no rigging or sails; the
wood of Nyvene's Wall was soaked in the blood of those
who had betrayed the realm. This was a place of execution.
Those condemned for treason were dragged to the wall by
black chargers and hoisted up on a gibbet, where they were
slowly choked with nooses—no quickly broken necks for
these men. They were cut down before they were dead,
then disemboweled by Black Willem, the traditional name
of the city's executioner. The condemned watched in horror as their entrails spilled out of their slit-open abdomens.
They were then beheaded and their limbs cut from their
bodies by Black Willem or men in his service, depending
on how many were to be put to death on any given Hanging
Day. Their severed heads were rammed onto shoulder-high
spikes placed in front of the wall, while their limbs and

entrails were nailed to the cross beams, where they stayed until only bones remained.

The bodies of five men currently graced the wall, spies who'd tried to sell secrets to the Threndish, according to the painted sign nailed up beside a severed leg. A scattering of bones littered the grass like dice that had been rolled and never picked up. Black carrion crows cawed from perches atop the wall and pecked at the rotting flesh. The stench was terrible: a thick, pungent odor of decay that infused the air in stubborn defiance of the ocean breeze. Claressa made a disgusted sound in her throat and covered her mouth and nose with one gloved hand.

"This is such an awful place," she muttered. "I hate it. It's so . . . offensive."

"You're *offended* by the corpses of traitors?" asked Therain. "I think you should view them with the contempt and hatred they deserve."

Claressa rolled her eyes. "You misunderstand everything I say. I'm offended that these criminals were stupid enough to commit crimes for which the penalty to *them* also serves to punish *me* by having to smell the stink of their corpses."

"Therain, you forgot the most important rule in our dear sister's life," said Gerin. "And that is that *everything* is about *her.*"

Off to the south he could see the wide sweep of the Samaro River. Between the river and the southern walls of the city lay a stretch of land called the Verge, a slope that transitioned from stone freckled with sprouts of hardscrabble grass to its exact opposite, a swath of greensward with bits of rock poking through. There was once a thick woods upon the Verge, but most of the trees had been cut down long ago to build a sprawling town called Gorlund, which huddled close to the Samaro's bank. The wooden buildings seemed in perpetual danger of losing their footholds and sliding down the slope and into the river's deep and sluggish current. Gorlund was where goods were offloaded from ships and barges coming down the Samaro from deeper in Khedesh, to be shipped up to the city proper.

Word had gone ahead that the king's family was approaching, so when they passed through the long tunnel beneath the Okoro Gate in the city's western wall, they were greeted by a cheering crowd thronging the side of the road and the nearby rooftops. Gerin waved from his horse, though his escort kept the people from approaching too close. The crowd parted before them as they proceeded down the Nathrad Road, the longest avenue in the city.

The buildings in this part of Almaris were made of stone quarried in northern Lormenien and brought to the city on barges floated down the Samaro River. Most of the structures were three or four stories high with flat roofs, separated by narrow alleys. Strung between many of the rooftops were lengths of rope and narrow wooden planks that allowed for quick passage around the city for those inclined to avoid the great press of people, horses, carts, wagons, and assorted animals that constantly jammed the streets. Of course, the roof roads, as they were called, were also used by thieves and other criminals, which in turn led to the regular patrols of the City Watch upon the roofs. Occasionally, some of the wooden gangways were torn down to hamper illegal activity, and once in a while, for good measure, suspicious characters were tossed to their deaths in the street below.

Gerin's entourage followed the road to the Azure Gate in the wall that surrounded the Old City, the ancient heart of Almaris. The Old City had once been a holy place of the Pashti, a citadel and pilgrimage site called Gal-Tendur, which had endured for thousands of years before the arrival of Khedesh and his warrior Raimen in the Dawn Age. The citadel and small city around it had been razed by Khedesh's son Alhared after a violent uprising by the Pashti, who were then driven from the region and forbidden to resettle there. Not until the time of Khedesh's grandson Selhouin were the foundations of the Old City of Almaris first set down on the ruins of Gal-Tendur.

Gerin wondered what the Pashti must have felt as they watched their sacred city burn, knowing they could never return to rebuild what was lost. How would he feel watching the Tirthaig burn, or the Temple of Telros, or Ailethon itself? It was not his place to question what Alhared had done—after all, the Pashti had risen against him. Still, as he passed through the Azure Gate his imagination would not let go of the images of Gal-Tendur consumed by fire.

Beyond the gate the road narrowed considerably, crowded on either side by tall buildings of stone and wood that cantilevered over the cobblestone street, creating a canopy over the travelers below. Though it was still officially known as the Nathrad Road, beyond the Azure Gate it was more often than not called the Needle by those who lived there, for a man standing at the end of the road and gazing toward the other would have the impression of looking through a giant thread hole.

Whether one chose to call it Nathrad or Needle, the road continued straight toward the hill upon which sat the Tirthaig, the vast and ancient royal palace of Almaris.

Vesparin's Hill, named for Khedesh's eldest son, stood at the western edge of the Cleave, where a sheer wall of granite three hundred feet high plunged into the waters below to form the harbor's inner rim. The Tirthaig's green-roofed towers gleamed like emeralds in the bright sun. The palace proper began three-quarters of the way up the hill's western slope at a narrow point set with a gate, from which it rose upward in a widening wedge shape formed of many terraces cut into the rock, the palace's overall profile that of staggered, rising buildings formed of white stone.

Two concentric walls circled the high rocky hill, with storerooms, barracks, stables, armories, foundries, and other buildings sprawled in the space between them.

The main gate of the Tirthaig opened into a circular courtyard bounded by a peristyle, its columns carved from gray-veined marble. Standards bearing the golden stag's head of House Atreyano rose high above the outer towers of the palace, whipping about in the ocean wind.

Above the columns of the courtyard were many terraces and balconies, filled with servants and courtiers who cheered when Gerin's procession passed through the gate. In truth, they were cheering Claressa, who rode in the center of an honor guard, looking, to Gerin's great annoyance, clean and unstained, as if she'd just emerged from a palace bath, as regal as a queen.

King Abran met them in the Grand Hall. He went first to Claressa and hugged her, telling her she'd grown even more beautiful since he'd last seen her, then to his sons. He greeted Gerin as if his older son were nearly a stranger. Gerin did not know what to think, and Therain gave him a look that said, *What was that all about?* Hollin remained back with Balandrick and the other guards; Abran did not greet him or even deign to look his way.

"Claressa, I'm sure you'll want to refresh yourself after your journey," said the king. He looked older since Gerin had seen him. There was more gray in his hair and beard, a few more lines creasing his face.

"Yes, Father, that would be wonderful. I'm famished."

Abran commanded some servants to take his daughter and her ladies-in-waiting to a private dining room, then see that their belongings were taken to the rooms set aside for them. Another group of servants were ordered to take Gerin and Therain's belongings, though the two were not invited to join Claressa.

"I'm pretty hungry myself, Father," said Gerin. "I'm sure Therain is, too."

The king did not reply. Instead, he wheeled about and marched toward a door at the rear of the hall. "Come with me. I have something interesting to show you both."

Gerin and Therain exchanged puzzled looks, then followed their father.

Abran led them to the kitchens first, where they hastily ate a few bites of roast chicken and gulped down some water. There was an odd, almost manic gleam in the king's eyes when he regarded Gerin that disturbed him.

They had barely finished when their father ushered them down several dark, twisting corridors. Abran handed a shuttered lamp to Therain and told him to carry it.

"Where are you taking us?" asked Therain.

"You'll see."

The final corridor ended at a small chamber with a single heavy door, watched over by a soldier. The man saluted as the king and his sons approached. "Your Majesty," he said, bowing. Then he unlocked the door and pulled it open on creaking hinges.

"These are the dungeons," said Gerin as they stepped onto a landing from which a staircase descended into the darkness. He had never entered them through this door before, but the oppressive stone walls, the low ceiling—the very air of the place—told him beyond doubt where they were going.

Abran took the lamp from Therain and unshuttered it. He gave Gerin another suspicion-laden look. "Your uncle Nellemar brought us a strange guest from Gedsengard."

They reached the bottom of the stair and continued through a short corridor with empty cells on either side. "Who is it?" asked Therain. "Did he capture that Threndish corsair who's been hounding the coast?"

"No, it's not Velgas or anyone else you might have heard of." It was clear Abran was not going to say any more.

They reached two guards sitting on stools in a small round room at the head of a dank corridor. They were playing cards, and rose to attention the moment they saw Abran. "Your Majesty," they said in unison.

"We're here to see the new prisoner," said the king.

"Yes, Your Majesty," said the senior soldier. He bowed his head, then led the three men down the corridor to a cell near the end. He unlocked the steel door and yanked it open, then stepped into the room.

There was a man in the cell, manacled to the wall and seated on a bench. He was disheveled and dirty, his hair unkempt, his beard wild and matted; yet there was a defiance in his expression as he stared at the men entering the cell, as if he were appraising each in turn and finding them all wanting.

"This man's ship crashed upon Harrow's Rock off of Gedsengard," said the king. "He was the only man to survive the wreck, though there were —"

The prisoner's gaze had been lingering on Gerin since his entry into the cell. His eyes suddenly went wide and he jumped up. The chains that held him fast did not permit him to move more than a few feet from the wall of the cell.

"It is you!" he shouted, staring at Gerin. He had a heavy accent that Gerin could not place, but he could understand the man readily enough. "You are the key! The one the Dreamer said has the Words of Making!" He strained at his bonds, his face livid. Spittle flew from his snarling lips.

The guard stepped forward and backhanded the prisoner across the jaw. The man was so focused on Gerin that he didn't even see the guard approach, and the blow caught him by surprise. His head snapped violently to the side and he slammed back into the wall and slumped onto the bench, dazed.

But he was not deterred. He shook his head to clear it, long strands of blood flying from a cut inside his mouth and splattering the floor, then returned his piercing gaze to Gerin.

"It *is* you," he said. "I saw your face."

"What in the name of the gods are you talking about?" Gerin spun toward his father. "Who is this man?"

He could tell from the shocked expression on the king's face that the prisoner's outburst had surprised him as well. "I don't know," Abran said at last.

"Where are the Words of Making?" demanded the prisoner. "I know you have them!"

"If you speak again without leave," said Gerin, "I'll have the guard beat you senseless."

The prisoner did not reply, but the arrogant, contemptuous expression remained.

"Watch him closely," the king said to the guard as he ushered his sons into the corridor.

"Do you have any idea about this?" the king asked Gerin when they were outside the cell. "Are these Words of Making something Hollin taught you? A spell?" There was more than a hint of accusation in his voice.

"I've never heard of them. If they're wizard magic, then they're something I haven't yet learned."

"He claimed to recognize you," Therain said to him. "Is that possible? Could he know you somehow?"

"I've never seen him before."

"I don't believe it's possible for him to know Gerin or any of us, if what Nellemar told me is true," said the king. "He claims to come from across the Maurelian Sea."

Therain made a snort of derision. Gerin said, "That's not possible. The Maurelian Sea is endless."

"I'm telling you what I know," said Abran sharply. "That man is also a wizard of some kind. Nellemar said he has the power to temporarily revive the dead."

Gerin returned to the cell. "How can you claim to know me?" he demanded. "We've never met before."

"Of course we have not met," said the prisoner. "I have traveled far from my homeland, across the breadth of the Great Sea, following the vision of the Dreamer. I saw the vision with my own eyes. You possess the Words of Making."

"Your Dreamer is wrong. I've never heard of the Words of Making."

The prisoner made a scoffing sound. "The Dreamers are never wrong. I *saw* the Dream. I *saw* your face. You have the Words, and one way or the other you will give them to us."

Gerin took a calming breath and drew magic into himself. The power filled him with warmth and vitality, made him temporarily forget his weariness. "Do not move," he said to the prisoner. He was going to test the truth of the man's words.

Gerin did not permit enough magic to flow through him to ignite his aura; the spells he planned to invoke would not require that much power. He did not believe that this man could be a wizard—his dark complexion in and of itself seemed to rule that out. At the Awakening of a wizard's magic, the flesh bleached to a bone-white color, and to the best of his knowledge nothing could be done to circumvent this particular effect. The Ritual of Discovery could put to rest once and for all the question of whether this man was indeed a wizard, but Gerin did not have a *methlenel* to perform the ritual, nor did he know the proper incantation; that test would have to wait for Hollin.

But there were still a few things he could do to sate his curiosity. He stretched his hand toward the prisoner and spoke softly in Osirin. Magic leaped from his hand. Gerin could

see traces of power flowing out of his fingertips, faint tendrils of shimmering, pulsing luminescence, but he knew that
to everyone else in the room his magic was invisible.

To his surprise, he found strange areas of emptiness
throughout the man's body that the seeing power of the spell
could not penetrate. They were not physically empty—he
was not missing organs or other chunks of his innards—but
rather, areas of slumbering power that Gerin's own magic
could not sense. Voids of some kind. He had never sensed
anything like it in any other person, wizard or otherwise.

Gerin changed the spell, altering the characteristics of
the Seeing in an attempt to illuminate what lay within the
strange voids. Nothing he did worked. He tried several different Seeing spells and even uttered three Words of Radiance—powerful and dangerous magic designed to pierce
shields, Wardings, Forbiddings, and other protective barriers—but nothing he tried could tell him what lay within the
voids, or what they could do.

"I can feel your mystical eyes upon me," said the prisoner.
"Your clumsy prodding of the *tendrashi* of Bariq. You see
that which makes me a Loremaster. Do you now believe
what I say?"

Gerin lowered his arm and halted the flow of magic
through him. He was tired. The Words of Radiance, especially, required an enormous amount of concentration to prevent their piercing power from losing its form.

Ignoring the prisoner's question, he turned to his father
and Therain, keeping his voice low. "There's something
strange within him, but I can't tell what it is."

"So he *is* a wizard?" asked Therain.

Gerin shook his head. "No. Not like me or Hollin. But
there is a power within him I don't understand."

"This is a dark and ominous turn of events," said the king.
There was venom in his voice as he added, "It seems magic
haunts us at every turn."

4

They made their way to the upper reaches of the palace. Nellemar and Hollin were brought to a small council chamber near the throne hall, where Nellemar related the story of Vethiq aril Tolsadri's capture upon the beaches of Gedsengard.

Gerin only half heard his uncle's tale. He kept returning to Tolsadri's conviction that he possessed the Words of Making—a conviction born of a vision by a being called a Dreamer. He grew angrier the more he thought about it. The idea that he was the subject of someone else's "vision" was far too close to the Neddari *kamichi*'s vision-quest that had resulted in a powerful compulsion being placed upon him. Once again he was a focal point for something he did not understand.

The end of his uncle's story caught his full attention. "He said that his ship was only the first of many, and that they planned to conquer us and force us to follow the gods they worship."

"An invasion," said Therain. "Do we have any idea how many ships, or when they might arrive?"

"No. He's made this fleet of his sound huge, but that's probably just bluster."

"Hollin, do you have any idea what these Words of Making are?" asked Gerin.

The wizard shook his head. "I've never heard of such a

thing. There are a few spells that have creative aspects to
them, but I doubt he is referring to those. There is certainly
no need to traverse the Maurelian Sea for spells of such limited use, assuming it was possible for him, or this Dreamer
of his, to learn of them in the first place."

They asked Nellemar a few more questions, then Gerin
and Hollin left to question Tolsadri further. The prisoner
looked hard at Hollin, then shook his head. "I do not know
your face."

"What are the Words of Making?" asked Gerin.

"Why do you ask *me*? You are the one who has them."

Gerin's frustration mounted. "I tell you I don't know what
they are."

"Then you lie."

"You'll show Prince Gerin proper respect," said the guard.
He stepped forward to strike Tolsadri, but Gerin waved him
back. He wanted the man able to answer questions, not bleeding and unconscious.

"Then perhaps I know them by some other name," said
Gerin. "But the name you give has no meaning for me."

Tolsadri considered this for a moment. Hollin waited beside Gerin with the *methlenel* in hand.

"Perhaps that is so," said Tolsadri at last. "Your barbarian
tongue was difficult to learn. It is like *pachu*, like mud in the
mouth. Perhaps the translation is not accurate."

"Then what *are* the Words of Making?"

"They are a weapon to battle the Great Enemy. A formidable power. Other than that, I do not know. The Dreamer said
only that you were the key to the Words, nothing more."

Gerin ran his hand through his hair. This was maddening.
How could he find out more about them if the man sent to
find them didn't know what they were?

Hollin put his hand on Gerin's shoulder. "I'm going to perform the Ritual of Discovery now. This man is no wizard,
but it may be that the spell will be able to identify these voids
within him more readily than your Seeings."

Gerin shifted his gaze between Tolsadri and the *methlenel*
as Hollin worked the spell. Tolsadri gave no indication he

felt anything or was even interested in what was happening. He slouched against the wall, his manacled hands in his lap, his eyes barely open. Gerin had to fight back a strong urge to march over and smash in the man's teeth.

He could see the shimmering trails of magic flowing from Hollin to Tolsadri, probing deep inside him. More deeply than was usually needed for the ritual to identify a wizard.

Hollin's eyes were squeezed shut in concentration as he directed the power through the body of the prisoner. Then he opened them and lowered his hand. As expected, the *methlenel* had not changed color. If it had, it would have signified that Tolsadri was a wizard, which was obviously not true. If he truly had come from across the sea, he could not be a descendant of the Atalari.

"I felt your filthy and vile power within me," said Tolsadri without moving from his slumped position. "But it is of no consequence. I allowed you to see. You have beheld the power of Bariq the Wise, but you cannot take it from me, or use it yourself. You are no Adept or Loremaster."

"What is he talking about?" Gerin asked Hollin. "What did you find?"

"We're finished here for now," Hollin said, and ushered the prince from the room.

"You will surrender all you know and all you have, Prince Gerin!" Tolsadri called after them. "No one long resists the Havalqa. All fall to us in the end. The Powers will not be denied. It is only a matter of time."

Out in the corridor, Gerin asked, "What did you find?"

"He is indeed a wizard of some kind. Not a descendant of the Atalari as we are, nor like any other practitioner of magic in Osseria."

"Could you tell what kind of power he has?"

"No. The voids within him were difficult to penetrate, and even when I did make my way past their boundaries, the nature of the power is so foreign to me that I can only guess its purpose.

"But," he said, raising his hand to cut off Gerin's next question, "based on what your uncle told us about Tolsadri reviving the dead, it seems the power contained in the voids are pockets of living energy. It's as if his own life force was splintered into many parts. I believe he can somehow direct those splintered bits of energy into the bodies of the dead, which allows him to animate them. They are not alive again in any sense that we would recognize. They are like marionettes controlled by a puppeteer. I don't think he can animate very many corpses at once. If he tried to animate too many, he would literally expend his own life out of him."

"So it has a limit. Is there anything else he can do? Or is that his only ability?"

"I would think he has other powers. The voids were the most obvious loci of his magic, but there were different, smaller areas that seemed capable of manipulating magic."

"You mean something like the *paru'enthred*?"

"No. They were nothing like a wizard's inner eye. His magic, as far as I can tell, is of a wholly different kind. Our magic works by using spells to manipulate power that we allow to enter and flow through our bodies. It is an inherently *external* force. The ultimate source of our magic comes from outside of us. But Tolsadri's magic is, I believe, mostly *internal*."

"I don't understand. If he's not drawing on some external reservoir of magic, where does his power come from?"

"I think he depletes some part of his own life to work his magic."

Gerin thought about that. It seemed very dangerous; too much power used, and you could exhaust your very life. It also seemed to set a practical limit of how much magic could be worked, since power drawn from one's own life energies could never be great enough to equal the kinds of spells wizards were capable of using. But without knowing more about exactly what Tolsadri could do, it was difficult to draw a firm conclusion.

Gerin was following a servant down the hallway outside the council chamber when he felt a strange emanation of magic from behind a closed door. He'd never felt anything like it, though the emanation brought to mind his journey through the subterranean levels of the Varsae Sandrova at Hethnost, when he'd taken the spells of the Baryashin Order so he could summon Naragenth's spirit from the dead. The passages of the lower levels had been saturated with magic that had seeped from the vaults over time, charging the air itself with a kind of vital potency that felt both exhilarating and dangerous.

He could sense a similar buildup from behind the door, which begged the question: What was magic doing in the Tirthaig?

"What is kept in that room?" he asked the servant.

"This is where the crowns for both king and queen are kept, my lord," said the old man. "And other items of great value to the royal family."

"Open it," said Gerin.

The man looked aghast. "My lord, I do not have the keys to open it! Only the king and first minister have the keys."

Gerin went to the heavy door and placed his hand upon it. He created a Spell of Knowing to penetrate the iron-banded wood and discern exactly how the door was locked. He could have easily broken down the door or blasted it to pieces, but did not think his father would appreciate the use of such brute force.

He closed his eyes, and the structure of the lock appeared as an image in his mind. He directed a thin current of magic to thread through the tumblers and work them until they fell into their open positions.

He pushed open the door and stepped inside. The servant started to protest, pleading that the crown prince should not enter without the permission of the king, but Gerin silenced him with a harsh glance.

The sensation of magical energy was much stronger within the room. He created a spark of magefire to illuminate the windowless space. The servant moved to the doorway of the room but would not enter, wringing his hands in agitation as Gerin looked about.

The chamber was not large—about twelve feet on each

side, with elaborate mahogany chests and cabinets lining the walls. They varied in height. Most were waist or shoulder high, but a few reached nearly to the ceiling. The tallest cabinet had doors inlaid with beveled glass through which he could see the royal crowns— though the kingdom had not had a queen in many years—as well as diamonds and other jewels upon cushions of burgundy velvet.

He paused, trying to determine from the sensation alone where the magic emanated. The power he felt was peculiar. It almost had a *flavor* to it, if something he sensed with magic could be said to have such a thing. He opened himself as much as he could to the wash of power that drifted in the air like a breeze only a wizard could sense, trying to follow it back to its source.

He shivered as he recognized what the flavor was.

Amber magic.

But how could amber magic be here? He was the only amber wizard alive in Osseria, and only the second to have ever lived, after Naragenth ul-Darhel.

Naragenth left something in this room, he realized. But why had such a thing never been found before now? In centuries past there must have been wizards near enough to this chamber to feel the power radiating from it. It seemed impossible that it could have gone unnoticed for so long.

Yet it was the only explanation. Gerin knew that he had not left anything in this place. Naragenth was the only other wizard who could have created something that radiated amber magic. To the best of his knowledge, there were no natural objects—stones, jewels, metals, or plants—that contained amber magic. Whatever was in here had to have been fashioned by a wizard.

Gerin continued to move through the room, pausing at each chest, until he reached the first of the ceiling-high cabinets. He pulled open the heavy doors and found himself staring at the Scepter of the King, the staff of office seen only at grand public events and occasions of state. He had only seen it a few times in his life, and not once since he became a wizard.

The scepter was the source of the amber magic. It threw off waves of amber power like heat.

He reached out and grasped the long ivory rod. The servant in the doorway gasped in apprehension.

Magic danced across his hand. The yard-long shaft had been inlaid with pearl and hair-thin filigrees of gold and silver. Its head was made of gold formed into the shape of a gull whose sleek wings were thrown forward so the tips nearly touched beyond the bird's beak. He'd never seen the scepter this close before, and found it a thing of beauty and quiet majesty.

What did you put in here, Naragenth? he wondered as he turned it in his hand, the blue-white light of the magefire sparkling like starlight on the silver and gold. *What secrets were you trying to hide?*

In the darkness of his cell, Vethiq aril Tolsadri brooded over this strange turn of events. He had met the man from the Dreamer's vision in the flesh and learned his name, something the Dreamer itself had not been able to discern with its arcane powers. Yet this man, Prince Gerin Atreyano, claimed to know nothing of the Words of Making. Tolsadri's powers as an Adept and Loremaster gave him unique insights into the hearts of men, and one of those insights was the ability to discern truth from falsehood. It did not always work, but he was right more often than not. And his heart told him that Gerin truly did not know of the Words.

He did not believe that it was an inaccurate translation, for even if Prince Gerin did not know the Words of Making by that exact name, he surely would have some idea about what they were. After all, according to the Dreamer, the Words were a weapon of vast, almost unimaginable power. That was why they were needed by the Steadfast—to be used in the coming battle with the Great Enemy, the ancient foe of Holvareh and the Powers who ruled the world in His Name. To think that Gerin could have them and not know what they were was preposterous.

Tolsadri knew he needed to learn more, but to do so, he

first had to escape from this cell. He'd remained captive in the hope that he could acquire information of use to his mission. A premature escape would have made him a fugitive on a forsaken isle, unable to gather any knowledge of the Words—and with the destruction of the *Kaashal* in that accursed storm, no way to return to the fleet—so he had decided to endure this humiliating confinement. He did not regret his decision. *Bariq be praised, I have learned more than I would have dreamed possible.*

But now it was time to take what he had discovered and return it by any means possible to the Dreamer and the fleet. Gerin would have to be taken, of course, and interrogated at length to get to the root of the dilemma between what he claimed he knew and what the Dreamer said he *did* know, but he was in no position to do that now. It would have to wait, though this did not trouble him. He knew Gerin's name and station, and the location of the city where he lived. Gerin would be taken in time.

Patience was often required when performing the work of the Powers. Delays were inevitable, but in the end the Havalqa always prevailed. It was their destiny as the rightful and natural rulers of the world, conquerors blessed by Holvareh Himself, Father of All. No people had ever successfully resisted them, and none ever would. Who could deny the Powers who had given shape to the world and devised the castes so that all men and women would know their place within it? And who would *want* to resist them?

Tolsadri shook his head. That was the greatest mystery of all. He did not understand why anyone would refuse the gift of the Havalqa, of rising from the darkness of ignorance and into the transcendent light of Holvareh and the Powers. Who, when shown the error of his ways, would not embrace the Havalqa as saviors? These heathens should be down on their knees weeping with joy that one such as he had come among them to show them the light. It enraged him that others would choose to wallow in the chaos of their imperfect societies when shown the evidence that a perfect one existed. But there was no accounting for the ability for men to deny the truth.

It was time for him to escape this prison.

His jailers had fed him barely enough to keep him alive, so he could not draw too much of his strength without risking true-death. If he died in this place, there was little hope that *al-fet*, his second life, could be fanned from the ashes of the old. He would perish, and all the knowledge he had gained would be lost. He had to proceed with caution, yet do his utmost to ensure his escape.

Tolsadri raised his wrists and examined the manacles. Their edges were rough, but not sharp enough for his needs. He required his own blood, but would not be able to draw it from the manacles or the chains.

He raised his forearm to his mouth and bit deeply into the flesh. Pain seared through his arm as hot blood gushed into his mouth. He did not bite completely through; there were some wounds that not even a Command could fully heal. But he needed his blood, and this was the only way to draw it.

He swallowed deeply several times, sucking the hot sticky fluid from the ragged rips in his forearm. When he was finished drinking he directed his thoughts inward, to the Eternal Mysteries that lay within him.

The Mysteries granted him control of his life and flesh. Charged with power, he used the secret Commands of the Loremasters to reshape the bones, muscles, tendons, and skin of his hands.

He clenched his teeth as his bones elongated and narrowed. The pain was exquisite, excruciating, but he did not cry out. His fingers stretched and thinned; his knuckles drew closer together; his wrists shrank in size. The bones and tendons made popping sounds as they obeyed his Command to stretch.

He stood and lowered his arms; the manacles fell to the floor. The sudden removal of the weight from his weakened wrists was a great relief. He commanded his hands to return to normal and once more endured the agony of transformation.

He sat back down, weary. The wound on his arm still bled, and he put it to his mouth and sucked once more. He regained some though not all of his strength. He commanded his arm to cease bleeding—he could have commanded it to fully heal, but that would have drained too much of the power he needed for the next step in his plan. He felt the flesh deep within the wounds knit themselves closed, though the open tears on the surface of his skin remained.

They will be coming soon, he thought. *To feed or torture me.*

They would be surprised at what they found.

Lem Derosa was almost asleep on his stool in the dungeons, his arms folded across his chest, his back leaning comfortably against the stone wall, head lolling forward, when Petros Ferouda, his fellow guard, smacked him on the shoulder and almost sent him sprawling across the floor.

"Wake up, you lunk," said Petros as he hitched up his belt. He was a tall man with broad shoulders and a broader belly. "Time to feed our guest." He gestured to the servant from the kitchens who'd just arrived, holding a tray of food.

"What'd you go and do that for?" said Lem irritably. "I was just about asleep. Why don't you feed him?"

"'Cause I fed him last time and now it's *your* turn," he said, jabbing a fat, hairy finger at Lem. Petros sat down with a contented sigh on the stool that Lem had just vacated. "I heard Tirel Hurent might be paying our guest a visit in a little while. Seems the king doesn't think the prisoner's been forthcoming enough with what he knows. Thinks he needs some additional motivation." He barked a laugh. "Hurent'll get him to talk. Always does."

Lem shivered at the torturer's name. Tirel Hurent was a gaunt, ghostlike man who drifted through the palace in his black clothing and black hooded cloak like the specter of Shayphim himself. Lem couldn't stand to have the man look at him, truth be told. The torturer's stare made him feel like a pig being sized up by the butcher for the Éalsteth's Day Fair.

"All right, I'll feed him," he said, taking the tray from the servant, who scurried out of the small room and up the stairs like a rabbit being chased by a hound. Scullions never liked to linger down here. It annoyed Lem—he would have liked some company from time to time other than Petros—but other than locking the doors so they couldn't leave, there wasn't anything he could do about it.

He marched down the corridor with the tray of food in one hand—a hunk of black bread, some thin soup that must have been cold by now, and a cup of water—and a torch in the other. He slipped the torch into a wall brace while he got out his keys and unlocked the door. He kicked it open, grabbed the torch, and stepped into the cell.

Once inside, he nearly dropped both tray and torch in shock. He could not believe what he was seeing. Or rather, what he was *not* seeing.

The prisoner was gone. Empty manacles—still locked, as far as he could see—lay upon the floor. Lem thrust the torch forward, casting a harsh, flickering light in the darker corners of the cell, hoping he would see the prisoner huddled there, trying to hide; but there was nothing. The cell was empty.

"Petros, get down here!" he bellowed. "The prisoner's escaped!"

Lem threw the tray to the floor and drew his short sword as Petros ran down the corridor. Even here, buried in the bedrock of Vesparin's Hill, the floor shook with each of the big man's footfalls, like the precursor rumblings of an earthquake.

"The gods condemn us, how did he get out?" said Petros. His massive frame completely blocked the doorway. "Was the door locked?"

"Yes, it was locked! So are his bloody manacles. Look." Lem pointed toward the empty shackles.

"The only way out is past us, and we would've seen—"

Lem heard Petros grunt, then emit an agonized groan the likes of which he'd never heard from the man. Lem wheeled to see what had happened—

—and was horrified to see Petros's sword protruding from his belly beneath his breastplate, buried in his flesh up to the hilt. Petros's face was ashen, his mouth hanging agape.

The sword twisted on its own and drew itself across Petros's lower abdomen, then was violently wrenched free. Petros collapsed in a heap and lay still.

Lem hadn't moved. He was immobilized by a kind of heart-gripping terror that until now had been beyond his ability to even imagine. Some part of his mind wondered distantly how he could experience such boundless horror and continue to live.

Petros's sword drifted in the air. Lem could see now that something held the weapon, a translucent man-shape that blurred the wall of the cell behind it.

The blur suddenly resolved itself into the prisoner, his face a snarling mask of hatred.

Before Lem could react, the prisoner lunged forward and sliced open his abdomen with a vicious swing of the blade, its tip ripping through leather and flesh. *He's killed me, same as he killed poor Petros!* thought Lem as his guts began to spill from his body. He dropped his weapon and the torch and instinctively covered his abdomen with his hands, trying in vain to keep his entrails inside him. They were hot and slippery between his fingers.

He fell to his knees, looking down in a strange kind of detachment at the bloody, shit-smelling mess piling up on the floor.

The prisoner picked up Lem's keys from the floor and grinned. It was a terrible thing to see. Lem thought about screaming for help. Maybe the scullion who'd brought the food was still close enough to hear.

The prisoner gripped the sword in both hands and swung it at Lem's neck. It seemed to be moving very slowly through the air. He tried to close his eyes, to deny what was about to happen, but his reactions felt slow and sluggish, like trying to flee from danger in a nightmare.

His eyes were still open when his severed head rolled against the wall of the cell.

5

Gerin threw open the doors to his father's council room and stormed in past the guards without waiting to be announced. He strode to the table and thrust the Scepter of the King toward the shocked faces of the men sitting across from him.

"There is magic—*amber* magic—in this, Father. I don't know how it's there, or why, but it can only have been put there by Naragenth himself, and it's something we need to talk about right now."

In addition to Gerin's father, his uncle Nellemar was at the table, as well as Jaros Waklan, Minister of the Realm, and Arilek Levkorail, Lord Commander and Governor General of the Taeratens of the Naege. They all shifted their gaze from Gerin to the scepter, trying to make sense of his words.

His father glowered at him, his face turning red as he fought to control his anger. "What are you doing with the Scepter of the King? You have no right to be touching it, let alone parading it about as if it were something *common*."

"Father, there's magic in this! And not just any magic, but amber magic! That means Naragenth had to put it there. I knew the scepter was old, but I didn't think it was *eighteen hundred* years old! The question now is, what did he put in here and why?"

The king grew so angry he trembled; his jaw clenched and a vein throbbed at his temple. Jaros Waklan made a calming motion with his old, wrinkled hands. "Please, Your Majesty, we need to step back and take account of what has happened here. Prince Gerin, for your elucidation, the Scepter of the King is well over two thousand years old, so it would most definitely have been in existence during the reign of King Naragenth. Now, please sit and tell us how you made this remarkable discovery."

Gerin sat down at the table and told them how he had found that the scepter contained amber magic. Abran's anger lessened somewhat as his son told his tale, but did not vanish entirely.

"I'm not sure I understand, my lord," said Arilek Levkorail. The Lord Commander's shaved head gleamed in the sunlight blazing through the windows behind him. He stroked the short beard along his chin. "Are you saying you can sense the magic from the scepter even now, in this room?"

"Yes. To me, the scepter is giving off amber magic the way a fire gives off heat."

Levkorail leaned back in his chair and folded his arms across his broad chest. "Strange. I feel nothing at all, and see no sign of magic in it."

"You're not a wizard, Lord Commander. The kind of magic I'm sensing is not something a nonwizard can detect. There are spells I can create that you can see or feel"—for a moment he ignited an open flame of magefire above the center of the table that blazed upward into the air like the end of an invisible torch—"but there are many more that are invisible to you."

Gerin dispelled the magefire as Hollin swept into the room. The older wizard bowed to Abran, then approached the table, his eyes locked on the Scepter of the King. "I was told you discovered a magical object," he said. "Is this it?"

"You mean you can't feel it?"

"I sense nothing coming from the scepter. It is as blank to me as the table." Hollin gestured to the chair next to Gerin. "Your Majesty, may I?"

"I suppose you must," he said with a dismissive wave of his hand.

Hollin ignored the king's rudeness and seated himself.

"You really can't feel anything from the scepter?" Gerin asked.

"No." The wizard stretched his hand toward the scepter and invoked a complicated Seeing. He examined the scepter for several minutes, making subtle changes to the spell as he directed his probing magic in and through the rod.

He lowered his hand. "Whatever magic is here is occluded from my power."

"How is that possible?" asked Gerin.

"There are ways to modify spells embedded in an object or a place that makes them impossible to detect by any means, or allows them to be sensed only under certain conditions, or by the right kind of power. You have not yet learned any of these techniques, and some of them you will probably never learn. Some powers are reserved for the rulers of Hethnost alone, for the safeguarding of secrets and their own hidden magics.

"I think the spells in the scepter were created by Naragenth—indeed, they could only have been made by him since the power you sense is amber—and that he modified the manner in which magic would leak from the scepter so it could only be detected by an amber wizard."

"Why would he do such a thing?" asked the king.

"Consider the era in which Naragenth lived," said Hollin. "He ascended to the throne of this kingdom just a few years before the beginning of the Wars of Unification, when all of Osseria was consumed in Helca's empire-building conflict. It was a dangerous time to be a sovereign king, let alone a wizard-king of Naragenth's stature. Look at the measures he took to hide his great library. He would have taken care to protect his devices of magic in case they fell into enemy hands. Remember, there were thousands of wizards in the world then, many of them aware of Naragenth and jealous of his power."

"So by changing the spells in the scepter so that they could only be sensed by an amber wizard," said Gerin, "he effectively made them impossible to detect, since he was the only amber wizard alive at that time."

"Exactly. And his protections worked surprisingly well.

Only now, nearly two thousand years later, have we learned that the symbol of the king is in truth a repository of magic."

"But *what* did he place there?" asked Abran. "What kind of spells are so important that he felt the need to hide them in such a way? Is the symbol of my power a *weapon* of magic?"

"That will take time to discover," said Hollin. "I have no means of seeing the spells directly, and Gerin has not yet been taught the techniques that we'll need to use to uncover them. We will have to proceed cautiously. It's probable that there are dangerous counterspells within the scepter that might injure or kill someone using brute force to determine its contents."

Gerin thought about what secrets might be contained within the scepter. What kind of magic would Naragenth have hidden in an object accessible only to the King of Khedesh? He had apparently done his work on it in secret, so that no others would even suspect that the scepter contained unique and powerful spells. Certainly there were no written accounts of his labors.

Spells for what? His father's question struck to the heart of the matter. What was Naragenth trying to hide?

Then it came to him. The answer, when he saw it, made perfect sense.

"Hollin," he said, keeping his voice even to mask his rising excitement. "I think the scepter might contain the key spells that allow entry to Naragenth's library, the Varsae Estrikavis."

6

Hollin took a moment to consider Gerin's idea. "Perhaps. It's a reasonable guess, to be sure. But we need to be as open-minded as possible when examining the scepter. It's also reasonable that the spells it contains have nothing to do with the library. They may contain secrets completely lost from history."

"Of course." But though he agreed that there were other possibilities, Gerin felt jittery with excitement. His idea just seemed *right*. What better place to hide the key spells for the Varsae Estrikavis than in an object only Naragenth had access to and that he'd carefully protected so only an amber wizard could sense its power? Nothing else made any sense.

"Your Majesty, with your permission," Hollin said, "I would like to take the scepter so that Gerin and I can study it in greater detail. Though I cannot say what it contains, I think we can all be confident it is something of great importance, considering the lengths Naragenth went to protect it."

Abran looked at the scepter for a long moment. "Though I'm loath to do it, I will grant you my permission, with certain conditions. First, I do not want the scepter removed from the palace grounds. Second, you are both to exercise *great* care in handling it, and I explicitly forbid you from using any kind of spell or test that might harm it. Next to Khedesh's sword, Tangeril, it is one of the oldest and most valuable heirlooms of our kingdom. I will not suffer any damage to it, no matter what promise of power or knowledge it may contain."

"Your conditions are quite reasonable, Your Majesty," said Hollin.

"We'll be careful with it, Father, don't worry."

They sent a servant to the room where the scepter was kept to retrieve its velvet-lined case. When the servant returned, Gerin placed the scepter in the case and closed and locked the lid. The gull sigil of the kingdom was stamped in gold on the polished rosewood.

"I need to rest for a little while before we get started," said Gerin in the corridor.

"I'll take the scepter and try a few spells," said Hollin. "But I don't expect to learn anything. I think its power will remain hidden from me no matter what I do. If we're to discover its secrets, you'll have to be the one to do it."

"I'll come to your rooms later this evening." He handed Hollin the case. "Remember, if you break it, I'm going to make *you* explain it to my father."

Hollin smiled. "I'll guard it with my life."

Gerin followed a young page wearing the orange and white livery of the palace to the rooms that had been prepared for him in the upper part of the Tirthaig. His belongings had already been brought there and placed in a walnut chest of drawers and matching wardrobe. There was a balcony running the length of the room that overlooked the Cleave. He stood for a long time at the parapet looking out over the eastern sections of the city, built upon the stony arms of Eigrend and Yethen, as the two headlands were called. He could hear the distant roar of water breaking against the cliff face far below him, like the thrumming pulse of the city itself.

The war galleys of the Khedeshian fleet bobbed in the harbor, their sails furled, oars drawn up and into the hulls. He could see sailors moving about on the decks, hauling coils of rope or rolling barrels of water or dried meat to the openings that led to the cargo holds.

I'll be king of all of this one day, he thought. It was a powerful, sobering idea that left him feeling a little queasy, faced so directly and bluntly with the enormity of it. He imagined himself sitting upon the sapphire throne for the first time, crown upon his head, scepter in hand, the room filled with nobles and courtiers who would look to him for guidance. What would they expect of him? And what would he provide? To whom would *he* turn for guidance?

He told himself he didn't need to worry about that now. He needed to rest so he could figure out what was in the bloody scepter. He pulled off his boots, stretched out on the bed, and soon was fast asleep.

It was fully dark when Gerin awoke. He sat up groggily in bed and rubbed his eyes, then lit the magefire lamp sitting upon the chest of drawers that had been unpacked from his belongings.

He just finished lighting it when there was a banging on his door. He opened it to find Therain standing in the corridor with a servant behind him carrying a large platter of food.

"Good, you're awake," said Therain.

"Just barely. Look, I need to see Hollin—"

"I know, but I thought you'd want a bite to eat first. The gods know I'm starving."

The servant entered, placed the platter on the table near the balcony, then scurried from the room. Therain picked up an apple and took a bite. "Before you rush off and lock yourself away with Hollin for who knows how long, I want to hear about what you found," he said as he chewed.

Gerin drank some water, then tore off a crust of bread and slathered some butter on it. "What have you heard? I'm already sick of telling this story."

"That you found some kind of secret magic hidden in the Scepter of the King."

"That's about all there is to know."

"What do you think it is? And don't tell me you have no idea, I know you. You've probably got six different ideas if you have one."

"I don't have six, but something did occur to me." He told

Therain what he thought about the spells it might contain.

"Do you mind if I come along?" asked Therain as Gerin got up to leave. "I'm curious to see how you study the thing."

"You're bored, aren't you?" Therain had never expressed any interest in his magic before, beyond a few general questions.

"Completely. Father's still holed up with his advisors and not seeing anyone yet, not even Aron Toresh, who's ready to beat down the door to talk with him about the wedding. Claressa's busy with half the courtiers in the palace, and I just have no desire to get involved in all that skulduggery and intrigue."

"I would think that skulduggery would suit you."

"No, as I recall, *you're* the one who sneaks around in the dead of night stealing dangerous spells and raising the spirits of the dead."

Gerin called for a servant and asked to be taken to Hollin's rooms, since neither he nor Therain had any idea where they were. The young boy silently led them through the corridors of the palace toward a nearby wing where guests of the royal family were accommodated. Gerin carried the magefire lamp with him, preferring its brighter light to the servant's dim candle.

They turned a corner and came face-to-face with their cousin, Marell Atreyano, Nellemar's eldest son.

"Hello, Marell," said Gerin. "It's been a long time. I trust you're doing well."

Marell folded his arms and glared at him, his eyes lingering on the magefire lamp. There was a mixture of fear and disgust in his expression, as if he'd just tasted something vile.

"My mother says you're a wizard," he said. Marell drew himself up straighter, but his height was no match for Gerin's. He was sixteen, with a slender build bordering on scrawniness. His face was round and bland; it reminded Gerin of unbaked dough that had been roughly shaped into the form of a face and then forgotten or abandoned before it could be finished.

"She says a wizard has no place on the throne of any kingdom, let alone one as great as Khedesh. She says wizards are beholden to foreigners with no love or caring for our people, and that you should be forbidden from ever becoming king."

Gerin stepped closer to his cousin until they were a hand's span apart. He towered over Marell. To his credit, Marell did not flinch or back away. Indeed, the hardness in his eyes only deepened.

"Then I'm thankful your mother has no say in the matter."

"She says you should choose, either the throne or your wizardry." He thrust his chin out defiantly. Marell's hands were clenched into fists, and for a moment Gerin thought his cousin might actually try to strike him.

"I will be wizard *and* king, cousin," said Gerin. "There is no law or tradition that says otherwise. Wizards have ruled Khedesh before, and will again. No one, not you or your mother or the Assembly of Lords, can force me to choose between them." Before Marell could reply, Gerin added, "Perhaps you should come with us to see my teacher and have him test you. You might be a wizard yourself."

Marell looked ready to spit on the floor. "I'll have nothing to do with blasphemous magic from foreign powers. My blood is pure, not polluted with the filth of some dead and vagrant race. And you'd do well to mark *my* words, cousin. The choice may be forced upon you whether you wish it or not."

Gerin's growing anger nearly spilled over. How *dare* his cousin speak to him like this! He wanted to grab Marell by the throat and shake him—

"And you'll find that being a part of the royal family will not provide you as much protection as you think if you continue to make threats against the crown prince," said Therain. "You'd be wise to shut your mouth now, Marell, before it's sewn shut for you and you find yourself in a lightless cell far beneath the palace, where even your mother would have trouble finding you. Such things have happened before to meddlesome princes who do not show the proper respect for the rulers of the realm. They are forcibly forgotten, expunged from the annals and family trees as if they did not exist. Do not forget it is *our* father who is king in Khedesh, not your mother or grandfather, as much as they might wish it were so."

Marell snarled and swept past them. The young servant who was guiding him rushed to catch up. He was gone in moments, but the sound of his boots clicking on the stone floor echoed down the corridor.

"I thought he was going to swing at you," said Therain.

"Believe me, I was *this* close to twisting his head around backward. But that wouldn't have done much for family harmony, would it?"

"To Shayphim with family harmony," said Therain. "The little brat deserved at least a bloody nose. Claressa told me once that Omara and her brood were dangerous, but I never imagined they'd be so open about it. I mean, he challenged your right to be king!"

"You shut him up nicely. Let's hope that's the last we hear of this nonsense."

Gerin and Hollin studied the scepter late into the night. The older wizard had tested the scepter while Gerin slept and had found no way to detect the presence of amber magic, let alone discern its purpose, which left Gerin to work all of the spells. Many were variations of Seeings, though more powerful and capable of being shaped and molded with greater flexibility. One moment Gerin was seeking for the signs of protective counterspells, and the next, with a few adjustments, looking for the telltale signs of key spells or Closings. It was difficult work. He'd learned many Seeings while studying with Hollin, but all of them were designed for a single purpose. This was the first time he'd encountered spells that could be modified while in use, and though he found them extremely helpful, they were also exhausting because of the care and concentration required to hold them together.

"I have to stop," he said, canceling the spell he was using and rubbing his eyes. "We'll start again tomorrow, but I just can't work any more magic right now."

"It's remarkable you've been able to go on as long as you have," said Hollin. "Sometimes I forget how much stamina you have. You should have said something earlier."

"I was fine until now." That was not exactly true. He'd been struggling for almost an hour, but was reluctant to stop because he wanted to make at least some progress before halting for the night. Now, however, he knew he couldn't go on any longer, in spite of the fact that they had found very little about the scepter.

Gerin was able to detect the presence of powerful counter-spells and other protections, but nothing beyond that. Many of the protections were Occlusions designed to prevent magical power from perceiving the nature of the spells hidden within the scepter. Hollin suspected that some spells were folded, which would make them invisible even to Gerin's magic. Folded spells usually required a specific type of magic to unfold and activate their power. Gerin despaired that they would ever be able to unlock the secrets of the scepter, but Hollin told him that their study had just begun and there were many more things they could try.

"There are layers and layers of carefully placed defenses and protections within this," said Hollin, gesturing to the scepter in its open case. "Whatever Naragenth has placed in here, he guarded it *very* well." Hollin closed the rosewood lid. "I think you should take this. There's nothing more I can do with it."

Gerin picked up the case, then paused. A distant, wistful look had come over Hollin's face. A look Gerin had seen more often recently. "Is everything all right?"

Hollin looked at him and smiled, but it was wan and mirthless. "I'm fine. A bit melancholy, that's all. Nothing to concern yourself with."

Gerin considered Hollin more than a teacher but not quite a friend; at least, not like Balandrick. He liked and respected the older wizard and often sought his advice, and though he had not officially named him a counselor, considered him one nonetheless. But Hollin was a guarded man and kept his thoughts and feelings private. Gerin could talk to him about wizards and magic, the running of Ailethon and its holdings or the governance of the realm, but they spoke very little to each other of personal matters.

Over the past few months, he had noticed Hollin's melancholy moods but said nothing to the wizard because he knew how private Hollin could be. But since the moods showed no sign of abating, he now felt compelled to ask about them. "Melancholy about what?"

The wizard shrugged and waved his hand dismissively. "It's nothing important, Gerin. I've been feeling a little out of place, that's all. Don't worry, it will pass."

At other times, Gerin would have made no further inquiry. But as he looked at the older wizard sitting at the table, surrounded by the darkness and gloom of the room, he suddenly felt that Hollin *should* be a closer friend than he was, and was not because he himself had made too few attempts to get the wizard to talk to him about such things.

"Are you sure?" he asked. "Is there anything I can do?"

He thought Hollin would give him a simple no, but instead the wizard paused. "I appreciate your asking. Truly. But there is nothing you or I or anyone can do. I'm lonely, Gerin. I miss Hethnost and the wizards there more than I thought I would when I agreed to teach you at Ailethon. A great break from our traditions, but it was necessary because of your station here in Khedesh. When I first came to your castle I was excited and invigorated to teach you, and it was thrilling to live outside of the fortress where I had spent so much of my life. Hethnost is a wonderful place, but it is also frozen in time, unable—perhaps I should say unwilling—to change its ways because of the vast weight of its history and tradition. And as you know, I was in a relationship with the Archmage herself that had been waning for many years. It seemed prudent to leave for many reasons, and I never intended to return, as I also told you.

"But now . . ." He shook his head. "I feel very much the outsider. That is no rebuke to you or your hospitality, or anything or anyone at Ailethon. It is a fine place to live, filled with many fine people. But my wizardry and long life set me apart in ways you can't yet appreciate. I thought I had moved beyond that particular problem, that without a wife and children whose mortality would remind me of my long life, that such things would no longer concern me. But they do. It's not just the brief lives of those around me. I haven't been at Ailethon long enough yet for that problem to manifest itself—having everyone I know age and die while I do not. But it *will* happen, and I cannot seem to stop dwelling on it. Time moves differently for me now. So much faster than it used to. I take what seem only a few breaths, and years have passed. Decades fall away like seasons. It feels sometimes that everything I experience and everyone I meet are but the fevered products of my own mind, that all of this"—he waved his hand across the room—"is little more than a dream."

Gerin was inwardly alarmed by Hollin's words. "Are you *sure* you're well? That doesn't sound good, if you think everything around you is a dream."

Hollin laughed. "Don't worry, I'm not delusional. It's very hard to describe. It's just a change in my perception. As I said, time does not move as it did when I was younger, but there's nothing to be done about it. I will adjust."

"Have you changed your mind about returning to Hethnost?" Hollin had once told him that he would remain with him once his training was complete if Gerin wished it. The Archmage still expected Hollin would return to Hethnost when Gerin was fully trained—he had not yet made his intentions to the contrary known to the wizards there. A careful hedging of his bets, Gerin realized.

"I don't know. I don't believe I will. I'm not sure I belong there any more than I belong at Ailethon. I don't think I could go back to Hethnost, for all the reasons I gave you." He shifted in his chair and looked Gerin directly in the eyes. "I do appreciate that you asked what was troubling me, but please don't worry. Things have changed for me, and I need to understand how I fit into the world again. I am fine, truly; just a little unsettled."

Gerin returned to his rooms and did his best not to worry about Hollin, but he could not help himself. What if Hollin in fact was growing delusional? People with delusions never *thought* they had them; that's what made them delusional in the first place. What if he got to a point where Hollin could no longer continue his training, or refused to? Would the Archmage send another wizard, or would she use that as leverage to try to force him to live at Hethnost while he finished his apprenticeship? She had not been pleased with his arrangement with Hollin. At one point the governing council of wizards had considered forcing him to remain there against his will, ostensibly for his own protection, and he worried it could become a problem again.

Gerin felt a presence suddenly behind him. He drew the dagger from his belt and wheeled about, wondering how someone had gained entry to his room.

A man stood near the balcony doors. He wore woolen pants and knee-high brown leather boots, and had straight black hair that fell to his shoulders and partially hid his face.

"Greetings, Gerin. We meet again."

7

Gerin lowered the knife. "I know you. You appeared to me on the road to Hethnost. The messenger of the Maker."

The man—if he was a man, which Gerin very much doubted—grinned. "You remember."

Gerin invoked a Seeing, and gasped when his spell revealed nothing at all. As far as his magic was concerned, there was no one there.

"I am beyond the ability of your powers to ken," said the man.

"The last time you appeared to me, time seemed to slow down before and after your arrival. I didn't feel that now."

"I have learned more subtle ways of entering the mortal sphere. You will not sense my presence in that manner again."

"Will you tell me your name?"

"My name in this realm is Zaephos."

Gerin had never heard the name before. It was certainly not the name of one of Khedesh's major gods, and not the name of any minor deity he knew.

"Why are you here?"

"I come to set you on a path."

Gerin tensed.

"I warn you, Zaephos, I will not be used by you or anyone else."

"I seek only to give you knowledge. I will not coerce you. Do you remember what I told you when we first met?"

"You warned me against the coming of an Adversary, the Enemy of the Maker. You said his power in the world was growing and that I should be mindful of signs of his presence."

"Yes. You must continue to be vigilant, for his power waxes even as we speak."

"Where is he? Can you tell me how to find him?"

"He is not in any place as you understand it. He is everywhere and nowhere. The Adversary has no physical form as yet. He is a spirit of illness and malice, a black wind in the night. There is nothing for you to find, or defeat. You must wait for him to take shape before you can act. Do you understand?"

Gerin nodded. He did not like the answer, but he saw the futility of seeking a disembodied spirit, or the wind.

"There is one other thing I told you," said Zaephos.

Gerin thought for a moment. "You said that even a prophet may not understand everything he is told."

Zaephos grinned. "Set your foot on the path, Gerin. It is the hope for the salvation of the Maker's work."

Then he was gone. There was no flash of light, no slowing of time, as at his first meeting with Zaephos. One moment he was there, the next moment the air where he'd been standing was empty.

Then he remembered: Viros Tennor and his letter of introduction to the Prophet. The Prophet of the One God! He'd completely forgotten about it, with all the other things that had happened since they arrived in the city.

The idea of being set on a path deeply troubled him. He had been forcibly set on a path by the Neddari *kamichi* who sought to bring their Slain God back to the world. He would not allow that to happen again. He would visit this Prophet—his curiosity would not permit him to stay away—but he would be cautious and wary. *One cannot avoid a path if one cannot see it,* he thought.

* * *

Gerin and Balandrick left the Tirthaig early the next day, headed for the district of Arghest and the Street of Poplars where the Prophet lived. Five Kotireon Guards—elite soldiers who protected the palace grounds and members of the royal family or important visiting dignitaries—accompanied them, their purple and gold breastplates gleaming in the bright morning sun.

The city streets were crowded, and their progress on horseback was slow. Not far from the palace they passed into the shadow of the Grael Citadel, a solitary tower of yellow-hued stone that rose from a courtyard enclosed by a square, five-story building. The chapter houses and guild houses of many orders were clustered here in Urlighest, a district within the confines of the Old City. They passed the chapter house for the Order of Laonn, of which Master Aslon was a member. It was smaller than the Grael Citadel, though still large enough in its own right. It had no tower, but was instead a four-story rectangular structure with a steeply pitched roof pierced with many chimneys. Beyond that was the headquarters for the Merchants Guild, followed by several other orders dedicated to the healing arts. Smaller guilds lined the street even after they had passed through the Wendin Gate and out of the Old City, soon to be replaced by a clutter of run-down homes, ill-looking taverns, and mangy brothels.

"I still don't see how he could have gotten out of the palace dungeons without help," said Balandrick as he kept a watchful eye on the throng of people around them. They were coming to the wide flat hill on the northern side of the city upon which the walled district of Arghest was built.

"There was no sign that anyone else was there. The guards were killed in his cell, not at the door, where you would expect if someone from the outside had come in to get him out."

"Then how did he do it?"

"He has powers we don't understand, Balan."

"Then why didn't he use them earlier?"

"I don't know. Maybe he was too injured. Or maybe he was just biding his time."

That morning, just as they were leaving the palace, they'd been told that Tolsadri had escaped from the dungeons sometime during the night. The bodies of two guards were found locked in his cell. He'd taken one of the guard's uniforms and armor as a disguise and managed, as far as could be determined, to escape the palace. Soldiers were sent at once to all of the city gates to prevent him from leaving Almaris, but Gerin was not hopeful they would succeed. If he wasn't already out of the city, he probably soon would be.

They reached a high wall set with iron braziers that separated Arghest from the districts surrounding it. The gates in the wall were manned with liveried guards, who bowed to Gerin and his escorts as they passed.

The Street of Poplars wound its way around the eastern side of the hill in a slowly rising curve. The Hill of Arghest was high enough to grant them a commanding view of the city.

At the end of the street was a walled manor, mostly hidden from view behind a grove of apple trees. Two men greeted them at the closed gate.

"Is this the home of Aunphar el'Turya?" asked Gerin.

"It is, my lord," said one of the men. Gerin doubted the man recognized him personally, though the presence of the Kotireon Guards indicated someone of importance was addressing him.

"I wish to speak to him. I have a letter of introduction from his servant, Viros Tennor." He held out the letter so they could see the seal, but did not give it to either of the men.

"Of course, my lord, of course." The men opened the gate and allowed them to enter a paved courtyard.

Balandrick and two of the Kotireon Guards accompanied Gerin as the man led them down a flagstone path toward the house. "May I have your name, my lord, so that I may tell the Prophet who is calling on him?"

"I am Gerin Atreyano, the crown prince of the realm."

The man's eyes widened and he bowed his head. "Yes, my lord. I am Orodren Fantal."

They turned sharply to the right, which revealed the house. It was three stories high and narrow across the front, with balconies on the upper two floors. To the left of the house was a long reflecting pool surrounded by paving stones.

Orodren led them to a small room on the first floor that was nearly overwhelmed by a massive granite table and many chairs. "Please, wait here, my lord. I will be back shortly."

"Make certain he knows it's the crown prince who has come calling," said Balandrick. "See that he does not make us wait."

"I will, good sir."

A short time later a serving girl entered with wine and fruit. "Orodren asked me to bring this to you, my lords," she said with a curtsy.

Gerin sipped the wine. "At least this Prophet shows good taste," he said. He offered a glass to Balandrick, but his friend declined. However, Balan did take one of the apples.

A tall woman appeared in the doorway. She had a slender shape and finely chiseled features that were a distant echo of Reshel's, though not quite as delicate or fragile. Gerin saw a fierceness of spirit in her dark eyes. Her wavy hair, thick and black, was pulled back from her face by a plain silver circlet. She wore a pale blue dress cinched at the waist with a ribbon of silk.

"May I ask what brings the crown prince to the house of my father?" she said from the doorway.

"You will address the crown prince as 'my lord' or 'my prince' to show the proper respect for his station," said Balandrick.

She inclined her head. "I apologize, my lord."

"I wish merely to speak to the Prophet," said Gerin. "And your name?"

"Elaysen el'Turya, my lord."

"I am pleased to meet you, Elaysen."

She stepped into the room. "I still must wonder, my lord, why the son of the king who despises my father has come to speak with him. It is odd, and troubling."

Gerin scowled at her accusation. "My father does not know I'm here, Elaysen. You said my father despises yours, and that may very well be the case. I do not know what his feelings are toward the Prophet because we have never spoken of it."

"Is your father in the habit of sending his daughter to antagonize visitors?" said Balandrick. "I am so far unimpressed with the hospitality of this house."

A man of middle years with graying hair and a clean-shaven face swept into the room. "Elaysen, how dare you harass my guests!" His face was scarlet with anger. Beneath bushy eyebrows that matched his gray and black hair were eyes of deep blue; the skin at their corners was deeply creased. He was lean, almost gaunt, his collarbone prominent beneath the top of his tunic.

Elaysen's demeanor changed at once. She lowered her head and stared at the floor, then folded her hands and hunched her shoulders together, as if trying to make herself smaller.

"I'm sorry, Father. When I heard the son of the king had come—"

"You dashed in here to make a fool of yourself and shame me in my own house." He turned from her to regard Gerin. "I apologize for my daughter's rudeness, my lord. She does not understand the concept of restraint and often forgets her place."

"It's no matter," said Gerin. "There is apparently some reason for her mistrust." He introduced himself and Balandrick.

"I brought a letter of introduction from your servant Viros Tennor." Gerin held out the sealed roll of parchment.

"Thank you, my lord, but that was not necessary." He broke the seal and read the brief message—more out of politeness, it seemed to Gerin, than any desire to know its contents—then placed it on the table.

"If you will excuse me, Father," said Elaysen.

"Please, stay," said Gerin. "You wanted to know why I was here. Don't leave just as I'm about to explain myself."

She glanced at her father. He made a dismissive gesture with his hand. "If the prince does not object, you may remain."

"Thank you, my lord," she said. Gerin noted that she did not sit near her father. "You are most kind."

8

Gerin paused. "I'm unsure where I should begin," he said. "I suppose I should simply get to the point. I've had several encounters with a divine being claiming to be a messenger of a god he called the Maker. Much of what he said I did not understand. Recently I heard Viros Tennor speaking about you and your belief in the One God, and some of what he said was similar to what the divine messenger told me."

A wild, hungry look came into Aunphar's eyes. "Indeed, my lord. Please, continue."

"The first encounter I had was several years ago in my rooms at Ailethon. I was awakened by the sense that there was some presence nearby, but I saw no one. A moment later a light filled the chamber that had no source I could see. The presence I'd felt grew stronger, and I could feel its attention bearing down on me. I sensed a vast amount of power, and somehow I knew that it was divine. I heard a voice in the light, which said, 'Gerin, your time is coming.' Then it and the light were gone.

"The second encounter was on the road to Hethnost, the fortress of wizards where my magic was to be Awakened."

Aunphar and Elaysen both looked surprised. "My lord, do you mean to say you are a wizard?" asked the Prophet.

Gerin rubbed his forehead. This story was growing more complicated by the moment. "Yes. I'll speak more of that later if time permits, but for now that has no real bearing on my tale." He wasn't sure exactly how true that was. After all, it was possible that he'd been singled out by the Maker precisely *because* of his magic.

"As I was saying, the second event happened on the road to Hethnost. I experienced a strange slowing of time, and then saw a man sitting on an outcropping of stone that had been empty a moment earlier. He said he was a messenger of the Maker and that his name was not for any man to know."

Aunphar paled. "My lord, would you please describe this being for me?"

"Do you think it's the same herald you met? Viros Tennor said you received your revelations at least in part from a divine herald."

Aunphar held up his hand. "Please, my lord. I would hear you tell me of this messenger before I say any more."

Gerin described the well-made but not opulent clothing worn by the messenger and the odd manner in which his dark hair had obscured part of his face. He did not mention the name Zaephos since he'd not reached that point in the story yet.

"Is this the same being who appeared to you?"

Aunphar nodded. "I believe so, my lord. But please, continue. I will tell you my own story when you are done, if you are willing to hear it."

Gerin paused to recall the words he'd been given. "This messenger told me that the gods are fickle creatures, that they may be powerless to save the things they have created. I was told that the Maker cannot reveal all the things He would have known, but the messenger did tell me that a being called the Adversary, who opposed the Maker at the beginning of time, was gathering strength within the confines of the world. He said the Maker needed people willing to serve His will because He could not strike the Adversary directly without undoing all that He has built, and warned me to be vigilant for signs of His Enemy's presence."

"Extraordinary, my lord," said Aunphar. "Viros Tennor said nothing to you of my own experiences?"

"No, and I did not speak to him of mine. But there is more. Just before he vanished, the messenger said to me, 'Even a prophet may not fully understand what he is shown. Be mindful of what you are told.'"

Aunphar looked stricken.

"The messenger vanished as soon as he spoke those words, and I have not been visited by him since—until last night." Gerin relayed the story of Zaephos's appearance and related his words.

A troubled look came to the Prophet's face. "I do not know what to make of this," he said. "What is it I don't understand?"

"I cannot say, Aunphar. I know little of what you teach or how you came to believe what you do. Perhaps that is a place to start. Tell me your tale and how you came to know this One God."

Aunphar nodded and poured himself a glass of wine. "I agree, my lord. Perhaps more will be revealed as you listen. Already, in some ways, you have been shown more than I. The being who appeared to me and set me upon my own path seems to be the same who visited you, though I was not blessed with the knowledge of his name."

"Has Zaephos appeared to anyone else? Do you recognize his name?"

"No. As far as I am aware, he has only appeared to you and me. And I did not know his name. It is not that of any known god of Khedesh."

"So what is your story?" asked Gerin. "How did you come to believe in the One God?"

For the next hour Aunphar told him how he had been a priest of Telros, as his father had been before him. He married the daughter of another powerful priest who thought the marriage would give him some measure of control over the young and influential Aunphar. "Harbeth died when Elaysen was seven, taken by the Scarlet Plague that ravaged Almaris during the Red Winter."

A look of distress came over Elaysen's face when her father

mentioned the plague. The disease had not reached Ailethon, but Gerin heard horrific stories about the plague wiping out entire villages and towns.

After his wife's death, Aunphar was a changed man. The priesthood mattered little to him. He took his daughter and moved to the town of Pelethar, in the forestlands of Haynaron. He often walked in the woods around his manor house, and one day was nearing the crown of a hill when he heard a voice call his name, but no one was there.

Then a blinding light filled his vision. A voice came from the light, but he also heard it within his mind, speaking with the voice of his thoughts. It said, *"Aunphar, I am the Maker, the One God, the High Father of gods and men alike. I have chosen you to be My voice to the world. It shall be your life's work to spread the word of My coming to all men so that they will know Me and life beyond this life. This is the path you shall walk. A darkness is coming to the world, and only through Me can mankind prevail."*

He asked how he would know what to say, and the voice said, *"You will know. You are my Prophet. There are signs all around you, and within you."* Then it was gone.

Gerin asked, "Why would the Maker, if He is indeed the creator of all things, remain unknown until now? Why was He hidden?"

Aunphar drew a long breath. "It's a question I have long pondered. I believe that ages ago He withdrew Himself from the affairs of the world. I think that He is *entering history*, that He is preparing to take a more active role in the unfolding of the future of mankind. I've studied many ancient sacred texts, searching for clues that may lead me to the answers I seek. The One God is never mentioned in them directly, but I've found passages that seem to indicate a divine presence greater than the gods of Khedesh. Some of the oldest texts speak of Telros entering the world *after* its creation, and choosing Khedesh to lead the Raimen into these lands to forge a great nation. It is never said explicitly who created the world, but it is apparent that Telros or the gods who came with him did *not* create it."

"What did He mean when He said 'spread the word of my coming to all men so that they will know me and know life beyond this life'?" asked Balandrick. "After death we go to Velyol in the dominion of Bellon. What else could there be?"

"The gods of Khedesh—in fact, all the gods of Osseria— are concerned with the earthly lives of men, achieving fame and glory, the conquest of enemies, the protection of the kingdom, while the goddesses are concerned with home and hearth and the raising of families. You are right, young man: all men when they die go to Velyol, where they dwell in gray silence. Never again to feel love or hate or joy or sorrow— only to exist as a shade in the dark Underworld. That is our belief, and what I learned and what I taught as a priest.

"I believe that the One God is granting the gift of eternal life to all who are worthy of it. Not the empty existence of Velyol, but a vibrant life of joy and happiness in His presence. True life beyond this life."

"Who is deemed worthy of this gift?" asked Gerin.

"Those who worship Him and aid Him in His battle against the Adversary. By worshipping the One God and living just and righteous lives, we move closer to Him and help Him enter the history of men."

"Why would He need help to do that?" asked Gerin. "If He is truly the creator of all things, then why could he not just enter His creation?"

"Because there are laws even *He* must obey. Laws the One God Himself created but that now bind Him as surely as both king and commoner alike are destined to one day die. I think that after He created the world, He left it to grow and change on its own, without His influence. To Him the world is like a snowglass with all of our lives, both gods and men alike, contained inside it. But even the maker of a snowglass cannot enter it without destroying it. The One God requires our help to fully enter the world, so that His own might does not ruin the very thing He created."

Gerin sat frozen, remembering his encounter with the Zaephos on the road to Hethnost: *There are restrictions even on the divine, rules by which they must abide, rules as inviolable as the law of death is to men. A god may find he is powerless to save what he has created even when that creation is threatened with annihilation."*

"Why would a god *want* to enter something he created?" he asked. "What could be served by doing such a thing?" It seemed a ridiculous thought, like a man trying to force himself into a drop of water.

"To become closer to His creation," said the Prophet. "He will no longer be *outside* of it, set eternally apart from what He has made. His divine power will suffuse our world and heal all the ills that have afflicted it since time began.

"And there is something else. Another reason He is returning now."

"The Adversary," said Gerin.

"Yes. A being dedicated to undoing all of the One God's work. This is another reason I was called to be His Prophet and spread the message of His return: to marshal men to oppose the Adversary. That is my mission: to proclaim the existence of the One God and make men know that He is deserving of their worship, and to battle the Adversary wherever his malign influence is felt. Worshipping Him and standing firm against the Adversary is the path men must follow in order to receive the gift of true life beyond death."

There was a long silence in the room. Balandrick was the first to speak. "You said you recognized the description Gerin gave to you of Zaephos, but in your story you heard only a voice."

"Ah, thank you for reminding me. That happened six years ago. I still lived in Pelethar, and was again walking alone when I felt a strange sensation that matches what you described as a slowing of time. When it ended I saw a stranger sitting on the trunk of a fallen tree near the path I was taking. He greeted me by name. I asked who he was, and he said to me, 'Many know who you are, O Prophet.' I again asked who he was, but he did not answer. He said that my fame was spreading throughout the land. I told him I was not concerned with my fame but rather the message of the One God.

'That,' he said, 'is why you must return to your birthplace. There you can do the most good spreading His word.' Then he was gone."

"What does this One God of yours want of me?" asked Gerin.

"He is not mine, my lord. Not in the essence that Telros is the lord of the gods of Khedesh, but not of Threndellen or Helcarea. The One God is above us *all*. All nations, all men, all gods. He is your God as much as He is mine. But as to what He wants with you *personally,* I cannot say. It seems He sent a vague warning to me through you, but why He chose you as His instrument is a mystery."

"Perhaps it has to do with Prince Gerin's magic," said Elaysen.

"Perhaps," said her father.

A servant entered and whispered into Aunphar's ear. He stood. "I'm afraid I must take your leave, my lord. I hope that we can speak again."

9

Elaysen remained seated at the table, watching
Gerin. "Does your magic grant you the ability to heal
wounds and sickness, my lord?"

"Yes. There are spells to accomplish healing of different
types, as well as devices of magic imbued with specific healing properties."

She asked him questions about magical healing. Did it always work? What kinds of things could *not* be cured with
magic? How many people could he heal at one time? Could
he remove disfigurements or flaws of birth, like a child born
deaf or blind or with no legs? Could he cure the insane?

Gerin answered each question in turn, explaining as best
as he could. Healing spells were some of the most complex
kinds of magic, and there was a great deal he still had to
learn from Hollin about that particular craft. As far as he
knew, they could not cure flaws *inherent* in a person. "Most
magical healing that I am familiar with is made to repair
an injury—to mend a broken bone, seal a cut, erase a burn,
things of that nature. A child born deaf or blind has no
healthy state to be returned *to*."

"My lord, what about someone who is blinded by injury?"
She grew more animated the more she spoke. *She speaks of
healing the way her father speaks of his religion,* he thought.
As if she were in the grips of a fever. "Could eyes plucked out
be made whole through your magic?"

"Perhaps," he said. "Some wounds are too grievous to mend, and some organs too complex for magic to properly rebuild. I still have much to learn about healing. Why are you so interested? Are you a healer yourself?"

She smiled and glanced down at the table. It was a warm, easy smile, and he liked it at once. It was the first time she'd smiled since he'd met her.

"Yes, I am a healer, my lord. What the common folk call a witching woman. I use herbs and potions and plant-lore to heal the sick, but when I go out among the people all I can see is how much I *cannot* do. I can set a broken bone, but if the break is not clean it is hard to make the bone mend correctly. I can cure fevers and stomach sickness, I can help a woman get with child or prevent her from doing so, I can make lotions and salves to help those with diseases of the skin. But I cannot cure blindness or deafness or heal a liver punctured by a knife. I can relieve the suffering of someone dying of consumption with Mandril's milk, but I cannot cure the illness that eats them from within.

"I would have that power if I could, Prince Gerin. I have dedicated my life to healing others. My father arranged for me to learn at the Grael Citadel and at other orders devoted to the healing arts. Many of the men would not help me— they felt a woman had no right to learn what they considered to be a man's work. But my father's influence allowed me past their doors, and what they would not teach me I taught myself in their libraries. I am good at what I do, but I also realize how much is beyond me." She leaned toward him, her eyes bright with excitement. "I beseech you, teach me as you have been taught. I do not want power for myself, only to help—"

Gerin held up his hand. "Elaysen, you misunderstand one important thing. Magic and wizardry cannot be taught to anyone who wishes to learn. It is not like reading, or your own healing arts, where the only true requirement is a willingness on the part of teacher and student." He explained about the Atalari and the mingling of their blood with races who did not have magic, diluting the potency of their powers.

"It is the remnant of Atalari blood that determines whether one can become a wizard, not the willingness of someone to learn. I could teach you hundreds of spells but there is nothing you could do with them because without magic flowing through you they are just empty words."

"How do you find those who still have the Atalari blood within them? Is it possible that some flows in my veins?"

"There is a ritual wizards use to test whether someone has the potential to become a wizard. Many of them spend their days scouring the kingdoms of Osseria for an ever-dwindling number of those with the ability. As to whether you have the potential, I cannot say. You would have to submit to the ritual."

Elaysen stood and bowed her head to him. "My lord, I ask that you test me as you were once tested."

"I do not have the ability to test you, but my teacher Hollin does. I will return with him when I can—"

"My lord, may I go with you to the Tirthaig? Is Hollin there now?"

He grinned at her eagerness.

"If you are of a mind to come with us, I will certainly not refuse you."

"Is there anything special I must do to prepare for this ritual?"

"No, nothing. But it's past time I leave."

"I will be back shortly, my lord," she said as she hurried to the door. "Please do not leave without me." Then she was gone.

Balandrick leaned toward Gerin's ear. "Are you sure you know what you're getting into, my lord?"

"I have no problem if she wants to undergo the ritual."

"That's not what I mean. I'm talking about this whole Prophet business," he said quietly, as if he suspected others in the house might be listening. "I don't doubt that you've both been visited by some divine power, but I'd say there's also little doubt that Aunphar is a bit mad. Maybe more than a bit. Have you ever seen any of the followers of Alamed, the sage who vanished at the Shrine of Labayas on Mount

Kail? They chant Alamed's name over and over and then fall on the ground, shaking and frothing at the mouth with their eyes rolled up into their heads. I thought Aunphar was going to go all frothy on us when he was talking about the One God."

"What would you have me do, Balan? Yes, I saw how he got when he talked. But he's the only other person who's had an experience like mine. I need him to help me understand what's happening."

"All right, my lord. I meant no offense, though I can hear the annoyance in your voice. I'm charged with protecting you, and that means I need to point out when I see danger, wherever it might come from. Just as long as you're aware of it, I'll say no more. Are you planning to tell your father about this?"

"That I've spoken with the Prophet? I won't volunteer it, but I also won't deny it if I'm asked."

"Then that's the position I'll take as well, my lord. No use stirring up the pot unless we have to."

Gerin felt he had enough problems with his father as it was. Even though he had perfectly legitimate reasons for his visit, his father would view it as fraternizing with a man the king considered an enemy of the realm. There was no reasoning with him when he got in one of his moods, and Gerin was certain that if word of his visit to Aunphar reached his father's ears, that mood would take him quickly and hard.

Elaysen swept back into the room, her cheeks rosy with color from running through the halls. She wore a light cloak across her shoulders. "One of the servants is bringing my horse, my lord," she said. "Are you ready?"

They followed her from the room and to the courtyard where the Kotireon Guards waited. A slender young man was there with a chestnut-colored mare. He held the reins while Elaysen climbed onto the saddle, then handed them to her and bowed his head. "Thank you, Kendren," she said.

"You're welcome, m'lady," the man said with another bow.

"Is no one escorting you?" asked Balandrick.

She laughed; Gerin liked the easy, throaty sound of it. "Of course someone is escorting me. You are. Men good enough for the heir to the throne are good enough for me. And before you ask, I'm often out in the city alone, tending to the sick or buying things I need for my medicines. I'll find my way back here without a problem, I assure you."

"I will see that you are provided an escort for your return," said Gerin. "It wouldn't do to have a guest of the palace way-laid on her way home."

They arrived at the palace and found Hollin in his chambers, staring at the Scepter of the King with an exasperated look. "There you are!" he barked when Gerin entered. "I thought you'd be back hours ago."

Hollin noticed Elaysen, who had stepped out from behind Gerin's larger presence. Gerin introduced her and told Hollin why she had come.

"Very good, very good," said the wizard. He disappeared into another room and emerged with a clear faceted jewel in his hand: a *methlenel*, the means by which a potential wizard's slumbering powers might be recognized.

Hollin gestured for Elaysen to step forward. "Did Gerin explain to you that it is unlikely that you have the potential to become a wizard?"

"Yes he did, Lord Hollin."

"Please, I am no lord. Hollin will be fine."

"Yes, Hollin."

"If you are a wizard, the heart of the *methlenel* will show the color of your magic, which is a rough gauge of your strength. If you are not a wizard, the jewel will remain dark."

As Hollin began the incantation, there was no fear in Elaysen that Gerin could see. He hoped she was indeed a wizard, though he knew the chances were slim.

Hollin finished the spell; no fire had lit in the heart of the *methlenel*.

"I'm sorry, Elaysen," said Hollin.

She stood frozen for a moment, then released her breath. "Thank you for testing me, Hollin. I'm no better or worse than I was." She faced Gerin. "And thank you, my lord, for graciously allowing me to accompany you. I will not forget it."

"I'm sorry that what you wanted is not meant to be."

He told Hollin he would arrange an escort for Elaysen and then return to help him with the scepter.

They walked a little in silence before Elaysen cleared her throat.

"I want to apologize for how I treated you at my father's house, my lord," she said. "I was inexcusably rude, and you've shown me nothing but patience and kindness in return."

He found a lieutenant in the palace guard and commanded him to prepare an escort for her. "I believe your man-at-arms has already done so, my lord, but I will check on it at once," said the lieutenant. They followed him to the courtyard within the palace gates, where Balandrick was waiting with Elaysen's mare and three soldiers.

"I was wondering when you'd show up, my lord," said Balandrick. He straightened and said to Elaysen, "May I ask how your visit with Hollin went?"

"I'm not a wizard, which is really no surprise," she said. But Gerin could hear a brittle glaze of disappointment in her voice.

"Are you ready to go home, my lady?" asked Balandrick.

"Yes, thank you."

"I will do my best to visit your father again before I return home."

"I would like that, my lord," she said. A quizzical look came over her. "Is your sword a weapon of magic?"

Gerin glanced down at Glaros. "No. Wizards eschew mundane weaponry for the most part. They consider their powers sufficient protection."

"I see. Then why do you carry one, my lord? Is it an heirloom of your house? Or does your role as crown prince require such accoutrements?"

"Both, truth be told."

"He just likes the feel of good steel at his side," said Balandrick.

* * *

Gerin was disappointed, but not surprised, to find that Hollin had failed to penetrate any further into the secrets of the scepter. He'd worked much of the morning on it, then given up to wait for Gerin's return from the city. "There's simply no point in me trying anymore," Hollin said in frustration. "I can't sense any of its power. Naragenth protected it too well for that. I'm afraid I'll trip a counterspell that will kill me, destroy the power the scepter contains, or both."

Gerin sat in a plush chair. He could not help but think about Elaysen, but tried to clear his mind and concentrate on the more immediate concern of the scepter. "We can't have that," he said. "What do you want me to try next?"

"I'm quite aware that she's an attractive and intriguing woman, but you need to concentrate. There are almost certainly lethal spells hidden here. I do not want to answer to your father if you are injured or killed, or the scepter damaged or destroyed, because you were distracted by a flash of cleavage."

"I'm not sure which one would make him more angry," Gerin muttered. "And what do you mean about Elaysen being attractive and intriguing? What has that got to do with anything?"

The old wizard rolled his eyes. "Your attentiveness to the young lady was evident to anyone with eyes. Are you ready to begin?"

Gerin decided to let Hollin's comment go unanswered. "Yes, I'm ready." And thought once more of Elaysen.

Gerin spent the rest of the day with Hollin, carefully prodding the scepter with various Seeings and key spells to see if he could uncover what lay within it, or perhaps unlock by chance one of the more basic protections. Nothing worked. He returned to his rooms well after dark, frustrated with their lack of progress. He was not tired, having used only small amounts of magic during the day, since both he and Hollin had been fearful of what larger amounts might inadvertently trigger, and had no desire to sleep as yet. His mind was whirling with thoughts of both the scepter and Elaysen, but he thought of Elaysen more.

The scepter was a mystery they would unravel in time, if the gods were willing. But Elaysen . . . he'd only been with her a few hours, but already missed her presence. There was strength in her, a steely confidence in her abilities that impressed him.

He saw Glaros in its scabbard, hanging on a peg in the wall. He got it down and placed it on a table. *Is your sword a weapon of magic?* It was a perfectly reasonable question to ask a wizard. He'd never given much thought to magical weapons. Wizards had their powers and own devices designed for battle. They did not use swords, spears, or knives.

Why not make a magic sword of my own? he wondered. A weapon worthy of an amber wizard. Glaros was an ancient heirloom and fine blade in its own right, but was it enough for him? Why be content with mere steel?

He wondered if any magical swords had ever been made, or if they existed solely in tales and legends. Wizards would not have created them for themselves but might very well have made them for others—kings or generals whose favor they curried in the days when wizards were members of many royal courts.

He thought about speaking to Hollin but decided against it. He wanted this weapon to be his and his alone, for better or worse, without aid from anyone else.

He drew Glaros from its scabbard and placed it on a table. The light from the oil lamp shone upon the naked blade.

He regarded it for a long while, planning what he would do to it. At last he drew magic into himself and began.

He decided to first strengthen the metal of the blade. He bathed the cold steel with magefire while imprinting it with preservation spells. The spells trapped the magefire within the blade itself so it shone with a pale silvery glow, as if he'd managed to capture stray starlight. He continued to work the magefire and the spells deeper and deeper into the blade until magefire, spell, and steel were inextricably woven together.

The effort was taxing and left him weary, but he was not

yet ready to stop. The act of making something new and unique had firmly gripped him. He picked up the sword and turned the blade back and forth in his hand. He was pleased by what he'd accomplished.

The sword was now a vessel able to contain spells.

He poured enormous amounts of unshaped magic into the sword so that it held its own reservoir of power. Once that was done, he created spell after spell and imprinted them into the blade. He fashioned the spells so they would become active when he sent a small bit of amber magic into the weapon. No other kind of magic would suffice, which meant he was the only one who could wield the power within his sword.

Once he sent his amber magic into the blade, the spells would not actually be triggered until he issued the commands to release them. In this way he could unleash spells one after the other much more quickly than he could otherwise, since he would not have to spend time *creating* them; they were already within the sword, waiting to be released. And he would not drain his own strength, since the spells would feed off the reservoir of magic within the sword rather than drawing from magic flowing through his body.

After several hours of work the blade was saturated with power. A nonwizard would sense nothing from the weapon, but a wizard would know at once that a potent source of power was near at hand.

Gerin examined his work. The silvery starlight glow of the blade brightened when he held it, and pulsed and throbbed with the rhythm of his heart. *It recognizes my touch somehow.* He wondered how that could be. Certainly the blade could not be aware of him in any real sense. Did the magic contained within it somehow sense his own amber power, even when he did not have it flowing through him?

There was a sudden flash in his vision, and he nearly dropped the weapon. He staggered back, blinking, and tightened his grip on the hilt.

The flash had not been of light, but something far more strange. He'd been peering at the blade when he thought he'd seen more than one weapon in the space occupied by Glaros.

There was no other way to describe it. For an instant it seemed as if dozens, hundreds, of swords were in his hand.

There was a room near the Sunlight Hall in Ailethon where two large gilded mirrors were hung upon the walls facing each other, with a great chandelier dangling between them. Someone looking into one of the mirrors would see the chandelier's image repeated in a recession that vanished toward an infinite distance. What he saw and felt with his sword was something like that. As if some impossible number of blades—similar but not identical to each other, of that much he was sure—were in the same space at the same time. He had no idea what to make of it.

The vision left him shaken. Midnight had passed hours ago, and fatigue rushed over him as the excitement that had fueled his endeavors evaporated like a morning mist.

But there was one more thing to be done. "You need a new name," he said aloud. Glaros meant "justice" in the old tongue of Khedesh. But this sword was very different from what it had been.

He stared at the dimly glowing blade when the name struck him: *Nimnahal.* "I christen thee 'Nimnahal,' Starfire in the tongue of wizards and the Atalari of old," he said quietly. "May you serve me true to the end of my days, and serve those who follow after me, for as long as House Atreyano endures."

He raised the sword and kissed the blade, then slid it into its scabbard with a clear ringing sound. He was about to return the belt to its peg on the wall when his door was flung open and Hollin rushed in with a look of horror upon his face.

"Gerin, in Venegreh's holy name, what have you done?"

✳ 10

Gerin was so surprised by Hollin's outburst that he could only stare at him and wonder what he was talking about. Then the weight of the sheathed sword in his hand registered. "You mean you can you sense this?"

Hollin approached the weapon as if it were a demon straining against weakening chains. His hair was wild from sleep, his cheeks stubbly with white whiskers. He wore a long nightshirt that fell to his knees. His feet were bare and pale against the wine-colored rug.

"Of course I can sense it," he said irritably. "What I don't know is what it *is* or how it came to be."

"I've made a magical weapon," Gerin said, trying not to sound defensive.

Hollin made an exasperated sigh. "Tell me everything."

Gerin slid the sword from its sheath. Its ethereal glow cast a wan light upon Hollin's face. The old wizard gasped.

"This is Ninmahal," said Gerin.

"What have you done to it?" he asked. He held his hand toward the blade but did not touch it.

"Why are you so upset?" said Gerin, ignoring Hollin's question for the moment.

"Because I was awakened from a lovely dream by a surge of magic I didn't understand and was shaken by it. Now tell me exactly what you've done."

Despite his weariness, Gerin recounted in detail how he'd

transformed his sword. He'd sheathed the blade once more and placed it on the table, where it lay between the two men like a silent, brooding omen.

"Just before you entered I saw a vision of some kind. For a very brief moment I saw hundreds of swords at once. I was holding the sword, and then I saw—I don't know how to describe it other than to say I saw hundreds of swords in my hand at the same time. I didn't *feel* hundreds of swords, but for a moment that's what was there. It wasn't a trick of the light or my eyes. I know it was real. Or as real as a vision can be. And they were not the same sword. They were similar but not identical."

Hollin gestured toward the sword. "May I?"

"Please. I want to know what you think."

Hollin grasped the hilt and drew the weapon from its scabbard. The blade shone with its watery light, but not with the pulsing intensity it displayed when gripped by Gerin. Hollin's powers did not resonate with it as Gerin's had.

"You have fused magefire with the steel of the blade," said Hollin. He placed the sword on the table and created a Seeing.

"It gets brighter when I hold it." Gerin wrapped his fingers around the hilt. The blade's light intensified and began to pulse.

"It senses the power that made it. Your amber magic feeds it and is contained within it." He continued to peer through the hazy circle in the air that marked the Seeing's power. "You've imprinted a large number of spells here. I'm impressed that you were able to do so much in just a few hours."

Hollin cancelled the Seeing and folded his hands. Gerin released his grip—

And the vision occurred again, an overlapping of hundreds of images of weapons occupying the same space as Nimnahal. Gerin jerked his hand away and cursed. Hollin stiffened in his seat and scowled.

"Did you see that?" said Gerin. "It just happened again."

"Yes, I saw."

"Do you know what it is?"

Hollin absently rubbed his chin. "Do you remember me teaching you about Telemardel Prethin?"

"Vaguely. He had some strange ideas about what happened to a wizard's spirit after death, if I remember."

"Among other things, yes. But he also had an idea that our world is but one of many, and that they all exist in the same space at the same time."

"You mean right now there are people from other worlds in this very room?"

"They're not *in* the room; they're on another plane of existence, but one that overlaps our own."

Gerin thought the idea was absurd. But then he remembered the thinning of the world on Maratheon's Hill when he'd blown the Horn of Tireon and had the strong feeling of having moved to some *other* place. He also recalled the blurring of the worlds of the living and the dead atop the Sundering when he'd confronted Asankaru, and suddenly the idea of another plane of existence didn't seem so ridiculous anymore.

"Prethin said these many worlds are similar to each other but not identical. You and I may be in many but not all of them, and in each of the ones we inhabit we may be changed in different ways. You might be married now, or not a wizard, or not the heir to the crown. He felt there could be an infinite number of variations. I think that what we've seen with your sword might be the first validation of Prethin's idea. When I saw your sword many times over it seemed that I was also seeing it in just as many *places*." The wizard folded his arms and his scowl darkened. "There were many swords, but you were right, not all of them were the same. And I didn't *see* different places, but I sensed very strongly that many of the images of the sword, the different versions of it, existed elsewhere."

"But what does it mean?" Gerin asked. "And how did I cause it?"

"I have no idea. It may be that you have so saturated the sword with magic and spells that it has somehow leaked into the other worlds of which Prethin spoke. Perhaps what we're sensing and seeing are all those worlds where you—and the other Gerins in those worlds—transformed your sword. Maybe the transformation is so powerful that the swords are somehow calling to each other across whatever boundary separates one world from the next. For a moment the boundary breaks down and we can see all of them at once."

Gerin did not like the sound of that. He also did not like the idea that there were other Gerins doing things of which he knew nothing. It seemed to cheapen his own existence, diluting the uniqueness of his personality. He tried to shake off the feeling, telling himself that these other worlds were not "real" in the sense of being places he could somehow reach, or that he could know what events transpired in them. Still, it was a troubling thought.

"Is this dangerous?" he asked. If he had done something to cause a boundary of some sort to break down between worlds that were never intended to meet, what kind of unforeseen consequences could result? He remembered the disastrous opening of the door between the worlds of the living and the dead, and a cold shiver ran down his spine. "Is this something I should try to undo?"

"I'm not sure you can," Hollin said. "You could rid the sword of its spells, but I can think of nothing that would allow you to unravel this unique blending of magic and steel. I think your only recourse would be to destroy it."

Gerin opened his mouth to object, but before he could speak, Hollin raised his hand. "*However*, I don't think that's called for, at least not yet. This is not a doorway between worlds, like the one you opened when you summoned Naragenth from the grave."

"I was just thinking about that."

"This is not the same. As I said, this is not a door, but rather a thing that exists in many worlds at once, whose different iterations are somehow unusually close to one another. But I don't see how anything could travel through the sword, or use it as a means of travel."

"I'm glad to hear you say that. I would not relish having to destroy an heirloom of my house." *Or explain it to my father,* he thought.

Hollin returned to his rooms, and Gerin slipped into bed. Despite his bone-deep weariness, sleep was a long time in coming.

Toward morning he dreamed. He sensed that it was no ordinary dream but a thing of truth, like the visions that had plagued him when the Storm King sent him the terrible sounds of the battle in which blood-crazed Atalari had exterminated Asankaru's people atop the Sundering.

In this dream he saw a mist-shrouded forest, still and quiet save for the chirping of birds and the rustle of animals moving through the underbrush. His view shifted to a wide lake nestled in the crook between two steep hills. The verdant slopes rose from the lake's edge without beach or break between land and water. The surface of the lake was as still as glass, with curling tendrils of mist drifting above the black water like lost and forlorn ghosts.

He saw two men standing at the edge of the lake beneath a sprawling willow tree. One was young, with a trim beard and large gray eyes; his face was hard, grim, and seemed burdened with great responsibilities and worries. He wore strangely fashioned plate armor over leather and bits of mail. There was scrollwork upon the chest plate and a crest of arms that Gerin did not recognize.

The other man was older, with hollow, wind-burned cheeks and a gray beard that reached to his collarbone. He carried a staff equal to his height and wore layers of robes bound with a thick leather belt; the outermost garment was embroidered with several arcane symbols that spoke to Gerin of magic. *That man is a wizard of some kind,* he realized, though not one descended from the Atalari.

The older man gestured to the younger and spoke in a language Gerin did not understand or recognize. The younger man waded into the water up to his thighs, then looked back at the wizard with curiosity and anticipation. Though there was nothing on his person signifying his identity, Gerin was suddenly certain that this young man was a king.

The wizard held out his staff and shouted a command. For a moment nothing happened. The forest fell utterly silent, as if all the world held its breath.

The water of the lake began to tremble a short distance from the young king, as though a fire had somehow been struck below its surface. The king and wizard watched the roiling water with hard, fervent stares.

A woman with flowing blond hair, wearing a white and gold dress, rose from the water bearing an unsheathed sword. Her eyes shone with a faint violet light. Gerin was startled to see that she was not wet. The waters of the lake bent around her legs in a swirling vortex, kept at bay by some invisible power he could not see or sense.

She turned the blade in her hand and extended the hilt toward the young king, who had knelt in the water at her appearance, his head bowed. Gerin could clearly see the sword. It was not Nimnahal—and yet it was. The blade was a bit narrower and slightly shorter than his own, and the hilt guards were angled differently and did not bear the same winged design that adorned his own weapon. Yet some part of him recognized this as Glaros-that-was, refashioned and reborn as Nimnahal, a weapon of such potency that its existence bled across worlds.

This was indeed a true vision and no mere dream of sleep. He was seeing his sword as it existed in some other place, where it was given to a king by a woman wizard who lived beneath a lake. Who were they? What was the story behind this particular weapon? He wanted to call out to them but could not; in this place he had no form, no voice.

The king took the sword from the woman and held it up before his eyes, a look of rapturous joy upon his face, as if he'd been handed a relic of unimaginable age and power. The female wizard lowered her head and immediately began to sink beneath the lake. The king turned to face the wizard standing on the shore, but then the dream faded as the power of the sword waned, and Gerin slipped into a normal, dreamless sleep.

* * *

Beneath the crescent-shaped curve of flat-topped hills ten miles north of Moriteri, the ancient capital city of the long-dead Helcarean Empire, an ancient being stirred from its millennial slumber.

The hills were surrounded by fields of wheat and pastures for cows and sheep, but the slopes themselves were barren save for tall grasses amidst the stones and sparse copses of oak and pine. The hills were not a natural part of the landscape, though no one now living knew that. They had been fashioned twenty thousand years ago, long before the coming of the Atalari or the Gendalos. The world had been a very different place, where beings of power and majesty had walked the hills and fields like gods made flesh.

The Atalari had shunned these hills and built no settlements within sight of them, having some sense of what lay buried beneath them. Many ages later, when mortal men had come here and built their first primitive communities, the hills had been prized for their commanding view; but those holds and citadels were later abandoned because of the haunted dreams and nighttime apparitions that had plagued every man, woman, and child who lived there. When the first city-state had been built where Moriteri now stood, a series of fortresses were raised upon the hills as protection from marauder clans who roamed the plains. Not long after their completion, hardened soldiers had deserted their posts; others had slain their fellow warriors for no reason, then taken their own lives. Eventually the fortresses were burned and the earth salted by priests invoking the power of their gods to cleanse the tainted land. Every few centuries another group made an attempt to settle the hills, unaware of the history and legends or defiantly ignoring them, and each time the attempt failed. The last had been three hundred years ago.

The trees that grew there were twisted and black, deformed by the ancient power of what lay beneath them. Animals who happened upon the hills quickly left for lower and less troubled ground; birds alighted in the trees for scant moments before flying off again.

The Helcareans of Formale—the name later given to the

region—called them the Bronze Demon Hills, though that name did not appear on any official map, which labeled them the Aplatoru, a word of dread and ill-omen in a tongue long vanished from Osseria.

The Vanil stirring to wakefulness was the Chieftain of the nineteen brethren who lay in the hills with him. There were similar hills scattered throughout Osseria, ancient barrows designed to hold them in a dreamless slumber until the time of the return. The Master would call to them once he had manifested himself in this world; that had been the promise. The call now stirring it back to life was changed, corrupted in some unknown manner from what had been expected, but it was enough to begin the process of awakening. As Chieftain, its duty was to awaken first and find the Master before summoning those who lay with it.

The Vanil's power began to wax and flow beyond the hills like poisoned floodwaters.

11

Claressa's wedding day was sunny and cheery, with a brisk wind blowing through the city. Tall clouds huddled on the horizon far out to sea, their distant tops tinted yellow by the sunlight.

Gerin, Therain, and a company of Kotireon Guards made their way from the Tirthaig to the Temple of Telros, the immense and ancient pile of stone and marble that was the earthly seat of power of the gods of Khedesh. Abran and Claressa had gone ahead earlier. Gerin hoped everything was fine; if something were amiss, he did not want to be near to feel his sister's wrath.

The Temple was nearly as large as the Tirthaig, and though it was not built upon a hill like the royal palace, the Pinnacle of Geled-Asulan rose from the Temple's central dome to nearly the height of the Tirthaig's tallest spire. The last time he had been inside it, his father was crowned king.

A group of high-ranking priests wearing robes of scarlet waited for them in a vestibule off of the main entryway to the Temple. The glowering priests did not speak. They gestured for the royal brothers to follow them—laws as old as the Temple itself forbid the presence of the Kotireon Guards any farther inside the holy place—and hurried off down a long, dim corridor.

They entered the Holy Sanctum of Telros and were led by the priests to the dais at the head of the room. The priests left them with an admonishment to be still and not offend the great gods who guarded the realm.

The sanctum was a rectangular room with two aisles of bench seating and a gallery; opposite them was the dais, which rose seven steps above the marble floor. The room had no windows; light was cast from candles in wall sconces and tall standing lamps. The high coffered ceiling was shrouded in a perpetual semigloom, far beyond the reach of the lamplight, which suggested to Gerin the mysterious and unknown, here at the heart of the gods' Temple. An enormous statue of Telros rose from behind the altar, his crowned head reaching nearly to the ceiling. Before him was an empty throne, the earthly symbol of his divine rule, and to either side smaller statues of the major gods of Khedesh, the ornamental lamps at their feet casting light upward onto their stern white faces.

He wondered about the One God and His relationship to other deities. Did these great gods of his homeland worship a being as greater than themselves as they were to him? He tried to imagine Telros kneeling in supplication and prayer and found it a difficult image to grasp.

The Temple quickly filled with nobles. Gerin saw Aron and Vaina Toresh and their daughter Morweil at the front of the sanctum. Aron absently stroked his thick moustache as he shifted his gaze between the rear of the sanctum and a narrow door at the foot of the dais.

The door near the dais opened and Baris Toresh, Claressa's husband-to-be, came through it, accompanied by another priest. His brown hair was bound by a pearl-laden circlet that Gerin assumed was an heirloom of his house. He wore layers of white silk and brocaded wool dyed a deep blue.

They were not waiting long when a group of heralds in the gallery sounded their trumpets. The audience turned toward the doors at the rear of the sanctum. High Priest Omman Salendiri entered, followed by Abran and Claressa. Gerin's father wore purple and gold and walked with his head high, his expression reserved.

Claressa was breathtakingly beautiful. There was no other way to describe her. The fall of her black curls, the porcelain smoothness of her skin, the snowlike purity of her gown, the radiant smile on her face, created an image of womanly perfection. He heard Therain take a deep breath at the sight of his twin.

When the high priest reached the top of the dais, he turned to face Abran and Claressa, who remained one step below him. Abran kissed Claressa's cheek and joined his sons. The high priest gestured for Baris to stand next to Claressa.

"In this holy house of Telros we have gathered to join this man, the son of a venerable and noble house, to the daughter of the king," he announced in a clear voice that carried through the room.

As Gerin listened to the ceremony, he felt that some of the nobles in the audience were watching him as well, wondering when the firstborn of the king and heir to the throne would be wed, and to whom. *Let them wonder,* he thought.

The day after Claressa's wedding, Gerin received a written message inviting him to a dinner at Aunphar's home to meet the members of his Inner Circle. Gerin told the messenger he would attend, then left to search for Hollin.

So far they'd had no luck in unlocking the secrets of the scepter. They'd learned a little about the nature of the first layer of protective spells contained in the Scepter of the King, but that knowledge was not enough to show them a way to penetrate the spells safely. "I fear that even if we took this to Hethnost for study, we would have little success," said Hollin glumly as the day wore on.

"We'll understand this eventually," said Gerin with more conviction than he felt. "Naragenth wouldn't have made the entry into the Varsae Estrikavis so difficult that no one other than himself could get in. What about the other wizards who contributed to the library? How would they enter?"

"Nevertheless, I'm afraid he might have done just that," said the wizard. "Perhaps Helca's wars interrupted their work, and he only had time to create access for himself before Almaris was besieged. Or maybe the other wizards took their keys with them, which were later lost. Certainly there is no record of them. I tell you, Gerin, I'm worried that even with these key spells literally in our hands, we may never find a way to unlock them."

Gerin, Balandrick, and a company of Kotireon Guards set out for the Prophet's home early in the evening.

Gerin was met by Elaysen and a solemn manservant. Elaysen wore a blue dress trimmed with gold and had braided her hair. "You look lovely," he said.

She grinned. "Thank you, my lord."

The manservant led them to a small dining room lit with many candles. Balandrick waited outside the door. The aroma of spices and incense drifted on the evening air.

Three people were in the dining room with Aunphar. All were men of middle years who regarded Gerin with wary and suspicious glances. He understood perfectly their feelings toward him. He would feel the same toward an outsider—the son of an avowed enemy of their religion, no less—who claimed to have been visited by the messenger of the One God, when they had not. It would be a difficult and bitter thing to swallow.

They were seated for dinner. Aunphar told him that among the Inner Circle all were equal. "There is no rank here, no station within the circle."

"Our esteemed Prophet has little faith in our abilities to rise above petty squabbles," said Hellam Ostreng, a slender man with thick gray hair and a white beard trimmed to a point. "He fears if he created ranks, we would be stabbing each other in the back within hours." He smiled as he spoke, but Gerin sensed his words were not said entirely in jest.

"You know very well what I mean," said Aunphar.

"I have no problem with the fact that we are all equal," said Hellam. "There is no need for rank or station among us; we are as yet too small to require it. We are bound by our faith, not a desire to replace you. There will never be another Prophet."

"This is an old argument, my lord," said Elaysen. "One my father and Hellam are trotting out for your viewing. I do believe they rather enjoy it, but after hearing this so often I do wish they'd attempt some other form of entertainment, like trained dogs or jugglers."

"I'm not so sure there will never be another Prophet," said Aidrel Entraly, pointedly ignoring Elaysen. He was a short man, well-tanned, with strong arms and shoulders and brown and gray hair cropped close to his head. "Aunphar became the Prophet because he was visited by the One God. We of the Inner Circle have never been so blessed, but now one comes among us who claims to have also basked in the One God's presence." He stared at Gerin. "It seems a succession has been implied, if not yet stated outright."

"I assure you I've no intention of replacing Aunphar," Gerin said as Aunphar glowered at Aidrel. "I am not even a follower of your religion."

"Yet you claim to have met the god of a religion you do not believe, my lord. An incredible claim, to say the least."

Aunphar's face darkened with anger. "Aidrel, Prince Gerin is here as my guest. I will not have you impugn his motives. *I* am satisfied that he was visited by the same messenger who appeared to me."

"This is folly," Aidrel said. "We are being used for a purpose we cannot yet see. Perhaps the king has sent his son to ingratiate himself to you, only to later undermine your work from within."

The Prophet's face turned scarlet with anger. "How dare you question my judgment!"

"Aunphar, it is quite all right," said Gerin. "I understand his suspicions. I would have the same concerns if our positions were reversed. I can only tell you that I am no spy or saboteur. Do you really think the king would send his son and heir to do such work? There are better and more subtle ways of spying, I assure you. Besides, I'll soon be leaving for Ailethon. I'd make a poor spy so far away from those I'm to watch."

"I for one welcome you, my lord," said Kurein Esdrech. He was a fat man with dark hair cut in severe bangs, like a curtain across his forehead, and a raw, ruddy complexion.

Aunphar looked around the table with an icy stare. "I will state again my unequivocal belief in Prince Gerin's sincerity. He is a man of high destiny, and not only because he will one day be king. The One God has chosen him for some purpose not yet revealed. I too have been chosen and shown my path. In time, Prince Gerin will find his." He faced Gerin. "My lord, because of this, I must make a request of you."

"I will listen, though I cannot say whether I will honor it."

"I would expect nothing less, my lord." Aunphar folded his hands as a kind of solemn weight settled over him. "I ask that you become a member of my Inner Circle."

Aidrel's head rocked back as if he'd been slapped. "Aunphar—"

"*I will brook no more dissent on this subject.* I have heard your objections. Either you follow my will or you step down from your position. That is your choice."

Aidrel clenched his jaw. After a moment he bowed his head. "I hear you and obey, Aunphar."

"I am honored by your request," said Gerin. "But I must decline. I know you feel my destiny is somehow twined with yours, or with the One God, but I am not yet convinced of that. I know nothing of your religion except its most basic ideas. I will learn more about the One God, but I cannot say yet whether I will become a follower. It would be inappropriate for me to join the governing body of something I scarcely understand."

Aunphar was silent for a long moment. "The One God's messenger has appeared to you for a *reason*, my lord."

"Yes, but that reason may have nothing to do with the religion you were charged to create. I cannot join your Inner Circle; I will not. Whether I am open to it in the future depends on a great many things."

"Very well," Aunphar said. "I will ask two more things of you, which I hope you will grant. First, I ask that you send word to me at once should the One God ever appear to you again."

"That is certainly a condition I can accept. And the other?"

"You said you want to learn more about the Way of the Faith, which I have named *dalar-aelom,* an Hodetten phrase that means 'holy path.' Those who follow *dalar-aelom* are called *taekrim,* the 'vigilant.' I want to send an emissary with you to teach you the ways of *dalar-aelom* so you may decide for yourself whether to become a follower."

"Viros Tennor is already near to my home. Why send someone else?"

"Tennor's charge is to spread the word of the One God to as many as he can. He cannot do that effectively and teach you personally."

"If that is your desire, I have no objection."

"Good. I will find an appropriate teacher and send word to you at the Tirthaig."

The next morning, Gerin was summoned to see his father. The king was in his garret room study near the summit of the Tirthaig. A brilliant blue sky was visible beyond the four dormer windows in the northern wall.

His father was at his desk when his servant, Yurente Praithas, closed the door behind Gerin. From the tightness around his father's eyes and the set line of his jaw, Gerin could tell that he was angry.

"You asked to see me, Father?"

"I've received word that you have twice now visited the home of a renegade priest. I'm troubled that you would even deign to visit such a man, and that, having done so, you further neglected to speak to me of it."

"Since I've arrived you've had Claressa's wedding to attend to. I didn't think there was any reason to tell you, and I certainly would have done so had I been asked."

His father's face twisted into a snarl of rage. "That *Prophet* is a menace to the kingdom! He was once a priest held in high regard, but he's turned his back on the Temple and everything it stands for, everything he was. His teachings undermine the Temple and undermine my own authority. I don't know why you felt compelled to see him, but you will not do so again."

Gerin was shocked at the change that had come over his father. It was as if he'd become possessed, overcome by some dark personality not his own. He sensed that something was deeply wrong with his father, other than simple anger at his visit to Aunphar.

"Father, are you feeling well? You seem—"

"I have a son who's consorting with traitors to the realm behind my back!" Abran was screaming now, and had risen partway from his chair. Spittle flew from his mouth. "How *should* I feel? Will you try to kill me with your magic? Make me die in my sleep so that no suspicion would fall on you? Is that—"

"Father!" He could not believe what he was hearing. Had his father gone mad?

"You will not see this priest again! He is after power, nothing more! There is no reason for you to see him, unless you wish to prove my suspicions."

For the first time in his life, Gerin felt unsafe in his father's presence. He could all too easily imagine the king having him arrested and thrown in the dungeons for treason. He'd never seen his father like this, and wondered again, this time quite seriously, if the king was losing his mind.

"He was visited by a divine being, Father," Gerin said, trying to keep his voice calm, which he found difficult to do. His heart hammered in his chest and fear tightened his throat. "He was told it was his task to spread the word of the One God to all men."

Abran made a scoffing noise and fell back into his chair. "That is what he *says*. I'm surprised, and more than a little disappointed, to find you so gullible."

"There is a reason I went to see him." His father's words hurt him deeply, and he decided he would not subject himself to any more of the madness that had gripped the king.

Gerin pushed back his chair and stood. He was about to reveal something that he had not yet shared with his father. He'd made no conscious decision to keep it secret, but the strain in their relationship since Reshel's death had left him feeling unable to confide in Abran.

"I believe him because the One God also visited *me*," he said, then marched from the room, leaving his father at his desk, speechless.

12

Later that day the king sought out Gerin in his rooms. "Explain to me what you meant when you said you've been visited by the One God." He was still angry, but not to the degree he had been earlier.

"It first happened a few years ago, when you were visiting Ailethon after your coronation," Gerin began, then went on to recount the later visitations of Zaephos.

"I believe we both encountered the same divine creature. What it wants with me is still uncertain, but Aunphar believes he's been tasked with spreading word of the One God's existence and preparing men for the coming battle with the Adversary."

"This has to do with your wizardry, doesn't it?"

Everything comes back to that and his regrets about Reshel. "I have no idea. If it does, Zaephos has not yet spoken of it."

"So now we have godlike creatures prowling the Tirthaig at will. You have left me defenseless in my own house. Your wizardry calls nothing but death and ruin to you and those around you. If I could cut it out of you I would do so without hesitation." He turned and left without another word.

"I hear you've been stirring up quite a lot of trouble," Claressa said to Gerin. They were in the courtyard of the Tirthaig, just inside the main gates. She faced her brother with a yellow parasol resting on her shoulder. Her husband Baris emerged from a colonnade with his mother and father and a number of servants with sealed chests in tow. She was leaving for the ship that would bear her to her new home in Tolthean, on the eastern coast of the kingdom beyond the immense cliffs of the Seawall. This was the last time Gerin would see his sister for a long time, perhaps years, and he did not want their parting to be angry or disagreeable.

She, however, was making that very difficult.

"I've done no such thing," he said.

She arched an eyebrow. "Oh? I suppose no one bothered to tell me that associating with troublesome, power-mad priests had recently become an acceptable practice among the nobility."

I really don't want her to drown at sea, I really don't, thought Gerin with his jaw clenched.

"And are you truly thinking about becoming a believer of this new religion? It's well and fine for the rabble, I suppose, but it's unseemly for the heir to the throne to consort with such ill-reputed characters."

Therain said, "By the gods, Claressa, if you treat your husband this way he'll throw you overboard before you come within a hundred miles of Tolthean."

The king appeared in the courtyard and strode up to Claressa with barely a glance at Gerin. She gave him a beaming smile and hugged him. "I was wondering if you were coming to see me off."

"Don't be foolish," said Abran. "Of course I would be here."

The Toreshes joined them. Gerin and Therain chatted with Baris for a little while before taking their leave. Claressa approached them, and he was surprised to see tears glistening in her eyes. "I'm sorry for what I said earlier," she whispered to him. "Cause all the trouble you want. It's what you do best." She gave him a hug and kiss on the cheek. "I'm going to miss you very much."

He felt suddenly sad at the thought of her leaving. Tears burned his eyes. "I'll miss you, too."

He stood with Therain and their father while the Toreshes, their servants, their baggage, and a retinue of guards departed the courtyard. Claressa looked back once from her saddle and waved, then disappeared around the curve beyond the gates.

The king turned to Gerin. His gaze was cold and hard. "The Scepter of the King will remain here when you depart for Ailethon. It's too valuable, and too important to the kingdom, for me to permit it to leave the Tirthaig. It is a symbol of royal authority, and as such cannot leave the seat of royal power."

"Father, if we can't take it with us to study we'll never unlock its secrets."

"You and Hollin may come here to study it. I will allow that much, and for that you should be grateful. That is my will, and it is final." Abran marched out of the courtyard.

"Looks like he's still mad at you about this Prophet business," said Therain.

"He's mad at me about everything."

"He'll get over it one of these days."

No, he won't. And not because of the Prophet. He'll never forgive me because Reshel is dead.

Gerin was up early on the morning of their departure after a fitful night of sleep. He was in a foul mood; the scepter had been locked away the night before, still greedily holding onto its secrets. And his nightmares about Reshel's death had returned. He'd suffered them almost nightly in the months after she died, but they abated after a time. In them he vividly saw her knife opening her throat, the blood pouring out in a seemingly endless torrent. In some of the dreams he tried to stop the bleeding with his hands, but it gushed through his fingers no matter how frantically he tried to hold the wound closed.

He wondered what she would make of their father's erratic behavior. Gods above, how he still missed her!

Balandrick joined him for breakfast. "My, someone's grouchy," he said as he caught sight of the scowl on Gerin's face. He tore off a piece of bread and sopped up the juices from a plate of sausages.

Gerin was eating a hard-boiled egg. He grunted at Balandrick and took another bite.

"I for one am in a very good mood, my lord," said Balandrick. "I like Almaris just fine, but I must admit I'm ready to go home."

They said good-bye to the king in the same courtyard where they'd bid farewell to Claressa. "A safe journey to you both," Abran said to his sons before wheeling about and vanishing between two columns. He'd said nothing about the scepter, and Gerin decided it would be best not to broach the subject again.

They made their way down Vesparin's Hill and out into the city, where Gerin was shocked to see Elaysen waiting for them on horseback, a baggage mule standing patiently behind her. She did not look pleased.

"What are you doing here?" he asked.

"I'm coming with you." Her voice was tight. "My father received your message about your departure and decided I am to be the emissary who will teach you the ways of *dalar-aelom.*"

Gerin had resigned himself to the fact that he would not see her again until his next return to Almaris; now she was here, prepared for the long road ahead.

"You don't look happy about it," Balandrick said to her.

"There are no experienced emissaries in the city who can accompany you. My father would come with you himself to teach you if he could, but that is impossible. So instead he has sent me."

"But you would prefer to stay here?" asked Balan.

"We all have our duties to perform, Master Balandrick, whether we agree with them or not. He is my father, and has charged me with a task. Do you think I should refuse him? Would you refuse Prince Gerin if he gave you an order you did not like?"

"Elaysen, stay here," said Gerin. "Have your father send an experienced emissary later. There is no pressing need."

She looked at him intently. Something had changed in her gaze, a subtle shifting of her anger. "It's true I feel my place is here, healing those in need. But I sense something else in your words, my lord. Do you doubt my ability to teach you?"

"Of course not."

"My lord, do you then doubt my father's judgment?"

"No, though even you said you feel your place is here."

"Perhaps there are things I can still learn from you about healing even though I am not a wizard. My father may see what I at first did not. And there must be people in your own castle in need of a healer. Surely you and Hollin cannot attend to them all."

Gods above, now she's arguing for coming just to prove she's capable of teaching me! He'd thought he was helping her to get what she wanted by refusing her, even though a part of him had been thrilled by the idea of her company.

"I was wrong to question my father's decision," she said. The anger had left her, replaced by a stern resolve. "I think now it will be best if I accompany you."

"You should cut your losses now and give in," said Therain to him. "I've seen that look before, mostly on Claressa when she's made up her mind about something. Elaysen's coming along whether you want her to or not."

Gerin frowned, despite feeling pleased by the outcome. "Very well. I seem to have been argued into a corner."

Balandrick—smirking far too much for Gerin's liking— ordered one of the servants to take charge of Elaysen's mule. She turned her mount and fell in beside Gerin as they started down the Needle toward the Azure Gate.

"Don't frown so much, my lord," she whispered to him. "It's not becoming on one of royal heritage."

He smiled despite himself. *Yes, I'm glad that you are coming with us.*

13

Rendo Pallan limped along the waterfront toward the Harbormaster's House, a two-storied box of weathered gray stone perched on Barresh Harbor's relatively sheltered southern side. The sun was bright and hot in the morning sky, beating down upon the wharfs, piers, gangplanks, walkways, decks, landings, and men scurrying across them.

And all of them trying to cheat the lord of his proper due, thought Pallan. *Every bloody last one of them. I know their thieving hearts, and may Paérendras take them all to a watery grave if they don't pay every last dera owed the lord.*

He grunted and placed his hand on his bad hip, run through with a harpoon nine years earlier while hunting whales in the open sea. He'd become harbormaster a year later, after old Temmen Frello had died of a fever. He missed the sea, but his ruined hip prevented him from doing much good on the deck of a ship, so harbormaster he'd become.

Over the years, he'd grown to love his position in his own gruff way. He wasn't filled with a hunger for power like old Frello, who'd never met a bribe he didn't like or a captain he didn't want to intimidate or, barring that, harass. That was not Pallan's way. Duke Nellemar Atreyano had entrusted him with the care of the harbor, and expected him to ensure that the duchy was paid its due. Oh, once in a great while he might accept some small payment to look the other way so an extra shipment of inland wool could find its way into a ship's hold duty free, but those times were few and far between, especially now that he'd paid off his gambling debts to that bastard Destronn. The duke had given him a job to do, and by the gods, he was going to do it to the best of his abilities, and to Velyol with anyone who gave him grief or tried to cheat him.

He eyed everyone with suspicion, felt that anyone he hadn't personally known for at least ten years was more than likely a pirate or brigand—or hungering to become one—and knew with the same certainty that he knew his hip would never be right that everyone—*everyone*—would try to cheat him out of the money he was charged to collect from the trade ships and merchants they dealt with here in Palendrell. No one wanted to pay their taxes. He knew that quite well, because when he'd been aboard ship he hadn't wanted to pay them, either. The siphoning off of his hard-earned wages, which would be better put to use on drink or food or a woman to hold for the night, had always been a bitter pill to swallow. But now it was his job to make sure the taxes got paid, so he and his men scoured the waterfront, checking manifests and storming through the dormitories and barracks that served as the land-homes of sailors to collect their silver. It was a hard job, but by the gods, he was going to do it *right*.

"'Mornin', Harbormaster," said a shirtless sailor on the deck of a two-master as he heaved a hawser to a companion. Other men were moving across the deck and climbing down from the rigging, their backs and shoulders as dark as old leather.

"'Morning to ya," said Pallan. He stopped and looked about. "Where in Shayphim's name is Haldes?" That damn boy was never where he was supposed to be. This was his section of the harbor to watch. He was to inspect every ship—

"Already in the holds countin' the cargo," said the sailor on deck. "Got here a few minutes ago."

"Oh . . . Well, good." He turned and shambled on. The perfectly good bit of anger and lather he'd been about to work up about Haldes's layabout ways was now ruined, so he yelled and snarled at two dockworkers napping in the sun until they jumped to and got busy. He finished the rest of his walk with a smile on his face.

Pallan grunted in pain as he mounted the stairs just inside the entryway of the Harbormaster's House. The second floor was a large open room jammed with wobbly piles of crates, boxes, casks, and other detritus that had accumulated over the years, and which he—and Temmen Frello before him—had neglected to sort or organize in any manner except to shift the piles about now and then to create narrow mazelike pathways through the room. Some of the piles reached to the ceiling and were so wedged in place it would more than likely take several stout blows to knock them loose. Grimy windows ran the length of all four walls, providing a panoramic view of both the harbor and the town.

Pallan made his way between several stacks of musty crates and sat down heavily on a rough wooden bench facing the harborside windows. It felt good to get the weight off his bad hip and leg.

He noticed a dark blotch on the horizon, off to the southwest. It was a ship of some kind, a big one to be visible from so far away. "Damn this bother, never a moment's rest," he mumbled as he lurched to his feet and rummaged through the papers and boxes piled atop a nearby table until he found what he was looking for: his spyglass. He extended the wood and brass tube and held the smaller end to his right eye, squinting his left eye shut.

The magnified view of the watery horizon jerked awkwardly back and forth as he tried to find the ship. After a few moments the vessel came into view. He steadied his hands and held his breath as he took in the sight.

Despite the heat in the room, the blood in his veins ran suddenly cold. He'd seen a ship like this once before, on a storm-ravaged night two months earlier. That ship had been smashed to bits upon Harrow's Rock, but he'd seen enough of it in the flashes of lightning that fractured the night to know that he would never forget it. Like that other ship, the one he saw through his glass was a massive vessel, larger than any ship in the Khedeshian fleet.

That other ship had carried a sorcerer of some kind and

hellish monsters from a foreign land, somewhere across the Maurelian Sea, if the stories he'd heard were to be believed. He didn't know about *that*—the Maurelian Sea was thought to be endless, haunted by vast monsters of the deep who waited beyond the shores of Osseria to devour any ship that came too close to their watery hunting grounds. Still, he was smart enough to know that the ship had come from *far away*, regardless of exactly where that was. Those were details that needn't concern him. He'd caught only a glimpse of an unconscious man being carried from the beach beyond the town's walls, but heard firsthand from some of the soldiers how the foreigner had brought the dead to life with his dark sorceries. And Pallan had seen the bodies of the dead monsters for himself, things straight out of a nightmare.

And now another of those ships was sailing for the harbor. *His* harbor.

He lowered the spyglass. "Come on, you old fool," he mumbled. "Make certain of what you're seeing." He raised the glass once more and sighted the ship.

He was not wrong. It was a sister ship to the one that had floundered and been smashed against the Rock.

He swore loudly when he saw what had become visible behind the first vessel.

Red and gray sails from at least a hundred ships formed a dark line like a storm upon the horizon. And he felt in his gut that even more were behind those he could see.

He swore again, then ran for the stairs as fast as his bad leg would allow, thinking, *Bellon take us all, we're being invaded!*

Standing upon the forecastle of his flagship *Uthna Tarel*, Mellam yun avki Drugal, the Sword of the Exalted, supreme military commander of the Steadfast invasion fleet, surveyed the rocky island directly ahead of him and pondered the fate of the *Kaashal* and its First, Vethiq aril Tolsadri. The Voice of the Exalted, a man of equal station and power in the Great Court of Kalmanyikul, was difficult at the best of times, but his death would nevertheless be a grievous blow. It did not bode well that the *Kaashal* appeared to be lost. Tolsadri's whereabouts were unknown, but Drugal assumed he was either dead or captured. Either way, for now Tolsadri was beyond his reach.

What they knew of these lands seemed to indicate that the inhabitants could offer only token resistance to the might of the Steadfast, but that knowledge was admittedly thin, and it was possible that these people were much more capable than their captured ships and crews had indicated. It was his sworn duty to ensure victory over whatever foes the Exalted and the Dreamers said he must conquer, but victory was best accomplished when his knowledge of his enemy was relatively complete. The fact that Tolsadri—sent ahead with the expressed purpose of filling in some of the gaps in their knowledge of these lands—appeared to be lost troubled him deeply.

They would see soon enough how capable these people were. The island toward which he was sailing was a rocky, desolate place, full of sheer cliffs and windswept highlands. A harsh place, where he was sure a harsh people must live. The harbor itself was well-sheltered, and Drugal approved of the castle built into the cliff wall behind the harbor town, visible through his seeing-glass. Its makers had built it well. An easy place to defend, and one difficult to conquer.

But conquer it he would. No one had ever withstood the might of the Steadfast, and it would not happen now. They were too strong. Holvareh the All Father and the Powers that served Him would come to their aid should they require it. Herol the Soldier would guide his heart and hand so he would stand true to his vows and overcome his enemies. They would conquer these lands and show them the light of the Powers. Every man, woman, and child would find their place in the natural order of things. They would swear their vows and don the proper attire and be taught the words of worship and the attributes of the Powers. Harmony would arise where now chaos must rein.

And we must find the Words of Making, the true reason for our long voyage across the perilous sea, he thought.

The island drew closer. Distantly, Drugal heard the distant peal of bells. *They are sounding a warning. Calling their men-at-arms to defend their homes against us.* He always felt a tinge of sadness before a new campaign. Why did they always resist? If only they could see the error of their ways and how much better life was as one of the Steadfast. He sighed, knowing it was not to be. People resisted change, no matter if it brought order and purpose to their lives. He'd conquered too many peoples to believe otherwise. But they would, in the end, accept the change, and eventually come to embrace it.

It took several generations before the old ways of life were forgotten. Not until then were the laws of the Steadfast welcomed completely. But it would happen. It had been that way for five and a half thousand years, since Metharog the Father had first appeared to Gleso in-Palurq in the desert wastes of Tumhaddi and demanded his obedience, in return for which Gleso would become the founder of the greatest people who had ever graced the world. It would not change now.

Drugal was a tall man with a shock of wavy black hair. His face had the high cheekbones, full lips, dark eyes, and olive-colored skin that marked him as a native of the Hantab region of northern Wasaaqti, near the forbidding Yeldrix Highlands. His people were natural fighters, forced from a young age to prove their mettle against foes both older and stronger. The Highlands were home to the voresh, winged predators as large as a man and black as crows. Their maws were filled with razor-sharp teeth, and their talons could eviscerate a man in seconds, spilling his guts onto the ground before he even realized he was dead.

Drugal had watched his older brother die at the hands of a voresh, which had disappeared with the body into the fog-shrouded Highlands. He had sworn vengeance and hunted the voresh for nine days before finding and slaughtering it in a vicious fight of knives and talons that nearly killed him. Legends has sprouted from that battle, which he neither confirmed nor denied. Let others think what they would, and if the tales made him more formidable, so be it. Killing a voresh single-handedly had set him on the path that led to his becoming Sword of the Exalted. He bore the scars from that battle to this day. Now, without thinking, he touched the long puckered gash that curved down the right side of his face like a dry riverbed. He thought of his brother's bones, carelessly discarded by the voresh after it had feasted, which Drugal had lovingly gathered and returned home for a proper burial. His fellow warriors said he was favored by Herol, that the Soldier would countenance no harm to befall him, nor allow him to lose in battle. Over the years he'd used those whispers to his advantage in his service to the Exalted. *A reputation can be a weapon in itself,* one of his teachers had explained to him during the third year of his training at the Cataar. *Use it as you would any other weapon. An enemy who fears you is already on the road to defeat.*

Gaiun Pizan, his Second for this expedition, appeared at Drugal's side. Pizan was a Kantu tribesmen, as tall and solid as a wall, with red-tinged eyes and yellowish teeth filed to points. A score of Pizan's kinsmen had been personally entrusted with the Sword's safety.

Pizan touched his fist to his heart and bowed his head. "Sword, Captain Gesed seeks your permission to order the fleet to launch the longboats."

Drugal scratched at the stubble on his chin. "Tell the captain he may begin the attack."

Rendo Pallan gripped a gnarled cudgel in one hand and a long-bladed knife in the other. He stood on a quay near the Harbormaster's House, watching as more than three hundred boats were rowed into the harbor. His shirt was drenched with sweat.

Haldes stood beside him, doing his best to prevent his hands from shaking. He too had seen the dead things dragged from the beach this past March and knew as well as Pallan that the boats coming toward them were apt to be filled with more of the monsters, only this time alive and lusting for their blood. Haldes's lanky hair fell in damp strands across his face. He shifted his weight from foot to foot as if standing on hot coals. In his right hand he held a short sword scavenged from the first floor of the Harbormaster's House, in his left a barbed hook used for hauling meat and carcasses.

"My bowels are churnin' like there's a storm in 'em," he said.

"Steady, lad," said Pallan. "The bastards haven't reached us yet. The Harbor Watch and garrison from the castle are going to fight them first. We may be doing nothing but cleaning up bodies."

"Do you really think so?"

No I do not. Not one little bit, Pallan thought, but did not say so aloud. The boy was frightened enough as it was. "Battles like this are tricky things, Haldes. They can turn in the blink of an eye. We hold the harbor, and they'll have to fight us for every bit of land they want to take. It's going to be bloody, all right, but most of the blood will be theirs." At least he hoped so.

The enemy longboats entered the harbor and immediately fanned out, putting as much distance between them as they could. Pallan realized they wanted to land in many places in order to disperse the defenses, spreading them thin in the hope of more easily breaking through.

He heard several lieutenants farther along the waterfront bark commands for their archers to release. Flaming pitch-tipped arrows shot across the harbor, leaving trails of dark smoke in their wake.

Many of the arrows fizzled in the water; others slammed into the rectangular shields raised by men in the longboats. A few struck the sides of the boats and kindled a flame, though these were quickly extinguished. Others punched through the flesh of those not adequately prepared to defend against the volley. Dead men tumbled into the harbor or slumped in their boats. Wounded men began to bellow in agony. Some of the boats were close enough that Pallan could see the monsters—*Bellon take them all, the damned bloody things!* he thought with a shiver of revulsion and dread—that seemed to be manning the oars, pulling them through the water with more strength and speed than any man could muster. He swallowed thickly at the sight and tried to keep his fear under control. Beside him, Haldes shook as if in the throes of a convulsion.

"Calm down, lad," said Pallan, sounding more steady than he felt. "It won't do you any good to rattle your bones to dust before the fighting even starts."

Haldes laughed sharply, a sound on the very edge of hysteria. *He's only fourteen, by the gods,* thought Pallan. *He should be frightened.* The boy annoyed him more often than not, but Pallan was still fond of the lad and had no desire to see him cut down. He said a prayer to Paérendras to protect them both in the coming battle.

Soldiers shouted again. Bowstrings thrummed, and a second volley of flaming arrows surged across the water. Perhaps twenty-five or thirty fell to the missiles, but the rest of the invaders and their boats remained unscathed. Pallan heard someone shout that arrows were to be held until the boats were at close range, at which time the archers could release at will.

"I just wish the fightin' would *start*," said Haldes. "All this waitin' is killin' me."

"It'll start soon enough. No need to be wishing it to hurry up any more than it is."

A quarter of a mile away around the harbor's rim, the first of the invaders' longboats reached the piers.

One of the enemy longboats crashed into a pier near the Harbormaster's House. Men of the Harbor Watch and a group of soldiers from Castle Cressan rushed to cut them off, but a dozen human invaders and five of the monsters had jumped onto the pier before the Gedsengarders could get there. The invaders met them in a headlong crash of steel and bone. Pallan and Haldes watched, too afraid to either rush to the fight or run away, as the monstrous creatures lunged forward, their narrow bony heads bobbing in a birdlike way upon their long necks. The human invaders followed close behind, their steel shields held high.

An archer standing at the end of the pier put down one of

the creatures with an arrow through its eye. It fell hard; its
pike skidded across the planks and dropped into the water.
The creature's fallen bulk blocked the invaders behind it.
The Gedsengarder archer sank an arrow deep into the neck
of another creature, which toppled on top of the first one,
thrashing about madly as it tried to pull the arrow free. It
shrieked wildly as it died, a strange mixture of a raven's caw
and the more guttural growls of a dog or wolf.

Before the second creature had ceased its death throes,
two of its companions shouldered it and the one beneath it
aside, dumping both into the bay to clear their path. Their
armor promptly dragged the discarded creatures to the bottom, leaving only a gurgle of bubbles behind.

One of the creatures snarled and reared back with its pike,
which it hurled toward the archer with tremendous force.
The pike's barbed tip took the man under the armpit as
he turned in a failed attempt to lunge aside. The tip burst
through his other side in a spray of hot blood. The man didn't
even scream; his lungs had been pulped by the huge head of
the pike.

The creatures roared and pressed their attack. The Gedsengarders could not get within the long reach of the pikes
on the narrow pier, and so fell back.

One of the creatures killed another defender, hacking
through his neck with the cutting edge of its pike. Haldes let
out a whimper of fear as the body crumpled to the planks.

Pallan heard a noise to his left. He turned, fearing that
somehow they'd been sneaked up on by the invaders.

He let out a groan of terror as the archer who'd been killed
with the thrown pike stirred and roused himself from the
ground. The other dead man twitched as if suffering a convulsion, then he too rose. Their eyes shone with a dim green-
ish light, like the ghost fires Pallan had seen once in a swamp
on the island's northern side.

"Paérendras protect us!" muttered Haldes. Pallan smelled
the acrid stench of urine and realized the boy had lost control
of his bladder.

The corpse with the pike through it could not balance well

or move easily because of the weight of the weapon, but the other corpse fared better. It grasped the sword it had dropped and turned on its companions. The closest Gedsengarder shrieked in horror as the dead man drove its sword through his mouth.

"Run, boy!" yelled Pallan, shoving Haldes away from the fighting. The boy stumbled and nearly fell, then gained his footing and sprinted toward the town. "Run! It's black magic, and there's naught we can do to fight it!" Terror clenched his bowels with such force he feared he would shit in his breeches. He hobbled after the boy as fast as he could, wondering how they could fight against their own dead. It was madness, madness.

Drugal watched the battle as the day grew long. His soldiers had taken control of the entire harbor front and were now working their way methodically through the town, disarming men who surrendered and making examples of those who did not. The Steadfast rules of war did not call for rampant, wholesale slaughter; that ran counter to their purpose of converting those they conquered to their ways, of showing them the wisdom and majesty of the Powers. Oh, on occasion a particularly intransigent town or city had been obliterated, the people too opposed to their Steadfast masters to be allowed to live. It was regrettable, but no different than having to amputate a gangrenous limb before the infection spread to healthy areas. Dissent was not tolerated.

But such annihilations were rare. He was certain that the town before him would fall, and then the castle. The Steadfast would move as quickly as possible to assume complete control and restore a sense of normalcy to the populace. Those who opposed them would be publicly executed as examples of what happened to troublemakers; those who helped them would be rewarded.

Then they would begin the process of determining in which caste to place every member of the population. That was the great gift of the Steadfast: order, and the absolute knowledge of one's place within that order. No fear, no doubt. Their strategies had worked for thousands of years, and he had no doubt that the same would occur here in due time.

Drugal felt a sense of calm settle over him as he thought of his place within the society of the Steadfast. He'd always been humbled by the honor of serving Herol, as well as the Exalted, who ruled in the name of Metharog, the Power to whom rulers swore their lives. Of course he was confident in his abilities to achieve victory no matter the odds against him: He was strong, smart, and capable; he understood a battlefield and knew how to motivate the men who would fight and die at his command. But he also knew that Herol was with him, showing him the way when the path to victory grew cloudy. He realized that the difference between serving Herol and being a minion of the feared and hated Harridan was not as great as some might believe.

As Vethiq aril Tolsadri had apparently believed. A scowl tugged at the scars on Drugal's face as he thought of the Exalted's Voice. He had always disliked Tolsadri, who was haughty and contemptuous of anyone not a follower of Bariq the Wise. He'd long wondered at the Exalted's reasoning in choosing Tolsadri as her Voice, the one who would speak for her to the peoples who had not yet been shown the ways of the Steadfast. Was his arrogant demeanor truly how the Exalted wanted to be seen in the greater world? Drugal shook his head. Apparently it was, as Tolsadri was favored in the Great Court of Kalmanyikul. But it was not his place to speak out about such things. He was the Exalted's Sword, sworn to conquer and obey. The intrigues of the Great Court were not his purview, though at times, by necessity, he had to play their games.

He wondered about Tolsadri's fate. Had the *Kaashal* even reached these shores, or had it floundered at sea and been lost? Perhaps they would find the answer when the island was taken. But his heart told him that they would never know what happened to the Voice of the Exalted, or be able to return his bones to the Sepulcher of Bariq beneath the Jade Temple.

Captain Gesed appeared at Drugal's side. His tanned faced

was creased with wrinkles as deep as knife slashes. Gold rings dangled from his ears, and a single small hoop pierced his left nostril.

"Honored Sword," he said in his raspy voice, as if his throat had rusted from years in the salty sea air, "the Dreamer commands that you attend him, and that you bring the hunters."

"Very well, Captain. Bring them from their ship and have them meet me at the entrance to the Dreamer's quarters."

Gesed bowed his head. "Yes, Honored Sword. At once."

Drugal watched the battle through his seeing-glass for a time. Only after the longboat returned bearing the hunters did he make his way toward the aftcastle of the ship.

He descended two sets of ladders that ended in a heavy wooden door inscribed with the *rhega*, the orange and blue spiral symbol of the Dreamers. Drugal did not know what the symbol or the word *rhega* meant. As far as he knew, it was a secret shared only among the Dreamers themselves.

Two black-armored Sai'fen guarded the door, the elite soldiers entrusted with the protection of the Dreamers, among the deadliest of all the followers of Herol. Their armor was spiked at the elbow and shoulder joints and had twin lines of serrated blades like shark teeth set along the vambraces. The sides of their helms were adorned with back-swept fans of narrow knives like the spread fingers of a hand. Even one such as Drugal had to tread carefully in their presence. The Sai'fen were not his to command. They served the Dreamers directly, and spoke to no one outside their order. They had their own quarters on the ship, apart from the rest of the crew; they even took their meals separately. No one but the Exalted herself was entirely safe around the Sai'fen, and some believed not even *she* was entirely above their all-encompassing suspicion. If Drugal were to act in a menacing fashion in the presence of the Dreamer, the Sai'fen would have no qualms about killing him. And because of their skill, he knew they would succeed.

A man and woman waited for him by the door, their hands

clasped before them, heads bowed. They wore the gray clothing that marked them as followers of Tulqan the Harridan, goddess of the outcast. She often opposed the other Powers for the simple reason of wickedness for its own sake. Drugal frowned when he saw them. *What trouble will they cause before they are done?* he wondered. It was the nature of the Harridan to sow the seeds of chaos and discord among the orderly ways of the Steadfast. He realized the Harridan had a vital role to play among the Powers—she encouraged the forces of Order to remain vigilant and united against her, lest all they had built fall to ruin—but he did not like it, and would never willingly embrace it.

These two, however, had been specifically chosen by the Dreamer for this hunt. The reasons had not been revealed to either Drugal or Tolsadri. In fact, Drugal knew little of the details of this hunt other than that it involved the Words of Making. Tolsadri had been honored by being allowed to witness a vision of the Dreamers before the fleet departed, but Drugal was away from the city at the time and had not participated. It galled him, and he felt slighted and insulted that such a thing had been done in his absence. But he could not utter his dissatisfaction without dishonoring himself, and Tolsadri chose to say nothing to him of what had transpired. Of the Dreamers he could ask nothing—they would either tell him or not, but he could not question them about such a vital matter as the very vision that had propelled the Exalted to invade these distant lands. The Dreamers kept their own counsel, and rarely did they share their motivations with anyone other than the Exalted herself.

"Come with me," he said gruffly to the two. "The Dreamer wishes to speak with us."

"Yes, Honored Sword." They spoke in unison, not lifting their gaze from the dark floor.

"Did you visit the Dreamer before we left Aleith'aqtar?" asked Drugal.

The woman glanced at the man, who replied for them both. "No, Honored Sword. We were told only that we had been chosen for a great task that would be revealed to us when we arrived at our destination. It was the Voice of the Exalted himself who commanded us."

Drugal forced down the renewed flame of annoyance that Tolsadri had withheld the knowledge of the vision from him. "It is time you learned the details of your task." He needed to learn them as well. "Be forewarned: the Dreamer is like no other being you have ever met. Attend to it well. Do not speak unless commanded to. If you have a question, ask it of me and I will relay it to the Dreamer. Do you understand?"

"Yes, Honored Sword," they said again.

"See that you heed my words. If you do not, you will suffer quick deaths." Drugal gestured to one of the Sai'fen, who withdrew a key from a chain around his neck and unlocked the door. He pushed it open and stepped inside, then gestured for the others to follow. The Sai'fen closed the door behind them and stepped to the side, his hand upon the hilt of his sword.

The windows were shuttered, as they had been for the duration of their voyage. Five candles burned on a table near the center of the room, the only source of illumination. Beyond the wan circle of light cast by the candles, the space was drowned in a murkiness that seemed to Drugal to be nearly a solid thing, as if darkness itself were assuming a physical form around them.

He crossed his wrists over his chest and bowed his head toward the far end of the room. "Great Dreamer, I have brought the hunters as you have commanded."

The creature at the end of the room was hidden from view by several layers of gauzy curtains that fell from ceiling to floor and ran the width of the chamber. The curtains swayed on mysterious, power-drenched currents; exhalations from the Dreamer contained energies that Drugal did not begin to comprehend. He understood how important the Dreamers were to the cause of the Steadfast. They could see outside of time—their visions had guided them since the days of Gleso in-Palurq himself—though it was not known if their visions were under their complete control or came to them unbidden, as did the ordinary dreams of men. The Dreamers revealed little of themselves and nothing at all of the extent of their powers. Much had been conjectured over the long history of the Steadfast, but little was known for certain.

Only once, fleetingly, had Drugal ever seen a Dreamer. They kept themselves hidden from all eyes save the Sai'fen and a few Loremasters of Bariq chosen to serve them, sworn to uttermost secrecy. The Drufar, as these Loremasters were called, had lit the candles in this room and served the Dreamers whatever strange foods they used to nourish themselves. They wore layers of deep blue clothing wrapped about their bodies in very particular and exacting ways, with a squarish head covering called a *huril* that covered neck, ears, forehead, and hair, like a burial headpiece with the face covering removed. They were also charged with preparing the windowless carriages used to move the Dreamers from place to place. The Drufar spoke only to each other and the Sai'fen; they did not acknowledge other Loremasters. They served only the Dreamers, as if nothing else in the world existed for them.

It was forbidden under pain of death for anyone other than a Sai'fen, Drufar, or the Exalted to see a Dreamer directly, though three years ago the curtains of the Dreamer he'd been speaking to had parted for an instant. Before he could avert his gaze, Drugal had seen the Dreamer clearly. That fleeting moment had *stretched*, lengthening somehow as if time itself had become malleable. As for what he had seen . . . to this day he could not truly describe it. His sight could not settle on the thing visible through the gap in the curtains, as if it were protected by powers that rendered it partially immune to his eyes. He saw its vague shape—the distended body, like a battlefield corpse swollen with gases, spiderlike limbs, and hints of a cluster of eyes upon a bulbous head—but could make out no details, as if in some way it was not wholly present in the room. The sensation was shocking to such a degree that he feared he would vomit upon the marble floor.

Then time had snapped back to its normal pace, and he lowered his head so quickly he nearly overbalanced and fell. *I have glimpsed a Dreamer!* he thought. His life was now forfeit. But though a Drufar had been in the room with him—striding over to close the part in the curtains with a defiant tug—no harm befell him. Drugal wondered afterward if perhaps the Drufar were somehow at fault for allowing the curtains to slip in the first place and thus spared him to cover his own error. He would never know, but he was nonetheless grateful for his life.

In the cabin of the ship, the being behind the curtains exhaled loudly, but the sound was unlike any human exhalation. It was deep, sonorous, like a wind blowing through a tunnel, transforming before it ended into an almost animal-like howl. The curtains rippled and billowed, but were tied down in such a manner that they did not open.

Drugal felt reality tremble.

Behind him, he heard the hunters take sharp, fearful breaths. He understood their trepidation. The powers of the Dreamers pierced time by weakening the foundations of the world, creating tremors that rippled outward through reality like the wake of a passing ship. For an instant of time between the beats of his heart, Drugal had felt himself grow insubstantial, in danger of vanishing completely from the world, unmade as reality itself was shredded to bits like a piece of moth-eaten cloth.

But reality did not tear. His heart beat again and he became solid and whole once more.

There was a strange musical sound like chimes from behind the curtain. Then the Dreamer spoke. Its voice had the breathy emanations of a flute.

"Do you know the fate of the Exalted's Voice?"

"I regret that I do not, Great Dreamer," said Drugal. "We have had no word from him and see no sign of his ship in these waters. It is possible that we will learn what happened to him and the *Kaashal* when we complete our assumption of this island."

"He is hidden from my sight," said the Dreamer. Drugal did not know whether it had a proper name. All Dreamers were referred to by that simple descriptive word, and when spoken to directly were called Great Dreamer. He did not know exactly how many Dreamers lived, though there could not be more than a few score inhabiting their own dark and forbidding wing of Pahjuleh Palace, from which they rarely ventured.

"The vast distance we have traveled obscures my powers," it said. "Now that our voyaging has ended I will be able to orient myself to the currents of energy upon which my visions depend, but for now too much is in flux, and my sight is dimmed.

"I have summoned you and the hunters so you all will understand the true reason for our long journey across the sea," it said. "Sword of the Exalted, you know some of the reasons, but the hunters do not. Step forward, hunters, that you may see."

The Dreamer exhaled its power, and the world around them shivered. The room wavered and grew indistinct, as if daring the knife edge of nonexistence. Once again Drugal felt himself become less than what he was; a sudden wave of nausea twisted in his stomach, and he fought back the groan that pressed to escape his lips. He saw the man clutch his abdomen, but neither he nor the woman made any sounds of distress.

In the next instant the chamber reasserted its solidity with an abruptness like a slap upon the face. Drugal remained steady, but the hunters staggered as if the ship had suddenly listed to one side.

A glowing mist appeared in the room between them and the curtain. It swirled about on currents of the Dreamer's power, a visible manifestation of its internal vision. The mist glowed with a faint rainbow sheen, like sunlight reflecting on a layer of oil, or the effervescent color of a soap bubble. Pale colors danced through the air, hypnotic in their movements.

Within the mist appeared the face of a man. Drugal did not know him. He had straight dark hair, deep green eyes, and a narrow nose. His flesh was extraordinarily pale, as if carved from white marble. He was looking at something they could not see with a fierce intensity. He opened his mouth and spoke to someone not visible in the vision, but there was no sound.

"Remember this face," commanded the Dreamer. Its voice had taken on an imperious tone, filled with an implied threat should they fail to heed it. "This is the man you must hunt. It is the reason you have been brought so far from your homes. Find him, and you find the Words of Making."

From the corners of his eyes Drugal saw the man and woman glance at each other sharply before looking back at the vision.

The man's face remained in the mist for a few moments before it blurred and vanished. It was replaced by a view of a hilltop castle, a large and well-fortified structure resplendent with towers and a winding road leading up to its shut gates.

"This is where you will find him," said the Dreamer. "Attend it well. The country in which you will hunt for him is large. You will need to stretch your skills to their limits if you are to succeed."

"Great Dreamer," said Drugal, "do you know the name of this man they are to hunt? Or the name of the castle in which he dwells?"

"No." The vision of the castle wavered and vanished, swallowed back into the mist. "Those have not been revealed to me.

"Hunters, attend. You will be taken to the mainland to hunt for the man you have been shown. *Under no circumstances is he to be harmed*. He must be captured and returned to me alive and undamaged. If you allow him to be injured or die, be sure to slay yourselves at once, for that death will be infinitely kinder than the fate you will meet should you return here.

"Go now. I am finished with you."

The mist faded from the room with a sudden chill. Drugal wheeled about and left the chamber, then climbed the ladders to the open deck of the *Uthna Tarel*.

Here in the sun he got his first good look at the hunters of the Harridan. The man's white hair and red-hued skin marked him as a Kelanim tribesman—outsiders called them "Blood Men"—from the forested valley at the southern tip of the Akska Mountains. He wore layers of leather and rough animal hide pierced here and there with bits of bone, all dyed gray to mark him as a Tulqani. The man raised his head to look at Drugal for the first time. The Sword of the Exalted saw flecks of yellow in his eyes that glinted like polished steel; they marked him as a maegosi, able to command the quatans who lived in the foothills of the Akska Mountains.

The woman stood with her head bowed and shoulders hunched, as if trying to withdraw into herself and disappear. She was small-boned, with narrow wrists and long, slender fingers. Her wavy black hair was tied in a thick braid that fell to the middle of her back. She had dark skin and large eyes above prominent cheekbones. She wore sandals, leggings, and a gray thigh-length tunic belted about her waist.

"You heard the Dreamer and partook of its vision," said Drugal. "Are you capable of accomplishing the task set before you?"

"Yes, Honored Sword," they said as one.

"Do you have questions before you depart for the mainland?"

"Honored Sword, are we also to capture these Words of Making?" asked the woman.

"Bring only the man," he said. "Make no attempt to find the Words yourselves. They will be taken in due time.

"Heed the words of the Dreamer. Allow no harm to befall the man you hunt. Now go, and may Ruren the Silent drag your souls into the deepest pits of Maniqarsa should you prove false."

✳ 14

The sun shone wanly through a heavy layer of clouds that hung in the sky like a veil of grimy glass when the ship that departed from Gedsengard Isle a day and a half earlier dropped anchor off a long stretch of deserted beach near the northern edge of Blackwater Marsh. Those upon the vessel did not know the name of the marsh—they referred to it simply as "the bog." The low expanse of soggy earth was veiled in mist, though the stench arising from it left no doubt as to its nature.

Two longboats dropped from the ship into the choppy waters. Thick-muscled men in sleeveless tunics rowed the longboats toward shore. The tattoos upon their faces and arms marked them as slaves in the caste of Keitru the Master and the property of Captain Gesed.

The male hunter, Kursil Rulhámad, was in one of the boats. Despite its size—twelve men were rowing, six on a side—it seemed about to sink at any moment, overcome by the weight of the four steel cages crammed upon it. Each swell sloshed seawater over the gunwales; the beasts within the cages growled and pounded their fists against the steel bars until Rulhámad spoke to them with his thoughts to calm and reassure them that the rocking back and forth would soon end. The creatures quieted, and Rulhámad turned back toward the shore, looking for signs of habitation. He saw none. Beyond the bog was a line of low cliffs shrouded in fog, like something glimpsed in a fevered dream.

He wondered how in this large and forbidding country he would find a single man. But find the man he would. He could not fail. He had journeyed too far, and too much was at stake. To find the man from the vision was to escape the bondage of the Harridan, to be elevated to the caste of one of the other Powers. He would be an outcast no more, able to own both property and slaves. He had dreamed of this freedom his whole life. Now that it lay within his reach, he would brook no thought of failure or defeat.

Rulhámad glanced at the other boat, where his companion hunter sat in the bow, hunched forward so that only her head and shoulders were visible. Though they both followed the Outcast One and had spent most of the long sea journey together, he felt only scorn for the woman, Katel yalez Algariq. She was a rival, one sent by their own masters to claim the prey and the glory and reward that would go with it. They had been sent, maegosi and soul stealer, not to work together, but to increase the chance of success—if one of them failed, the other would continue on. He did not know if the other ships of the fleet carried hunters of their own; such knowledge would not have been given to him even if he had asked.

They might work together for a time, helping each other find their way in this foreign land, doing what they could to remain alive, but he would be scheming against her, just as he knew she would be doing the same against him. But with his quatans—he looked back at the mighty creatures, bound to his thoughts by the nature of his being, waiting patiently to be freed of their cages—he would be more than a match for her when the proper time came.

The water in the longboat has risen almost to his knees when they finally reached the shore. The Keitruni jumped into the crashing surf and dragged the boat onto the sand. Once the boat was beyond the edge of the waves, Rulhámad told the men to get back. "I will open the cages. The quatans are irritable and hungry. Keep your distance if you wish to remain alive." He wondered if there were animals nearby on which the quatans could feed.

The Keitruni moved back into the surf. Rulhámad threw back the thick bolt on the first cage, sending his thoughts to Evi, the dominant quatan within, to calm and reassure it. Behind Evi, Haru lurked in the corner of the cage. For a long time Rulhámad had wondered if the quatans would be able to survive the long sea journey, but after falling deathly ill the first few days of the voyage, the creatures had recovered most of their strength. They had not thrived on the crossing, but neither did they waste away as he had feared.

Evi jumped down to the beach, followed a moment later by Haru. Their thoughts erupted like a fire in Rulhámad's mind as they unfolded their limbs, flexing their daggerlike fingers and toes.

Quatans did not think with words as men did, but Rulhámad could understand them well enough: they were overflowing with joy to be on land once more, and filled with a deep, ravenous hunger. Rulhámad released the other quatans, eight in all. The longboat rocked violently as each creature leaped to the sand.

The other longboat had already beached. Algariq and two of her rowers cautiously approached Rulhámad as he clambered over the side.

"So the hunt begins at last," she said. "I wondered if this day would ever truly arrive."

"As did I. The voyage was long."

"We should head for—"

Before Algariq could finish, one of the Keitruni stumbled in the surf. Evi spun about and leaped into the water with incredible speed, opening the man's throat with its claws before Rulhámad could respond. The man fell back, blood jetting through his fingers. The quatan lunged forward and pinned the man's shoulders with its upper arms while its lower limbs ripped open his abdomen. The frothy waves turned pink with blood and viscera.

The other Keitruni ran from the carnage as Rulhámad

reached out with his mind. *Leave them! We will find food for you soon.*

Rulhámad gave the quatan no admonishment for its kill. The others fell upon the corpse and in a few quick minutes had devoured it. Tattered bits of flesh and clothing churned in the surf while the creatures crunched on bloody bones.

Algariq shouldered a large pack and waited. She did not ask when he would be ready to depart, or when the quatans would be finished with their meager meal. *At least she has some self-control,* he thought. *She does not blather like so many women who only love to hear themselves talk.* He could admire that quality in her. It would make their journey together—for as long as it lasted—easier on them both.

Without taking their eyes from the quatans, the Keitruni approached the longboat that contained the empty cages. Rulhámad eyed them with amusement. He enjoyed the fear his quatans stirred in others; even those of higher castes, who, if their gaze happened to fall upon him, could not help but show a glimmer of fear if they glimpsed the creatures who lived and died at his command. *And fear them they should,* he thought. *A single thought from me would snuff out their lives in an instant.* Of course, if he did such a thing, he would quickly follow them into death, something he was not eager to do. So he held his shame and his anger within him, a smoldering fire he dare not let rage unchecked.

"Hold!"

The shout came from the grassy dunes behind them. Rulhámad wheeled about as the quatans sprang forward, snarling. He commanded them to stop and not attack. There was something familiar about the voice. That single word had made him deeply afraid, and he would not risk any of his quatans attacking until he knew who was approaching.

The man had also spoken Havalos, Rulhámad realized, which meant he was not a native of these lands. But who could have arrived here ahead of them, and how?

"Hold, I say! In the name of the Exalted!"

The quatans held their places, their long torsos hunched forward, their muscles trembling with the desire to spring forward and mete out a quick and bloody death. But Rulhámad maintained a grip on them like an iron fist. He knew who was coming, though he could not imagine *how* Vethiq aril Tolsadri, the Voice of the Exalted, had arrived here, alone on a deserted stretch of beach in a foreign and hostile land.

They could see him approaching across the sand. He'd crested the dunes and now walked toward them with a stiff gait. Rulhámad stole a glance at Algariq to gauge her reaction to Tolsadri's sudden and unexpected arrival, but her face was an emotionless mask.

When Tolsadri drew nearer, Algariq knelt and lowered her head. Rulhámad cursed himself for a fool and quickly knelt beside her. He heard the longboat creak and sway as the rowers made obeisance to one of the most powerful men in Aleith'aqtar.

Rulhámad kept his head lowered until he could see Tolsadri's battered boots appear in his vision a few feet ahead of him. "Rise, wretches of the Harridan," Tolsadri said. "And attend."

They did as he commanded. Rulhámad was shocked by the other man's appearance. Tolsadri had been on a different ship ahead of the main fleet, sent to pave the way for their arrival in these strange lands. He had seen the Voice of the Exalted but a few times before their voyage began, but Tolsadri was not a man easily forgotten.

Whatever had happened, Tolsadri was changed almost beyond recognition. Aside from his torn and battered clothing—encrusted with so much dirt and grime it seemed more filth than cloth, in danger of dissolving away at its first thorough washing—he had shriveled away until what remained was little more than a skeleton painted with a thin layer of flesh. The skin of his face had shrunken and tightened to such a degree that it seemed a fierce skull set with two livid eyes stared back at him rather than the visage of a living man. His beard was wild and tangled, like those of the madmen of Holkesh who lived in the caves near the Tumhaddi Desert and ate beetles and scorpions in accordance with their perverse vows. His fingers were desiccated, and reminded Rulhámad of walnuts strung together with bits of gristle. He did not see how the Voice could remain alive in such a state. But Tolsadri was no ordinary man, he reminded himself. He was an Adept of Bariq the Wise, Loremaster of the Mysteries, a man of subtle and potent energies far beyond Rulhámad's ken.

Algariq swung her pack off her shoulders. "Great Master, please allow me the honor to offer you my food—"

Tolsadri spat into the sand. "Leave your pack and step away. I will get what I need. I would not deign to sully myself with your unworthy food if my predicament was not so dire."

Algariq bowed her head and took five steps back. Tolsadri knelt and rummaged through the pack, trying to touch as little of it as possible with his skeletal fingers. He withdrew several pieces of dried fruit and strips of jerky. "This will suffice."

When he had finished the food, Tolsadri regarded them in turn. "You are the hunters tasked with finding the man in the Dreamer's vision. Were you shown the face of this man before you left your ship?"

With a slight nod of her head, Algariq deferred to Rulhámad. "Yes, Honored Voice," he said. "The Sword of the Exalted commanded us to join him and see the Dreamer's vision with our own eyes. We know the face of the man we hunt."

Tolsadri regarded him with utter contempt. "And how do you plan to seek this man? You have been taught the uncouth language of this country. Will you attempt to describe him to any travelers you come across and ask if they know him? Will you knock on every door in the towns and cities you will visit? Come, what is your plan now that you know his face?"

Rulhámad felt himself redden. He understood the problems they would meet, which Tolsadri had just used to mock them. Without more knowledge of their prey, finding him would be a daunting task.

"Honored Voice, I made something while we waited for our longboats to be prepared," said Algariq.

"Show me."

Rulhámad was incensed as the soul stealer bent down to her pack and removed a tightly rolled piece of parchment from an inner pocket. *What has she done?* he wondered. He feared that she had already outmaneuvered him in some crucial way, that his quest was lost before it had begun.

She unrolled the parchment. On it was a charcoal drawing of the man from the vision. It was a very good likeness. Rulhámad felt sick with envy, but could not deny how clever she had been.

She held it toward Tolsadri, who bent closer to examine it but made no move to touch it himself. "A passable likeness. You have some wits about you, at least."

"Thank you, Honored Voice. I plan to show the drawing and ask those I speak to if they know the man's name."

"As I said, you show some wits. But your drawing will not be needed. I know the name of the man. I have met him myself, in a city several days' journey to the south. He is Gerin Atreyano, a prince of some sort in this heathen country."

To Rulhámad's surprise, Tolsadri deigned to give them an abbreviated account of how he came to be on the mainland and how, in turn, he found them. He said the man from the vision examined him with some kind of mystical powers. "Different from my own, or those of any Loremaster. Take heed when you find him—I do not know the extent of his abilities."

Rulhámad knew this was not said out of any concern for his or Algariq's well being; Tolsadri warned them to help ensure that they succeeded in their mission to capture this Gerin Atreyano. If both of them perished in the attempt, the Voice of the Exalted would give them no more thought than he did to the grains of sand he crunched under his worn boots.

After escaping the city he had ventured into the hills they could see in the distance, where he had cast about with his thoughts for other Steadfast. A day earlier he had sensed the unique powers of the hunters as they neared the coast. "You cannot cross the swamp," he said, gesturing toward the fetid, shrouded bog. "You will have to climb those hills from the north, where the ascent is not so steep as these formidable cliffs."

As he listened, Rulhámad was astounded by how much Tolsadri had recovered from such a small amount of food. His face had visibly filled out, the tendons of his neck—so prominent upon his arrival, like a tent of spears beneath his flesh—had receded, and his fingers no longer looked in danger of simply dropping off his hands for want of support. He wondered if the exertion of so much of his power had contributed to Tolsadri's wasted appearance in the first place. It did not seem enough time had passed for him to have grown so emaciated from lack of food alone, even if he had eaten nothing since his escape, which seemed doubtful; surely an Adept could have found food of some sort from this foreign country. Rulhámad had heard rumors and whispers that Loremasters needed to replenish their strength with arcane rituals lest their powers overwhelm them. Perhaps Tolsadri's appearance was a telling sign that the rumors were true.

"Start at the city," commanded Tolsadri. "It is your best hope for finding him quickly."

15

"Balandrick, do you think you'll ever marry, or are you going to remain a bachelor soldier to the end of your days?"

Therain asked the question in a frivolous, teasing way as he chewed a dry crust of bread. They were seated around their camp's cookfire in the western reaches of Neldemarien. The servants had finished erecting the tents and had scurried off to eat and bed down for the night. Donael Rundgar prowled about the tents, his back to the fires to keep his eyes adjusted to the darkness. Guards stood along the camp's perimeter in groups of two, talking quietly to one another to pass away the long, idle hours of the night.

Therain and Balandrick had finished sword practice a little while ago and were sitting down to eat their evening meal when Therain aired his question. He was surprised by the darkening of Balan's expression, almost a look of pain. Balan sat down on a small folding stool and stirred the steaming chunks of deer meat and carrots with a wooden spoon, staring into the bowl as if expecting it to speak on his behalf.

"I'm sorry, Balan, I meant no offense," Therain offered. From across the fire, Hollin watched the two of them with interest.

"Oh, none taken, my lord. I was considering how best to answer you." He took a bite of meat and chewed methodically. "I believe I will marry one day, but not soon. At least I do not see it that way, though where women are involved, things may change in the blink of an eye with no forewarning." He glanced toward Gerin and Elaysen, sitting by themselves near the open flap of Gerin's tent. "I think that someday I'll marry, but for now it's difficult to consider." He paused, and for the first time looked directly at Therain. "You know that I had strong feelings for the lady Reshel before she died. And she had feelings for me as well."

"Yes, I knew some of that. Gerin told me." Therain silently cursed himself, annoyed by his stupidity. Only then did he recall their sighting of the Daughters of Reshel near Padesh and Balandrick's reaction to them. It was hard to believe that this broad-shouldered, bearded soldier and his delicate sister Reshel had loved each other. And deeply, from what he could tell.

"We had even talked of marriage," Balan continued, "though both of us knew it was unlikely to happen. But still we hoped that one day when her training was completed we would find a way to be together, but then the bloody Storm King appeared . . ."

Therain's gaze fell once more on Gerin and Elaysen, huddled next to one another, speaking in hushed tones about the gods only knew what. *Her father's religion, most likely*, he thought. But they seemed awfully cozy to be discussing matters of doctrine and the machinations of the divine. He wished for Gerin's acute sense of hearing, that he might eavesdrop—just for a bit—on their conversation. "Maybe all it will take is for you to meet the right woman," he said to Balan.

"I already did, but she is lost," he said. "I'm sure I'll find a woman who will make me happy. But Reshel still seems so much a part of me.

"I've thought about this a great deal, and it's hard for me to put into words, but I will try. It's as if, when someone close to us dies, we lose a little of ourselves because part of how we understand who *we* are is by seeing ourselves through the eyes of those who love us and who we love in return. I didn't say that well, and don't know if it makes sense, but I feel that part of *me* is diminished by her death. That some vital measure of my essence has been lost."

Therain was surprised and moved by his words. Who would have thought Balandrick, of all people, would utter something like that? He understood a little better why his sister had fallen in love with him, if he had shown her this side of himself. Reshel had been an inquisitive, intellectual young woman, a lover of books and history and ideas, and would have positively melted if Balan had revealed himself to be nimble and almost poetic in his manner of thought.

"No, it makes sense, Balandrick. In fact it's rather profound, at least to someone like me."

"That was insightful, and stated with grace and eloquence," said Hollin. "Are you sure your talents are not wasted on soldiering? Perhaps you should be a philosopher."

Balan laughed. "Me? No, thank you. I'm quite content to be a soldier. I'll leave the philosophizing to others. Soldiering comes easy to me. Thinking and philosophizing is hard."

"All the more reason to do it," said the wizard.

"No, soldiering is what I know and love. Maybe I'll wax philosophic in my gray years, and write down profound thoughts that will befuddle scholars and wizards for centuries to come."

"I'll drink to that," said Therain, hoisting a mug of beer. The others joined him.

"And what about you, my lord?" asked Balandrick as he wiped a froth of beer from his lip. "Is Laysa Oldann still the woman your father wishes you to marry?"

Therain rolled his eyes. "The gods only know. I thought for certain there would be an announcement while we were in Almaris, but not only was nothing said publicly, nothing was said to me privately either. She's a nice enough woman—she was in the city for Claressa's wedding and we were able to speak a few times—and I think I'd be happy enough married to her. I'm sure it will happen, but I'll be damned if I know when."

"Your father's so angry with your brother that maybe it's driven all other thoughts from his head," said Balandrick.

Therain shrugged. "Perhaps. His anger is wearying, even to me. He seems almost . . . unhinged in some of his actions. I'm sure Gerin is ready to throttle him. It's a good thing we've left Almaris or we might have a patricide on our hands."

"Would it be a patricide or regicide?" asked Balandrick. "Which comes first, father or king?"

Therain looked to the wizard. "Hollin?"

"Take your pick, I would say. If there is some rule for such things, I do not know it. But I also think it's in poor taste to speak of it, even in jest."

"Oh, you're right, but it *is* wearying," said Therain. "Gods above me and below, my father needs to *forgive*. Reshel made her own choice, and it was brave and selfless and he should honor that. You'd think Gerin had slit her throat himself, the way he acts. Death can come for any of us at any time, no matter how much we may wish it otherwise, to highborn or low alike. In the end, we are all food for the worms and must pass into Bellon's mansion. That is an immutable law of the world if ever there was one.

"He was always hardest on Gerin. Pushing him to be the best, to be *perfect*. And for a while he was, and I freely admit now I resented Gerin for it, and resented my father for focusing so much of his attention on him. But now I think I prefer it this way. I would not want him this angry at me for so long. I would wither under the weight of it. And I worry that my father's anger is becoming like a consuming fire within him, feeding on itself in a way that is beyond his control and will leave him with nothing *but* anger in the end."

"More wise words from the young," said Hollin. "I have known men like that, devoured by their passions. But there is nothing that can be done to help them. Those fires cannot be quenched by others; only those in whom they burn have the power to extinguish them."

"Such cheery talk before bed," said Balandrick. "You will both give me indigestion and a poor night's sleep. I'll probably have nightmares of men with blazing fires in their guts."

"He's right," Therain said. "We should turn to lighter matters before a cloud of gloom settles over us. And what of you,

Hollin? Shouldn't you be teaching Gerin spells of one kind or another?"

Balandrick bent his head in Elaysen's general direction. "He seems to have been usurped."

Hollin pressed his lips together tightly. "Women. I love them dearly—*dearly*—but they are a distraction to young men the likes of which even magic cannot overcome."

"Not only to young men," said Therain. "I saw you cast an admiring glance or two at the impressive bosom of Mistress Islem back in the Tirthaig. It might have even been three or four glances. I doubt the thought of magic ever crossed your mind."

Hollin assumed a look of shock and indignation. "I may be *old*, Master Therain, but I am not yet *dead*. And 'impressive' is hardly the word I would use to describe Mistress Islem's bosom. In fact, I'm not sure the word exists that can adequately convey the magnificence of her cleavage. I do not think I've ever seen better, and I assure you I've seen many in my long life."

"This is more like it," said Balandrick. "My dreams tonight are beginning to look up."

"I for one am shocked that there are no spells that can overcome this sort of affliction," said Therain. "You mean to say with all of the power at your disposal that you can't manage to wrest Gerin away from an admittedly attractive—"

"And smart," added Balandrick.

"—and smart young woman? What have you wizards been doing all these years? It seems you lot have been sorely lacking in priorities. It's obvious you need to be managed better if you're ever going to find a cure for these inconvenient lapses in attention brought about by the mere presence of smart and attractive women."

"And cleavage," said Balandrick.

"Oh, there are many spells that can take care of this problem," said Hollin. "But most would leave Gerin unconscious, slack-jawed, drooling, and perhaps half-witted."

"Then I'm not impressed by your magic," said Balandrick, "since I could accomplish the same thing by cracking him on the head with the flat of my sword."

* * *

"They're talking about us," said Elaysen as the three men sitting around the campfire laughed loudly at something Balandrick said.

"Ignore them," said Gerin. "I'm sure they mean nothing."

"It doesn't bother me, my lord. I find it amusing, actually, that two grown men—and one very old wizard—can still act so much like *boys*."

Gerin understood her meaning, though another part of him wanted to end their lesson for the night and join his friends so *he* could act like a boy, too, and laugh and carry on and forget duties and responsibilities for a little while. But then he would have to forgo Elaysen's company, and since the desire to remain in her presence was the stronger of the two, he stayed where he was.

"Anyway," he said, "you were telling me that to be a *taekrim* means to be ever watchful for signs of the Adversary's presence. Is that all there is to following *dalar-aelom*?"

"No, there is much more. There are acts to perform that purify the body and mind, prayers to be made to the One God, tithes to support the emissaries and the tabernacles and temples my father is building. But for now we will focus on the Adversary, since that is the reason the One God spoke to my father. And to you, I believe."

"So how do you look for signs of the Adversary? What are we to be vigilant *for*?"

"We are to be mindful of evil in all its forms, and to thwart it wherever we encounter it. The Adversary himself is not yet fully here in this world. He is still *becoming*, slowly building his power until he is strong enough to manifest himself in a wholly physical incarnation, but because he is not yet fully here does not mean the evil he brings with him is absent. It is not. Right now my father believes he is a bodiless spirit of malice and corruption, spreading his evil the way a poison spreads through the air or water. It corrupts our hearts and minds and makes us spurn others in need of help and treat them with hatred and contempt."

"Are you saying that the Adversary's evil takes root inside of us?"

"Yes, but it is not *of* us. As I said, it is like a poison, but instead of killing us or making us ill, it corrupts our hearts."

Gerin frowned. "I have a hard time believing that. Your father has said the Adversary has only recently entered the world. Yet people have been evil as long as there have *been* people. How could the Adversary have been the cause if he wasn't here?" He remembered the annihilation of the Eletheros in their once beautiful city atop the Sundering, and a little boy skewered on an Atalari spear, slain simply because of what he was.

Elaysen was shaking her head. "I didn't explain myself well. Yes, the Adversary is only now making himself manifest, but his evil has been here since the beginning of time, a taint like oil on water that lies over all of Creation. When the One God made the world and all that is in it, the pure vision of His Creation was thwarted by the Adversary, corrupted by his malign influence. *The world is broken.* It is not as it should be, as it was meant to be. It has been marred by the power of the One God's Enemy. He is returning so that he may further distort the purpose of Creation, but his taint has been here since the beginning. *That* is why men act in evil ways. Because the world was broken and its purpose distorted."

Gerin pondered this. He decided to accept that explanation for now, though his heart told him something was missing from it.

"What are we to do once the Adversary regains his body? Is there any way to prevent that from happening, or is it inevitable? And if it is inevitable, how are we to fight him? From what you have said, we would be facing a god clothed in flesh."

"I don't know. It may be that by being vigilant we will somehow discern the presence of the Adversary before he has completely entered the world, but my father is far from certain about this." Her eyes grew wide. "Perhaps *that* is the reason you have been singled out! Your powers as a wizard may provide a way to discover the Adversary while he is yet weak and vulnerable and grant us a means to overcome him."

"I don't know how I would find the growing power of a divine being. Hollin has said explicitly that divine power is hidden from our sight."

"A way may be shown to us that we cannot yet see. We must have faith, my lord."

"If we are to face a divinity upon a field of battle, we would do well to have an army."

Elaysen laughed, but the sound was glazed with a kind of nervous unease. "That is exactly what Aidrel has called for. He and my father have argued bitterly over it. He says that we must prepare an army now if we are to have any hope of defeating the Adversary when he arises. He grows impatient with the emissaries. He feels we should use force to convert all of Osseria to belief in the One God so that we will face the Adversary united."

"Conversion on the sword is not the answer. Those converted against their will would be ripe for betrayal at the first opportunity."

"It is even more than that. My father believes that a forced conversion will not allow their spirits to enjoy true life beyond death in the One God's presence. They must *want* to follow him, and to fight evil. They cannot be forced to."

He thought of the Pashti. For thousands of years they had been a conquered people, living in poverty in slums and ghettos, scratching a meager living in remote areas of the country, and working as servants for the nobility and the wealthy. For most of his life he'd never given them a second thought; they were of no more interest to him than a piece of furniture.

But then, after witnessing the eradication of the Eletheros, he'd vowed to do what he could to help them. He felt that what had happened to the long-vanished Eletheros could have easily happened to the Pashti—his father once remarked that he thought it would have been better if Khedesh had killed all of the Pashti when he conquered them, a sentiment that now left Gerin aghast. *No race should ever have to die,* he thought. *Or suffer needlessly simply because of what they are.* He'd vowed to do what he could to right the wrongs that had been done to them, at least in some small manner. But so far he'd been unable to think of any practical way to do so. He'd spoken to a number of the Pashti servants at Ailethon, asking them what they wanted from their lives, but they all said they were content to serve, since they knew nothing else and felt that was all they could do. He could see that they feared the question, perhaps believing that if they spoke the secret desires of their hearts to this powerful Khedeshian lord they would be punished for it. No matter how much he reassured them, their answers did not change.

"I have another question for you."

"Go on, my lord."

"What exactly *is* the Adversary? When Zaephos appeared to me on the road to Hethnost he said that the Adversary opposed the One God at the beginning of all things and was thrown down in darkness and defeat, but wasn't destroyed. Your father teaches that the One God is the creator of everything, including other gods like Telros. So how does the Adversary fit into this? If he was strong enough to have opposed the One God, does that mean he is of equal strength? It seems he existed before Creation happened, otherwise he could not have tainted the world when it was made. So is he a being that is equal to the One God—which to me would indicate He is not truly the 'One God' but at least one of two—or something else?"

"My father believes the Adversary is *not* the equal of the One God but is of the same essence, of a like kind but of lesser strength. This too has caused problems among the Inner Circle."

"Aidrel again?"

"Yes. He's the one most often at odds with my father. From early in life he believed he would be called to a great purpose, and when he heard the message of the One God from my father he felt that he had found his calling at last. He is a capable and intelligent man, full of passion for my father's cause, but I also think he feels slighted that the One God has not appeared to him directly."

"What does Aidrel think about the Adversary?"

"He believes the Adversary was created by the One God and is in no way an equal to Him. He feels very strongly that my father is in error about this. He finds it blasphemous to even consider that they could possibly be similar. My father has argued with him about this at length, but neither will move in their positions."

"It seems, then, that the answer to my question is that no one is sure exactly what the Adversary is."

"Yes, my lord."

And it was possible that both were wrong and the Adversary was something else entirely. Aunphar had to be wrong about *something*. Zaephos's warning said as much.

Later that night Gerin awoke in a sweat and took a shuddering gasp of air. He'd dreamed of Reshel's death again. He rolled over and wiped the tears from his eyes. He wondered what she would make of Aunphar's religion and his own involvement in it. He tried to have a conversation with her in his mind, to see if he could discern what she would have thought, but he had no penetrating insights to her answers. They seemed a pale reflection of what the real Reshel would say, which saddened him even more.

16

Rulhámad waited for Katel yalez Algariq's return with increasing impatience. She had been gone for two days, swallowed by the city perched upon a forked rocky plateau overlooking the sea. The city, though not as immense as sprawling Kalmanyikul, was nevertheless impressive in size, ringed with two high defensive walls pierced by well-fortified gates.

Having nothing else to occupy his time, he'd studied the city since Algariq's departure. He wondered how old it was, how many people lived there—he guessed somewhere between 300,000 and half a million—how many soldiers were garrisoned within, how well it was provisioned in case of a siege, where its wells, cisterns, granaries, and warehouses were located, from what direction its main supply lines came, and other observations he would take back with him when their task was complete. All the Steadfast of every caste who ventured forth to the lands of unbelievers were taught what to look for so their observations could aid the warriors of Herol, to whom the task would eventually fall of conquering fortified positions—whether villages, towns, castles, fortresses, holds, or cities. It was one of the few areas in which every follower of every Power was charged with the same duty, so they could work together for the betterment of all. Even Tolsadri would have made observations about those who had captured him; no different, Rulhámad reflected, than he himself was doing now.

Meli appeared beside him. The quatan's jaws were slick with blood from a deer it has just slaughtered and eaten. Rulhámad could sense its contentment.

After Tolsadri had commandeered one of their longboats, Rulhámad and Algariq left the coast and made their way inland, past the bog and cliffs to the wooded slopes of the hills. There had been plenty of game in the rugged lowlands that formed the skirts of the hills, and the quatans feasted on fresh meat. But something in either the meat or the water in the streams from which they drank made three of the quatans violently ill. It had unnerved Rulhámad to see his powerful companions stricken so, their ribs heaving with each breath, their tongues lolling from their mouths as they whimpered in pain.

A few hours later he and Algariq had also fallen ill, afflicted with terrible stomach cramps, vomiting, and diarrhea. He suspected the cause of the sickness was in the water, since he and Algariq had eaten only supplies they brought with them. They did not move for two days, hiding in a deep tree-shrouded gully while their bodies purged themselves of whatever had ailed them. Once they were feeling well enough to move, they made their way southward into the rising wooded folds of the hills. They traveled slowly as their bodies acclimated to the water—perhaps the very air—of this new land. More than once Rulhámad had shat large quantities of blood and felt so ill that he feared he might die, shivering uncontrollably while his body burned with fever.

But he did not. Neither did Algariq or any of the quatans. They were a hardy people, used to arduous tasks and enduring great torment and suffering. They crossed the hills and arrived at this spot, where they had debated how to proceed.

"I will go to the city to find out what I can of our prey," Algariq had said that night. "You stay here with your beasts until I return."

Rulhámad feared treachery from her. *She will find him and leave me to pursue him on her own.* "No. We will both go."

She gave him a look that said plainly he was behaving like a fool. "And what of your quatans? How far does your bond with them extend? If you are in the city, will you be able to sense if they are in danger, or injured? What if they are discovered by a party of hunters, or worse, a patrol of soldiers? I will go. I give you my word that when I've learned all I can, I will return."

He made a sound of disgust. "And what good is your word? You are a wretch of the Harridan, the same as I."

Algariq fixed him with a cold stare. "We can have honor among ourselves, even if others do not honor *us*. You know the game we play; we both hope to be elevated to a higher caste by completing our task. But what good will it do us to be raised to a better caste if we do not act with honor? By behaving with honor now, we show ourselves worthy of the reward we seek."

"And what if you find him while you are in the city? What if you turn a corner and find yourself face-to-face with this Gerin Atreyano?"

A grin spread across her face, but the coldness did not leave her eyes. "Then I will take it as a sign that the Holvareh Himself has given His blessing to me, and the prey will be mine and mine alone. But do not fear, Rulhámad. I do not think in a city so vast that such a thing is likely."

He had regarded her for a long moment, trying to discern the truthfulness of her words. He reached out to her with his bond, but it failed to touch her mind, as it always did when he tried to use it upon human beings. He was a maegosi, his power reserved for quatans alone. Her heart and her thoughts were closed to him.

Their conversation, and Algariq's departure, had occurred two days ago. Evening was coming on. A vermillion stain was spreading across the cloudy western sky. He felt a slow rage burning within him, certain that he had been betrayed after believing a worthless vow from her.

Rulhámad was pondering his options as the sky darkened when he spied a rider on horseback moving in his direction from the plain. He took cover behind a tree and sent a command for his quatans to hide themselves as best as they could. The wind was in his favor, and would hide the scent of his quatans until the horse and rider were almost upon them.

When the rider was perhaps fifty yards away, Rulhámad relaxed and stepped forward. Algariq was upon the horse. She was an adept rider, and he wondered where she had learned such a skill.

"Hail, Kursil," she said as she swung down from the saddle.

"Hail, Katel," he said in return, holding his right hand to his breastbone and bowing his head. "I see you found yourself a steed."

"I felt the need for haste," she said as she tethered the horse to a sturdy tree limb. She brushed some dirt from her sleeve as she made her way to him through the underbrush. "I had spent too long in the city by my reckoning, and I knew you would be restless and fearing betrayal. Besides," she reached out and stroked the horse's long neck, "he is a beautiful creature."

"How was your hunting?"

"Frustrating. This Gerin's name is well known, but not his whereabouts. When I made inquiries, most pointed to a palace on a hill and said he was within its walls, with his father the king. A few thought he had left the city, but they were not certain and I did not want to act until I knew for sure where to find him. I scouted the palace and drew the attention of its guards with my questions and darker skin. I do not look like these pale people, and many were suspicious."

"You did not use your power upon them?"

She shook her head, frustrated at the recollection. "There were too many others about. I could not take so many. I had to withdraw. It was not until this morning that I found a soldier of the palace alone where I could work my power on him. He told me that the prince left the city nine days ago."

Rulhámad stiffened. "So long? Where is he headed? Did the soldier know?"

"Yes." She turned and gestured to the plain below them. "He is upon that western road, and his destination is a place called Ailethon. I believe it is the castle shown to us in the Dreamer's vision."

"We cannot tarry," said Rulhámad. "We must set out at once." He turned to summon the quatans, but Algariq stopped him with a forceful grip on his upper arm.

"Before we set out, we must decide who will make the first attempt to capture him. I have kept my word to you that I would join you here and tell you what I learned rather than use it to my advantage. But now, before we go further, one of us must take precedence."

He regarded her warily. "What do you suggest?"

"*Kanilé.*"

Rulhámad tried to conceal the triumphant grin he felt spreading across his face. *She chooses trial by combat. I can defeat her easily. She is no match for me.* He nodded solemnly. "I accept. We will decide by *kanilé*. Do you know *ilé-asurdath*?"

"I do. And you?"

"Yes."

"Do you wish to fight now, in the dark?"

"I would not have us waste any more time. Our prey already has a considerable lead. I would prefer to overtake him on the open road rather than pry him loose from his home."

"Very well. There is a clearing a short distance from here that will suffice for our combat."

Rulhámad set off through the woods, up toward a depression barren of trees. The floor of the depression was rocky, with tufts of weeds and grass poking up like straggling hairs on a balding man's head. The trees ringing the hollow were tall and leaned inward over it, so it seemed that the broken ruins of a leafy dome hung above their heads.

The quatans lingered at the edge of the trees while Rulhámad and Algariq made their way to the center of the depression. They faced each other, their hands flat at their sides, and bowed.

"*Kanilé* is a fight of honor," said Algariq. "No matter that it is we of the Harridan who are engaged, we will follow the ancient rules. We may not use weapons of any kind: no blade or spear, no bow, no rocks from the ground. Neither may we use our powers. We fight with hands and feet alone. Our bodies are our weapons, and will either prove our worth or deny it. A violation of these rules means forfeiture of the right to hunt and take captive our prey. Do you agree to this?"

"I agree. My quatans will not enter this clearing. Neither will you use your powers as a soul stealer upon me." He unbuckled his belt and tossed it toward the trees. Algariq removed her own belt and several knives hidden in her sleeves and the tops of her boots. He sent a strong command to the quatans to remain where they were and not interfere. *I am not in danger. If you move you will anger me greatly.* He sent a flicker of pain through the bond as a taste of what they would incur should they disobey him.

"We fight according to *ilé-asurdath*, the Code of Herol the Warrior and those who follow him," she said. "Though we are not of that caste, we will show honor to Herol and ourselves by abiding by the rules handed down long ago. The first to knock the other to the ground gains the right to hunt our prey without interference from the other. Only if the first fails shall the other be free to hunt. Do you agree to this?"

"I do."

They assumed the ritual stance of *ilé-asurdath*: knees bent, right foot forward, the left foot turned outward at a right angle, hands up with straight and rigid fingers.

"We begin on your word," said Algariq.

"Begin."

The word had barely left his mouth before Algariq shot toward him with dizzying speed. He raised his arm by reflex and was just able to deflect a blow from her right hand that might have knocked him unconscious had it landed on his jaw as intended. A flare of pain erupted in his forearm where the rigid side of her hand struck it. *Ruren's breath, she is fast!* Much faster than he had thought.

He backed up several paces, keeping his stance wide to maintain balance and his hands raised to ward off blows. She pressed her attack, jabbing toward his face and torso with blinding speed. He was able to deflect most of the blows, but one landed on his ribs with numbing force; he grunted, then tried to clip the side of her head with his right hand. But she rolled her head back and danced away so quickly that his fist swung through empty air. He overbalanced slightly, his swing twisting him around farther than he had intended, and before he could square his body to her, she landed two blows on his lower back. The pain was excruciating. His knees buckled. He swung his arm backward savagely in an attempt to backhand her, but once again she leaped beyond his reach.

He knew he would have to go on the offensive immediately or else lose the fight. The pain in his back burned like a brand, but he ignored it and lunged toward Algariq, hoping to surprise her and use his longer reach to knock her down before she could react.

The lunge did surprise her; he could see it in her eyes. Instead of striking her, he tried to grasp her around the waist, planning to lift her into the air so she would lose all leverage and then slam her down on her back.

He got one hand around her back, but before he could close with the other, she spun wildly to her right and chopped down on his elbow, forcing it to bend and freeing her from his grip. He snarled and lunged again, but this time she was ready for him. She crouched low and kicked toward his hip. He spun to the right and narrowly avoided the blow.

She liked to kick. It told him how he could defeat her. Kicks could be put to deadly use in *ilé-asurdath,* but when used in *kanïlé,* they could be turned against the kicker.

Rulhámad pressed his attack, trying once again to use his slightly longer reach to his advantage. But Algariq was simply too fast. He could not land his blows. She blocked every one with furious movements of her arms, forcing his attacks to fall wide while she quickly counterpunched before backing outside of his reach. One of her blows came so close to his face that he could feel the breeze of its passing on his cheeks.

She was wearing him down. That was her strategy. To use her speed to land blows and force him to pursue her until he grew tired and careless. And it would work. He could sense it in the growing leaden weight of his arms. She did not seem nearly so spent, her blows coming as fast and hard now as they had at the start.

He had to take a risk, otherwise all would be lost.

He lunged at her again, spreading his arms wide to make her think he was attempting once more to grab her around the waist and throw her down. By doing so he dangerously exposed his torso to an attack, which was his intent.

She took the bait. She kicked up with her right leg, aiming for his breastbone.

It was exactly what he'd hoped she would do. Even before she launched her kick, he'd begun to bring his arms inward; as soon as her foot shot forward, he spun to the side and grabbed her ankle with both hands. He used her own weight to balance himself as he twisted her foot and shoved her backward with all of his might.

Algariq let out a cry of surprise as her arms pinwheeled in an attempt to remain upright, then extended her left leg, hoping to raise her body far enough from the ground to give her time to get her right leg under her. But she could not regain her balance and fell to the ground, her back slamming hard into a rock protruding from the dirt like a clenched fist. She rolled over, writhing in pain, and got to her knees.

"A valiant fight," he said, panting and wiping sweat from his face. "But I win."

A short while later Algariq watched him leave, surrounded by his grotesque quatans, headed for the westlands and their prey. *Her* prey. Gerin should be hers. She cursed herself for letting him best her at *kanilé*. She should never have been so careless. She knew that kicks were dangerous in *kanilé*, that one should never let balance become that precarious. But he'd left himself so vulnerable that she'd felt the risk had been worth taking.

Clearly, his apparent exposure and vulnerability had been a feint. She could see that now. He'd lunged at her, fully expecting—*hoping*—she would do what she did.

She sat at the edge of the clearing, her head bowed in defeat. She had lost her chance. Now she could only hope that he would fail, but she did not think that likely. Rulhámad was a resourceful man, and his quatans were formidable creatures. And if he failed, what did that say about her own chances of success?

She thought of her mother, dead for eleven years now, an outcast woman buried in a common grave near the sawtooth hills of Ulram Wadeli. Mulai ibel Algariq had died a bitter, lonely death, shunning her daughter and grandson out of spite for her own wretched condition and guilt for what she had brought upon them. *Better I had never had you than bring you into this world as one of Tulqan's spawn*, her mother had said the final time they spoke. *Your son will suffer as we have, and there will be no end to our torment. I curse my mother's name and rue the day I took my first breath.*

Not long after, Mulai had vanished from their hovel in the slums of Kalmanyikul, leaving no word or note of where she had gone or why. A year passed before Katel's uncle appeared in her doorway to tell her that her mother had flung herself from a cliff in the Ulram Wadeli. He had buried her in the lich yard reserved for those of the Harridan. There was no marker or gravestone to show where she lay; such accoutrements were not permitted for members of her caste.

Katel had not visited the lich yard where her mother lay. There was no point. There was nothing to see, nothing to mourn. She had her memories, and they would suffice. Her mother was gone, devoured by her loathing of herself and her inability to accept what she was. She had offered her daughter little in life. Her death served only to end her torment. Katel hoped it had done so, but doubted that Ruren, god of the Underworld and master of the dead, would be so kind.

Katel herself refused to give in to her mother's despair. Yes, life in the caste of the Harridan was hard and unjust and unfair. One could either accept it or choose to change it. She had chosen the latter. She wanted a better life for herself and her son. She sighed again as she thought of Huma, his dark curly hair and dark eyes so much like his father's, a man who had vanished into the slave warrens of Kenset six years earlier, never to be seen again. She missed her son so keenly sometimes it was like a wound in her heart, an ache so deep within her she wondered, when the pain was at its worst, how she could continue without him. *I am doing this for him,* she would remind herself. *For us. So that we can have a better life. That he will not live forever with the shame and humiliation of being Tulqani.*

If she were the one to capture this Prince Gerin, as a reward she would be elevated to another caste, one without the harsh stigma of the Harridan. As would her son. They would be cleansed, their past washed away and forgotten. They would no longer have to live as outcasts, shunned and despised.

But I was careless, and Rulhámad bested me. And now all is lost. I will never see Huma again. Despair welled up within her. For the first time, she understood her mother's choice to end her life rather than continue in such pain. She saw only darkness before her, a black doom that swallowed all light, all hope. Rulhámad would capture their prey, and the best she could hope for was to return to Aleith'aqtar in shame and dishonor, though more likely she would either be left here or killed outright for her failure. She could only hope that little Huma would find the strength to achieve the freedom for himself that his mother could not.

A sob escaped her, and a tear rolled down her cheek. The thought of never seeing Huma again was too much to endure. This long separation from him had been difficult enough, but she had gone with the hope that she would return to him victorious in her quest and raise him to a new and better life. But now that hope was gone.

She wept bitterly, and hated herself for it. This was how her mother would react, bemoaning her fate and the injustice of her life. Katel had always thought herself stronger than that. *Yet here I sit, weeping and cursing. I am no better than she was.* Her mother had never done anything to help herself or her only daughter. From an early age, Katel had vowed always to fight for herself. Better that than passive acceptance.

When Huma's father was lost in the slave dens, she had wept for one night and one night only, then continued on with her infant son. She had to be strong for him. She had to *live* for him, and to *hope* for him. To do anything less was a betrayal of everything she believed in and how she saw herself. Her love for Huma knew no bounds. How could she not do everything in her power to give him a better life?

Yes, how could I not? She straightened and wiped the tears from her face. *I am strong. All is not yet lost. I must be ready if Rulhámad fails. If I do not follow then I will have forfeited my right as second and any hope that I may yet succeed. I cannot throw my chance away, no matter how slim it may be. I must always hope.* That had been her mother's failure, and undoing. She had lost the ability to hope.

Algariq made her way through the trees to the horse she had taken in the city. It raised its head when it heard her approach and watched her as if impatient for her arrival, its tail swishing lazily. She untied its tether and mounted.

She would not betray Rulhámad or try to thwart him—if she desired to rise above the caste of the Harridan, she must at all times behave as one higher than she, or else she was deserving of the hatred and spite shown to her by others who considered all followers of the Harridan to be betrayers and oathbreakers. But she would watch and wait, and if he failed, she would be ready to claim their prey for herself.

Algariq rode along the edge of the trees toward the west. She would not take the road for fear of being stopped by soldiers. She could not risk capture. She would ride fast and hard until she caught up to Rulhámad. He would be most displeased to see her, but could not deny her right to accompany him. Together they would find their prey, and she would hope that her chance would come.

She could do nothing else. She loved her son too much.

17

Tolsadri stepped from the rocking boat and climbed the wooden rungs that had been hammered into the algae-covered pylons that disappeared beneath him into the murky, sloshing waters of the harbor. Six rungs brought him onto the weather-beaten planking of the pier. He straightened, brushed his hands on his thighs, and marched down the pier toward the murdrendi and human soldiers lounging at its far end. They snapped to attention when they saw him; Tolsadri's face was well known, and even in his current withered condition—though he had recovered much of his strength during the trip back to this accursed island—he was still easily recognizable to most of the common soldiers who were part of the invasion fleet.

"Voice of the Exalted, you have returned!" said the commander at the pier's end. The man saluted and bowed. "The Veiled One truly watches over you. We believed you were dead."

"Your belief was in error." He did not deign to look the man in the eye. Instead, he surveyed what he could see of the harbor front and town beyond it. Much of his view was occluded by three squat towers of brick separated from an equal number of warehouses behind them by a narrow cobblestone avenue. Wooden scaffolds had been erected on the avenue, and from them several dozen naked bodies hung.

Great flocks of crows swarmed through the air like a feathered black cloud and picked at the dead flesh.

"Where are the Dreamer and Sword of the Exalted?" he said to the commander, still without looking at him.

"They are in the castle upon the cliff, Honored Voice."

Tolsadri sighed. These lands felt too strange for him. He had never before ventured so far from his home, and was disquieted to discover how much he was unsettled by this place. He felt that his connection to Bariq was somehow lessened, thinned like a taut rope fraying in the middle and threatening to break. His powers were as strong as ever, yet there was nevertheless some indefinable essence that seemed to have vanished from him. Holvareh and the Powers were everywhere in the world, which was theirs to govern through their servants the Steadfast. Yet he also felt that the presence of the Powers was distant in these lands, like the cold rays of the sun in the heart of winter.

"I am still recovering from my travails," he said. "Summon a sedan chair to take me to the castle."

The chair was hastily assembled from one of the ships while he waited—apparently the Khedeshians of this isle did not use this mode of transportation, since none had so far been found, though Tolsadri had seen such conveyances during his escape from the city. He settled into the cushions and let his mind wander as he was carried through the streets, swaying gently with the motion of his bearers. From time to time he parted the curtains with his hand to peer at the town through which he passed.

He saw columns of Steadfast infantry marching through the streets, while other soldiers stood watch at intersections and alleyways and at the doors of buildings that were occupied by their commanders. Groups of Khedeshians sat in rows in a small square waiting to be examined by Tolsadri's fellow Adepts, who would use the *burquai* and *tel'fan* to determine which caste would be most appropriate for them. His gaze fell upon the burned, smoke-stained ruins of several buildings, their interiors and roofs having collapsed into charred, smoldering piles of wreckage like bones in an os-

suary. Farther on he saw more soldiers patrolling the wall
that encircled the town, with the high cliffs looming behind
them blotting out much of the sky, and two naked men manacled to a wall where they were being whipped, their backs
flayed open and streaming blood while their screams echoed
through the canyonlike streets.

Tolsadri lowered his hand and allowed the curtains to
close. The town did not matter. If the disobedience of its inhabitants could not be adequately quelled, then they would
be slaughtered and the town burned to the ground. Isolated
as it was, it would not make an ideal example to others, but
the bodies they would hang along the harbor, in front of the
charnel house they would make of the town itself, with signs
proclaiming this was done because of their disobedience,
would still have some effect on ships coming here. He smiled
at the image of the dead town, and some part of him hoped
they *would* resist enough that they drew upon themselves
such a harsh punishment.

He dozed for a while as his bearers carried him out of the
town and up the slope to the main entrance to the castle.
In the forecourt, he exited the sedan chair and saw several
Sai'fen stationed along the castle's walls and within its large
entrance chamber. He both hated and feared the soldiers of
the Dreamers because they neither feared nor acknowledged
him. The knowledge that they could and would kill him under the right circumstances, and do so with impunity, fueled
his hatred, though he could never let his hatred, or his fear,
be known.

He commanded a Keitruni slave to take him to the Sword
of the Exalted. The woman led him through a labyrinthine
maze of corridors, zigzagging stairways, and narrow passages to the windowed, west-facing chamber he had seen
only briefly during his imprisonment here. Despite his loathing for this country, he could not help but admire the commanding view from the room.

Mellam yun avki Drugal was standing at a massive black
table inlaid with filigrees of silver and pearl, poring over
maps that had apparently been found within the castle itself,

as the Steadfast themselves had no maps of these new lands. Several aides were seated at the table, studying parchments and taking inventory of the contents of several small steel-banded chests. When Drugal saw Tolsadri approach him across the length of the long room, a look of astonishment came over his face.

"Tolsadri! We thought you dead!"

"A common sentiment, it seems."

"What happened to you? Have you been on this island all along?"

"No. I only just returned."

Drugal swiveled toward a Keitruni lurking near an archway in the naked rock wall opposite the windows. The sun was low in the sky, and it seemed the stone was awash in a coppery flame. "Bring the Voice of the Exalted food and drink at once!" He turned back to Tolsadri and clasped his hand. "I am pleased to see you. I am not one to parley with foreigners."

"I have already had my fill of the people of this country," Tolsadri replied. "They are proud and stubborn and will never willingly submit to our ways. It is, as always, the Sword that shall conquer them, not the Voice." *And you are not glad to see me,* he thought. *You have always despised me and coveted my closeness to the Exalted. Do not feign friendship where you desire none.* But he said nothing. It was in his best interest to work in unison with the Exalted's Sword, so the conquering of new lands went as smoothly as possible. In that way his own power and influence was increased. He planned, one day, to maneuver the Exalted to place a minion of his own as her Sword. Of course, the Exalted would believe she was acting of her own will, but Tolsadri had her ear, and with each victory she relied upon his counsel that much more. Until the right moment presented itself, he would bide his time and continue his discreet search through the ranks of up-and-coming followers of Herol for the one both strong enough to become the Sword yet malleable enough to be swayed by his own power. Tolsadri knew it was a dangerous game, for Drugal himself was no doubt seeking the man who would one day assume his role and would certainly destroy without hesitation anyone who had the remotest connection with him.

But precisely *because* it was dangerous, Tolsadri relished every moment of it. It was while playing games of power within the halls of the Jade Temple and the Pahjuleh Palace that he felt the most alive. Drugal was an effective Sword in some ways: a competent battlefield commander, able to devise and improvise strategies in the churning ebb and flow of combat, and pious almost to the point of absurdity. Yet he was a remarkably boring man, unimaginative in any aspect of life unrelated to warfare, with no real ambition—though it could be argued, Tolsadri conceded, that he'd had enough ambition to become Sword, and having reached that pinnacle, had no need for more. Still, power required that those who held it exercise it as well, if only to gain more of it. It was a law Tolsadri understood well, and that Drugal did not understand in the least. He did his tasks effectively and efficiently, but nothing more. Tolsadri had destroyed many men during his rise to power. Some had been competitors, some adversaries, and some he had destroyed simply to see if he could. Drugal stood one step below the Exalted herself; to eliminate him would be a monumental achievement. Yet the man refused to play the game! That in itself was unforgivable, and deserving of the fate Tolsadri was determined to deal to him in due time.

Drugal nodded, then gestured to one of the chairs. "Please, sit, and tell me what happened to you."

Tolsadri slumped into a seat and in a clipped, bored tone related the story of the sinking of the *Kaashal* and his subsequent capture, imprisonment, and interrogation in the capital city upon the mainland. "I have met the man from the Dreamer's vision and know his name," he said bluntly. He enjoyed the look of shock that spread across Drugal's face at his pronouncement. "He is Prince Gerin Atreyano, the son of the king of this country. I found the hunters upon the mainland and told them where he could be found."

"Holvareh guide us, it seems your capture was more a

thing of good fortune than ill. Were you able to learn anything about the Words of Making?"

"He claims to know nothing of them."

"I will send additional men to seek for him. I was never comfortable with trusting such an important task to spawns of the Harridan. Her will can turn the surest blade-thrust from true."

"It was the Dreamer's will that these hunters were brought with us."

"I know, and I should not question it, yet Tulqan is still a Power and may distort even the visions of the Dreamers."

An aide entered the room and bowed before Drugal. "My lord, a large ship was sighted approaching the island. When they saw the fleet they turned about and retreated toward the mainland. The *Kretpur* and *Ja'lar* are giving chase, but it is doubtful they will overtake the ship before she reaches her destination."

"We should begin the assault upon the mainland as soon as this island is secured," said Tolsadri. "Take their capital and their king. If the hunters have not succeeded in finding Prince Gerin, having his father as a hostage will draw him out."

Drugal straightened. "Tell me everything you can of the city where you were captive so that I may prepare a plan of attack."

18

King Abran Atreyano stood before a window in his garret room, staring across the sun-drenched city. His attention was preoccupied with thoughts of his son. It had been apparent from a very early age that his eldest son and heir was gifted. A big child who grew quickly, he was walking before he was a year old and speaking short words not long after. But Gerin had always been a problematic child for him, and Abran had feared his son even as he marveled at him. Not that he had ever expressed his fear aloud, even to his late wife Vanya, who had doted on Gerin before the arrival of the twins and the inevitable shift in her attention to the younger children.

Now, however, with so much wrong between the two of them, so much broken, Abran faced it squarely: he feared his son. Feared that Gerin would eclipse his own accomplishments to such a degree that it would be as if he had never lived. He knew that fathers should wish for their sons to achieve greatness in their own right, that they needed to step out of their fathers' shadows in order to become men. Perhaps it was a flaw of his character that he could not truly hope for such a thing.

He turned away from the window, sank into a nearby chair and drummed his fingers along one wooden arm. He no longer understood Gerin. The business of magic was bad enough, and had led to the untimely death of his precious

Reshel. But now Gerin was involving himself with the apostate priest who styled himself a prophet of a new god that Gerin claimed had appeared to him as well. An outlandish, ridiculous claim, yet Abran feared that it was indeed true—even the divine were paying attention to his son, marking him for some unknown and unfathomable purpose. He did not know where this involvement with the priest would end, but he could see no good coming of it.

The question was, what, if anything, could he himself do about it? Gerin would live for centuries if the damned wizard Hollin were to be believed. What would it do to the kingdom to have a king's reign last so long? Would Gerin step aside so that a son of his, yet to be born, could rule when he was fully grown, or would Gerin deny that birthright to his heirs? Even if he himself did the truly unthinkable and passed over Gerin in favor of Therain to succeed him, Gerin would still be a man of power with a life that would endure for hundreds of years. And what was to prevent Gerin from using his power to simply take what he wanted?

Abran thought once more about his son's involvement with the apostate priest. When he'd first heard of the Prophet of the One God, he dismissed this new religion out of hand. It seemed little more than a thinly veiled ploy for a fallen priest of the Temple to both antagonize those who had cast him out and try to regain some measure of respect and power. That Aunphar's teachings had become popular so quickly with the commoners had dismayed both him and the Temple hierarchy. Something in the man's teachings was resonating among the people with incredible power. His popularity has soared to such heights that it was now impossible to move against him without risking a full-scale riot in the city. He considered Aunphar a power monger, especially after he'd learned that the Prophet had sent emissaries not only to other areas of Khedesh, but to other nations as well. It seemed the Prophet's ambitions knew no bounds, that he was determined that his teachings of the One God would sweep across Osseria like a fire through dry kindling.

He had never considered that Aunphar was truly sincere in

his belief. But Gerin not only believed Aunphar completely, he claimed to have been visited by the very same One God— or his messenger, if he understood his son correctly—of which the Prophet preached. It forced him to reevaluate the matter in an entirely different light. If the Prophet were truly sincere, and if Gerin's experiences were correct in supporting the Prophet's teachings, then there was a new and powerful god becoming active in the world. One who had singled out his son. Abran forced himself to take it very seriously. He had not taken Gerin's or Reshel's wizardry seriously enough at first, and look at the disaster *that* had caused.

He shook his head in dismay and anger. Gerin had become an outsider. There had been times during Gerin's stay in the Tirthaig when he had feared to be in his son's presence, worried that the magic flowing in Gerin's veins would rise up like a demon and command his son to strike him down.

I do not know him anymore. He is becoming a threat to me; I can feel it in my heart. He scorns me because I do not have his power yet still have authority over him. It chafes him like a slave collar, and he will not endure it forever. Not with Hollin always whispering in his ear.

The question was, who would take action first: Abran or his son? Hard decisions would have to be made.

What would he do? What *could* he do? To pass Gerin over in favor of Therain would not solve the fundamental problem of Gerin's magic. His sister-in-law Omara had perceived this before any of them. Because of his strained history with her, he'd been quick to dismiss her ravings, but for once her perception was accurate; he would grant her that much.

The more he thought about the ways in which Gerin had become so utterly different from the son he had been, the son he had wanted, the angrier her got. He felt betrayed. Gerin was becoming something dangerous, something . . . monstrous. It was intolerable. The son he'd raised and trained and disciplined with his own hand no longer existed. He had been replaced by a creature of magic, under the tutelage of a wizard from a foreign land.

Gerin could not be controlled forever, and could not be ignored. He submitted to his authority for now, but that would not last. Eventually Gerin would decide that his own power was greater than the king's authority. It was inevitable.

Abran's temples ached, and he squeezed his eyes shut in a vain attempt to quell the pain. He thought and thought, but could see no way to undo what had happened, to release Gerin from the snare of his wizardry. It had consumed him utterly. Gerin was lost.

It might be that his son would have to die for the good of the realm. He could not let the Sapphire Throne be sullied by a man who had turned his back on both king and country to willfully embrace foreign magic and a mongrel religion. He would betray all those who came before him if he allowed such a thing to occur.

Ah, my son. How has it come to this?

Hard decisions indeed.

Nellemar held his wife's upper arm in a firm grip to steady her as they crossed the gangplank from the *Rising Dawn* to the pier in Almaris where the ship had just docked. His sons followed behind them, quiet and sullen. *And when are they not?* he thought. *They are too much like their mother, always dark and brooding. And when they do speak, they are haughty and arrogant. Omara has poisoned them.* He grew annoyed with his petulance toward his children. They were nevertheless his sons, and perhaps it was a failing of his that they were not more what he would wish them to be. Still, considering what had happened, he had reason to be short-tempered.

"This is a disaster," said Omara as she stepped off the gangplank onto the timber and stone foundations of the waterfront. "Our home beset by filthy foreigners looting our treasures. And it's the fault of Gerin and his magic, drawing this evil to our shores."

"Hush, Omara. We will not speak of this until we reach the Tirthaig. The king must know what has happened before word spreads through the streets."

She made a scoffing noise. "The men aboard ship will be

telling everything they saw within the hour, over an ale in the nearest inn or as they lie between some whore's thighs. There is no need for me to—"

"You will be *silent*," he said through clenched teeth. He squeezed her arm more tightly. "The men will not be leaving the ship, and no one else will be coming aboard. Let the dockhands think what they will, but they will hear nothing from the *Rising Dawn* until I give the command."

"If you think—"

He stopped and whirled her toward him with such violence that she flinched and widened her eyes in alarm. "I *think* that if you say another word before we are within the walls of the Tirthaig, I will have my guards bind your mouth and hands and carry you the rest of the way over their shoulders. Do not open your mouth again, Omara, or I swear by Paérendras and all that is holy that I will do exactly what I promised. Our sovereign lands have been invaded, which has already placed us in a state of war. I am in no mood for your foolishness or your loose tongue. The king must be made aware, and he will be informed *first*. Do you understand me?"

Still shocked, she nodded once, and did not speak again until they reached the palace.

"How many?" Abran asked after hearing his younger brother's news.

"Well over a hundred war ships, similar to the one that crashed on Harrow's Rock a few months ago," said Nellemar. "And dozens of smaller ones. The harbor was choked with them."

"What of Palendrell and your castle?" asked Abran. "Could you determine their fate?"

"I saw some smoke, but the town did not appear to have been burned. Or the castle."

"Now that they've taken Gedsengard, what is their next move? The island cannot support so many indefinitely."

"They will use it as a staging area. Once they have it firmly in their control, they'll strike out against the coast. They will need to establish a foothold on the mainland in order to keep themselves provisioned. And since these Words of Making they seek are not on Gedsengard, they'll have to search elsewhere."

"What will you need to retake the island?"

Nellemar made a scoffing sound. "The entire Khedeshian fleet, and as many mercenary ships as we can pay for. Abran, their armada is immense. By the time we summon the number of ships we will need, they will have long since attacked. They know they cannot stay there."

Abran swallowed his ire at his brother's reluctant stance. *In the name of Telros, he needs to grow a backbone! The grand admiral of the navy is conceding his own castle to our enemies!* "We cannot just wait for them to strike. Summon the navy. Every ship you can get, as quickly as they can be sent. And yes, I will open the treasury to pay for mercenaries, but only *after* you take full stock of the available ships and determine our needs. I will not suffer invaders to hold our lands while we do nothing. Fulfill your duties, Nellemar, or I will find someone who will."

Nellemar bowed his head. "Yes, my king. I will see it done."

19

Gerin pulled a blanket over his chest and closed his eyes in the darkness of his tent. Another day, maybe a little more, and they would be home.

He missed Ailethon deeply. He remembered the day they had left to make the long sad journey to Almaris when King Bessel lay on his deathbed. His father's eyes were full of tears as he passed through the Gate of the Gray Woman. Gerin, riding beside him, had asked if everything was all right.

"My father is dying and I'm leaving this place, my home, forever," his father said curtly. "Yes, I will become king soon, but there is a price to be paid for such things, Gerin. Always there is a price. Remember that when you make this journey."

He now understood those words much better. It would be hard to leave Ailethon now; he could scarcely imagine how much more difficult it would be decades hence. And he would be married by then, with a wife and children to uproot and move across the kingdom.

He thought of Elaysen. A woman he admired and had become increasingly fond of during their journey. But she was in many ways a mystery to him. Melancholy moods came over her with surprising swiftness. There was passion in her whenever she spoke of healing and helping others, but also a hint of anger. Hollin had also noted her sudden dark moods, and asked her once if she were well, to which she had said cryptically, *I live, which for some is enough,* before vanishing into her tent. No one knew what to make of it, and though Elaysen later apologized to Hollin, she refused to explain herself.

He had almost drifted off when he heard shouts from the perimeter of the camp, followed quickly by animal growls and a blood-freezing scream.

It was the sound of a man dying in terror and pain.

They were under attack. He threw off his blanket, drew Nimnahal from its scabbard, then ran out of his tent.

It was very dark on the flattened hilltop where they had made camp—most of the fires had dwindled—and he paused to allow his eyes to adjust.

Balandrick, Hollin, Therain, and Elaysen had emerged from their tents as well. Gerin pointed toward Elaysen and bellowed, "Get back inside!" She scowled and ignored him.

He could not afford to keep his attention on her. The sounds of fighting were coming from just over the lip of the hilltop, where the outermost guards were stationed. He could hear screaming and animal snarls and soldiers shouting for help.

He sprinted toward the sounds of fighting. Balandrick shouted at him to fall back as he chased after him, but Gerin did not break stride. He drew magic into himself and felt Nimnahal respond, warming in his grip and growing brighter as his power flowed into it.

Two soldiers appeared over the lip of the hill, running toward the camp. This was no orderly retreat. They were running for their lives.

A second later Gerin saw what they were fleeing from.

Monstrous shapes pursued the Khedeshians. Gerin had never seen anything like them. He stared at the nearest creature as it raced forward; time seemed to slow down as he struggled to understand what they were.

Four grasping, claw-tipped arms extended from a bare torso bristling with dark hair. It ran with such speed that the lower set of arms brushed the ground to help keep its balance. Bony, silver-tipped spurs jutted from the thing's back like knives and extended the entire length of its spine.

Its head was low and flat, its eyes set on opposite sides

of flaring jaws. Slender articulated tentacles longer than a man's arm rose from the back of its skull, writhing like a nest of angry vipers. Gerin recoiled when he realized that the tentacles ended in tiny fang-filled mouths.

The lead creature crouched low and sprang forward, its arms extended toward the closest Khedeshian. Four sets of claws pierced the screaming man's back and ripped out bloody chunks of flesh. It sank its fangs into the man's neck while the snakelike tentacles whipped forward and bit into his face. The soldier had stopped screaming but still seemed to be alive.

The tentacles began to suck. Gerin could see the muscles contracting along their lengths, drawing . . . something from the dying man.

"Where are the bloody archers?" shouted Therain. "Ah, Shayphim take me," he said, then dashed toward his tent.

Balan readied his sword and spread his stance as the creatures charged. Hollin took a step forward and unleashed a lance of golden fire from his hand that contained enough power to burn through any living being.

Yet instead of striking the creature, the lance of power bent *around* it and seared a smoking hole through the trunk of a tree on the hilltop's edge. Gerin did not understand what had happened. Neither did Hollin, by the puzzled and alarmed look on his face. He tried again, but the second lance was deflected away like a stone skipping across the surface of a pond.

Gerin attacked it himself and could only stare in disbelief as his magic dissipated a foot from the monster's body.

Somehow these creatures were immune to magic. He did not know how that could be, but he could not worry about it any longer. Men were shouting all around him. He saw Therain emerge from his tent, bow in hand and quiver on his back, an arrow already nocked. Other creatures were appearing all around the rim of the hilltop. Gerin tried to determine how many were attacking, but they were moving too fast through the darkness.

Balan jumped back from another creature as it charged

him and thrust his sword toward it, hoping to lop off one of its outstretched claws, but it nimbly darted out of the sword's reach. As it flew past Balandrick it lashed out at another soldier coming from the other side and ripped open the man's thigh down to the bone.

Gerin attacked it again with magic, not wanting to believe what he had seen. His power was deflected away from the creature and nearly killed one of his own men. Cursing, he sprinted back toward Balandrick and Hollin.

He wondered where Elaysen was. He had lost track of her in the fighting.

Another creature sprang in front of him. The tentacles formed a gruesome halo around its head. Blood and other fluids dripped from the tiny sucking mouths as they reared back.

Gerin unleashed a Forbidding contained in his sword. The shimmering barrier appear in the air in front of him, a translucent wall visible only to wizards.

The thing slammed into the Forbidding at a full sprint. Gerin was startled when the barrier buckled; concentric waves spread outward from the point of impact as the spell began to fail.

The collision stunned the creature, but only for a moment. Its feral eyes gleamed with fury as they focused on him once more. Then it lunged toward him through the collapsing power of the Forbidding that it had somehow, beyond all reckoning, managed to thwart and pierce.

Gerin lunged toward the creature with Nimnahal. The thing swiped at the blade but also retreated several steps, which was what Gerin wanted it to do. He released another Forbidding from his weapon and formed it beside the thing. When it tried to move away, it crashed into the barrier. Startled, it turned its head to see what was blocking its path.

That was all the opening Gerin needed. He stepped forward and swung his blade with all his strength. Its glow left an arc in the air like a ghostly crescent moon as it sheared through the creature's neck, nearly severing its head. It collapsed in a heap, the tentacles falling limp.

Gerin brought the blade down again and cut its head off completely, then kicked it away in disgust.

Meanwhile, two other creatures were rampaging through the center of the camp. Gerin caught sight of Therain as his brother shot an arrow at one, but the creature had snatched another soldier in its powerful arms and Therain's missile struck the helpless man in the shoulder instead. A moment later the nimbus of tentacles around the thing's head sank into the man's face and neck and began to feed.

Therain nocked another arrow. Gerin created a blazing white flare of magefire next to the creature, which turned and exposed its side to Therain. His brother sighted and released.

The arrow sank into the thing's chest. The creature roared in pain and surprise and dropped the Khedeshian. Therain nocked another arrow and fired. This one struck the base of its neck. The thing fell to the ground and thrashed about madly.

Hollin unleashed a death spell. Gerin could see the spell's power shimmering in the darkness—to his eyes it looked like shards of glass streaming toward the thing from the wizard's outstretched hand. The spell sank into the creature's body and attempted to shred its organs, as it was designed to do. But whatever powers protected these beasts from their magic was strong enough to prevent the spell from having its intended effect. It hurt the creature, which howled as some of the spell's power penetrated its protections, but did not kill it.

Balandrick was heading toward it with his sword raised, but before he reached the creature, Therain shot yet again. This arrow pierced the thing's right eye and punched out of the back of its head with bits of brain clinging to the arrowhead.

Gerin caught sight of Elaysen running from her tent with her pack of medicines. She knelt by the soldier whose leg had been ripped open and started to fashion a tourniquet. Two more of the creatures were fighting a cluster of soldiers a short distance from her, but she paid them no attention.

Gods above me, she's going to get herself killed! Gerin started to run toward her, but had gone only a few steps when he heard something to his right. By the time he turned to look it was too late for him to raise his weapon or unleash magic; he saw only claws and a whiplash strike of a dozen tiny mouths streaking toward his face.

"One of them has the crown prince!" shouted a soldier behind Hollin.

Hollin had seen the creature appear from the darkness and attack Gerin. The mouth-tipped tendrils from the thing's head lashed out with blinding speed and latched onto the prince's face. Gerin had gone slack at once, Nimnahal dropping from his limp hand.

He's dead. Venegreh preserve us, the amber wizard is dead. Rage filled Hollin, and he lashed out at the creature with his magic, but once again it curved away from the thing and blasted a smoking hole in the earth.

What lorecraft was protecting these beasts? How could they be immune from his powers? Such a thing was unheard of. He'd seen his death spell inflict harm upon the creature, but it should have reduced its insides to a bloody ruin. That it had survived at all was something he could not comprehend.

The creature that had latched onto Gerin cradled him to its chest with its lower set of arms, then turned and dashed away. The other creatures had eviscerated the soldiers they'd attacked within seconds, but this thing was carrying Gerin almost protectively.

He was still alive. Perhaps he could yet be saved.

"Bloody buggerin' ugly things," Therain muttered from behind him. An arrow whistled by Hollin's head, alarmingly close. The wizard flinched, and his heart fluttered with momentary alarm. *Damnation, but that boy takes chances!*

The arrow sank into the calf of the creature, just below the knee. It let out a howl of rage and fell as its leg collapsed beneath it. Therain nocked another arrow, but his line-of-sight was no longer clear—Balandrick and two other soldiers were running frantically toward Gerin, and though Therain bellowed for them to get out of the way, they either ignored him or could not hear him over the noise of the battle. Therain swore and sprinted past the wizard.

Hollin, uncharacteristically, was unsure of what he should do. With his magic rendered useless, he felt a kind of vulnerability and mortal dread that he had not experienced for many generations of men. *I should not be afraid! I am a wizard of Hethnost, a descendant of the mighty Atalari of old. I will not allow my fears to conquer me.* He ran after Therain, still uncertain of what he could do but knowing he had to do *something.* He could not stand paralyzed while the battle raged around him.

With his greater speed, Hollin had almost closed the distance to Therain when another creature appeared from behind one of the soldiers' tents and charged the prince. Therain, carrying his bow in his left hand, reflexively thrust it toward the creature as he tried to duck out of the way. He was not fast enough, and the beast's jaws closed down over his hand and wrist.

A second later Therain rolled free, clutching the bleeding stump of his arm.

The beast chewed the fresh meat it had in its mouth as it stalked closer to Therain, who was screaming now.

Hollin created another death spell and sent the shards of power into the creature. It howled in pain and wheeled about to face him, injured but very much alive.

He created another death spell and hurled the magic into the beast. It was not as powerful as the others because the first two had already taxed a great deal of his strength. The spell did not kill it, but hurt it enough that it did not move closer to the wizard, perhaps confused at how it was being harmed.

Seeing Therain's sword lying on the ground, Hollin snatched it up. Other than briefly handling Nimnahal to examine it, he had not held a sword for nearly two centuries. The weight was strangely satisfying in his hands. The weapon was well-balanced, and he could discern the keenness of its edge. But in all his long life he had never wielded one in battle. *Now my life depends on it,* he thought as the thing took a step toward him, the tentacles rising stiffly behind its head, the tiny mouths all pointed at the wizard as if they were eyes focused upon his death.

Behind the beast, Therain writhed on the ground, holding his arm and screaming.

Hollin's spells seemed to have blinded one of the thing's eyes, which was milky and shot through with dark veins of blood. And its right arms did not seem to be working; they hung limp while the others were held forward, claws grasping.

Donael Rundgar appeared from the darkness. "My lord!" he shouted when he saw the prince upon the ground.

"Kill it, Rundgar!" said Therain in a hissing breath through clenched teeth. "Kill the bloody thing!"

Rundgar shrieked with rage and plunged his sword into the thing's right side. It raised its head and bellowed as the captain's weapon sank into its flesh all the way to the cross guards.

Hollin saw his chance and took it. He brought Therain's blade back behind his shoulder, then swung it with all his might, cutting through hair and flesh and bone. The thing's bloody head rolled across the ground.

Rundgar knelt by Therain, but Hollin waved him away. "I will tend to him," he said.

Therain's face was white and slick with sweat. He shook uncontrollably. The thing had bitten through his right arm about two inches above the wrist. Hollin could see the bones of the forearm poking through the ragged end of flesh. It was not a clean cut; his flesh had been chewed and torn.

"Therain, I'm going to do what I can for your arm. It will hurt, but I must do it."

The prince nodded through gritted teeth.

Hollin tore a strip from his long overshirt and tied it around Therain's arm above the wound. He saw a dagger dangling from Therain's belt and pulled it free, then slipped it into the tourniquet and twisted until it was tight.

"I thought you'd be using magic," commented Rundgar.

"There are some things better done without magic. This is one. Besides, I need to save all my strength for healing what I can of . . . this."

The wizard took a deep breath, summoned magic into himself, and got to work.

Balandrick halted about twenty feet from the thing holding Gerin. It had collapsed near the slope of the hill. He'd never seen anything like this—a monster straight out of a nightmare, carrying Gerin away from the camp. And it looked as if it were being careful *not* to injure him, despite the tentacles hooked into his flesh. The world had gone mad.

More soldiers reached them and spread out to surround the thing. None of them, he saw ruefully, had a bow. Or a pike.

The creature became more guarded when it saw the soldiers, but it did not release its grip on Gerin's limp, unconscious form. The sight of the tentacles latched onto the crown prince's face made Balan shiver and sent a queasy flutter through his stomach.

"We'll do whatever we must to rescue the prince unharmed," he said to the soldiers. "Timel, you and Pirren get behind it and keep it where it is."

The two men swung wide around the creature's flanks and down the slope of the hill. The remaining soldiers took a step closer. The tentacles grew rigid as the contractions along their length halted.

"Here's what we're going to do. I'm going to *slowly* move toward it. Mikel, you and Vaz position yourselves on either side of it and get ready to stab it on my command. Just run the bloody thing through. Try to hit its heart. I want it dead before it can do something to the prince."

Balandrick lowered his sword, holding it point down along his leg. He held his free hand out in front of him, the fingers opened as if he were moving toward an unfamiliar dog rather than a nightmarish thing. The creature made a throaty, growling noise and glared with a malevolence that chilled him. *What in the name of the gods* are *these things?*

He continued forward until he was less than two yards

from Gerin's legs. The thing had fallen on its side, but held its grip on the crown prince with its lower set of limbs.

It tried to back away from him. Timel and Pirren made their presence known and jabbed at the thing's back with their swords, but then both men yelled in surprise as the creature lashed out with its good leg and one of its arms, the claws cutting through the air like daggers. "Shayphim take me, that thing moves fast!" Pirren said.

Balan could see the thing getting desperate and preparing to take action of some kind, though he had no idea what it might try. It was now or never. "Mikel, Vaz, go!"

The two men lunged forward and drove their swords into the creature, sliding their blades between its ribs. It tried to strike both men with its upper arms and caught Vaz across the throat. He tumbled backward, gurgling as blood gushed from a gash that opened his windpipe.

Balan dashed toward it, keeping his eyes on the thing's jaws.

The tentacles lifted suddenly from Gerin's face and whipped out toward Balandrick, the small fangs within the rings of flesh slick with blood. Balan sliced through a third of them with a single swing of his blade, then drove the point through the creature's mouth and out the back of its head. The thing's body spasmed violently, then was still.

Gerin was still unconscious, his face covered with round bloody welts where the tentacles had bitten into his flesh. The welts were beginning to bruise and swell, and Balan feared that the thing had released venom or poison.

Four of the men lifted Gerin as gently as they could. It was only then that Balandrick saw Hollin and Elaysen kneeling over Therain. The expression on Donael Rundgar's face told him all he needed to know, and his heart felt like a stone within his chest.

Gerin felt a cool pressure on his face and open his eyes. Panic surged through him, clutching coldly at his heart.

The pressure he felt was Elaysen rubbing a salve onto swollen, painful welts.

"You are well, my lord, and safe," she said in a soothing tone. "The attack is over. The creatures have fled."

He touched one of the welts. "I remember those things striking my face . . ."

"Yes, my lord. It tried to drag you out of the camp. Balandrick rescued you."

Gerin sat up slowly. "Indeed? Balan, come here!"

The captain, who'd been speaking quietly with three of his men, hurried to Gerin's side. "Yes, my lord. I'm glad to see you're awake."

"Tell me everything that happened."

Elaysen reached out and touched his shoulder. "My lord, there is something you should know first. Therain was grievously wounded."

Gerin's expression hardened. "Take me to him. Right now."

✦
20

Elaysen and Balandrick helped Gerin to his feet.
"I can feel your medicine in my wounds," he said as they
made their way toward Therain's tent. "It burns a little, but
I can tell that it's working." His entire face felt swollen and
tender, which made talking awkward.

"Hollin determined there was no venom in the bites," she
said, "but was too exhausted from helping your brother to do
any more for now."

Donael Rundgar stood at the entrance to Therain's tent at
rigid attention, a grim expression upon his face. "I'm glad
you are well, my lord," he said.

"Thank you, Captain." Gerin could clearly see on the
man's pained face that he felt he had failed in his duties to
protect Therain.

A number of lamps had been hung from the tent poles.
Therain was stretched out upon pillows with a light blanket
thrown over him. He was unconscious and moaning in a fevered sleep. Gerin could see the blood-soaked bandages that
encased his ghastly wound.

Hollin, seated on a stool beside him, stood as Gerin moved
toward his brother. "I can scarcely believe you are unharmed
after seeing those . . . things attached to your face," said the
wizard, "But I am certainly pleased."

Gerin did not want to talk about himself. "How is he?"

"His wound is severe, and he is very weak. I have done
what I can for him, but he may die."

The thought of Therain dying drove all the air from Gerin's lungs and made it difficult for him to take a breath. *By all the gods in heaven, what will Father say?* He knew it was a selfish thought—he should be worried about Therain, not how the king might react to the news of his second son's death. First Reshel, and now Therain. Was his family cursed? He imagined another burial ceremony and wondered where Therain would be interred. At their ancestral home at Ailethon, or Agdenor, the castle Therain had ruled as a duke for several years now?

He did not want to know the answer. Tears sprang to his eyes and rolled down his cheeks. He remembered all the times they'd fought as children, and the way Therain had resented him, something they'd only put behind them in the last few years, after their father had become king. *I want him to live.*

Elaysen put her mouth to his ear and whispered, "Be strong for him, my lord. He will need you." Gerin nodded, not trusting himself to speak. He felt overwhelmed with sadness and dread.

Elaysen rummaged through her pack and pulled out four stoppered vials and a small porcelain bowl. "I need warm water," she said as she opened one of the vials and sprinkled its contents into the bowl—dried leaves of some plant Gerin did not recognize.

"What are you making?" he asked.

"Something to give him strength."

She poured the water one of the soldiers brought her into the bowl, then began to mix in the powders in the other vials. A strong medicinal smell wafted up from the mixture.

When she was finished she lifted Therain's head and slowly poured the elixir into his mouth. Her hands were steady and confident, and she managed to get the unconscious prince to swallow it all.

Hollin studied Therain through a Seeing. "It has already steadied his breathing. Remarkable. Once again I'm impressed by your lorecraft."

"I will stay with him," Elaysen said. "The two of you need to rest. Especially you, my lord. I will wake you should his condition change."

* * *

Gerin slept until dawn. The camp was quiet and still. Mounds of freshly turned dirt marked the graves of the soldiers who had died during the attack. The men were still wary, keeping a watchful eye on the surrounding countryside for signs of the creatures.

"How is he?" he asked as he entered Therain's tent. Elaysen and Hollin were sitting with Therain, who was still unconscious.

"Better," said Hollin. "Elaysen's elixir was potent."

"How do your wounds feel, my lord?" she asked, gesturing to his face.

"I'll be fine." He faced the wizard. "Do you have any idea what those things were or where they came from?"

"I don't know what they were, but I believe they came with that man Tolsadri who escaped from the Tirthaig."

"But Tolsadri was the only survivor from his ship."

"He also told your uncle his was but the first ship of a fleet. Those creatures can deflect a wizard's magic. If they existed anywhere in Osseria, that fact would have been widely known at Hethnost. Besides, we were not randomly attacked. We were chosen for a reason."

"They were trying to capture you, my lord," Elaysen said to Gerin.

"Yes," said the wizard. "Think about it. They killed or tried to kill every man they attacked *except* you. They came here for you, and retreated only when they could not achieve their goal."

"But if you're right," said Balandrick, "then those things had to be smart like men. Otherwise, how did they know he was the one they wanted instead of you or me?"

"Tolsadri knows Gerin's face," said the wizard.

"Then the prince is being hunted," said Elaysen.

"They want me captured alive so I can give them the Words of Making."

"Yes," said Hollin. "It's the only thing that makes sense. We must take precautions. You must be even more carefully guarded than before."

Balandrick stood. "We need to get back to Ailethon as

quickly as possible. We're too exposed out here. I want you surrounded by walls with easily defensible entrances. We're going to ride hard until we get there."

"Elaysen, listen to me," said Gerin. "I want you to return to Almaris. I will send an escort to protect you. You're in danger if you stay near me. By the gods, look what happened to my own brother."

"I will not leave you, my lord. I've been given a task and I will see it done."

"I do not want anything to happen to you because of me."

She looked up at him, a fierce resolve in her eyes. "And what of the dangers to Hollin, or Balandrick? Will you send them away as well? I take my duties seriously, Lord Gerin. You had best remember that."

He was quiet for a time. Reshel had made a similar demand when she vowed to accompany him to the Sundering and his confrontation with Asankaru. And ended up dead because of it.

Hollin called out from behind them, "Gerin, your brother is awake."

Quietly, he said to Elaysen, "You may stay for now. But if the situation grows more dire you *will* go."

Therain was lying very still beneath a blanket. His skin was sallow and drawn, and it seemed his eyes had sunk even farther into his skull.

"How are you?" asked Gerin.

Therain held up his ruined left arm in front of Gerin's face. "How do you think I am? I'm missing my hand, Gerin! My gods-damned bloody hand! I can't even begin to tell you how that feels, or how much it hurts! Hollin's done something to help with the pain, and I can only imagine what it would feel like without it because it bloody well hurts a lot right now!" Tears spilled over his eyes and down his cheeks. "Just like that, and I'm a cripple. What in the name of all the gods *were* those things?"

"We're not sure. We have some ideas, but now's not the time to talk about it. We need to get moving."

Gerin gestured for Hollin to step away from Therain, then took him aside. "Is he well enough to ride?" he asked.

"For a while, I would think. But I don't know for how long or how hard. It's a serious wound, Gerin. My healing spells will take time to work, and they will weaken him as they do."

Gerin turned back, knelt again by his brother and took his right hand in his own. "We're going to be moving out soon. Do you think you can ride by yourself?"

"I'll take him, if the prince wishes it," said Donael Rundgar.

"What does it matter now?" said Therain. "I'll ride, and if I fall off you can strap me to Rundgar and be done with it."

21

The quatans were almost upon Katel yalez Algariq before she heard them. Her horse had whickered uneasily, catching the scent of the creatures a few moments before she heard them racing up the hill toward her. *By the Harridan, they can move quietly,* she thought as she stood to meet Rulhámad and congratulate him on his victory. Her stomach was sour. He would be elevated to another caste, freed of a life of servitude and scorn. She thought of how far she had traveled, and how close she'd come to achieving her goal. *It was all for nothing. I'm sorry, Huma. I've failed you.* She longed to see her son, but it would be many months before she could return home. Tolsadri might even kill her outright. But if that were his will, she could do nothing to change it. Her life was not her own; it had not been since the day she was born.

When she saw how many quatans were with him, she realized he had suffered losses. She tried not to feel satisfaction at this—after all, the quatans were only following his commands—but it was there nonetheless.

She saw no other man with them.

"Where is the prey?" she asked. Her heart thumped within her breast. Could he have failed? She did not want to lure herself with false hope, but she could not help it. "You did not kill him, did you?"

The expression on the maegosi's face and every movement

of his body projected barely contained rage. "No, he is not dead, curse his black soul. This man we are to take is a Loremaster of some kind, but with power unlike any I have ever seen. It was not enough to penetrate the natural barriers that protect my quatans, but it made the task that much harder. And his men fought bravely in the face of my attack. I had him in my grasp . . ." He clenched his fist, then punched at the air in frustration.

"Tolsadri warned us that the prey had powers unlike any he had ever seen."

Rulhámad wheeled about, and for a moment she thought he would strike her. "I know that! I remember as well as you. But he didn't say *what* those powers were, or how they could be used against us. I have never seen the like before."

"Tell me everything that happened."

When he finished, she said, "I will wait until he is back in his castle before making my attempt. He will feel safe there and not expect one lone woman to be a threat."

"*Your* attempt? I am not finished—"

"Yes you are, Rulhámad. That is the law of *kanilé*. The victor may make one attempt, and one only. You have made yours. Now it is my turn."

"You are twisting the law—"

"I am doing no such thing! You will submit and allow me my chance, or I swear I will kill you where you stand." Her right hand fell to the hilt of her knife. He knew she could kill him in an instant if she desired. He might command his quatans to tear her apart in the moment before her knife found him, but he would still be dead.

He straightened a little and bowed his head. "All right. By the law of *kanilé*, I will stand aside for you. You treated me with honor when you returned from the city rather than hunt the prey yourself. I will honor you in return."

She bowed, but her hand did not leave her knife. "I require one last thing of you before I leave."

His eyes narrowed with suspicion. "And what is that?"

"My powers wane. If I am to have any hope of success, I must replenish my strength. You must help me with this."

"Ah, yes, your powers. Drawn from rutting like a whore."

She did not react to the insult. "You know how draining it will be for you. Are you prepared now, or would you prefer to rest first?"

He shrugged. "Best to get it over with. Take what you will from me, and then I will rest and mourn my quatans who died at the hands of these infidels."

They disrobed in silence. Algariq grew calm and detached from herself. It had always been this way, from the time she learned she had the powers of a soul stealer, a latent talent made active by an Adept of Bariq when she was eleven years old. Her power was renewed through sexual union, a unique ability that was scorned throughout the world—but since her powers were useful, she and others like her were tolerated.

She did not kiss him as he pressed his naked body against hers; there was no love here, no affection. Only a duty to be done so she might complete her task. She felt nothing for him, and she knew he felt none for her. She had loved only one man in her life: Hurilan, the father of her son.

She stroked Rulhámad until he became hard, then stretched out on her back and spread her legs. He slid inside her and began thrusting with his hips. She concentrated on receiving the essence from him that would replenish her power, the vitality that only a man could give when he spurted his seed into her. The process of taking the vitality from his seed left them dead, so there was no possibility of becoming pregnant. Only if she closed off her power could that happen, and she had only allowed that once.

She felt the heat of her power grow within her, becoming greater with each of Rulhámad's thrusts. She clutched his back and felt the first draining of his vitality—what the Adept had told her was called *fetwa'pesh*, the secret heart of a man that granted her, for a time, the ability to seize the souls of others—a line of power that connected them in the most intimate of ways. Rulhámad grunted as he felt her power begin to work in him. She wondered what it felt like, to lose a little of his life though the act by which life was created. She had asked some of the men who had replenished her to describe the experience, but they either refused to speak of it or said it was not something they could ever truly explain.

She would not bother to ask Rulhámad. She knew he would say nothing.

The line of power that drained the strength from his *fetwa'pesh* continued to strengthen until in her mind's eye she saw a living tendril of white light connecting their bodies. Rulhámad grunted with each thrust now, but it was not a sound of pleasure. His life was quite literally being taken from him, a little at a time. He fought against it, but it was impossible to resist—men had no ability to fight back against a soul stealer. They had no defenses. Once sex had begun, there was no stopping it until she had taken the strength she needed. Twice she had killed men. Not on purpose, but her needs had been so dire, and her strength so low, that the men who were to replenish her had lost too much of themselves and died. She was not that weary now, but Rulhámad would be exhausted to the point of collapse by the time she was finished.

He screamed and came inside her. Her power flared in that instant, taking the life from his seed and revitalizing her diminished strength. She gasped as the renewal flowed through every part of her body. He collapsed atop her. She pushed him aside—he was already unconscious—stood up and dressed. She threw a blanket over the maegosi, then gathered her things, climbed onto her horse, and rode off toward the east.

Toward her prey, and the promise of a new and better life.

22

They reached Ailethon late at night. King Olam's Road was familiar to Gerin and Balandrick and well-maintained, so though it grew dark, they decided to continue.

Therain was weak, and as they rode on, grew weaker. But he managed to ride all the way by himself, occasionally lingering on the edge of sleep while in the saddle. Donael Rundgar rode next to him and from time to time reached out a hand to steady his lord. Therain's head would snap up then and he'd mutter, "I'm fine, I'm fine," feeling his captain's hand upon his shoulder. Upon setting out he'd kept his wounded arm curled protectively against his chest, but as he wearied, it drooped and eventually rested upon his thigh. At a brief midday stop, Elaysen changed Therain's dressings and sprinkled some mauro-root powder on it to minimize the blood loss, and Hollin worked several spells to speed the healing and prevent infections.

"I will do more for you when we reach Ailethon," he had said to Therain, who winced as Elaysen rewrapped the wound. "But if I do too much now you'll be too weak to ride."

"Is there any spell that can regrow my hand?"

"No, Therain, there is not. Magic can strengthen the body so it returns to health sooner, but there is nothing to be done for something as devastating as the loss of a limb."

They entered Ailethon with little fanfare. Matren Swendes, the castellan of Ailethon, appeared in his nightshirt and apologized for not having a proper welcome prepared for them. "I had no idea you'd be returning in the middle of the night!"

"Neither did we, Matren," said Gerin. "We're weary and my brother is injured. Hollin is tending to him for now, but have Master Aslon visit him in the morning to see if there is anything he can do to help him."

Matren saw Therain's bandaged arm and gasped. "My lord, what happened?"

"We were attacked on the road home," said Gerin. "I will tell you the details in the morning." He gestured for Elaysen to step forward. "This is Elaysen el'Turya, daughter of a man called the Prophet of the One God."

"I've heard that name," said the castellan. "He has an emissary in Padesh." He bowed his head to her. "I am pleased to make your acquaintance, Lady Elaysen."

"Thank you. But please, Elaysen is fine. My father is a priest, not a noble."

"Have a room prepared for her at once," said Gerin.

"How long will she be staying, my lord?"

"I'm not sure. Some time, I would imagine. She's come to instruct me in the ways of her father's religion."

Matren arched an eyebrow. "Indeed. If you will follow me, Elaysen, I will take you to your chambers."

Gerin said good night to her, then made his way to his own rooms. He wondered when the next attempt to take him would come, and what form it would take. *Let them try to get me now,* he thought. *Let them batter themselves to death against Ailethon's strong walls. I'll take whoever comes for me and learn what I can from them. I will not live in fear, jumping at shadows, wondering when they will strike next. These invaders must be dealt with, and will receive no mercy from me.*

They'd brought the carcass of one of the creatures with them for Hollin to study. He discovered that the bony spurs along its spine contained the substance rezarim. "The ancient Gendalos discovered it during their wars with the Atalari," he said to Gerin in a ground floor workroom in Paladan's Tower. The stench from the carcass was almost overwhelming and made Gerin's eyes water. "They mined it as a metal and worked it into their weapons and armor. Without it they would have had no chance against the powers of the Atalari. Rezarim disrupts our magic in ways that are not well understood, since we can't use magic to study how it works."

"Are there any rezarim weapons still in existence?"

"Probably, but as you can guess, wizards did all that they could to find and destroy them. It is a weakness of ours that has mostly been forgotten."

"Is there anything we can do to counteract the rezarim?"

"No. If we meet these creatures again, we will have to face them with mortal weapons alone."

Gerin spent the next few days attending to the needs of the castle and its holdings. Master Aslon, Hollin, and Elaysen tended to Therain. Hollin worked spells to ease his brother's pain and speed the healing of his wound. Elaysen and Master Aslon engaged in long discussions about different medicinal plants and their properties, and what potions and elixirs would best help Therain maintain his strength in light of the sapping nature of Hollin's spells. Therain was still too weary to travel, so he remained at Ailethon rather than returning to Agdenor.

One evening, Gerin asked Elaysen to dine with him alone. She was escorted to the dining room by a young female servant. She wore a simple rose-colored dress accented with a gold necklace and earrings, and had tied her hair back with a black velvet ribbon.

"My lord," she said, bowing her head and executing a well-practiced curtsy. "Thank you for the invitation."

"I wanted to thank you for helping Therain and the soldier who later died of his wounds, though I know you did all you could for him. It was brave of you to venture onto a field of battle."

"Isel Trelmen, my lord."

"What?"

"That's the name of the soldier who died. I make it a point to know the names of the people I am helping, even when they die."

They ate some bread and poached eggs, and drank some wine. "Was that your first experience in battle?" he asked.

"Yes, my lord. In the way you are speaking of it. But I have helped men and women who were slashed or stabbed by knives or throttled about the neck not only by strangers intent on robbery but by those they thought loved them, fathers or husbands whose hearts were black and evil. I've done what I could for those trapped as fires spread through their homes, and their walls and ceilings tumbled down upon them, the heat so intense that their flesh melted and ran like wax. I've helped people with blood sickness and the Red Plague, though in most cases all I can do is ease their pain before the end. So while the attack by those creatures was the first time I was involved in a military battle, it is far from the first time I have witnessed such horror. And, truth be told, it was far from the worst."

"The Red Plague took my grandmother, the queen," said Gerin. "I have never seen it, but heard it is a terrible thing. You show great courage to treat those so afflicted."

Elaysen lowered her eyes and seemed to draw inward.

"I apologize if I've said something to offend you."

"No, my lord," she said. "The Red Plague killed my mother when I was seven. I was with her when she died."

"That must have been horrible. I am sorry."

She looked up at him, her eyes bright with tears. But they were hard as well, glittering like cold stars in a winter sky. "My mother and I were both sickened with it. My father took us to a plague house, where we were locked in with other victims. There were so many people that we slept leaning against one another—there was no room to lie flat on the dirty floors. It seemed someone died with each breath I took. The Red Plague is a disease of the blood. Death is accompanied by a great outpouring of blood from the nose and mouth and other orifices, and sometimes the eyes and ears.

"My mother died on the third day. Almost half of the house was dead by then, the bodies lying where they died, covered with blood, the floor and walls sticky with it. And the smell . . . it was terrible, my lord. Something that haunts me to this day. More than the sight of the blood or the bodies of the dead, it is the smell that lingers.

"I was there for two weeks. Everyone else was dead by then, their bodies rotting in the heat. I will not describe to you the horror of that place. I had only scraps of food to eat, and almost no water. They were about to burn the house to the ground when I began to scream. At first they were going to burn me with the rest, but then someone decided to pull me out before the fires engulfed me. My father says the spirit of the One God moved the man to save me for some great purpose."

"Is that what you believe? That you were singled out for salvation?"

"No. Because then everyone else had to die because of me. My mother did not die as a *sign*. The One God is not so capricious. I do not know why I lived, but those who died did so because of the Adversary. Because the world is broken."

"We are going to be in so much trouble," said Rukee as he and his younger brother Tremmel hurried along the dirt road toward their homestead. Twilight was deepening into full darkness, with a mere sliver of wan orange light lingering above the western prairies. "It's all your fault."

"Is not!" yelled Tremmel.

"Is too. You were supposed to wake me up before it got dark."

"I couldn't help it. I fell asleep too. I was tired."

"Tell that to Papa's belt."

Tremmel whimpered. Rukee was about to make a whipping motion when he saw a flash of light in the hills to their left.

"What was that?" asked Tremmel, seeing it, too.

"I don't know." It had looked from the corner of his eye like lightning, but the sky above was clear, with not even a hint of rain in the air. There also had been no thunder, just a faint sizzling sound, like frying bacon.

The flash occurred again. It *was* lightning, though he would have sworn it had come out of the ground rather than down from the sky. It also looked red, like a bloody crack in the darkness. The sizzling sound was a little louder this time.

"I'm scared," said Tremmel.

Another flash. It had come up from the ground; he was certain of that now. From the Bronze Demon Hills. Rukee hated those hills. There was something wrong about them, something diseased, as if there were a black, rotten heart beating sluggishly beneath them, poisoning the land with its vile blood. At times he thought he could almost hear the heart like a thudding whisper in the back of his mind. Just looking at the hills made his skin crawl, as if something might stare back at him from beneath the tortured trees clumped along the slopes.

Over the past few weeks he'd had terrible nightmares about the hills. He understood now how they'd gotten their name. In his dreams he'd been stalked by a bronze-skinned demon with flowing back hair and baleful yellow eyes. And no matter how many times he awoke in terror, gasping for breath, as soon as he fell back asleep, the demon was there, waiting for him.

That was why he'd wanted to sleep a little today while he and Tremmel were on their hike. And Tremmel had ruined it by making them late.

The silent red lightning erupted from the ground again, brighter than before. Tremmel flinched and squeaked in fear, then tugged on Rukee's sleeve.

"Please, let's go . . ."

The lightning flashed again, and again, and again. Rukee could now see that each lance of light was ripping open the earth, forming an ever-widening wound. He was both fascinated and terrified by the sight. He felt unable to move. The hole out of which the lightning burst looked *deep*, a ragged, black-walled tunnel into the hill's black heart. Its edges burned with small fires; from his vantage point it looked like a burning eye.

"Please, Rukee . . ."

Rukee felt the demon a moment before he saw it. A cold dread slithered through his bowels like a snake. Beside him, Tremmel began to cry.

The demon rose from the smoking pit like a king ascending to his throne. As soon as he saw it, Rukee realized his nightmares had been true, that there actually was a demon beneath the hills whose slumber had somehow bled into his, infecting his dreams with its own.

"Rukeeeeeee . . ." Tremmel was crying so hard that Rukee barely recognized his name.

The demon was massive, at least as large as the statue of Miestos that stood in the square of Konfatine. Rukee gauged it to be ten feet tall or more. It was broad-shouldered and heavily muscled. Each leg was as thick as Rukee's entire body, and its metal-banded arms looked strong enough to crush granite. It wore a sleeveless black tunic and sandals that laced up its calves.

The demon started down the hill toward them, moving with an easy, powerful stride, its yellow eyes glinting in the darkness. Rukee smelled the hot stench of urine as Tremmel lost control of his bladder. Then his brother dashed down the road, wailing in terror.

Rukee continued to stand there, unable to tear his gaze from the demon's eyes as it stalked down the hill. He could sense power enveloping it like a wreath of smoke.

It reached him and halted. Rukee craned his neck to stare up at its broad face with its wide, flat nose and prominent cheekbones. Its black hair was so dark it was like a hole in the night, an absence of something rather than a thing unto itself.

It spoke to him. When its lips parted a faint reddish glow emerged from its mouth, as if a fire were smoldering deep in its throat. The sound was so deep Rukee felt it in his bones as much as heard it. But he did not understand its speech.

It spoke again, the sound harsher this time, tinged with anger. Rukee could only shake his head. "I don't understand . . ." he whispered.

The demon extended a long-nailed hand toward him and touched his shoulder. He knew he should run away as Tremmel had, but he could not bring himself to move.

The demon spoke a single word, and Rukee collapsed to the ground like a broken scaffold. He was dead before his head thumped against the dirt, his soul, the very essence of what made him who he was, ripped violently from his body.

As the Vanil marched away to the south, its body wavered and shifted as though wading into murky water, then vanished as if it had never been.

Upon the Bronze Demon Hills, the hole in the earth continued to burn and smoke.

Rahmdil Khazuzili, Warden of the Archives of Hethnost, was humming to himself as he wandered along a flagstone path toward the Varsae Sandrova. It was a crisp clear morning, the sky unbroken by clouds, and he could smell the tulips beside the path, their yellow and pink petals bending toward him as if bowing in respect.

He moved slowly, leaning hard on the sturdy oak cane he now used because of his lame left leg. But he did not let the limp or nagging pain that shot through his thigh and knee affect his disposition—at least not most of the time. He was a wizard, after all, and had been blessed with a long and glorious life.

His failing eyesight was more bothersome for the sole fact that it made his work harder. If he could not see, then he could not read or study the many glorious artifacts contained in the library. Eventually, one of the few remaining novices would have to read to him, assuming his sight gave out before his heart. He preferred to read rather than listen, but would do whatever was necessary to continue his work. He had no greater joy in life.

Rahmdil said hello to several wizards on the path before

he reached the Varsae Sandrova. He continued to hum "The Merchant of Mintora"—his favorite song since childhood, and one all of his own children had loved—while he shuffled through the long halls toward his private library and work chamber.

Once inside, he sat heavily upon a divan and let out a sigh. He leaned his head back and closed his eyes, planning to nap for a while before resuming his translation of a manuscript recently brought back from the seaport of Athram by Abaru Mezza. It was an exquisite find: a two-thousand-year-old diary of the famed wizard Menoch Isul. Until now, no extant writings of Isul's had ever been found. All that was known of him and his discoveries had been written by his contemporaries and later historians. Abaru's find was one of the most important of the last hundred years, perhaps more.

But almost as soon as Rahmdil closed his eyes he opened them again. Something was wrong. He was not sure exactly what, but he knew this room better in some ways than he knew his own face, and something was most definitely not as it should be.

He sat up and moved his gaze slowly across the tall shelves that lined the round chamber beneath its painted dome. Though they were jammed with books, scrolls, parchments, chests, animal skeletons, and a variety of magical objects, he was certain he would notice at once if anything were out of place or missing. But nothing caught his eye.

He stood and walked the length of the table that occupied the center of the room; a silent command from him brightened the three magefire lamps upon it. The diary of Isul was where he'd left it, cocooned in powerful preservation spells that kept the brittle pages from crumbling and the ink from fading further. The table was a mess—he needed to let a servant in here to remove some of the dishes, but was always so busy and never seemed to remember when a servant was around—but he could see no obvious change in the clutter spread across the dark, scarred wood.

Then he felt something behind him. A tickle of magic, so faint that at first he ignored it as an ordinary itch on the back of his neck. Only after he attempted to scratch it did he realize that the tingling on his skin was being produced from a magical source.

One he did not recognize.

The itch had produced a subtle sense of alarm in him, but it was unlike any tocsin spell he'd ever experienced. Puzzled, he renewed his search of the work chamber, moving methodically along the bookcases, probing gently with his own powers to determine the source of the strange magic.

"Aha, there you are," he said after he'd gone halfway around the room. He was staring at a small box peeking out from behind a bound sheaf of parchments. The box was about the size of his hand and fashioned from bronze that had been carved with symbols whose meanings had never been discovered. It was in the room when he inherited it from Warden Taeknos, and it had been decades since Rahmdil had opened it. He had to shuffle through his memory before he could recall what was in it. He thought it was an amulet, though he could not remember any details of its appearance, and did not think it had any magical properties.

He took the box to the table, wiped off the thick layer of dust that had settled upon its lid, and opened it.

"Curious," he muttered as he lifted the amulet from the box. It was circular, made of silver, with an oval jewel half the size of his thumb set in the center.

The jewel was glowing with a pulsing red light.

"So you are a warning device," he said as he gazed at the light. "What, exactly, are you trying to warn us about?"

23

Mori Genro was asleep on his stool just inside the postern door beside the Gate of the Gray Woman, slumped against the stone wall, his head lolling on his shoulder, when he was wakened by a knock on the door. He spluttered and came to, jumping to his feet and reaching for his halberd, which leaned against one corner of the narrow room like a sleeping pet. He rubbed his eyes, wondering if he'd imagined the sound. He waited a moment in silence, then heard the knock once more.

He pulled back the shutter that covered the narrow eye-level slot in the door and peered through it. It was too dark to make out anything beyond the door. He had no idea of the time, but knew it was late, at least midnight if not later.

"Who's there?" he said. "And state your business."

"I'm a traveler," said a woman's voice from the other side. "I was injured on the road. Can you help me?" Genro stood on his toes to look down through the slot—her voice had come from below him, so she was either short or crouched down—but he could see nothing, even when he held up his lamp.

"Please, can you help me?" She spoke with an accent he did not recognize. It was strong enough that it took him a moment to understand what she was saying. He wondered where she was from.

"What are you doing out so late at night?" He didn't like this one bit. Captain Vaules had explained about the attack against the prince's party on the road home from Almaris and ordered the castle guards to be alert for anything out of the ordinary. While he didn't think the woman herself was a threat, it was possible she was a decoy for others.

"Please," she said. She did sound as if she were in pain. "My husband and I were camped near the road when we were attacked. One of the men cut me but I got away and ran here. Please, let me in. They might still be after me. And you need to send someone to help my husband."

Something about her story rang false to him. "Go find the constable in Padesh," he said. "He'll help you. The castle is closed for the night."

He was about to close the shutter on the eye slot when he saw something on the other side. It was just a smudge in the darkness, but it made him pause.

"Please, I can pay you. Take this. Just let me in."

He could now make out that the smudge was a closed hand, but could not see what she was holding. "Pass it here. I'll look at it, but I make no promises."

She stretched her fingers through the slot. Her skin was dark, even darker than a Neddari or the nomads of Hunzar. She was not holding a coin or even a weapon, but rather, a small statue carved of dark wood. Wondering what could be so valuable about a bit of wood—even if hollowed out and filled with gold, it was too small to be worth much—he reached up to take it so he could inspect it more closely.

When he grabbed the statue, she slid her fingers forward until they touched his own. He felt a sudden coldness in his hand, as if her touch had drawn all the warmth from it. He tried to pull away from her but found that he could not move. He saw a flash of light behind his eyes and felt a part of his being leave him.

She pulled her hand back through the slot. "Open the door," she commanded, no longer sounding injured.

He obeyed without question. He would do anything she asked. A part of his mind knew that somehow she had taken control of his body. But that part was far away, as if locked in a deep cell, and could only watch helplessly as his body moved to pull back the large bolts and single heavy cross beam that sealed the postern. The larger part of his mind was under her complete control. No matter what she commanded, he would do it in an instant, even if she told him to pluck out his eye or fall on his blade. She could not be denied.

He opened the door. A dark-skinned woman in plain brown clothing slipped inside. "Close it quickly." Once he had done so, she commanded him to sit on his stool. "I am going into the castle," she told him. "I will be leaving later with one other person. You will remain here and help me when I need to get out. If you see anyone else, you will say nothing about me. Do you understand?"

"Yes."

"Now, tell me where I can find Prince Gerin's private rooms."

Katel yalez Algariq left the guard by the door and made her way down the narrow corridor that snaked through the castle's thick outer wall. She held the statue tightly in her right hand, the *putan* into which she placed the souls that she stole. It was an image of Holvareh the All Father given to her by her mother when she was five. Any material object could suffice as a *putan*—the power resided in her, after all, and not the object itself. And in her heart she knew it was not truly a soul that she stole, but rather the *volition* of those she touched, their ability to think and act independently. She took that from them for a time, substituting her own will for theirs, so they became little more than her puppets.

It was possible for soul stealers to take too much from a victim, removing not only conscious will but the more deeply buried, innate abilities of the body to keep itself alive. She had known others of her kind who had killed inadvertently when they took their prey's ability to breathe or keep their hearts beating. She had come close to killing her first quarry, but altered her touch at the last moment so as to only take the man's conscious mind. It was a delicate process, taking the will from another and placing it in an object for safekeeping until her powers waned or she deliberately returned what she had stolen. Holding onto a stolen soul became more difficult as time passed, until it simply became too hard for her to retain and it slipped from her grasp like water through opened fingers. It returned then to the man or woman from whom it was taken, no matter that they were separated by half the world. Distance did not matter. That was simply the way of such power.

Algariq stepped onto a wide swath of lawn that separated the outer wall of the castle from the inner one. There were a number of buildings here, storerooms and barracks, from the looks of them; a trampled area of grass that looked like a practice yard of some kind; as well as several towers. She saw the dark throat of a tunnel in the inner wall and started toward it, moving as quietly as she could. There was no one about that she could see other than a few guards upon the outer wall, but they were all looking outward, beyond the castle.

She was fortunate they had not seen her approach. For days she had scouted the castle to determine the best way for her to make her move against the prince. It was the castle she had seen in the Dreamer's vision. She'd stood near a bridge that crossed a narrow but deep river and regarded the hilltop fortress from almost the same vantage point that she had seen in the Dreamer's hold on the ship. She had shivered at the sight, at the sense that vast powers were arrayed around her, herding her toward the completion of her goal. That even the treacherous Harridan was smiling upon her. She would be patient. If she failed in her first attempt, it was unlikely she would live to make another.

Having taken note of the guards upon the walls during her surveys, she had waited until a cloudy, moonless night to make her approach. She clawed her way through a bracken-choked gully that cut up the hill near the road and then made a quick dash through the darkness from the gully to the gates. No one saw her. So far, her planning had worked well.

She needed to minimize the number of people she ran into on her way to the prince. Though she had recently replenished her power by having sex with Rulhámad, she would quickly deplete it if she were forced to take too many souls in a short period of time. If others in the castle got in her way, she would use her power only as a last resort. She put the *putan* in her left hand and kept her right near one of the knives she had hidden beneath her dress, near a seam she pulled loose so she could reach it quickly. The prior owner of the dress—a woman from the town below the castle who had met her end on Algariq's blade—had kept it well, and Algariq had been careful not to tear the fabric with her knife when working the threads loose. It was the least she could do.

The inner tunnel was neither guarded nor closed. *The Harridan watches over me,* she thought. But the Harridan was a tricky patron, and her favor could turn on the slightest of whims. She knew she would have to be cautious and not rely too much on Tulqan's help. Preparation and planning were her most trusted allies.

She saw a number of guards wandering about near the keep. She made her way closer to the wide steps leading to the keep's main doors, pressing herself along the sides of buildings that huddled close together on the inner ring of the castle. But when she reached the edge of the final building, there was still an open area nearly fifty paces wide that she would have to cross before she reached the stairs. She wondered if there were a second entrance to the keep that she could get to more easily, and decided to see what she could find.

Algariq followed a pathway around to her right, along the eastern side of the keep. The open area had narrowed until it was barely twenty paces wide, bordered by a flagstone path and a line of trees. It was exceptionally dark save for the yellow light coming through a few windows high up the keep's wall.

She paused behind the slender trunk of a birch tree. Descending from the side of the keep was a steep stairway with high stone walls on either side. The stairs led to a recessed door. She saw no guard or watchman. After checking to make sure the path was clear, she dashed across it and up the narrow stone steps. When she reached the top, she pressed herself against the cool wood of the door and paused to listen for any indication that she'd been seen. She took five long breaths, then pressed the latch, saying a quick prayer to Tulqan to ease her passage by making sure the door was unlocked. She had other means to open it should it prove necessary, but then would have to expend some of her precious power.

The latch clicked and the door swung inward on creaking hinges. She mouthed a silent thank-you to the Harridan, then slipped inside.

The darkness was absolute, but the air felt close; she guessed she was in a small chamber. She stepped forward carefully, hands outstretched, until her fingers struck a wall, then felt around until she found the wood of another door, which she opened just a crack so she could peer out.

She saw a corridor with a flickering light at its end that spilled out into a wide entrance hall with a few torches held in brackets along the walls. The main doors of the keep were to her left. She saw no guards or servants as she crossed the hall, keeping out of the dim light as much as she could, and made her way up the stairs.

The guard's directions to Gerin's private rooms had been maddeningly imprecise—it seemed he lived and worked in the outer edge of the castle and had only been inside the keep a handful of times. She followed the stairs up several stories, then made her way down a long torchlit corridor toward another stairway at its end.

She'd gone about halfway down the corridor when a guard appeared in front of her from a branching hallway. "What are you doing here?" he demanded.

Algariq blinked her eyes rapidly and acted as if she were coming out of a daze. "I'm . . . where am I?"

"What do you mean, where are you? Are you a simpleton?"

She rubbed her forehead. "I'm sorry, good sir. I sleepwalk sometimes. I must have—"

She took a step forward and with a single deft motion plunged her knife up under the man's jaw. Blood jetted down the front of the guard's tunic and mail shirt. She caught him as he slumped, already dead, and pulled him against the wall. She quietly tried the latch of the door closest to her and found a storeroom for linens. Sliding her hands under his arms, she dragged him inside, hiding him in the back as best as she could. Then she wiped her knife on his thigh, returned it to its sheath, and stepped back into the corridor.

She encountered no one else on the way to her prey's rooms. The guard had told her they lay in the upper west corner, beneath one of the keep's squat towers. The man had not known if the prince's sleeping chambers were in the tower itself or the rooms below it.

She followed one stair, a corridor, then another stair, hoping that her sense of direction had not gotten turned around in the dark. *The turn ahead should take me to the western corner of this place,* she thought as she placed each foot silently upon the rug covering the stone floor.

Algariq peered around the corner and saw a single guard standing at a door in the hallway's end. She pulled back before he saw her and contemplated her best course of action. He was at least ten strides away—too far for her to rush him before he could shout an alarm or awaken her prey.

She withdrew a smaller knife from the top of her boot. From her brief glimpse of him, the guard had been wearing a mail shirt over a leather jerkin. *Tulqan, you have helped me greatly this night, but I must ask you to guide my hand now so that my throw will be true.* She did not question the irony of praying to a goddess to help her achieve a quest that would allow her to leave the goddess's service.

Algariq paused to steady herself. In her mind's eye she pictured exactly what she must do until it seemed a memory of a thing already done.

She stepped around the corner and threw her knife. The second she released the blade, she sprinted toward the guard, her larger knife already in hand.

The guard did as she had hoped he would when she stepped into his view—he froze for an instant. But the Harridan's blessing failed her. The man reached for his own weapon and reflexively shifted to one side. Her knife, which otherwise would have pierced his neck almost dead center, merely grazed the side of it before sinking into the door behind him.

But fortune had not abandoned her entirely. He made a gasping sound and clutched at the blood flowing from his wounded neck. His weapon was free, but his attention was split between her mad rush toward him and trying to determine the seriousness of his wound.

Then she was upon him. He swung at her with his blade, deciding that the madwoman who had just tried to kill him with a knife and was still trying to kill him with a second blade was more deserving of his full attention than the cut upon his neck.

He swung high, aiming for her head. She ducked beneath the swing and came up inside his reach before he could bring his weapon back around. He chopped down at her neck with his other hand and connected hard with the edge of his palm. The impact numbed her shoulder and made her right leg buckle. In another moment he would be upon her, and with his greater size, weight, and protections, she would be lost.

She rolled to her left and slashed violently across his throat. He tried to draw back but the door behind him blocked his movement and he could not get outside the reach of her blade. The tip cut into the gristly meat of his voice box and through his windpipe. A mist of blood flew from the end of her blade. His eyes grew wide as blood poured from the new mouth she'd cut into his throat. He dropped his weapon and covered his wound, but already the life was leaving him.

Algariq pushed him facedown onto the floor. As soon as he thumped against the rug, she drove her knife into the base of his skull. She pulled a set of keys from his belt, and after four attempts found the one that opened the door.

She took the lamp from its hook and carried it with her into the room. She knew she had to move quickly now, and could not afford to waste time fumbling in the dark.

Algariq made her way through two rooms until she found the prince's bedchamber. He was sleeping—alone, fortunately—on a massive canopied bed. The corner posts were thick and intricately carved with images of vines and leaves. After placing the lamp on the floor, she stepped closer to the bed, the *putan* firmly in hand.

He was asleep on his side, his face pressed into a feather pillow, with one arm curled beneath it. She reached forward to touch him—

He sprang awake and recoiled from her before her fingers reached his skin. He moved blindingly fast, like a striking cobra from the Tumhaddi Desert, drew back across the bed and held up his hands in a fighting position. "Who are you?" he said.

She lunged toward him with her open hand. She held no weapon and prayed that he would react the way she hoped.

Instead of drawing back farther, he took note of her lack of a weapon and lashed out with his own hand, wrapping his fingers around her much smaller wrist, planning to pin her down and call his guards.

It was exactly what she wanted him to do.

Her power required only the slightest touch to work. She unleashed it the moment he touched her. His soul, his conscious will, became hers, flowing from him into her, and from her into the *putan.*

One floor below them, Hollin came awake suddenly. He'd been in the grip of a dark dream about his long-dead wife Katara. In the dream, she had accused him of withholding the gift of life from her so he could be rid of her.

He'd had the dream more and more often of late. It troubled him and awakened long dormant feelings of guilt that he was unable to grant her the one gift of his magic that he had been so desperate to share. *She is gone. This is not her spirit speaking to me. I know she would never say such a thing.* He wondered if watching Gerin and Elaysen—a wizard and a mortal woman, like himself and Katara—had triggered these feelings in him again; that his dreams were a means of displaying the concern he felt for them both.

He rubbed his eyes and pushed the thoughts of his dream aside. Something had awakened him. Power of some kind, a momentary surge of magic that had drawn him from sleep. The faintest trace of it lingered around him, at the very edge of his senses. He frowned when he realized he did not recognize it. He tried to concentrate on the power so he could better understand it, but in a moment it was gone, like a wisp of smoke dispersed upon the wind.

He wondered what it could have been. Was Gerin making more changes to that infernal sword of his? It was already too dangerous by half. He supposed he should go and see what his inventive apprentice was up to now. He doubted he would get back to sleep until he found out what had awakened him. Besides, he needed some time to clear the dream from his head. The last thing he wanted was to fall asleep and see Katara's accusing and hate-filled stare.

Hollin got up, pulled on a dressing robe, and slipped from his rooms into the dark hallway, carrying a magefire lamp to light his way.

"Release me and stand up," Algariq said. "Do not speak."

Her prey did as she commanded. There was a tremendous amount of power in him of a kind she had never before experienced.

"What is the power I feel within you? Answer me, but quietly."

"It is my magic."

"What were you going to do with it?"

"Hold you with a Binding spell."

"Release your magic. You will never use it against me. I control you now. I have captured your soul, and until I release it, you are mine."

She sensed his power recede like water slipping down a drain. She could sense no resistance from him, for which she was glad. Those in her power should not be able to mount even a token effort to thwart her. Their conscious wills were hers, so there was nothing within them to resist *with,* but she had worried that his great power would grant him some ability to defy her or accelerate the weakening of her control, and she was relieved to discover this was not the case.

"Your guard is in the hall. Bring him in here, before he is found."

He obeyed her in silence, moving quickly and efficiently to perform his task. He was a strong man and had no difficulty carrying the guard's corpse into the room.

She felt time pressing down on her like a weight upon her

shoulders, growing heavier with each breath she took. She needed to get out of the castle now, with her prey, before everything unraveled.

"Get dressed. Wear traveling clothes. We are leaving now and have need of haste."

He removed his large nightshirt and pulled clothing from a wardrobe standing against one wall. It was not long until he stood before her in a linen shirt beneath a leather vest, brown wool trousers, and leather boots.

"Do you usually carry a weapon?"

"Yes. My sword."

"Then bring it. But like your magic, you may not use it against me. You will use it to protect us should it prove necessary, and then only at my command."

He buckled on a worn leather belt from which hung a two-handed blade. She did not give it a second thought. He could no more harm her with it than he could leap to the moon.

She placed the *putan* deep in her pocket. "Come. It's time to leave."

Hollin trudged up the stairs and around the corner that led to Gerin's chambers. At once he realized something was wrong. The guard was missing, and he caught the cloying stench of blood in the air. He drew magic into himself and hurried to the door.

He called out, "Gerin!" and threw open the door.

The prince was standing in the short entry hall to his chambers, fully dressed. He looked dazed, as if he were sleepwalking, or in a trance. A small dark-skinned woman Hollin had never seen before stood beside him, carrying a lamp.

"Gerin, what's going on? Where's your guard? Who is this woman?" Then he saw the guard's body lying on the floor behind them, slumped against the wall.

The woman pointed a rigid finger at Hollin and said, "Attack him!"

24

Even as the woman issued her command, Hollin was lashing out with a Binding spell. Her arms slapped against her sides as he closed his fingers to constrict the tendrils of magic flowing from his hand. She struggled against her imprisonment, but he ignored her and looked about frantically for her accomplices. Who was she shouting for? He didn't see—

Gerin held out his hand toward Hollin and called magic into himself. Hollin realized Gerin was going to attack *him* and threw himself backward while invoking a Warding. His magefire lamp fell from his hand and shattered in a sudden flash of light.

Gerin's Blindness spell smashed into the partially formed Warding and destroyed it, then struck Hollin full in the face. He felt it bore into his eyes, and his vision darkened until he could see only a dim spark of light from the lamp the woman had dropped when his own spell had taken her. His Warding had inflicted some damage to Gerin's power, otherwise he knew he would have no sight at all.

Hollin took another fumbling step backward and invoked a Forbidding, hoping the more powerful protection would provide a hardier defense against Gerin's amber magic.

He had to drop the Binding to concentrate on the Forbidding. A moment later a blast of raw magic slammed into his defenses like a hammer blow. The force of it knocked him to his knees, and he felt his Forbidding weaken and then shatter beneath Gerin's power.

"Help!" he shouted. "The prince has been—"

A hand touched his shoulder. He shuddered and fell silent, no longer able to do so much as lift his finger. He had been perfectly immobilized by a power he did not understand. It was no wizard's magic. It must be the woman.

"Stand up," she said. Her accent was thick, similar to Tolsadri's. "You will not speak."

His body obeyed her, no longer his to control. It was not a Compulsion, as he understood them. Compulsions were exercises in brute force, overpowering the victim's active will. This was very different. He *had* no will of his own, at least as far as his body was concerned. He could not struggle against this because he had no means to resist. He'd been reduced to a mere spectator, trapped within the prison of his own flesh.

"Get into the room. Quickly."

He started forward and smacked his knee against the door, which he could not see. He took another step and nearly tripped over what felt like an outstretched leg. The dead guard.

"What is wrong with you?" she demanded angrily. "Speak quietly."

"Gerin attacked me with a Blindness spell. I defended myself, but my vision is mostly gone."

"The Harridan's favor is turning from me," she muttered. She shoved him several paces deeper into the room and told him to lie down. Part of Hollin was fascinated by how compliant his body was, how it perfectly obeyed her will. What would she do to him? Slit his throat?

"It brings ill fortune to kill a follower of Bariq the Wise," she said. "Though you are not the same, you have powers like an Adept, and I will not risk either Bariq's or the Harridan's wrath by killing you." She pressed her mouth almost to his ear. "You will not move or speak until I release you from my power. When you are free, you should thank me for your life. It is mine now to take, yet I leave your blood unshed."

He felt rather than saw her pull away from him. She picked

her lamp up from the floor, and then she and Gerin were gone, leaving him in absolute blackness.

Gerin could not believe what had just happened. He had *attacked* Hollin, his teacher and friend. He had shouted *No! I won't!* when this woman had issued her command, but the shout had only been in the small part of his mind that remained his own; no sound had come from his mouth, and his body obeyed her without hesitation.

It reminded him gallingly of his plight upon the Sundering, when Asankaru's war priests had brutally taken control of his body and forced him to sound the Horn of Tireon to activate the dormant power of the Baryashin Order, black wizards who had long ago used forbidden magic and murder in their quest for eternal life. Asankaru had hoped to use the power of the horn to take possession of his body so he could live once more as a being of flesh and blood and not merely as a spirit of vengeance.

And his failure to stop the Red Robes, to prevent the blowing of Tireon's horn, had ended with Reshel's death by her own hand so that Osseria itself would not perish. Who would pay for his failure this time?

"Take us out of this castle as quickly as you can," she said. "Do not draw attention to yourself. If you are stopped, say you could not sleep and are going for a walk."

They left Hollin immobile on the floor—he thanked the gods she had not made him kill the wizard—and hurried to a nearby door that opened to a downward spiraling stairway. She handed him the lamp and told him to go first. They descended in silence. He tried to think of a way to break the power that gripped him, his thoughts growing increasingly frantic with each step on the wedge-shaped treads, but there was nothing. He could not reach his *paru'enthred* no matter how hard he tried. But she could control his magic, he realized, otherwise he could not have fashioned the Blindness spell.

They reached the ground floor and exited near the kitchens. Gerin led her through a cluttered passage and several

storage rooms until they came to a door in the north side
of the keep that opened to a walled courtyard. She had him
extinguish the lamp when they left the keep. Just as he was
about to open the gate, she placed her hand on his arm to stop
him. "Does your . . . *magic* have any way to conceal us? So
that we are not seen leaving this castle?"

"I cannot make us invisible, but I can create an Unseeing.
We will not be invisible, but beneath the threshold of their
vision unless we are right in front of them."

"Make it."

He felt his body open to magic and create the spell. "I do
not feel anything," she said. "Have you done it?"

"Yes. The Unseeing is around us both."

They moved along the eastern side of the keep. The guards
on duty did not take note of them as they passed. Gerin
screamed in his mind, but his body marched along calmly
with his captor, as if nothing was wrong. They might as well
have been bodiless spirits moving silently in the darkness,
their passage unseen by mortal eyes.

At the postern in the main gate they found a guard seated
on a stool, his eyes open but unfocused. When the woman
stepped before him, he seemed to come awake, as if rising
through the mists of a trance.

The guard opened the postern at her command. "You will
forget that you have seen us this night," she said. "You will
remember nothing of my presence here, or Gerin's leaving
this place, until you are released from my power."

They passed through the thick door and started down the
dark road. The thud of the door closing behind him was like
the sound of his doom. Gerin wanted to turn his head to look
at his home, fearing it would be the last time he would ever
see it. But even that small gesture was denied to him. He
could only follow her in silence as she led him away.

25

"And why isn't the crown prince here to defend his land from the invasion *he* caused?" spat Omara to her husband as a servant buckled his belt in their dressing room in the Tirthaig. Ten days had passed since his return to the city, bringing word of the fall of his island. He'd sent messages to the sea lords of Khedesh, commanding them to ready their ships and soldiers, which they were to bring to Almaris as soon as they were able so they could begin the assault to reclaim Gedsengard.

"Nellemar, are you listening to me?"

"How could I not, the way you're bellowing?"

"Then answer me!"

"There's nothing to say to your foolishness. Gerin is not yet aware of the invasion since his father has not yet written to him. As for him causing this, you're not only wrong, you flirt with treason. I would watch who you flap your tongue to, Omara, or you may find it plucked from your head. My brother will not suffer such dissension as you seem intent on stirring."

"The king is beginning to see what his son has become."

"And what do you mean by that?"

"You know exactly what I mean."

"The king requires my presence." He strode past her and out of the room. He had loved his wife once—or at least her beauty, which still had the power to stop him in his tracks like a cold slap on the face—but that love had withered and finally died in the frosty air of her endless ambition and scheming.

But she was right about one thing: Abran's feelings toward his eldest son had changed, and not for the better. The king had become unpredictable in alarming ways, prone to violent outbursts and tirades against what he saw as the incompetence of those around him. Abran had privately mentioned to him that he feared plots to unseat him, and hinted strongly that he thought Gerin was behind them. Nellemar knew that was nonsense and had been alarmed by the accusations, but Abran dismissed him before he could voice a single objection.

The king was meeting with his privy council. When Nellemar entered the council chamber, Abran and Jaros Waklan were leaning over several maps spread out on a long table. Arilek Levkorail and Ademel Caranis, the Lord Captain of the City Watch, were seated at one end, speaking quietly about the defense of the city and how the duties would be divided between the Watch and the Taeratens should their enemy lay siege to them.

Caranis was a decade older than the Lord Commander, with a thick white moustache he kept waxed and curled. He was a stern, humorless man who worshipped Telros with the passion of a priest and loathed corruption with equal fervor. Any man who tried to bribe him quickly found himself on the receiving end of his cudgel or in the dungeons of the Watch House. Caranis's incorruptibility was the primary reason Abran had named him to the post when he'd become king. The previous Lord Captain, Bron Indrelani, had used the men of the Watch to turn entire districts of Almaris into his personal fiefs, forcing payments from merchants, guild houses, shop owners, thieves, and brothels. Those who did not pay were beaten, some found their buildings burned, and a few ended up with knives in their backs, the murderers never found. When Indrelani saw that Abran was serious about cleaning up the corruption of the Watch, he fled in the middle of the night. He was rumored to be in Trothmar now, selling what knowledge he had to the Threndish.

While there was still corruption in parts of the Watch, the changes Caranis had wrought throughout their ranks—with nearly thirty commanders remanded to Osgayle Prison and nine to Black Willem's tender ministrations—were little shy of miraculous.

Despite his incorruptibility, Nellemar couldn't stand the man. Caranis was more dour than the most solemn priest, and his many affectations—his moustache, cudgel, overly mannered way of speaking, and the ridiculous number of rings he wore—annoyed him to no end. But Nellemar grudgingly admitted he was effective, and had done an exemplary job of carrying out the tasks given to him.

"Nellemar, come in," said the king. "I've received word from Baron Thorael that the invaders have landed south of Castle Pelleron. He writes that a massive force has taken a large stretch of beach, from which they are making forays deeper into Khedesh."

"Have they made any attempt to take Pelleron itself?" asked Nellemar.

"Not when Baron Thorael wrote to me," said the king. "But that may have since changed."

"His castle is well-protected upon its bluff," said Nellemar. "They may decide to bottle him up and prevent him from leaving rather than trying to take the castle."

"Indeed," said the king. "That is exactly what the baron thinks they will do, though treachery is ever our enemy and he may be betrayed from within. But there is nothing we can do to help him. We are cut off." He looked at Nellemar squarely. "What word have you from the lords of the fleet? When will our ships arrive?"

"I've not yet heard back from all of the coastal lords," said Nellemar. "Those who replied are gathering their forces, but I would not expect the ships from Istameth for at least another month."

"That is too long," said the king.

"Men and ships can only move so fast, Your Majesty. The hills of Istameth are far from here, and it will take them time to gather their vassals and set sail, prepared for war. Have you sent word to your vassals yet to march to the defense of the city?"

"No. I sent them word of the fall of Gedsengard and warned them that an invasion of the mainland was imminent and to prepare, but I have not yet given the command to march."

"I would suggest, in light of the news from Baron Thorael, that you now issue that command, Your Majesty," said Waklan. "We must keep our supply lines to the city open. If their fleet is as large as Lord Nellemar says, and they use it to blockade the city, we will only be able to receive supplies overland."

"Have they sent an embassy to Baron Thorael?" Nellemar asked the king.

"No. Thorael sent some of his own men under a flag of truce, but they were taken by the invaders and not permitted to return. But we know what they want. If that man Tolsadri hadn't made it clear enough, Gerin's letter to me certainly did." Abran clenched his jaw in fury. "They want my son, so he can give them these Words of Making they seek."

"And to convert us to their beliefs," said Nellemar.

"It is an odd thing," said Waklan. "For a people to travel so far for such a strange purpose. I don't know what to make of it."

"I care nothing for their purpose," said the king. "I care only that we drive them from our kingdom with such harrowing rage that their great-grandchildren will fear to return here, or even speak our name." He glared at each of them in turn. "And if you are not the men to see that done, I will find those who will."

26

Shortly after dawn, a Pashti servant woman named Reila Kitmi noticed that the guard was missing from Prince Gerin's door. She thought little of it, assumed he'd dashed off for a bite of breakfast or a quick cuddle in the arms of a woman, but she scowled when she noticed a pile of broken glass and metal against one wall. It looked to her like a broken lamp. Just like a soldier to break something and walk away.

She knelt beside the largest pile of broken glass. It was evident from the shards and the shape of the iron base that it was not like any ordinary lamp, and she wondered if it was one of the magic lights the wizard used. She placed her hand in something wet and sticky on the rug that ran the corridor's length, pulled it back quickly and sniffed her fingers. Her old nose wasn't what it once was, but she knew blood when she smelled it. *Tendur save me. A man has died here.* Was it Prince Gerin?

She was suddenly so afraid she did not think she could move. *Curse my old bones!* She pushed herself upright, her knees popping and creaking, and looked at the prince's door. Should she go in? What if he were dead inside? Or what if the killer was still there?

The last thought decided for her. She turned and ran for help as fast as her old legs would carry her.

* * *

Balandrick was in a fury. Gerin was gone, Hollin injured in some way that left him completely unresponsive, and two guards were dead. Someone had infiltrated the keep *right under his bloody nose*, killed his men, and spirited away his lord and prince—the man he'd sworn to protect with his very life—all without being seen by a single person. It was unfathomable. Unthinkable. It could not have happened.

But it bloody well *did* happen, and Shayphim take him by nightfall if he didn't figure out exactly how it happened and how to get Gerin back.

He was in the Sunlight Hall questioning Jeril Horthremiden, his second in command. Matren Swendes was there as well.

"No one saw the prince himself leaving in the dead of night?" asked Balandrick. "All the gates were closed, were they not?"

"Yes, sir." Horthremiden stood with his helm beneath his arm, sweating profusely.

"And the gates were guarded?"

"Yes, sir."

"Then how in the holy name of Telros did he get out? Did he just walk through the bloody walls? Fly off like a bloody crow? Tell me, commander, how did he get out?" He'd risen from his chair and was shouting only inches from the man's face.

"I don't know, sir. I'm at a loss to explain it."

"Send every guard to me who was on duty last night. If we can't explain it, our heads deserve to be on pikes above the Gray Woman."

Horthremiden swallowed heavily. "Yes, sir. I'll send them at once."

Elaysen and Master Aslon were with Hollin, trying to determine the extent of his injuries and how to revive him. When Balandrick had spoken to them earlier, they were puzzled by the wizard's condition. "There's not a mark on him," Elaysen had said. She'd probed beneath his hair with her fingers and found no lump, bruise, or other sign that he'd received a blow. "It's like he's sleeping but unable to awaken."

"Find a way to rouse him," Balandrick had growled, more roughly than he intended, but he made no apology. "We need to know what happened here, and he's probably the only one who has any answers." He was also troubled by the thought of someone overcoming the wizard. He'd seen Hollin's powers at work and knew they were not to be taken lightly.

It was times like this, when his stress was high and the world around him seemed chaotic and out of control, that he missed Reshel the most. He'd always thought of her as a voice of reason, with her intelligent, logical mind, full of insights that escaped the scrutiny of so many others, himself included. She'd been able to see many different sides of a problem, and could make intuitive leaps to arrive at conclusions he knew were far beyond his ability. His mind simply didn't work that way. He dealt with what was in front of him and reacted accordingly. It was what made him an effective soldier. But he also knew that such a way of seeing the world had its limits. When he did not have enough facts from which to draw a conclusion, he was lost.

This situation was a prime example of that. From the few facts he had—guards dead, Gerin missing, Hollin injured—he could not figure out a sequence of events or understand how the abduction had happened. Oh, it was obvious that the dead guard they'd found in a closet had intercepted the intruders and had paid with his life, and that the guard at the prince's door had been an obstacle to be removed. But that gave him no insight into how they'd gotten into the castle unseen to begin with, or how they'd injured Hollin, or forced someone as powerful as Gerin to depart against his will without leaving the slightest trace. He had ordered the castle to be sealed immediately and searched in case they had not yet escaped, but it soon became evident that they were no longer here. The search then expanded beyond Ailethon. He had men scouring the nearby lands, some with bloodhounds who'd been given Gerin's scent.

He'd wager a handsome sum that Reshel could have figured something out of this mess. Her wildest guesses were usually better than someone else's well-reasoned thoughts.

His attention was drawn back to the sun-drenched table when the first of the guards were escorted in. "We'll do this one at a time," he announced to them. "Have a seat. It's going to take a while."

* * *

"I don't remember anything, I swear," said Mori Genro after an intense round of questioning from Balandrick. "I was at the postern the whole night. I may have dozed once or twice, but I had my feet across the door, which was locked. No one could have come in that way without my knowing it."

"The intruders didn't come in or leave by the larger gates," said Matren, taking over from Balandrick, who had slumped in his chair, disgusted at his lack of progress.

I should resign my post, Balandrick thought miserably. *Gerin attacked on the road where Therain loses his bloody hand, and now this. I'm not fit to be the Captain of the Guard. That's assuming I can get him back so I can give him my resignation.* "That leaves the postern doors," he said.

"It wasn't mine, I swear it," said Genro. "I didn't leave my post."

They'd been questioning the men for hours, with no progress. Everyone was where they should have been, no one saw anything. Balandrick wanted to pound his fist on the table until either the wood or his hand broke, but refrained from such an outburst and satisfied his urge by drumming his fingers on the table's edge.

Abruptly, he stood and stretched his back. Genro was the last man they questioned, and they had learned nothing. "I'm going to see how Hollin is doing," he said to Matren.

The wizard had been examined in Gerin's chambers where he'd been found before being taken to Master Aslon's tower.

The Laonnite Master's tower lay within the inner bailey, nestled near an angle in the bailey's western wall. Balandrick found Aslon and Elaysen in a small bedroom. Hollin lay on a narrow bed beneath a large east-facing window. It was getting toward evening, and a number of candles and lamps had been placed on a table near the head of the bed.

"How is he?"

Baelish Aslon faced him, his milky eye glowing eerily in the light of a nearby candle. "Unchanged. He exhibits no signs of poison and seems otherwise strong and healthy. But we cannot rouse him from this slumber."

"Is there any word of Prince Gerin?" Elaysen asked Balandrick.

"No. I received the first report from our scouts a little while ago. No trail's been found so far. I'm sure they're headed east, but I had some men sweep around Padesh and further west to make sure they aren't hiding out there to throw us off their scent."

"Do you have any idea how they were able to take him?" she asked.

Hot anger and frustration seethed within him anew. "Not yet. It's a mystery, and so far I am lacking clues to help me understand it. I'm hoping Hollin can tell us something when he's able to speak."

"It had to be magic of some kind," she said. "That's the only way I can conceive of someone taking him against his will."

"Is Hollin under a spell?" asked Balandrick. "Is that why he won't awaken?"

"I would say that's probable," said Aslon, "but I have no means of testing for magic."

Feeling the need to do something, Balandrick left the tower and made a circuit of the castle's outer wall. He visited the postern door near the Gate of the Gray Woman and inspected it for signs of being forced open. He climbed to the wall-walk and looked out over the dark lands below Ireon's Hill. *You're out there somewhere,* he thought when he turned to the east. *I'll find you, my lord. I swear it. And the people who took you will pay dearly.*

He walked the complete length of the outer wall, stopping to talk to some of the guards, trying to see if anything looked out of place from this vantage point, any small clue that might tell him how the perpetrators had gotten in and out of the castle unseen. But there was nothing.

Later that night he was in a deep, troubled sleep when he heard a pounding on his door. He got out of bed groggily. It felt like the hours before dawn, but he had no way to be sure.

A breathless guard stood wide-eyed in the hall. "Captain,

the Master has asked you to come quickly. The wizard is awake."

"How did you manage to rouse him?" asked Balandrick as he entered the wizard's room.

"We did not," said the Master. "He awoke on his own."

"The power that held me has released its grip," said Hollin. He was sitting up in the bed, leaning against a thick pile of pillows. Elaysen was still in the chair where she'd been sleeping, but was now wide awake and focused intently on the wizard.

"What happened?" asked Balandrick. "Who took Gerin? *How* did they take him?"

"He was taken by a woman."

"How many were with her? Do you know how they got in?"

"I saw no one with her, and believe she acted alone."

Balan made an incredulous noise. "How could a single woman force Gerin to leave here against his will?"

"Her power is potent, Balandrick. With a single touch she took complete control of my body and mind. I could do nothing to thwart her. If she had commanded me to leap from the tallest spire of the keep, my body would have obeyed her without hesitation. She's used the same power on Gerin." He told them how the prince had attacked him on her order, and how she had touched him and commanded that he remain unconscious until she released him. "I'm sure she used the same power to help her enter and leave the castle."

"You mean there are guards who *helped* her get in? But none of them remembers a thing!"

"She could have commanded them to forget."

"Is there any magic that can find Prince Gerin?" asked Elaysen.

"I'll create a Farseeing, but I have little hope that it will help. They have too much of a head start."

A soldier admitted Mori Genro to the room. His face was flushed with embarrassment. He fiddled nervously with a felt hat and kept his eyes locked mostly on his feet.

"What is it?" asked Balandrick.

"I remember now what happened at the gate, sir," he said. "I don't know why I didn't remember earlier, I swear I don't. I mean, she told me to forget, but I don't know why I listened, it's not like I wanted—"

"It's all right," said Balandrick. "We know why you didn't remember. Just tell us what happened."

Genro recounted the appearance of a woman asking for help and how, after she touched him, he became completely obedient to her commands. "I swear I didn't want to let her in, I just couldn't help myself!" Tears stood in his eyes, and his lip trembled with fear. "Please don't execute me, sir! I swear I ain't no traitor!"

Balandrick put a hand on his shoulder. "We know. She used magic to cast a spell on you."

Genro finished his story with the departure of Gerin and the woman and her admonition to him that he forget that he had seen her.

"Hollin, why do you think that you awoke and Genro's memory returned now?" asked Balandrick after the guard had gone.

"The woman said she would release me from her power. I assume she is far enough from here to feel safe, or else she can no longer maintain her hold on us."

"Perhaps the prince has overwhelmed her," said Master Aslon.

"We can hope that is so, but I would not count on it," said Hollin. "We need to follow them at once. We should head to the east. That is the only reasonable direction for them to take."

"I would already be gone," said Balandrick, "but I thought it best to remain until you were awake to find out what you know."

"I'm going with you," said Elaysen. "Don't even think of saying no. I was helpful in the fight against those . . . things. You might need me again."

Balandrick and Hollin exchanged knowing looks. "I wouldn't dream of refusing you," said the captain.

27

Gerin trudged behind his captor, wishing with all his heart and soul that he could draw his sword and run it through her back, or at least club her senseless with it, since there were several dozen questions he wanted to ask her if he knew she could not capture him again. But he could not afford the risk if he were able to break free of her spell; he would kill her the moment he could. He would not risk this . . . slavery again.

She'd pushed them mercilessly once they were off Ireon's Hill. She had two horses hidden among some trees at the hill's bottom, and they rode them hard to the east. They'd kept to the road during the darkness and part of that first morning, but as noon approached, she took them into the Ossland Plains north of the road. She had not spoken a word to him since they began riding, and the spell she'd cast upon him prevented him from speaking. He could only obey her, and as she climbed onto her horse her single command had been, "Follow me."

The plains soon yielded to more hilly country as they made their way eastward. They stopped only for the briefest of meals and to allow the horses to rest and graze a bit before resuming their journey. *She's a cold one,* he thought. Even the most reticent jailer would have said more words to his prisoner than this woman had uttered to him.

She finally allowed them to stop when it got too dark to

travel without risking the horses. "We spend the night here," she announced in her strange accent. "Once you lie down, you will not move until dawn." After picketing the horses, she curled up on the grass beneath a blanket and fell asleep almost immediately.

Gerin was exhausted. He tried to fight his fatigue, hoping to figure out some means of escape; but there was no crack in her grip on him that he could find, and after a little while he fell asleep himself.

He awoke to darkness, startled by sudden movement near him. She was sitting up with something in her hand. Even with his sensitive eyes, he could not see what it was. "I have released the other two whose souls I took to get to you." He could see a sheen of sweat on her face and throat. "I can no longer hold onto so many at once."

So her powers do have limits, he thought as she lay back down. Hope smoldered within him for the first time since his capture. *Maybe there's a way to weaken her further.*

They rode hard as soon as dawn broke. He spent the morning wondering if there were some way to force her to overextend her power that would allow him to break free. He noticed that by having his conscious mind so completely severed from the workings of his body, he could more deeply concentrate on the problem of escaping. It was not much of a consolation, but in his present circumstances he would take what he could get.

Unfortunately, despite his effort, he could not break her grip upon him. He prayed to Telros for guidance, and later the One God; but they were silent, and he was left alone, a prisoner within his own flesh.

They stopped at midday in a sheltered depression in the base of a high rounded hill. She sat down with her back against a tree and watched him with more interest than she had yet shown. "Sit by me," she said, and handed him a bit of jerky as he obeyed.

"I had a dream of you last night. I believe it was no ordinary dream, but one sent by Parel himself, the Lord of

Dreams, who alone of the Powers touches all the castes when he wills." She chewed for a moment before continuing. "I saw you step through a door of light and vanish. It felt true, as the dreams of Parel do.

"Tell me of these Words of Making the Exalted seeks. What are they, and where do you keep them? Are they in your castle? I was told to bring only you, but it seems that something as important as the Words would be kept in your home, safely guarded. I'm curious why I was not tasked with retrieving them as well. You may speak."

It seemed a wall fell away in his mind, allowing in light and air to a prisoner who had been without both almost to the point of death. His consciousness—the part of him that was still *him*, and not under this woman's control—surged forward. He sensed that his voice was his once more, but before he spoke he tried to lunge for his sword with the fervent hope of driving the point of Nimnahal through her throat.

His body did not exert even the slightest effort to lift his hand. The attempt was less than a wish.

"Speak to me. There are things I wish to know, and if you answer well, I will let you ask me questions in return."

He put aside his effort to regain control of his body. Maybe there was some vital bit of knowledge he could glean from talking to her, something she might let slip that he could turn to his advantage.

"I know nothing of the Words of Making. I never heard of them until I met that man Tolsadri and he accused me of having them."

"How could you not? The Dreamer saw that you had them in a vision. A Dreamer's vision is truth."

"Truth or not, I have no idea what they are."

"No matter. It is not my concern. The Voice and Sword of the Exalted will know what to do once I have brought you to them." She gestured to him. "You may ask me questions."

"How did you take control of me? What is the nature of your power?"

"I am a soul stealer. I take your soul with my touch, and until I return it you have no will of your own save for that I grant you. But my power is not important. You cannot break it. Tell me of *your* power. I would know more of it."

"Are there many soul stealers in your homeland?"

"You have not yet answered my question. Do not forget who is the master here. Answer me or I will silence you. If you please me I will allow you to continue speaking."

He decided not to argue. "I am a wizard."

She frowned. "I do not know that word."

"I can use power others cannot. We call this power magic." He explained about the Atalari and the intermingling of that race with those who had no magic. He did not lie to her—he had no idea whether she could detect deception in him—but neither did he speak in any detail. His accounts were brief, cursory. He did not tell her that the number of wizards had dwindled until they had reached their present, sorry state. He preferred to leave her with the impression that there were thousands upon thousands of wizards all across Osseria.

He was still talking when she commanded that they resume their journey. "You will speak as we ride, but if we are seen by others you will remain silent. You will not cry out or seek aid in any capacity. Now, continue with your tale."

She asked him a few questions about how he summoned his powers and what he could do with them, but mostly she listened as they wound their way through the low hills.

"You asked how many soul stealers are in my homeland," she said when he paused to sip from his water skin. "There are few of us. It is believed the first soul stealer was created when a demon possessed a young girl in the lost city of Mapei. She proved stronger than it had thought. She trapped the demon within her and would not let it depart her body, believing it would grant her great powers and fortune. The demon would not bow to her, and whenever she touched another, it tried to take possession of that person in an attempt to escape. But the girl thwarted the demon and drew the others into her instead. She learned that this granted her control of others, and she used it to her advantage. Those in Mapei considered her cursed, and condemned her to the caste of the Harridan though she had been a follower of Yendis the

Mother. She in turn cursed them and left Mapei, which was later buried beneath the sands of Nubar and lost to the world, destroyed by Tulqan and the power of the girl's curse."

"Who or what is the Harridan? And Yendis, and Tulqan? I don't know those names. For that matter, what is *your* name?"

She shook her head. "I still cannot believe that these lands live in such darkness, without the light of the Powers to guide them. Do you not feel lost, not knowing your place?"

"I know my place. I am Gerin Atreyano, crown prince of Khedesh."

"You have given me your name and your title, but that is not what you *are*. No matter. I am Katel yalez Algariq, of the caste of Tulqan the Harridan, who is one of the Powers of the world."

"Where are you taking me, Katel?"

"To the Sword and Voice of the Exalted. You have already met the Exalted's Voice: Vethiq aril Tolsadri, also a Loremaster and Adept of Bariq. A 'wizard,' you might say, though his powers are unlike yours."

"Who is the Exalted? Is he your king?"

"The Exalted is to a king what the sea is to a drop of water. She is the supreme ruler of the Havalqa, Those Who Stand Fast. Her name is Tareq elin Wasaqta. She is the earthly presence of the Powers, the manifestation of their will in the mortal world. It is by her decree that I will have the curse of the Harridan lifted from me when I hand you over to the Sword and Voice. I will at last be free."

They rode in silence for a while through a narrow meadow of high grass and colorful wildflowers that twisted its way between the hills like a river. Flocks of geese flew above them, and he could hear birds singing in the copses that capped the hilltops. The sky was almost unbroken by clouds, and a gentle breeze blew from their left, bringing them the scent of the wildflowers.

The far end of the meadow ended in a sharp rise of two hills, between which was a boulder-strewn culvert too dangerous for the horses to attempt. Algariq led him up the less steep northern slope, on the far side of which lay a ridge that ran almost arrow-straight to the east, like a raised roadbed.

"Who is this Harridan you serve?" Gerin asked once they were on the ridge.

"She is Tulqan, one of the Powers. There are ten who rule the world in the name of Holvareh the All Father. They are Metharog the Father, god of those who rule our empire; Yendis the Mother, spouse of Metharog and the goddess of virtuous matrons; Bariq the Wise, Lord of the Mysteries; Elqos the Worker, whose followers are laborers and servants; Ruren the Silent, Master of the Dead; Ruren's brother Parel, Lord of Dreams, who has no caste of his own and touches any and all men with his dreams, like the one I had of you; Herol the Soldier, the master of men who fight, both soldiers and mercenaries; Meitha the Maiden, worshipped by young women and virgins; Keitru the Master, god of slaves; and finally Tulqan the Harridan, goddess of the outcast. In her spite, she often opposes the wishes of her brethren, and many of her followers are wicked for its own sake because they know no other way."

"Are you wicked, Katel? Do you savor stealing the lives of others?"

"I am no more wicked than you. I do what I must, what is demanded of me. Have you never killed?"

"Yes, I've killed. I've ordered men put to death for their crimes—it is one of my sworn and solemn duties as lord of these lands—and I've killed men in battle. But I have never stolen a man from his home in the dead of the night to deliver him to his enemies."

"These men you put to death for their crimes . . . you did this to protect those you love, did you not?"

"Among other reasons, yes."

"That is why I have taken you. Our reasons are no different. I do what I must for those I love."

"You said your Exalted would free you from the Harridan if you deliver me, but are you not free of her now, here in these lands where your gods have no power?"

"You know nothing," she said in disgust. "Be silent."

At her command, he receded within his own mind behind the wall that separated him from the volition to control his body, and could speak no more. But he was not displeased. There was something in her reason for taking him that he needed to understand. *I do what I must for those I love.* Yes, the key was there, in those words, a fulcrum he hoped he could use to pry himself loose from her grip. *She wants to be free,* he thought. *Maybe I can show her that she already is.*

"You may speak again," she said at mid-morning the next day. "But do not try my patience or I will silence you at once."

The wall in his mind fell away, and the will that was still his own came forward once more. "I don't want to try your patience," he said. "I want to understand you and why you're doing this to me."

"We have already spoken of this. There is nothing more to say."

"I know what you were commanded to do, but I still don't know what you hope to get out of it. You said you would be made free, but are you not free now? You are your own master in these lands. You're not a slave. You could stay here and forget about the Harridan."

She laughed and shook her head. "Your ignorance is wider than the sands of Great Tumhaddi. You truly know *nothing.*"

"Then tell me, Katel. Make me understand."

He could see her thinking about what, if anything, she should say to him. He thought she would not speak, but then she made a scoffing noise and gave him a piercing stare. "I am no slave. To be a slave is to be Keitruni. To be a wretch of the Harridan is to be lower than a slave. We are beholden to *anyone* of *any* caste. If a child of Yendis commanded me to steal the soul of another child who teased her, I could not refuse. To do so would result in torture, and repeated refusals would end in death."

"But here we have no castes. We—"

"You either lie or delude yourself. You are noble born. I

learned this in your city. Are there not servants in your castle? Merchants who sell you goods? Men who till the earth? Soldiers and mercenaries? Criminals, outcasts, and murderers? Of course you have castes. You are not so very different from us, but you have not been shown the Light of the Powers. Your way is but a shadow of the truth, a mockery of the order of the world set down by Holvareh in the beginning of time. You will fall to us eventually. No one has ever resisted the Havalqa. You will be conquered and your people placed in their proper castes so the Light of the Powers will shine where now there is only darkness. You will become us. It is inevitable.

"But even if I wished for a time to break the bond of my caste, the Powers are in these lands, biding their time until their faithful servants bring their Light here. They are weakened but present nevertheless, even now. The Harridan could still punish me here—there is no place in the world beyond their reach. And when your people become one with the Havalqa, what will happen to me then? I would be tortured and killed for my betrayal. And my son as well, who remains behind in Aleith'aqtar. When I am raised from this caste he will be raised with me, freed from this wretched life. Then I will no longer be a soul stealer. Once raised, I will forgo my powers forever. No, you have nothing to give me except pain and death for myself and my son."

Gerin did not wish to argue with her about the likelihood that Khedesh, or any kingdom of Osseria, would fall to the invaders. It would be a pointless debate. But he now understood the passion that drove her, the reason she had come so far from her own home to kidnap a man she had never met. She did not hate him. This was not about a difference of ideas, or a need to take land, or a ransom, or a personal vendetta. He was a means to an end, the only way she could free herself and her son from their captivity. He realized he did not have any argument to counter with. The love of a mother for her child was a powerful thing.

He was surprised when he felt a stirring of pity for her. *She doesn't deserve my pity,* he told himself. *She's kidnapped me*

from my home. She deserves my blade through her heart.
Yet he could not help but feel sorry for her. The tragedy of
her situation, and her desire to better her life and the life of
her son, touched him. He found himself unable to hate her.
But he would free himself from her, he vowed. And if that
meant he must kill her, so be it. She was doing what she felt
she must, but he could do no less.

Toward evening they reached a tree-crowned hill. They were
nearly to its summit when two of the grotesque creatures
who had attacked Gerin appeared a short distance ahead.
Gerin wanted to draw his weapon and summon his magic,
but he could do nothing.

"You have nothing to fear," she said. "They will not harm
us."

The things backed away from them as they crested the
summit. Their horses grew skittish but did not bolt as Gerin
feared they might. A man approached them from the trees.
He was small and thin, with white hair and bloodred flesh.

He did not looked pleased to see them. "So you have succeeded where I failed," he said to Katel. He gave Gerin a
withering, hateful look, then turned away. *That is one who
would just as soon stick a knife between my ribs as look at
me,* thought Gerin. If the man chose to murder him, he knew
he could do nothing but watch. He did not know the relationship between the two, if one was master of the other. The
creatures had tried to take him first, and when they failed,
Katel had come.

The man bowed stiffly to Katel. "I salute your capture.
The hunt is yours."

The two did not speak to him the rest of the night. They sat
apart from him, talking quietly in their native tongue. Once
in a while Katel gestured toward him while presumably relating the tale of his capture.

They spent the next week traveling hard toward the coast,
keeping off roads and avoiding any towns or villages. Gerin
assumed that Balandrick and Hollin were searching for him,
so he tried to come up with some means of leaving a trail,

but Katel's control over him was so complete that he could not even leave bits of uneaten food on the ground. When she commanded him to eat, that was exactly what he did, with no ability to deviate from her instructions.

He learned that the man's name was Kursil Rulhámad and that he was a maegosi, able to control the beasts he called quatans with his mind. For the most part, the creatures kept away from them as they traveled.

She let him speak almost every day. He asked questions of them both, being careful in his wording, not wanting to risk angering them and losing his ability to communicate.

He learned that Rulhámad was another follower of the Harridan, though he made no mention of his reasons for pursuing the prince. Gerin assumed they were the same as Katel's: to free himself from the bondage of Tulqan. But if he had any other reasons, like a family or companion he also wished to free, he would not speak of them.

On the morning of the tenth day since leaving Ailethon, Gerin noticed that Katel seemed drawn and weary, as if she had not slept well. There were dark circles beneath her eyes and her skin seemed ashen, almost waxy. Her condition worsened visibly throughout the day. She slumped forward on her saddle as they rode, her shoulders rolled forward as if she were carrying some terrible weight. He wondered if she was ill. She had not given him permission to speak that day so he could only ride, mute, and observe.

She and Rulhámad spent most of the day in silence, punctuated here and there with hushed bits of conversation in their own language, which sounded harsh and unlovely to Gerin's ears. He thought from the man's gestures that Rulhámad might be asking her about her condition. If she was ill, it had not lessened her control of him in any appreciable degree. He was as firmly in her grasp now as when she'd first taken him.

Katel nearly tumbled from her horse when they stopped for the night. Rulhámad reached out to steady her and spoke harshly to her. He thrust a finger at Gerin and spoke again, then pointed to himself. She nodded wearily.

"I must replenish my power," she said to Gerin. "Rulhámad refuses to assist me, saying he has helped me enough. He says now that you are mine, you should be the one I use. And he is right. Someone whose soul I have taken will give me greater power than someone who is free.

"Disrobe."

Even as Gerin's body calmly moved to obey her, his thoughts were frantic. What was she intending to do? Was she going to torture him in some way to replenish her power?

Rulhámad had left their small camp area to be with his creatures. Gerin's attention snapped back squarely on Katel as she too began to undress. He noticed that her dark skin was blemished with scars across her shoulders, back, and legs.

When they were both naked, she stepped close to him and began to stroke his penis until he grew firm. "This is the means of replenishing my power," she stated matter-of-factly as she continued to stroke him. His body was calm and responsive to her, but he was screaming in his head for her to stop. "Sex with any man will suffice, but sex with one under my power will grant me the greatest replenishment."

She stretched out on her back on the blanket she had placed on the grass. She did not seem uncomfortable or awkward about her nudity in front of not only a stranger, but her captive. "Lie on top of me," she said as she spread her legs. His body obeyed. She grabbed his penis once again, rubbed it against the delta of black hair between her legs, then slid him inside her.

She then commanded him to thrust until he climaxed.

Images of Elaysen's face appeared in his thoughts as his pelvis drove against hers. *Please forgive me, I can't stop this. There's nothing I can do.* She spread her legs farther and pulled back her knees with her hands. She closed her eyes and parted her lips. As Gerin continued to thrust, he felt a nebulous haze of energy build around them. It began as a kind of skin-prickling sensation but soon resolved itself into an invisible line of power between them.

And it was drawing something out of him.

His limbs began to tremble as he weakened. His life was

literally flowing into her through the magical connection she had established.

His trembling grew worse. The part of his body under her control released a reflexive grunt of pain. His arms shook so badly he thought he might collapse upon her.

Then he climaxed, spurting at the end of a deep thrust into her. Some invisible power within her flared with heat and energy before it vanished.

"Get off of me," she said. His shaking body complied. "Get dressed and eat. You will be weak for a while. Sleep soon. It will help you recover."

She turned away from him and began to pull on her own clothes. Feeling miserable and defiled, Gerin could only rage at her in his own mind.

28

On the foredeck of the *Uthna Tarel*, the Sword of the Exalted peered through a spyglass at the coast they were approaching, taking in every detail of the land, planning how he would turn what he saw into a tactical advantage against his enemies, or guess how they would attempt to use the lay of the land against him. He saw nothing remarkable. The city they were approaching was large and commanding, and looked to be well defended and fortified with strong walls. *No matter,* he thought as he lowered his glass. *They will fall.*

High Admiral Dragno kan-tel Urit would blockade the city by sea. Later, once the ground forces were in place, Drugal would choke off the city's land supply lines, then work to batter down its walls. It would take time; sieges always did. But time was on their side. They were a patient people. The Havalqa had not conquered two and a half continents on the far side of the sea by being hasty or rash. They knew they were in the right, and that Holvareh and the Powers who served Him watched over and blessed all that they did. Even when they suffered setbacks, their faith in their cause did not waver. They were destined to prevail.

He thought of his home in the Kandurq district of Kalmanyikul, near the massive sandstone walls and terraced pyramid of the Cataar, where the most elite warriors of Herol received their training. Outside of the Pahlujeh Palace itself, the city within a city that was the home to the Exalted, Kandurq was the largest and wealthiest part of Kalmanyikul. Its cobbled streets were broad and open, the squares filled with fountained pools and palm, date, and tanqu trees. Begging was not allowed in Kandurq, nor were any wretches of the Harridan permitted within its border, under pain of death.

His home was perched upon the summit of the Hrajna Hill, a sprawling palace with more than one hundred Elqosi and Keitruni to maintain the grounds and run his household. He wondered how his wife Nelim was faring, and his sons Tureq and Dalma. They were both training at the Cataar now—Tureq as a Second Sword and Dalma as a Knife. Dalma was only six, but he was big and strong for his age, and very quick. *He will do well,* thought Drugal. *He is like me when I was that age. Strong and hungry and full of fire.* Tureq was more thoughtful than his younger brother, taken to contemplation rather than action, but he could more than hold his own with a weapon when necessary, and would go far as a strategist or tactician. He missed them all, but they understood that his duties took him far from home to carry out the Exalted's will.

His sons had never visited the hot sands of Hantab where he grew up. *How far I have come,* he thought as the sea wind blew across his face. *Herol has truly blessed me.* He looked at this new land and felt his destiny calling to him again. He always felt this stirring before a campaign began, a sense of his place in the world and the inevitability of what he was doing.

Tolsadri's arrogant presence aboard his ship fouled his mood, and he'd done his best to maintain a distance from the Exalted's Voice without going so far as to offend him. He knew little of the Voice's life in their homeland. He had no family, no wife or children, at least none that he acknowledged. He was rumored to be a cruel man, taking delight in the torture of prisoners. Drugal had no problem with torture—it was a necessary part of dealing with one's enemies—but some deep part of him was offended by the idea of someone of Tolsadri's rank and stature taking joy in inflicting such pain. It was . . . unseemly.

As if summoned by his thoughts, Tolsadri appeared on the

deck. "When will you send your embassy to demand their unconditional surrender?" Drugal asked without looking over at his counterpart.

"I am not," Tolsadri said flatly. "When I was held captive by them, I presented to their king our terms. I was refused. They will not surrender to us. In our long history, has anyone ever surrendered without a conflict?"

"No. But the laws of in-Palurq must be obeyed."

"You are tedious almost beyond measure. The law has been followed. It is a mystery to me why the Exalted chose one such as you to be her Sword."

"Strange. I was just pondering your own numerous shortcomings."

Tolsadri wheeled on him, furious. "You know nothing of me!"

"Perhaps I will have to rectify that."

"Know this, Sword Drugal," hissed Tolsadri. "One day I will destroy you utterly. I will ruin your name and your house. And before you die, you will know that I have done this to you, and that no harm will come to me because of it."

"Better men than you have threatened me before, Tolsadri. Loremasters die like any other men, though in your pride and arrogance you may think otherwise." Drugal dropped his hand to his sword's hilt. "I will give you this warning but once: threaten my family again and I will separate your head from your shoulders before the breath of your words has left your mouth."

Tolsadri stormed from the deck. Drugal turned back to the sea. The Loremaster had been right: he did know nothing of him. That was something he *would* change; he needed to know the Adept's weaknesses, his points of vulnerability. He would treat him the way he would any enemy he faced upon the battlefield.

He'd considered Tolsadri little more than a deviant, but realized now that he was much more dangerous. To Tolsadri, the games of power were like an oasis to a man dying of thirst in the great Tumhaddi; they were necessary to survive.

Drugal decided he would have to find a way to kill the

Voice. Certainly the Loremaster was plotting the same for him. Wars were dangerous, and even the highest sometimes fell. It might become difficult if suspicion fell on him and the truthsayers became involved, but that was a necessary and unavoidable risk.

Tolsadri would be a casualty of this campaign. When word of his death reached Kalmanyikul, he would be mourned by the Exalted and her court. Great things would be said about him, and then he would be replaced and forgotten. Such was the way of things.

He would see to it personally.

"There is nothing in these records, Warden," said Abaru Mezza as he straightened from the stack of loose parchments he'd just read through in meticulous detail. He stretched his massive arms and rubbed his weary eyes.

"We'll just have to keep looking, Bar," said Rahmdil. He was seated at the table opposite Abaru, with several piles of books spread out around him. He too was tired. He removed his spectacles and pinched his nose between his thumb and forefinger.

"I feel like we've read through half the library," said Abaru.

"I admit, I thought we would have found something by now." Ever since Rahmdil had gone to the Archmage with the alarm amulet—his name for the object he'd found in the bronze box, since it had no name that he could discover— he, Abaru, and a few other wizards had carefully combed through records in the Varsae Sandrova to learn what the amulet was trying to tell them. The Archmage had been adamant that they discover its purpose as soon as possible, but so far they had found nothing other than a single reference to its age.

At first Rahmdil had refused to believe that lone account. He could not imagine that something so ancient had been tossed on a shelf and forgotten. A careful review of the catalogs of the work chamber's contents showed that the amulet was brought to Hethnost by a wizard named Gillen Ulsvar, who also brought records with him that purported to trace the amulet's history back to the time when the Atalari first came to Osseria some fourteen thousand years ago.

But an exhaustive search for Ulsvar's records had turned up nothing. They located several references to the records, but the accounts themselves were nowhere to be found. It was maddening.

Highly specialized and dangerous spells had been used to attempt to determine the amulet's age. Rahmdil was shocked when the spells indicated that it was indeed many, many thousands of years old.

They redoubled their search for Ulsvar's records, again without success. He did not know what to think. Had they been stolen? He wondered if the accursed Baryashins had taken them, or one of the wizards who over the centuries had left Hethnost to live among ordinary mortals. It was forbidden to remove materials from the Varsae Sandrova without the permission of the Warden of the Archives, but over the years valuable objects had mysteriously disappeared when wizards left. A few were later recovered, but most were not.

He returned his spectacles to his nose and, with a heavy sigh, once more began to read the inventory list of the library's subterranean chambers, hoping the answer lay somewhere in a long-forgotten vault.

Rahmdil was alone in his work chamber on a rainy afternoon when Kirin Zaeset, the Warden of Healing, strode in through the open door. He looked shaken. He held in his hands a small book bound in black leather. The book was oddly shaped, and despite being saturated with preservation spells that Rahmdil could sense from his seat, it was near to falling to pieces.

"Kirin, are you all right?" he asked. Kirin had decided he would physically search the vaults below the library in case there were items not in the indexes.

"I found what the amulet is for." He placed the book on the table. It was written in an archaic form of Osirin. The ink had almost faded completely from the pages. Rahmdil had to hold the book an inch from his nose to read it.

"Where did you find this?"

"In one of the fourth level vaults. I think it might be one of the records Ulsvar brought back with the amulet itself. It's the diary of an Atalari who went off to fight in the Last Battle of the Doomwar. He was an aristocrat of some kind. Before he left he bequeathed the amulet to his young son. This"—he pointed toward the faded writing—"is his account of that."

"Is this the *original* diary?"

"I believe so. If not the original, then a copy made almost as long ago."

Rahmdil was aghast. "How could we have overlooked this! This might be older than the Ammon Ekril!" It seemed a lapse of inconceivable incompetence that this ancient diary should have been misplaced.

"Please, Rahmdil, read it."

Rahmdil squinted through his spectacles and read what he could. Some words he did not know; others had faded beyond legibility. But he could read enough to understand it.

> *Tomorrow I leave for . . . to meet the Aestanulinar and make ready for our march against the dragonlord and his . . . beasts . . . fire. Earlier I gave Brethe the Vanilë-torgaetha, the oldest heirloom of our house, brought from the lost . . . lands . . . by . . . said to be blessed and invested . . . grace of . . . by Emunial herself. Brethe understands how precious . . . shed many tears. He knows I will not return.*

Rahmdil lowered the book. "The 'Siren of the Vanil'? That cannot mean what I think it does. Is he talking about the mythic beings of prehistory?"

"As far as I can tell, that is exactly what he is referring to."

Rahmdil paused to gather his thoughts. The Vanil were creatures of legend that inhabited Osseria millennia before the Atalari migrations. There were fragments of records from the Forgotten Years in which the Atalari spoke of the Vanil with great fear, but it was never clear whether the Vanil were actual beings or fearsome creatures of myth. They were no longer in Osseria when the Atalari arrived, but there were accounts of the Atalari finding long-abandoned ruins tens of thousands of years old that struck them with such dread that some considered returning to their homelands in the West beyond the Barrier Mountains. Rahmdil had never given those accounts much credence; they seemed stories or legends rather than descriptions of actual events.

Somehow the Atalari had learned that the Vanil devoured the souls of other sentient beings. To be killed by a Vanil was to be denied the afterlife, to be consigned to oblivion and nonexistence. It was not known what had happened to the Vanil. If such knowledge had ever existed, it was lost to history.

"So this amulet, this Siren of the Vanil, is telling us what, exactly?"

"There is a description of it later in the diary. I won't make you strain your eyes any further trying to read it. The amulet is an alarm, set to activate when a very specific condition is met."

"And what is that condition?"

"When a living Vanil returns to the world."

29

As they neared the coast, Gerin and his captors saw increasing signs of large-scale troop movements through the country. *My father has summoned his vassals,* he thought as they rode across the days-old path of several hundred armored men and horses heading southeast. The signs of their passage could not be missed: a wide swatch of earth churned from the shod hooves of heavy destriers on either side of the narrow hard-packed road that emerged from the hills to the north like a winding ribbon, the charred remains of cook fires, the smell of burned wood still lingering faintly in the air, the gnawed bones of hastily eaten meals, latrine trenches buzzing with flies, bits of torn tent fabric, and other telltale signs of the passage of armed men. These would have been the soldiers of Earl Tulweck of Feormel. His gaze followed the path back to the northwest. From their present location he could not see the hillock atop which perched Castle Geithos, the earl's home—the castle lay at least a dozen miles distant, and was hidden behind an undulating line of forested hills, but there was no one else who could have mustered so many men in this region of Neldemarien.

His heart sank at the thought of more warfare in Khedesh, ravaging the country, killing the gods only knew how many good men, called from their hearths and homes to fight for the lords to whom they had sworn fealty. How many villages and towns would be put to the torch? Images of the

Eletheros slaughter atop the Sundering appeared unbidden and unwanted in his mind, the agonizing extermination of an entire race. *I will not let Khedesh suffer that fate,* he vowed. *Never.*

From his conversations with Katel and Rulhámad over the course of their journey, he'd learned that the goal of these Havalqa was not conquest for land, riches, or vengeance. They would kill only those they had to, to defend themselves or make examples of those who defied their might and righteousness. Their goal, instead, was the conversion of those they conquered to their beliefs and social structure. And if these two were to be believed, the Havalqa had subsumed entire cultures.

Tolsadri had said much same thing, but he had been dismissive of him, assuming his words were little more than boasting because of Tolsadri's haughty arrogance. But then the bastard had managed to escape the dungeons of the Tirthaig itself, a feat never before accomplished in all the long centuries since the palace had been built upon the burned ruins of its predecessor. Clearly, they had underestimated his abilities, which led Gerin to wonder what else about these strange people they might underestimate, to their sorrow. A single woman had managed to come into his castle and steal him away in the dead of night from his very bed. An amber wizard, the most powerful in all of Osseria, captured and held in the unbreakable bonds of this soul stealing witch from across the sea.

It doesn't matter how many other kingdoms they may have conquered and converted. They won't conquer us. We're a strong people. We'll stand together and fight them until they give up and go home. We will never yield. The others they've conquered did not have our resolve. We are the people of Khedesh, descendants of the mighty Raimen of old. The price of our blood will be too high for them.

His heart skipped a beat when he realized that the Pashti, the ancient people who had lived in these lands when Khedesh arrived here and were later conquered by him, might have vowed the very same thing when the Raimen armies first appeared, not realizing they were harbingers of their doom. Did any conquered people ever believe such a thing was possible? Even as they fell, did they hold faith that their own strength or their gods would deliver them from their fate?

When, finally, did a people know they were conquered?

When they came within sight of Almaris they could see a train of at least three thousand soldiers entering the city, along with their squires, attendants, servants, baggage mules, and wagons, threading their way between gawking peasants who had lined up to watch the spectacle or to beg for coins from the lords.

They watched from the skirts of the Tervasé Hills. Rulhámad's creatures were well-hidden farther up the slopes. Gerin could just make out a large number of ships in the Gulf of Gedsuel beyond the city. They were too far away for even his eyes to discern the details of flags or standards, but they were not Khedeshian ships. He realized that the enemy had blockaded the city. From the size of the vessels, and how closely they were arrayed, he doubted that any Khedeshian ships could run the blockade without being captured or destroyed. Still, the land routes were open, and he was sure his father had summoned the navy to break the blockade. Sieges were tests of endurance, and in that they would prevail.

The memory of the Storm King battering through the gates of Agdenor Castle and taking the well-defended fortress in just a few days caused his certainty to falter. His brother had no way of knowing that Asankaru could hurl twisters at the castle, and had no means of defending against them. What surprises did these Havalqa have for them? Did they have powers that could cause the walls of the city to shiver and crumble as if made of no more than sand?

"Defenders march to your city's aid," Rulhámad said to him. "They are fools. To save lives, they should surrender to the Sword now. Defiance is useless."

Katel had not given him permission to speak that day, so he could make no reply to the maegosi. In his mind, he raged

at the small man. *Would the Havalqa surrender if they suffered an invasion? Would you lay down your arms and give
up the only way of life you've ever known because someone
else told you* their *way was better? If you have ever found
a people who surrendered to you without a fight, then they
were not worth the effort of conquering.*

Gerin was taken aback by the size of the invasion force
sprawling across the plains of Hurion a few miles inland from
the sea. He guessed close to twenty thousand men were in
the massive camp, whose miles-long perimeter was bounded
by a palisade of sharpened timbers set atop an earthen rampart. A scarlike trench around the palisade had been filled
with sharpened stakes set at angles in the trench's floor. The
palisade was not yet complete, but more than three-quarters
of the camp was enclosed, and the rest soon would be. There
was a single gate set in each wall, and several watch towers
had been built behind the ramparts. The sun was setting, and
fires were sparking to life in the long shadows cast by the
palisade.

"This is but a fraction of a fraction of our might," said
Rulhámad. "The *vanguard* that marched into the Lurash Ge-
sos numbered more than 100,000. The power of the Exalted
is limitless. The Herolen number more than the stars in the
sky or the grains of sand upon a beach. You would do well to
remember it in the days to come."

Gerin thought it odd that a man condemned to a caste he
loathed so intensely that he had traveled to another continent
for the chance to elevate himself from it would speak with
such pride of the society that kept him beneath its heel and
treated him as something lower than dirt. But as he pondered
the seeming contradiction while they made their way down a
treacherous, rocky slope toward the plain below, he thought
he better understood the maegosi's situation. Of course he
was proud of his people. He loathed his position in his society—he'd made that much clear during their journey, letting
slip occasional comments about the injustices done to the
followers of Tulqan—but that was a predicament he hoped to

change. He craved to move upward in that society, to climb to a caste where he would be both respected and accepted, two things that were now missing from his life. If he hated the society itself, there would be nothing driving him to improve his lot within it. That was why he praised this Exalted of theirs; she represented his ultimate goal. To gain her approval, even indirectly, by becoming part of a caste that she respected, would validate his existence in a way he could not now achieve.

In contrast to Rulhámad, there had to be those who were dissatisfied with the society and its structures and would lash out against it. They would become rebels, insurrectionists, defying the strictures of the culture from without rather than trying to abide by its rules. He wondered how many of the Havalqa chose this option, turning their backs on the rigidity of their world. Did they simply leave, going to lands not yet conquered by the Exalted's apparently long-armed reach? Or did they do what they could to sabotage the society from within?

Rulhámad and his quatans were first to the foot of the hill. He was met by a company of armed soldiers who challenged him in an unfriendly manner, their spears and pikes leveled at him and his creatures while he spoke and gestured up the hill. The soldiers relaxed only a little as they waited for Gerin and Algariq to reach them.

The armor of the soldiers looked odd to Gerin. The Herolen—those who followed the Havalqa's soldier god, Herol, he had learned—wore overlapping plates on their shoulders of intricately scribed steel. Some of the plates were black, others red, but they were not the same from man to man. If they denoted rank, Gerin could not make sense of it. Some of the markings on the plates were etched with silver, but he could not tell if they were words or symbols of some kind, spells of protection, or perhaps a blessing from the god. To his eye, their helmets were elaborately decorative, almost to the point of ridiculousness. They, too, were of black steel, edged in red lacquer, with great amounts of detail molded into the metal. They had a vaguely birdlike shape, with forward-sweeping cheek-guards whose sharp points nearly touched beyond the wearer's nose. The chest plates had ornamental ridges flowing across the steel and were painted with sigils. Skirts of black chain mail hung to their knees over quilted leggings.

The man Gerin assumed was commander of the company, from his attitude and several unique markings upon his armor, began to question Katel as soon as she reined her horse to a halt, his hostility apparent. She hunched her shoulders and stared down at her hands as he spoke, refusing to meet his gaze. They were speaking in their own language, so Gerin had no idea what was being said.

The races of the Herolen were unlike any Gerin had ever seen. The commander himself had skin as black as night, with long straight hair as fine as silk flowing from beneath his helmet, bound between his shoulder blades with a yellow piece of cloth. His nose was long and narrow above thin lips. Above his prominent cheekbones, his eyes slanted upward in the outer corners and were shaped in such a way that the folds of the eyelids disappeared when open. He had an exotic quality that made him seem almost unearthly, as if he'd descended to this sphere of existence from the realm of the divine.

Four or five of the other Herolen were similar in appearance, but others were different. Many had olive skin and looked somewhat like Neddari, with tattoos upon their necks, faces, arms, and hands. Tribesmen of some kind, Gerin guessed, but of course, of what tribe and from where, he could not say.

Others had paler skin, like his own, though with subtle variations to their features that gave them a mysterious, foreign appearance. Some had mouths wider than he was used to seeing, and a few had the tilted eye shape of the commander. Their strange facial features, coupled with their exotic armor, made them look like warriors of legend.

The commander finished his interrogation of Katel and gestured for them to go to the closest gate into the camp. Katel commanded Gerin to follow. The look in her eyes was like that of a dog that had just been beaten, but he hardened his heart against her.

Rulhámad, who had waited patiently to one side with his quatans, bowed to Katel but made no move to join her or Gerin as the company of Herolen parted to let them pass. He said several words to her; her reply was a single nod of her head.

"He goes to find his fortunes elsewhere in this land," she said to Gerin as they crossed the plain toward the camp. "The victory of your capture belongs to me alone. He cannot share it, so there is no need for him to accompany us further."

From behind them, Rulhámad shouted, "Perhaps I will capture your father the king! That would be a prize worth rewarding! Not as great as you, but perhaps enough for my wish to be granted!" His laughter dwindled behind them. Still forbidden to speak, Gerin could say nothing, though inwardly he seethed with hatred at the thought of those terrifying quatans anywhere near his father.

They followed a hard-packed path that led across the trench, up the slope of the rampart and through the open timber gate. Herolen were everywhere: archers, pikemen, infantry, and cavalry. There were thousands of tents within the camp, whose center was occupied by more permanent wooden structures. He saw men and women without armor or weapon—servants or slaves of some kind—scurrying through the lanes formed by the tents. Some of them were Khedeshian, forced to adopt the ways of the Havalqa, but they paid him no heed, and if any recognized him, they did not show it.

One section of the encampment was devoted to the monstrous creatures that Tolsadri had named murdrendi. While some of the creatures were intermingled among the human soldiers—standing guard or patrolling the camp's perimeter—most of them remained separate in their quarter. They were fearsome in appearance, but once he got past his initial revulsion he noticed that there seemed as many varieties of murdrendi in the camp as humans. He could see at least three distinctly different sizes of creature. The largest was gray-skinned, with a head noticeably wider and flatter than the others, and with thicker limbs. The second largest had mottled skin the color of rust. This variety hunched over more than the others when they walked, and had longer arms and hands. Their heads were the roundest of the three, their necks the shortest. The smallest murdrendi had a head crest whose bone flared outward at its peak to form a blunt, rounded end—almost like the rounded tip of a human thigh bone—in contrast to the much sharper crests of the other two. Their legs and feet were shaped differently as well. Their skin had the dark tones of polished mahogany shot through with streaks of yellow. And each variety of creature also had its own distinctive armor. He thought there must be at least five thousand murdrendi in the encampment and the grounds surrounding it.

They passed a group of murdrendi that were eating, huddled over something he could not make out. He did not want to, either: it stank of a charnel house. Flies buzzed around the creatures in clouds so thick they partially obscured his view. They were all bent low, and he could hear wet, tearing sounds as they ripped at whatever meat they'd been provided.

Katel led him through the camp to the coast of the gulf. They left their horses with black-garbed servants and walked across a wide stretch of rocky ground that ran parallel to the beach. Beyond the rocks were the first of two dunes anchored by slender grasses that swayed in the constant breeze. The beach itself was littered with thousands of longboats. Farther out in the gulf, a score of warships were arrayed to protect the encampment from a seaborne assault.

She led him to a group of men loitering near a cluster of longboats. She spoke to them quickly and quietly. They did not verbally disparage her the way the Herolen commander had, but their dislike of her was evident from their expressions.

Four of the men began to drag one of the longboats toward the surf, hauling it with two heavy ropes they held across their shoulders. Gulls whirled overhead, filling the air with their caws, while some of the birds scampered across the sand in search of food.

"I am to take you to the island where we first landed," she said. "I've been told that both the Sword and the Voice of the Exalted are with the fleet that is blockading your city, so a second boat will be send to inform them of your capture. Come with me."

Gerin followed her across the sand and into the waters of the gulf. He climbed into the boat after her, and they were soon rowed toward one of the larger ships anchored at sea. He was overcome with a sudden, deep dread. He did not have the Words of Making, or any knowledge of their existence. Once they realized this, what further use would they have for him? Despite his protestations to the contrary, he feared he would die at the hands of his foes, far from his home, his body thrown into an unmarked grave and forgotten, never to be found or honored.

✦

30

"What news of the king?" shouted Balandrick to a group of men on horseback protecting several wagonloads of goods. They had the look of mercenaries to Therain—hard, heavily muscled men, all of whom were armed with a variety of weapons.

He noticed blue sashes bound about their waists, the mark of Elloharan mercenaries. He knew that less skilled swordsmen sometimes adopted the sashes to make others believe they had been trained in the elite fighting camps that dotted the plains between Serel and Avelneyur, but to attempt such a charade was risky. If true Elloharans happened across them—and they spent much of their time on the roads scouring for signs of impersonators, who only served to harm their reputation and lower their asking price—the imposters would be tortured, sometimes for days. They would eventually be executed, their severed heads impaled on spikes, the false sashes tied across their mouths.

"He was well when we left the city," shouted the lead mercenary. He sounded Elloharan to Therain, speaking with the short clipped accent of someone raised west of the Graymantle Mountains. Now that they were closer, he could also see the kemtar throwing knives arrayed along the man's belt, another sign that the men were genuine Elloharans. The exquisitely crafted knifes were forged for the mercenaries alone—they were not for sale to anyone else, at any price.

"Almaris is preparing for a siege," said the mercenary. "The king's vassals have flooded the city, and both the Taeratens and the City Watch have been mobilized. The invaders have blockaded the sea lanes, and so far it has not been broken."

"What of the Khedeshian fleet?" called out Therain.

The man shrugged. "The bulk of it is still weeks away. Truth be told, I have no idea who these invaders are, or what their grievance is with Khedesh. I've heard rumors that they come from across the sea, but that's nonsense."

Therain was not about to waste time trying to change the man's mind. He could believe what he wanted about the Havalqa. It made no difference.

"Do you know anything about a man named Aunphar el'Turya?" asked Elaysen. "He is also called the Prophet of the One God."

"Don't hold much with religious men. They tend to frown on my line of work. Until they need to pass through dangerous country, that is. Then they want the best, which is always us, and then they always cry foul when they hear our price and try to haggle us down to show respect for their god." He spat onto the ground.

"But to answer your question, no. Never heard of him. I don't think any of my men has either." He glanced over his shoulder at his companions, each of whom shook their heads.

A steady stream of travelers, many of them merchants fleeing an impending war zone with as much as they could haul away, were moving westward along King Olam's Road. The number of people on the road had been increasing almost by the hour for the past two days. They were perhaps a day from the city itself.

But Therain knew that Gerin's kidnapper would not take him to Almaris. It was out of the question. Where, then, would she take him?

"A final question, if I may," said Hollin.

"It better be," the Elloharan replied. "Any more will cost you."

"Do you know if the invaders have reached the mainland yet?"

"Come on, Graezin, we don't got all day," said one of the other mercenaries. Graezin shot him a heart-stopping glare, then turned back to the wizard.

"That *will* cost you," he said. "That's not common knowledge. I've got my sources, and it costs *me* to keep them happy. You can ask a hundred different people behind us, and you'll get a hundred different answers."

"And how do I know your information is any better than theirs?"

Graezin tensed, and for an instant Therain feared he would attack Hollin for insulting his honesty. *We don't need a bloodbath here, wizard. Don't do something stupid.*

"Do you know what this sash means?"

"It's the mark of a sell-sword from Ellohar," said the wizard. "I grant that you are renowned for your fighting abilities and your loyalty to those who pay you. But that says nothing of the accuracy of the information you or your companions claim to have. Why should I believe what you say any more than someone else on this road?"

Graezin's fingers hovered near the handle of one of his kemtar knives, but he made no further move to draw it. "I have contacts in almost every city in Osseria. They're well paid to provide me with the information I want, and if they lie to me, they learn very quickly how costly that is. I have a bag of ears in my saddlebag. Along with a few fingers and a nose or two. Shall I get them for you?"

A grim smile touched Hollin's lips. "That won't be necessary."

"Then when I tell you that the information I have from Almaris is reliable and worth paying for, you can be assured I am telling you the truth. I've given you some leeway, stranger, but don't think to insult me again. Unless you don't mind if your tongue joins the ears in my bag. Maybe it can whisper to them how sorry it is!" He and his men laughed.

Hollin tossed three silver deras to the mercenary. Graezin caught the coins neatly out of the air, examined them, then deftly slipped them into a small satchel around his waist. "The invaders have landed a sizable force on the Hurion just north of the Tervasé Hills. A thousand score of men at least, and growing. Raiding parties have been making incursions into Ulkreon and Delvasi, pillaging villages and towns. From what I've heard, they are taking everyone they find as slaves or captives."

They thanked the Elloharan, then moved off the road to the north and halted in a meadow to confer.

"She's going to take Gerin to the Hurion plains," said Therain. "That's the only thing that makes sense."

"Should we go to Almaris first and get help from the king?" said Elaysen. "He could give us soldiers to mount a rescue."

"Even if he gave us five thousand men—which he won't, since the city's about to come under siege—that wouldn't help," said Therain. "We're not going to get him out using force."

"Do you think they'll keep him with the troops marching on Almaris, or hold him at the landing area?" asked Elaysen.

"They won't take him on the march," said Balandrick. "These invaders are not fools. They may even hold him on a ship to keep him more secure."

"We need to get to the Hurion and see what's going on there before we can decide how to proceed," said Therain. "We're not going to Almaris. My father can't give us anything that will help, and going there will only delay us." No one voiced an objection. "We'll skirt the Whispering Wood and enter the Tervasé Hills from there. They're not as rugged this far west, and we'll be able to cross them quickly. Once we're on their northern side we'll keep to the hills until we reach the Hurion. I hope that by avoiding the plains we'll avoid the raiding parties."

"Elaysen, do you still wish to accompany us?" asked Hollin. "You could go to your father if you wish. No one would blame you."

There was a long silence as Elaysen pondered what she

should do. "My heart is divided," she said. "My father is capable of looking after himself, and if I go to Almaris I'll be trapped there once the siege begins. I would be able to help in the city—healers are ever needed in times of war—but I can also help here. If I leave you now, I don't foresee any way of joining you later." She folded her arms. "I'll come with you. It's not in my nature to abandon a task once begun."

"Very well," said Therain. "Now that that's decided, we ride hard toward the Tervasé Hills."

The first few days of their ride out of Ailethon had been brutally difficult for Therain. Not only did he find it hard to control his horse Peros with only one hand to hold the reins, but his strength was still not fully returned, and by midday he was sweating and exhausted, his wounded arm throbbing with pain. Donael Rundgar rode close by his side in case he wavered and fell, which left him feeling helpless and humiliated. Hollin worked a number of spells to help his pain, but they also dulled other senses, so that he felt as if he rode through a wavering dreamscape, the sounds around him coming to him as if from a great distance, the colors of the grass and trees and sky muted and dreary, as though a shadow or veil had been pulled across the world. Elaysen gave him an elixir each night to help him sleep soundly and restfully, and after he'd described some of the effects of Hollin's spells—which the wizard admitted he could do little about—she fashioned a mixture of powders that would alleviate some of the symptoms. He took the mixture with his water in the morning, and to his astonishment and gratitude, her potions worked just as she said they would.

As the days passed he grew stronger and needed Hollin's spells and Elaysen's medicines less and less. By the tenth day of their journey Therain felt better than at any point since the attack.

They rode along a rutted wagon path that led toward several farms and a small town in the shadow of the hills. If the Elloharan mercenary had been right, their chances of finding Gerin were negligible. How in the holy name of Telros could they hope to get to the Havalqa's most valuable prisoner? He did not think of it as a suicide mission—certainly he had no intention of throwing his life away in a gesture if there were no hope of actually reaching Gerin—but the chance of success seemed bleak, at best.

Still, he had to try. He had a great deal to prove, both to himself and his companions. Besides, it would all be worth it just to see the look on Gerin's face when his little brother rescued him from the clutches of the enemy. *He might almost prefer to remain a captive than have to thank me for saving him. And then he'd have to tell Father!* He laughed aloud, imagining the look of shock.

"Is everything all right, my lord?"

"Fine, Donael. Fine."

They were almost to the northern side of a long-ridged slope when Balandrick caught their first sight of their enemy: a lone rider, maybe a messenger or courier, hunched low in the saddle, riding his horse fast to the east.

Hollin cast a Farseeing and placed it so all of them could peer through it. The view disoriented Balan a little. Hollin turned one hand to keep the spell focused on the rider as he galloped along.

"Definitely not Khedeshian," muttered Donael Rundgar.

Within the misty-edged confines of the spell they could see the rider as if he were but a few yards away. He rode a black and gray charger and was perched in a saddle of odd design. He wore a short gray cloak with blue trim but no other markings that Balan could see.

"Take him alive," said Therain. "We need information. He's no use to us dead."

They watched the rider from a line of trees about a mile above the plain. Between them and the flatlands below lay a sharp-sided gully like a dry riverbed, its bottom choked with rocks overgrown with brambles and thorns. The gully was too deep for the horses to descend into, and just wide enough that they dare not attempt to jump across. But about a thousand yards to the east some resourceful locals had built a small wooden bridge. It wasn't pretty—it had no rails or curb, and was in truth little more than planks nailed to heavy timbers that had been hammered into the earth on each side of the gully—but it looked to be in decent repair, solid enough to support horses moving single file.

"I should remain with you, my lord, in case there are other of these Havalqa about," said Rundgar. "Captain Vaules can handle one lone rider."

"I agree," said Balandrick.

"That's fine, but *get moving* before he disappears! He's riding like Shayphim's Hounds are nipping at his heels."

Balandrick took Hollin and five of the soldiers to intercept the rider. He was already far ahead of them, a distant smudge on the darkening horizon. Balandrick pushed his horse as hard as he could. He was in the lead, with Nerilen and Torrick a few paces back, and the rest behind them. As they neared the bridge across the gully, the soldiers formed a single-file line. Balandrick did not slow at all, and hoped the bridge was as sturdy as it appeared.

He dashed across the planks, which buckled beneath his horse's weight but otherwise held firm. He heard the others cross behind him, the sound of their shod hooves echoing down the gully like a rumble of thunder.

The Havalqa rider was still far ahead of them, but they were slowly gaining. They'd closed the distance to about a hundred yards when he glanced back and caught sight of them. He did not panic or alter his course, merely responded by managing a little more speed out of his horse. Balandrick, however, could see that the rider would not be able to sustain the increased pace for long. Unless there were other Havalqa a lot closer than the coastal encampment, he and his men would overtake him.

Balandrick saw the rider reach carefully into his saddle bag and remove a small object. He did something with it in his hands, then hurled it in a high arc over his head, back toward them.

It struck the ground about twenty yards in front of them and exploded in a column of red and orange flame, churning up a cloud of dirt and smoke. A wave of heat and a sudden press of air washed over them. Aven reared and nearly threw Balandrick from the saddle. The other horses reacted in terror at the sudden explosion. Two of the soldiers were thrown from their mounts and landed hard in the grass.

"Hollin!"

"I don't know what it is!" shouted the wizard, who had managed to remain on his horse and was now riding next to Balan. "Something like Fierel's Fire, only more combustible."

Balandrick didn't care one whit what the wizard thought the explosive was. "Can you take that man down before he throws another one at us?"

"It's hard at this distance while moving, but I'll do what I can."

Hollin extended his right hand. Balan expected to sense the calling of magic, or see some sign that power was being used—a glow or aura around the wizard, a flash of light from his hand—but there was nothing.

Hollin clenched his fingers, and ahead of them the rider fell off his horse backward, as if he'd been tied to a tree and the rope had just extended to its full length. He slammed down hard on his back and did not move. His horse continued to run.

"Can you stop his horse?" Balan asked. "I'd like to see what those things were he threw at us."

"Not easily. It's difficult to hold him while I'm moving like this. To bind his horse as well, while it's running so fast . . ." He shook his head.

"All right. We'll get the horse ourselves."

When they reached the fallen rider, who lay on his back with his arms pinned to his sides by Hollin's power, Balandrick and his men dismounted, drew their swords, and approached warily. "Nerilen, check him for any weapons. I don't want him to blow himself up before we can question him."

Nerilen gave Balandrick a long look, then took a step toward the fallen man. "You sure you're holding him good and tight?" he asked the wizard.

"He can't so much as move his fingers until I release him."

Nerilen crouched down and began to search the man, who let out what was obviously a string of curses in his native language, which Nerilen ignored. "Funny. I can feel something wrapped around his torso, but I can't see nothing at all."

"The power of a Binding is invisible," said Hollin. "Only another wizard could see its presence."

Nerilen grunted and nodded, then resumed his search.

The Khedeshians who'd been dismounted had recovered their horses and arrived. Balandrick sent them after the man's horse. "For the sake of Telros, be careful! That exploding device he threw at us came from his saddlebag. Don't be careless and blow yourselves to Velyol."

Nerilen had recovered several knives and a short sword, but found none of the explosives. The man continued his cursing, and spat once at Nerilen, who cuffed him hard enough to draw blood from his nose.

"That's all he's got on 'im, Captain," said Nerilen as he rose from his crouch.

Balandrick stood over the man and held his sword point toward his throat. His skin was the color of hammered copper, a shade quite unlike anything he had ever seen before. He was young and thin, and not very tall. *Less weight for a faster ride,* he thought. There was a downy fall of beard along his cheeks and chin, and his hair was thick and curly and as black as his armor, with bits of deep reddish hues mixed in.

"What is your name?"

"Kalq'alam sunara azim bar'abathel tulvesam," he spat. *"Talasiq pûl Tulqani!"*

"I don't know what you said, but it doesn't sound very nice," said Balandrick. "Do you understand me? Can you speak Kelarin?"

He snarled again in his native tongue. Balan turned to the wizard. "Can you understand him? Is there a spell that can translate what he is saying?"

"No."

"Any suggestions?"

"None that I can think of. We don't know his language, and if he doesn't know ours, we are at an impasse."

The two soldiers arrived, leading the man's horse, about the same time Therain and the others reached them. "Have you learned anything?" asked the prince as he dismounted.

"Not a bloody thing. This one doesn't speak Kelarin."

"Is anyone hurt?" asked Elaysen. "We saw him throw something that exploded."

"We're fine," said Balandrick. "No one's injured unless Dren or Phaylen bruised their asses when they fell off their horses."

They found two of what they believed were the explosive devices but nothing else of value. There were several folded papers kept in a watertight leather satchel, indicating that the man might well be a messenger, but the writing on it was as alien as his speech. Hollin looked at the pages but could not read a word of it. He took the bag with the devices in them and held them carefully at his side.

"Do you understand me?" said Therain. This time the man said nothing. He simply stared straight up into the sky, refusing to acknowledge their existence. "If you do not speak to us, we'll have no choice but to kill you. I ask again: do you understand me?"

Elaysen looked aghast at Therain's threat. Balandrick wondered how Reshel would have reacted. Would growing up in a royal household with a father who was charged with ordering the executions of criminals have hardened her to this? He knew she had dealt out death herself, on the road home from Hethnost when they found the men who murdered a helpless family in their home. He'd never seen her so furious. Elaysen might believe Therain was bluffing, but Reshel would have known better. The prince meant every word of what he said. The man was no use to them if he could not give them information, and it would be treasonous to release an enemy into the countryside. If he proved useful, they might take him with them for a time, but if not . . .

"My lord, don't you think that —" began Elaysen.

Balandrick put a hand on her shoulder and shook his head once, emphatically. "Not now," he said quietly.

The man refused to speak or look at Therain. The prince repeated his question one more time. Again, the man said nothing. "Hollin, is there anything you can do?"

"I can use a Compulsion to force him to speak, but it won't help us if he doesn't understand Kelarin."

"Will that prove definitively whether he speaks Kelarin or not?"

"Yes. If he knows it, the spell will force him to speak it."

"Go ahead."

Hollin handed the saddlebag containing the devices to Balandrick and stepped closer to the man. Balan held the bag gingerly, worried that he might accidentally set off the remaining explosives. He couldn't decide whether they should take the bag with them so they could use the explosives themselves or simply set them off now, somewhere safe, and be rid of them and the danger they posed.

Hollin still held out his right hand with his fingers partially clenched, gripping the Havalqa in his invisible Binding. He began to speak in Osirin, falling into a lilting singsong chant that Balan found oddly soothing.

Golden fire burst from his left hand. Everyone jumped, including the prisoner, whose eyes were now firmly locked on the wizard. He said something in his native language that sounded like a question.

Hollin continued the incantation. Beads of sweat appeared on his forehead. The chant rose to a fever pitch, then he clenched his fist and thrust it at the prisoner, who flinched and cried out. The flame vanished from his hand.

The wizard straightened and visibly relaxed. "Can you understand me? Do you speak Kelarin?"

The prisoner no longer looked afraid. His expression was blank, the emotionless mask of a corpse being laid to rest.

When the prisoner spoke again, his voice was calm, almost soothing. He continued to use his native tongue. His glassy eyes stared at Hollin though he did not actually see him.

Hollin asked a few more questions, but each answer was in

the man's language, and all sounded the same to Balandrick. *He's probably saying, "I don't understand you." Pity for him. And a shame for us.*

The wizard looked at Therain. "Even if he knows where your brother is being held, he has no way of telling us."

"Then we have no more use for him. We ride on. Captain Rundgar, dispose of the prisoner."

"My lord!" said Elaysen. "Are you truly going to murder this man?"

Therain's expression was grim. "This is not murder. It is the execution of an invader who has set foot upon Khedeshian soil. We are at war, and he is our enemy. I will not set him free, or bind him and allow him to be found by his fellows and set free. He has no information for us, therefore he is of no use." He moved closer to Elaysen. She did not flinch or step farther away. "Do not think to accuse me of murder again. I carry out the king's justice. I will allow it this once, because you are new to the ways of war. But this is the only warning you will receive. If you utter such a thing again, you will regret it."

"I understand, my lord. Forgive me. I misspoke."

"Yes, you did." He turned away from her and climbed back on his horse as Donael Rundgar drove the point of his sword through the prisoner's throat. Blood spurted up the blade in a dark geyser. The man gurgled, his eyes wide, then was still. Hollin lowered his hands and released his magic. Elaysen looked at the prisoner and visibly paled.

She's learned a thing or two today, thought Balan as he tied the dead man's saddlebag to his own with deliberate care. *And I'd wager she'll learn a few more before all is said and done.*

That night Hollin studied the explosive devices they'd taken from the Havalqa rider. They were hardened ceramic spheres filled with at least three distinct substances. "One appears to be similar to naphtha," he said. "But I have no idea about the other two." The substances were separated within the ceramic sphere by flexible membranes. There was a single punch hole in the spheres, which was also covered with a membrane. It appeared that by pressing a finger through the hole, the interior membranes were punctured, allowing the compounds to begin to mix together to create a volatile, explosive substance that either detonated in a few seconds after the mixture began or upon a jarring impact, like slamming into the ground. Hollin could not be sure.

"Should we keep them with us?" asked Balandrick. He'd been nervous riding with them, wondering if a sudden jolt from his horse would blow him to pieces.

"They might prove useful," said Hollin. "The fact that the rider carried them at such a furious pace shows they're relatively stable. But I will carry them if that makes you feel better, Captain."

Balandrick did not hesitate. He made a shooing motion with his hands. "They're yours."

Elaysen sat away from everyone else, eating quietly. She'd said nothing to anyone since they stopped to make camp. Balandrick went over and sat down beside her. "It was a hard thing we did today," he said. "Don't think Prince Therain is heartless. It's never an easy thing to order a man's death, even when he deserves it. I know you don't think that rider did anything to bring on his death—not in the way a murderer or cutpurse does, I mean. But just by being in our lands is a death sentence for foreigners like these. You heard the stories from those people fleeing into the hills. These invaders have killed by the hundreds, and there are tens of thousands of them getting ready to march on Almaris, if they haven't already done so. It is our sworn duty to kill them and drive them from our lands. You have to understand that. Leaving that man alive was not an option."

She nodded without looking at him. "I know that. I truly do. But at that moment it seemed so . . . cold. So casual, as if the man's life was less than nothing."

Balandrick shifted so he could look into her eyes, and sighed heavily. "That is how a soldier thinks, Elaysen. You don't think about an enemy as a man who has a mother and father, maybe a wife and children. You can't. He's someone you have to kill before he kills you. A soldier thinks about *his* mother and father, *his* wife and children, and how he needs to protect them."

"Don't you think our enemies think the very same thing?"

"Of course they do. A soldier is a soldier no matter the land of his birth."

"Then who is in the right? If soldiers are all the same, how can one side be said to be better than the other?"

"You know the answer to that. *They* invaded *our* lands, without cause. We didn't even know these bastards existed. They can't say we've wronged them in any way, that they've come here to claim reparations or some nonsense like that. Besides, it's not a soldier's job to figure out who's right. A soldier's job is to follow orders and win the day. It's for princes and kings to know the *why* of war."

"So did the Raimen wrong the Pashti when they came to these lands and conquered them in the name of Telros? The Pashti did nothing to the Raimen; they did not even know those 'bastards' existed."

"I won't argue history. What's done is done. All I can do is protect our country and our families."

She looked at him at last. "I don't know whether you've made me feel better or not, Balan."

"War's not something you're supposed to feel good about. But you do need to understand it. There's more killing to come. That I guarantee. And you need to understand that and come to terms with it, or it will be the end of you."

Toward evening two days later they neared a long ridge across their path. Balandrick halted their company before they reached the summit and sent Nerilen and Torrick forward on foot to see what lay below. The men dropped to the ground and arm-crawled their way to the gentle drop. They lay there for several minutes before returning.

"It's hard to see, what with it gettin' dark an' all," said Nerilen. "The far side of the ridge drops away toward a wooded valley. There's enemy soldiers in a camp near the edge of them woods."

"You're sure they're not Khedeshians?"

"Not unless we started enlisting monsters, sir. There're some things down there that definitely ain't human."

"And you weren't seen?"

Nerilen looked offended by the question. "Shayphim's blood, no sir! We're not fools. We know how to hide right and proper."

"I want to take that camp," said Therain. "We still need to find out where they're holding Gerin."

"Is there a way to get down the ridge without being seen?" asked Donael Rundgar.

"The ridge is pretty flat," said Nerilen. "Most of it's just grass an' some rock, but to the right a few hundred yards away there's a fairly thick line of trees that runs most of the way down to the valley. Should provide cover. Are we plannin' to move at night? We're sure not to be seen then, unless Captain Vaules decides to fart or sneeze at a bad time." He gave Balandrick a wry smile. Balan ignored him.

"I think we should move now," said Therain. "We can get closer to them and take them by surprise. If we wait for daylight, they'll be moving again and we won't be able to hide our pursuit."

They formulated a plan as the darkness deepened around them. Hollin would lead them down the slope since he had the most night-sensitive eyes and could most easily find a clear path. Therain wanted to join the attack, but Balandrick and Donael Rundgar would have none of it. "These aren't the men holding Prince Gerin," said Balandrick. "You'll get your chance, my lord, but not here, not now. They may know nothing at all about him, or be unable to speak Kelarin. You're not going to risk yourself on something that may have no value to us."

Balandrick could see Therain fuming. "You're right," the prince said at last. "I don't like it, but I'll stay here with Elaysen and Captain Rundgar. Take the rest with you. You'll need them more."

The captains decided that two additional soldiers would remain with Therain in case they were happened upon by other enemy troops. When they were ready, Therain wished them luck. They left their horses and followed the rim of the ridge—far enough back from its edge that they could not be seen from below—to the point where the line of trees made a meandering descent. "We'll be done soon," whispered Balandrick. Then he followed Hollin into the trees.

The land beneath the trees was a treacherous stretch of ground, with rocks and the gnarled tree roots poking from the dirt. Hollin made his way down as silently as a cat, but even though Balandrick tried to place each foot where he thought the wizard had placed his, it seemed he was as loud as an enraged bear. The men behind him fared little better. He realized that what sounded loud to him more than likely did not carry even through the trees, and certainly could not be heard in the camp, whose just-lit fire gave them a nice bright goal they could use to orient themselves for their approach.

After what seemed an eternity, they reached the valley floor. "We'll move a short distance into the woods to mask our approach," Hollin whispered to him. Balandrick nodded, then gestured for the other men to follow and keep close.

The footing in the woods was even more treacherous than on the slope. It seemed that dry twigs snapped beneath every other footfall. Balandrick winced each time he heard one. Small animals fled from them, creating more noise as they crunched across fallen leaves and deadfall. But there was nothing to be done. It would be nearly as loud if they left the trees and skirted along their edge, with a much greater chance of being seen as they got closer.

They saw a perimeter guard about thirty feet from them, staring out into the darkness away from the trees, oblivious to their presence. Using hand signals he hoped his men could see in the dark, Balandrick ordered the four men with crossbows to take up positions at wide intervals at the edge of the woods. When everyone was in position, he gave Hollin the signal to proceed.

A second later Hollin used his magic to make the fire flare into a raging pillar of light extending at least thirty feet into the air. Balandrick could feel the sudden wave of heat on his body. The flare lasted only a few seconds before it consumed its fuel, but that was all the time they needed.

The perimeter guards spun around to see what had happened. Balandrick and the others had averted their gaze so their night-adjusted vision wouldn't be completely ruined by the sudden brightness. As soon as the fire collapsed, he turned his head back to survey the scene. The reflex that had the perimeter guards wheel toward the bright light wrecked their vision for a brief time, as planned. But these Havalqa were well-trained. The guards all spun back around almost immediately, aware that the fire might be nothing more than a diversion.

Balandrick heard the sound of crossbows firing, followed by the dull thuds of four quarrels striking their targets. The two nearest perimeter guards went down, as well as two of the creatures nearer to the edge of camp. He thought these must be the same beings Gerin's uncle had fought on Gedsengard—murdrendi, he thought they were called. Sprinting through the trees, he crouched low, no longer concerned about sound but in moving as fast as he could. He counted to four in his head and heard the crossbows fire again.

The camp had erupted in confusion when Hollin worked his magic on the fire, which had since been reduced to smoldering cinders that cast only a dim red light. The soldiers recovered quickly, drawing their weapons and assuming a defensive posture around the central tents. The nearest Havalqa heard him and wheeled around, but it was too late; Balan's throwing knife was in the man's throat.

Another volley of quarrels took out the Havalqa bowmen who were nocking their own arrows. Balan saw Hollin charge out of the trees on his right, his hands wreathed in golden fire. *That's a sight that should give them pause,* he thought, then had to focus his attention on another Havalqa who was sprinting toward him. He feinted as if lunging left, then threw his weight to the right and crouched low, swinging his blade around in an attempt to cut the man's legs from under him. The soldier, prepared for the feint, swung his sword low in a backhanded arc, deflecting Balan's blade with ease. Balandrick regained his feet as his opponent's momentum carried him past. The huge, thick-armed man with streaming black hair turned about and raised his sword to defend against the thrust he knew was coming. He caught some of Balandrick's blade, but not enough to fully stop it. The sword slid against the man's own weapon with a shrieking noise of steel on steel and drove into his left side, just below his ribs. A serious wound, but not immediately fatal, or even enough to incapacitate a soldier such as this one, caught up in the heat of battle. Balan yanked his long curved knife from his belt and slashed it across the man's throat before he could recover. Blood gushed from the wound as the soldier's head fell backward.

Hollin had captured three or four men with his magic, presumably the commanders and those most likely to know Gerin's whereabouts and to speak Kelarin. He'd also erected defenses around himself. Balandrick saw one of the Havalqa hack at the wizard with his sword, which rebounded off an invisible barrier. A quarrel thudded into the man's chest just as he raised his weapon to attack Hollin again. The sword flew out of his hand and spun wildly through the air as the force of the quarrel drove through his breastplate and lifted him off his feet. A fine mist of blood sprayed through the air and landed upon Hollin's barrier, where it dripped down as if on glass.

The Havalqa had by now realized the attack was coming solely from the woods, but it was too late for them to use that to their advantage. Balandrick and his men had already killed more than half the company and were now fighting mostly man-to-man throughout the camp. His men were clustered around the murdrendi, who were using their pikes to devastating effect. A number of the Khedeshians were down, run through or slashed viciously by the creatures.

Hollin was using what extra magic he could spare to create fleeting barriers to impede the movements of the enemy soldiers. Balandrick watched as one man fell down in front of him, as if he'd tripped over a taut ankle-high rope, though nothing visible was there. The man sprawled in the dirt. Balandrick knelt down and clubbed him hard on the back of the neck, then threw his weapon into the grass. He wanted as many alive as possible.

He turned to see a murdrendi bearing down on him. The thing thrust its pike toward his breastbone. Balan barely managed to deflect the thrust with his own weapon. He leaped to his left and slashed at the murdrendi's exposed leg, opening it to the bone. The thing shrieked in rage and pain and swung its pike in a sideways slashing motion. The shaft of the pike slammed into Balandrick's ribs with bone-cracking force and knocked him from his feet.

The murdrendi tried to impale him as he lay there, but he rolled to the side and it missed, the point of its pike embedding in the ground. Balan then hacked off its left forearm below the elbow; dark blood jetted from the stump. He was about to drive his sword point into the thing's heart—or where he hoped its heart was—when its head fell cleanly from its shoulders, as if its neck had been sheared through with Black Willem's sharpest axe.

"What in Shayphim's bloody name . . . ?"

"I thought you could use the help," called out Hollin.

"What did you do?"

"I created a Warding through its neck. It's an ancient form of execution once used by wizards."

"It's definitely handy."

Balandrick heard someone running toward him from behind.

"Captain, are you all right?" shouted Torrick.

"I'm fine." He looked around. The camp seemed almost calm. "What about the attack?"

"Looks to be just about done, sir. We won."

✳ 31

The rest of the night was a blur for Balandrick. Five Khedeshians had fallen. Three had been slain by the murdrendi, the other two by enemy quarrels before the crossbowmen could be taken out by his men. Seven others were wounded, though none seriously.

Hollin still had the commanders held in Bindings. They were on the ground near the embers of the dying fire. They were conscious, and furious, to judge by their expressions.

The wizard looked exhausted. "I'll see to your injuries shortly," he said. "I'm sorry, I can't do anything more until I release these Binding spells. It would help me greatly if you would have your men tie them up."

Balan coughed and saw more blood on his hand. Behind him, the other Khedeshians were tending to their wounded, binding the injured or unconscious enemy soldiers, and making sure that those who appeared dead really were by driving their sword points through their throats.

"Right away." Balan barked orders. His voice was hoarse and low, his throat slick with blood. *I hope Elaysen gets here soon,* he thought. *Maybe she can do something for me.* He could feel the grinding of his broken rib with each step he took. The pain was excruciating, and several times he thought he might pass out.

When the enemy commanders were bound with rope, Hollin visibly relaxed. "Lie down, Balan. It will be easier for me to see what's wrong with you."

Hollin created a Seeing spell to determine the extent of Balandrick's injuries, then set to work repairing his rib and a slight puncture in his lung. Balan felt a liquid warmth coursing through his torso, the heat blossoming in the areas where his injuries were the most severe.

"Your rib will be fragile for a few weeks," said Hollin when he was finished. "Have Elaysen bind it for you when she arrives."

"Gods above me, Hollin, I can't keep my eyes open . . ."

"That is the way of healing spells. They draw upon your own strength to help your body mend itself. Sleep for a while. I'll tell Prince Therain what happened when he gets here."

Hollin's final words sounded very far away. Balandrick's eyes were already closed, and before he'd taken five breaths, he was asleep.

He woke groggily. He forced his eyes open and saw Elaysen peering down at him, smiling. "Welcome back," she said. "Hollin told me about your rib. Sit up and I'll bandage it for you."

He did as she asked, waiting patiently while she wrapped a linen cloth about his torso. "I've made an elixir I want you to drink," she said as she tucked in the end of the bandage.

He propped himself up on his elbows. He felt light-headed and a little dizzy. "Thank you." It was still fully dark. The fire had been rekindled to provide some light. "How long . . . ?"

She shrugged. "An hour, maybe. It's hard for me to judge at night."

He sipped the foul-smelling cup Elaysen handed him, his nose wrinkling. "Gods above me, this tastes awful."

"Don't be a baby, just drink it down quickly."

He did as he was told. "Have they spoken to the Havalqa commanders yet?"

"They tried, but they aren't talking. Rundgar hurt one pretty badly. He broke all of the man's fingers on his right hand, then cut three of them off before Therain told him to stop." She spoke matter-of-factly, but there was a tightness around her eyes and mouth that made it clear she did not like what she had seen. "The man had barely broken a sweat. Hollin seems to think they've been trained or conditioned to withstand torture."

"No one can be trained to hold out against torture. Every man can be broken. Always. It's only a matter of time, but that's one thing we don't have."

He struggled to his feet. The bandages were heavy and tight; it was hard for him to draw a deep breath.

She helped him over to the fire. "How are you, Captain?" asked Therain.

"I'll be fine, my lord. Hollin and Elaysen have patched me up nicely."

"You did good work here. We tried to interrogate one of the men, but he proved resistant to Captain Rundgar's persuasions. Hollin will use a Compulsion once he's strong enough. I think that will be faster and more effective than trying to break him by other means." Therain faced the wizard. "Do you feel up to questioning these men yet?"

"One, at least. We'll see how my strength holds."

All of the bound Havalqa commanders were still awake and glared at them with naked hatred and contempt. Hollin stepped closer to one of the men and extended his hand, then began the Compulsion incantation. Golden fire enveloped Hollin's hand as the spell neared its completion. The prisoners watched with a mingled look of terror and wonder. The man to whom Hollin directed his magic trembled in his bonds.

When the prisoner relaxed and regarded Hollin expectantly, the wizard asked, "Do you understand me? Do you speak our tongue?"

The prisoner nodded. "Yes. It was taught to me, and most of command rank, in preparation for our voyage." His accent was heavy and strange, but he was perfectly understandable.

Therain stepped forward. "Where is my brother being held? Prince Gerin Atreyano. He was taken by a woman who can take control of the minds of others."

"The soul stealer. A wretch of Tulqan, but useful. She was

commanded to transport him to the island we have captured.
I do not know its name."

"Gedsengard," said Therain. "What else do you know of
my brother? Has he been well treated? Do you know where
on the island they're holding him?"

"I can say nothing of his treatment. I did not see him. As to
where he is being held, I do not know. There is a castle on the
island, built into the side of a cliff, that overlooks the town. I
would guess he is there."

The prisoner spasmed, his muscles going suddenly taut,
as though a fire had been kindled beneath him. Hollin shook
his head as if to clear it. "My lord," he said quietly, "the
Compulsion is beginning to fail. Finish soon, or we'll have
to resume this later."

Therain nodded without looking at the wizard. "Is my
brother on the island or still within your encampment?"

"He is gone. He sailed five days ago."

So we're off to Gedsengard, thought Balandrick. *And
what if they decide to take him back to their homeland,
wherever that is? Can we chase him across the Maurelian
Sea?* For the first time since they'd set out to reclaim Gerin,
Balandrick felt overwhelmed with despair. *I will never see
him again. Our cause is lost.* When they set out, they were
chasing a lone woman who had managed to spirit away the
prince. It seemed a relatively simple thing to overtake them
and wrest Gerin from her clutches. After all, from what Hollin and Mori Genro had said, it appeared that she needed to
touch a man in order for her power to work. There was no
way she could touch all of them once they were found, and a
well-placed arrow in her chest would put an end to her powers quickly and permanently. He thought they would rescue
the prince in a matter of days.

But then word had come of the massive invasion of Havalqa,
the impending siege of Almaris itself, and the situation became a great deal more complicated. Their own country was
now dangerous for them, filled with invaders they needed to
avoid. And what if they did take Gerin to their homeland?
What then?

No, they will keep him here, in these lands, he told himself. *They need him to find the Words of Making, which they said are here in Osseria. Taking him away accomplishes nothing. They have control of Gedsengard. That's why they took him there. To ensure that he did not leave until he gives them what they want.*

Therain asked a few more questions, about the number of soldiers in the encampment and how well it was fortified. When he was finished, he gestured to Hollin, who released his hold on the Compulsion. The man spasmed and lapsed into unconsciousness.

"There's nothing more we need from them," said Therain. "Kill them, and the rest of the invaders. I'll not be saddled with prisoners on this journey."

"Aye, my lord," said Donael Rundgar, who quickly and efficiently slit the prisoner's throat. Hollin relaxed as he released the draining power of his Compulsion. Balandrick saw Elaysen turn and walk away while the rest of the prisoners were executed.

He's grown hard, thought Balan as he regarded Therain. The prince stared coldly at the corpse of the man who'd answered his questions, his expression stony and pitiless. *Paying them back for the loss of his hand. And who can blame him?*

Balandrick remembered the boy Therain had been, living in his older brother's shadow for so long it seemed he would be lost there, swallowed by the darkness, never able to step into light of his own. A young man unsure of himself and his place in the world. A royal son, yet a second son, an afterthought in many ways, both to his father and everyone else. Not that Abran had ever been cruel to Therain—most of his ruthlessness was spent on Gerin, preparing the son who would take the throne after him—but Balan realized that being ignored for most of one's life could be a different kind of cruelty. Therain had always questioned his worth because of it. Claressa held such a high opinion of herself that Telros himself could not persuade her otherwise. It was as if in the womb she had leeched away Therain's confi-

·dence. The gods knew she had enough for two or three men, at least.

But to look at Therain now . . . he was scarcely the same person. The Neddari War and the siege of Agdenor had been an incredible trial for him, a hard test that burned away any softness. Still, to Balandrick it seemed that some of the prince's old doubts and uncertainties had awakened within him again. *He wants to rescue Gerin as a way to prove his own worth,* he thought. *To show his father—and himself— that he is deserving of the name Àtreyano.*

The last of the Havalqa soldiers was dead. "What is your command, my lord?" said Balandrick.

"We rest for now, and ride hard at dawn. And the gods help anyone else who gets in our way."

32

The following morning they came across a group of homesteads nestled along the knife-edged hills separated from the dense tangle of woods by a long strip of relatively open land. The houses, barns, sheds, and a small tabernacle dedicated to Volraneth and Merel, were completely deserted. There were no bodies, no freshly dug graves, no dead livestock.

"The enemy has taken them," said Therain as he and Donael Rundgar emerged from the largest house.

"Slave labor for their camp, most likely," said Hollin. "They have no value as hostages."

How many other homes are like this? Therain wondered. *Empty, abandoned, the people snatched from their beds, weeping with fear, wondering why the might of Khedesh wasn't smashing the invaders to bits.* He felt his blood grow hot. *I will see them all dead, I swear it!*

"How, exactly, are we going to reach Gedsengard?" asked Balandrick when they stopped later that day to rest and water their horses. "We have no ship, and the Havalqa hold the coast ahead of us. We can't go back to Almaris because of the blockade, which means we'd have to go even farther south to find an open seaport."

"Let's eat, and then I'll tell all of you what we're going to do," said Therain. He sat down with his back against a tree and sipped some water from his water skin. The others, sensing his dark mood, left him alone.

When they finished their meager and hasty meal, Therain removed a watertight leather cylinder from his saddlebag. He untied one end and unrolled four maps he'd brought with him from Ailethon. "Master Aslon provided me with these before we left," he said as he placed stones on the corners of one to hold it flat. It showed the forested valley they were in, as well as the rocky highlands to the north. On its right side, the map showed land all the way to the Gulf of Gedsuel; the waters had been painted a pale blue-green. There was a large open area to the north of the Blackwater Marsh, sandwiched between the bog and the highlands. The valley they were in widened into a barren plain—the Hurion—a dozen miles before it reached the coast.

Therain pointed to the open area along the beach. "That is where the enemy encampment is. Gedsengard lies seventy miles or so off the coast, though it's not on any of the maps I have here." He produced another parchment, which showed the hills to their north, all the way into Threndish territory. There was an emblem of a castle in the high hills near the coast. "This is Castle Pelleron, the home of Baron Thorael. It's very well-protected, seated on high bluffs with only two means of approach. Both are winding stairs cut into the cliff face on either side of the promontory it sits upon. I doubt the enemy has taken it. It seems their attention is turned to Almaris for now. They may try to bottle the baron in, but I'd bet a hundred deras he still holds the castle itself."

"How does that help us?" said Elaysen. "Even if the baron is unmolested in his castle, if the enemy is between us and them . . ."

"There are paths through the Belkan Hills," said Therain. "I'm hoping we can avoid the enemy in the rough terrain and make our way to the southern stair."

"I see no other alternative," said Hollin. "Any other course will simply delay us further, and we cannot afford to lose any more time."

"My lord, does the baron have access to ships?" asked

Elaysen. "I'm afraid we'll reach his castle only to become trapped there with him."

"There's a sheltered inlet to the north of Pelleron that's home to a small fishing village. I can't remember its name, and it's not on this map, but I was there once with my father when he visited the baron. Thorael keeps several ships there. That's where the northern stair from the castle leads. I'm hoping we can get one of those ships to take us to Gedsengard."

"Assuming the invaders haven't taken the fishing village, or the baron hasn't sent all of his ships to the defense of Almaris," said Elaysen.

"Ever the pessimist," said Balandrick, but Therain saw him wink at Elaysen to show he was teasing her. "There are unknowns in any direction we might take. This is the best option available to us."

"I understand. I'm not trying to be contrary, but it seems to me that any path we take is hopeless."

"Not hopeless," said Therain. "Difficult, yes, but not hopeless."

"It's just unfortunate that the chase has to end on that gods-forsaken isle," said Balandrick. "Too bloody far to swim, that's for sure."

"I have faith in you, my lord," said Elaysen. "Where you lead, I will follow."

A few miles on they found a narrow, meandering line of hard-packed dirt that led up into the Belkan Hills. It was not on any of Therain's maps, but he decided to take it anyway. "Best to get out of this valley before we run across more patrols," he said. "There's bound to be more of them the closer we get to the coast."

That night they camped in the shelter of a narrow canyon. Just beyond their campsite the canyon bent hard to the left, then angled up toward the summit of one of the higher hills in the area. Balandrick had scouted ahead before it grew dark. "This canyon empties out onto a rocky shelf a few hundred yards below the top of the hill. In the morning we'll have a good view from there."

Heavy clouds rolled in during the night, and though it did
not rain, the next day was gray and overcast, the light dim.
They followed the canyon to the summit of the hill, but their
view was obscured by a veil of haze. They heard thunder
grumble in the distance and saw several flashes of lightning
to the northeast. "That looks to be coming our way," said
Balandrick, gesturing toward the charcoal wall of clouds
that formed a backdrop against which the lightning flashed.
"Rain will be here by midday at the latest."

"We should get down from the heights," said Hollin. "It
will be dangerous up here once the storm arrives."

A torrent of rain washed over them early in the afternoon.
They continued awhile before stopping for the day and hud-
dling against a vertical rock face that offered some scant shelter from the wind, though none from the rain. They waited
there, wet and miserable, while sheets of rain poured across
them and thunder boomed across the hills, some blasts so
loud the rock beneath their feet seemed to tremble.

The storm abated sometime in the night, moving off to the
west, and they awoke to clear, cool skies. They proceeded
deeper into the hills, moving always to the northeast, at least
as much as the terrain allowed. At times they had to nearly
double back on their path to circumvent impassable spires of
rock or cliff faces as high as the walls of Almaris. "It's like a
bloody maze in these hills," Therain heard Balandrick mutter after they'd had to double back for the third time that day.
The prince wondered if he'd made a mistake taking them
into the hills as early as he had. He'd hoped to find a more
or less straight path toward the castle, but the Belkans were
proving to be a formidable obstacle.

"We're going to have to swing back toward the south
soon," he said one evening. They were high on the slope of a
granite-capped peak that rose like a spear point from the
lower hills surrounding it. His eyes were moving between
one of the maps he held and the hills to the east. "The Belkans are just too rugged north of here. We won't be able to
get to the castle's northern stair. That leaves the southern
stair, the one that leads up from the plain at the end of the

valley we were in. I was hoping we could reach it through the hills, but I don't think we can." He pointed due east. "Look at those peaks. They're like knife blades. The hills between us and the stair are just too difficult to cross. We have to move closer to the valley to find the stair."

"But then we'll have to worry about Havalqa patrols again," said Elaysen.

"Yes, but we'll take a southeastern path out of the hills, which should put us pretty close to the stairs once we reach the valley. We won't have much open land to cross. Not nearly as much as we would have had."

"The base of the stairs is likely to be watched by the enemy," said Balandrick.

"Improvising is one of the great arts of soldiering, is it not?" said Therain. "Nothing is ever as simple as we would like. Once we see exactly what we're facing, we'll figure out a way to get to Pelleron. One step at a time, Captain. One step at a time."

Once back in the valley, they saw signs that a large company of riders had recently passed. "At least a hundred horsemen," said Balan as he surveyed the trampled grass. "Moving quickly but orderly. I'd say not more than a day in front of us."

"Are we sure they're enemy troops?" asked Elaysen. "Maybe they're Khedeshians."

Balandrick straightened and rubbed the stubble along his jaw. "It's possible, but doubtful. There aren't any garrisons near here, and if there were, they should be riding toward Almaris."

"They could be vassals of Baron Thorael, summoned to his aid," said Donael Rundgar.

"True, but we can't take that chance," said Therain.

The valley here had grown to several miles in width. To the south, the Tervasé Hills were little more than a faint line rising above the forest in the distance.

They continued for the better part of a day and saw no sign of either friend or foe. The Belkan Hills here were more

gentle on their southern face than their brethren to the west;
to the north were the knifelike peaks that had defeated them,
massive faces of sheer-sided stone and shadow-filled clefts.

"Castle Pelleron is in those higher peaks," said Therain,
pointing to the northeast.

"How far to the stair?" asked Elaysen as they climbed the
first of the hills.

"Hard to say," said Therain. "I was only there once, and
didn't come from this direction. I'd guess from where we are
and what these maps say, it's perhaps ten miles ahead."

They found a hunting path and decided to follow it. A few
miles ahead the path paralleled a meandering stream whose
banks were lined with old willow trees, their long drooping
branches dangling over the water like the arms of old men
too tired to straighten. A bit farther on the stream hooked
sharply to the left, across their path, and disappeared into a
rocky cleft. The path continued on the far side of the stream
and around the foot of a long humped-backed hill. The path
turned again at the far end of the hill, opening into a broad
shallow valley.

That was when they caught their first sight of the village.

It was ringed with a patchwork of farming fields and fenced
grazing pastures. The village was comprised mostly of timber houses with thatch roofs, though one or two buildings
appeared to be made of fieldstone. The houses were huddled
together, like soldiers who'd closed ranks to form a defensive
perimeter, though a scattering of homes and other buildings
fell outside of the central area, dotting the landscape like
lone sentries.

"I don't see anyone moving down there," said Balandrick.

"Neither do I," said Hollin. "Four or five of the houses appear to have been burned. The place is deserted. The people
have either fled or been taken by the enemy."

Therain swore silently, overwhelmed with a sudden, helpless rage. "Let's see what we can find," he said through
clenched teeth.

The path continued all the way to the village, threading
through rows of half-grown wheat. When they were closer,

they could see that the damage to the village was more extensive than they first thought. In addition to the burned houses clustered together along one of the larger avenues, most of the windows in nearly every building had been cracked or shattered, and many of the doors battered down or torn from their hinges. Two broken-down wagons, their wheels splintered into little more than kindling, littered the square at the center of the village like wooden corpses.

There were signs of fighting everywhere. Pitchforks and knives lay in the dirt. They entered a few of the homes and saw overturned and broken furniture, and dried blood on some of the floors, but no bodies.

They split up as they walked through the village. Behind one of the houses, Therain's group found fresh graves. Nineteen in all, laid close together. "At least they had the decency to bury those they killed," said Elaysen.

"Small comfort to those who find themselves with Bellon," said Therain. "Or to the survivors taken away in bondage."

Elaysen bowed her head and said a prayer for the dead.

"My lord, should we camp here for the night?" asked Donael Rundgar.

Before Therain could reply, Hollin, who had moved off by himself, returned, racing toward them. "There are enemy troops coming from the south, heading this way," he said, gesturing.

"Shayphim's bloody Hounds," said Therain. "Where are they? How close?"

"At the edge of this valley. Here, see for yourself." Hollin spoke quickly and held up his hands about two feet apart. A Farseeing appeared in the air and resolved into a view of the southern slope leading out of the valley.

Therain could see well over a hundred Havalqa soldiers marching toward the village in formation. "At least there are no horses. Do they know we're here?"

"I don't think so. They don't seem in a hurry, and aren't making any attempt to conceal themselves. Thank Venegreh we haven't lit any fires."

Therain turned to Captain Rundgar. "Gather everyone on

the north side of the village. Hurry, and be quiet about it. Come on, Hollin."

He, Elaysen, and the wizard rushed through the town square and up the wide rutted avenue toward the village's northern end. A few soldiers were already there, waiting in their saddles. The remainder of the company arrived quickly. Hollin created another Farseeing to check on the approach of the Havalqa. They'd covered about a third of the distance to the village but still did not appear to have seen the Khedeshians.

"What is your command, my lord?" said Balandrick.

Therain looked to the northern rim of the valley, whose flat floor rose up in several waves of increasingly higher hills, like a rug bunched up against a wall. Beyond these lower slopes were rockier hills. Therain thought he spied a cleft in one of the rock faces but could not be certain because of the failing light. "Hollin, can you show me what's there?" he said, pointing.

Hollin cast another Farseeing. It showed a narrow cleft between two sheer-sided hills. It looked as if the cleft passed deep into the hills, but even with Hollin's power magnifying their view, they could not be sure because of the gloom within it.

They could not stay here and fight the enemy in this village. "We make for that cleft," Therain announced. "It will force them to narrow their ranks so they won't be able to surround us. They won't be able to go around us either, unless they can fly. Those hills are too steep for them to climb."

They set off across the fields, keeping their horses to a quick trot. "I sure hope that cleft doesn't dead-end a hundred feet in," muttered Balandrick.

"We'll worry about that if and when the time comes, Captain," said Therain.

"Yes, my lord. Sorry, just mumbling out loud."

They had not gone far when Therain heard men shouting in the distance behind them. *Shayphim take them all,* he thought. *They know we're here now.*

33

They galloped in a mad dash for the cleft. The Havalqa soldiers had reached the village and were rushing through its center. Therain heard the distant thrum of bowstrings and flinched instinctively, waiting to feel one pierce him between the shoulder blades. He managed a glance back and saw several missiles fall to the ground fifty yards behind them. "Faster, damn you all, or we'll be skewered before we get to the first hill!"

They reached the edge of the shallow valley, raced up the first gentle slope, then made their way over each successive hill until they reached the entrance to the cleft, where they paused. It was nearly as black as night within it. The ground was uneven and strewn with rocks and scree. Balandrick lit a torch. "We need to see where we're going or we could break out necks," he said when Therain gave him a questioning glance. "Besides, it's not as if they don't know where we are."

"Fine. You go in first."

"I'll bring up the rear," said Hollin. "I can create Wardings behind us to protect us from their arrows."

Torch in hand, Balandrick made his way into the narrow defile.

The walls were tall and sheer, formed of dark stone gouged with deep fissures and narrower cracks. The horses picked their way carefully along the rubble-covered ground. Their pace had slowed to little more than walking speed. Therain clenched his teeth and bit down a desire to shout for them to hurry up.

The defile followed a crooked course. At any one time they could not see farther than thirty or forty feet ahead of or behind them. It made Therain even more nervous, and he echoed Balan's fear of a dead end—that they would come around a turn and find a solid wall in front of them, with no means of escape.

The company was spread out along a sharp turn when the men ahead of him came to a stop. "What's wrong?" he asked. "Why are we stopping?"

He heard a murmur travel down the line of soldiers. Dareth Bryndal turned to him and said, "The path narrows considerably around the turn, my lord, and Captain Vaules feared it had closed completely. But he went through and apparently it remains wide enough for us to pass through single file."

"Thank Telros for that bit of luck," said Therain quietly. "Hollin, have they reached your Wardings?"

"Not yet."

"Can they prevent those men from following us? Is there a way you can bottle them up in here?"

The line began to move forward. "For a while, yes. But as time passes and I move farther from the Warding, I have to increase the amount of magic used to maintain it. At some point it will collapse. There are other, stronger spells, of course. Forbiddings, and certain Words of Power. But those will tap my strength even further."

"Just hold them as long as you can."

"I have some plans ready for when they reach us. It's only a matter of time before this becomes a fight. I don't think we can outrun them."

Therain entered the constricted length of the defile and was swallowed by darkness. He looked up and saw only a narrow strip of stars far above him. He stretched out his right arm and touched the wall. The rock felt crumbly against his fingers, packed with loose dirt.

The path narrowed so much at one point that he had to shift his saddlebags in order to squeeze through, and felt a cold touch of fear that he would become stuck, choking the

passage like a bone in a throat. His horse whickered rest-
lessly in the constriction, but then he was through.

A few yards farther on, the defile widened to about twenty
feet across and remained that way to its end, which he could
see ahead of him. But its width was also a detriment for Hollin. The wizard explained that he would quickly exhaust
himself if he created a Warding large enough to cover the
entire area.

Beyond the end of the defile was a boulder-strewn clearing ringed with a dense line of trees. Rugged hills rose all
around them. *There are ways out of here, but none of them
will be quick,* thought Therain as he surveyed the terrain.
The company had gathered toward the clearing's center,
waiting for the prince.

"What is your command, my lord?" asked Balandrick.

"We make a stand here," he said. "The enemy is bottle-
necked in the defile. There's no way they can overwhelm us
with their greater numbers. Captains, position archers at the
entrance to the defile. I want that narrow passage choked
with bodies when they start to come through."

"My lord, should we use the explosive devices we recovered from the rider?" asked Balandrick. "We might be able
to block the defile completely."

Therain considered it. "Hollin, could you use your powers
in conjunction with the explosives to seal that passage?"

"Perhaps."

Therain gave him a grim look. "Never one to fully commit
to anything, are you, wizard?"

"I prefer never to make promises I am not completely sure
I can deliver."

"Very well. Get the archers in position. Hollin, go with
them and get the explosives ready. I don't want to use them
until we see the first of the enemy coming through. That way,
even if the passage doesn't completely close, we'll at least
take some of the bastards down in the blast. Everyone else,
array yourselves around this clearing. Make it a killing box.
The rest of the archers and crossbowmen, set up a cross fire
over the entrance to the defile."

The company got into position. Therain waited with Donael

Rundgar at his side. The archers had crouched low behind
boulders near the defile's mouth, arrows nocked but not yet
drawn. Hollin had positioned himself a dozen feet into the
defile. *I hope he's got himself well protected,* thought Therain. *If he gets himself killed . . .*

They did not have to wait long for the enemy to arrive.

The Khedeshian crossbowmen and archers waited until the
first enemy soldier had cleared the bottleneck before firing.
They'd decided upon a firing order before getting set in their
positions, so they would not waste several arrows on the
same man.

The first man who cleared the bottleneck went down with a
quarrel through his breastbone. He dropped his torch, which
fell on his leather armor and began to smolder. The men behind him let out a shout of warning and raised their shields,
then rushed forward.

Hollin punched his finger through the membrane of the
first explosive, then hurled it into the bottleneck. Therain saw
it strike the wall and carom once before it erupted in a brilliant flash of fire and smoke. Men screamed, and a tremendous boom rolled out of the defile. Before the enemy could
recover, Hollin threw the second one, which exploded a little
deeper in the bottleneck. Smoke billowed out of the defile as
if coughed from a giant's throat.

Hollin immediately delivered several powerful blasts of
searing golden fire at the location he'd struck with the explosives. Waves of pressure thumped against the prince's chest
as the magic pouring from Hollin's hand chewed into the
rock wall of the passage.

But the stone was proving to be stubborn. It split, cracked,
and dropped chunks of rock and dirt into the passage, but
the full-scale collapse that Therain had been hoping for did
not materialize. The dust and smoke was so thick that he
could not see any of the enemy soldiers, but he could hear
their shouts as they tried to avoid being buried by what was
falling.

Hollin sent several more blasts into the passage before re-
treating, then joined the prince, a look of anger on his face.

"Some power was opposing me," he said. "That path should be completely buried by now. I could sense some other will shielding it."

"They have a wizard with them? A Loremaster?"

"I would guess."

The Khedeshian bowmen had paused while the smoke and dust cleared from the throat of the defile. Therain could see the dim flickering of a few torches deep in the smoke, bobbing up and down wildly as the soldiers clambered over the rubble Hollin had managed to bring down. He thought he heard scrabbling noises high along the walls of the bottleneck and wondered what was happening. Arrows began to fly out of the defile, forcing the Khedeshians to duck their heads while the enemy advanced through the smoke. A score of Havalqa soldiers had cleared the bottleneck and were spreading out into the widened area of the defile, taking cover behind rocks, firing arrows, then advancing. Two Khedeshians went down. More enemy soldiers spilled from the bottleneck and reached the forwardmost archers. Close fighting erupted, but the Khedeshians were quickly overwhelmed and soon lay dead to a man. The rest fell back into the clearing, dashing for the cover of the trees.

Arrows began to land among them from a high angle. "What the . . . ?" said Therain. Then the smoke cleared enough for him to see that the scrabbling sounds he'd heard earlier had been made by enemy soldiers climbing the freshly damaged walls to gouged-out sections in the rock, which they now used as sheltered positions from which to shoot quarrels and arrows in a clear line-of-sight over their advancing companions.

"On the walls!" he shouted to his own men. They began to fire at the enemy positions, but the narrow angle of entry made them nearly impossible targets from this distance. He yearned for a bow of his own, but his missing hand made that impossible.

The forward line of enemy soldiers surged into the clearing. The Khedeshian archers made them pay mercilessly for each step of ground claimed; bodies littered the mouth of the defile in a widening crescent, like detritus left by the tide. But they could not stop the flow completely, and the defile behind them was filling fast with more soldiers. Soon there would be enough men to simply rush through the clearing and overwhelm them with sheer numbers.

"Hollin, whatever you were planning, I suggest that now—"

The wizard held up a hand to silence the prince. He rose from behind the fallen trunk he and Therain had been crouching behind. One of the Havalqa spotted him and released a quarrel, but it bounced off the Warding protecting the wizard and tumbled crazily through the air.

Hollin then shouted, *"Pranal-iveistu!"*

His shout was as loud as a clap of thunder. It echoed through the defile like the cry of a demigod. Therain flinched and covered his ears. At the same instant, he was gripped with a sudden, cold terror. His bowels became watery and he was paralyzed with a deep but indefinable dread. A startled cry escaped his lips; he nearly dropped his weapon.

Then it passed, as if it had been nothing more than a foul wind, leaving clean air in its wake.

Before him, the enemy soldiers had collapsed to a man, screaming and trembling with terror. Some clawed at their faces or throats. Some looked to have blinded themselves, gouging out their eyes with fingers that now dripped with gore. Others vomited uncontrollably. One had set himself on fire with his torch and lay on the ground shrieking.

Without taking his eyes from the clearing, the wizard said, "Get down. I'm going to have to drop my Wardings to create the next spell."

Therain obeyed without hesitation. *I must have caught the edge of that magic, whatever it was. Something that filled them with stark terror.* He in no way wanted to sample what was coming next, and crouched even lower.

"This defile was a boon to us," said Hollin. "Without it, they would have been too spread out for this to work."

The wizard drew back both his arms, then threw them forward; as he did so, his body exploded with golden fire that blinded Therain with its brightness. It went out after a moment, as if Hollin had been doused with water, then the wizard collapsed to the ground, falling stiff and hard.

But the spell—whatever it was—worked. Therain saw a wave of force rush across the clearing like a shimmering wall of heat. When the rolling wave struck the enemy soldiers, they fell instantly dead. The wave continued down the defile, killing every man it touched. It traveled some distance into the bottleneck before dissipating.

Therain scrambled to Hollin's side. The wizard was conscious but weak, barely able to speak. "I have spent my power. There is no more I can do now. If there are any left, your men will have to kill them."

"I understand. You did better than I could have dreamed. Are you all right?"

Hollin nodded. "Drained, but nothing rest will not cure. I don't think I will be making a spell for days, though. An Illumination and Word of Death made so close together . . . my brethren at Hethnost would be horrified at my recklessness, but our need was great."

Therain stood and surveyed the clearing. It was littered with bodies. He noticed for the first time that Hollin's spell had been indiscriminate: the scrub grass over which the spell had traveled was dead as well, brown and dry, so brittle it crunched and broke beneath his boots.

"Put out that fire," he said to the Khedeshians emerging from the trees. He was pointing to the dead Havalqa, whose body still burned, filling the clearing with the stench of roasting meat. Rundgar appeared at his side. "Send some men into the defile to make sure everyone back there is dead."

"Yes, my lord."

Khedeshians were smacking out the fire with blankets, while others moved methodically through the litter of corpses, making sure they were dead. Captain Rundgar was relaying Therain's command to a cluster of soldiers when the prince heard someone shout in fear.

He looked, and drew a hissing breath when he saw some of the bodies twitch and then slowly rise from the dead earth.

34

Balandrick stepped forward and lopped off the head of one of the corpses before it could fully rise. The body did not falter in its movements. It continued to push itself up to its feet, groping with blackened hands for a knife in its belt.

"How do we kill the bloody things?" he shouted. There was an edge of panic in his voice. "They're already dead!"

The other Khedeshians had backed away from the rising corpses. The headless body in front of Balandrick succeeded in drawing its knife. The captain did not hesitate. He chopped off the thing's hand at the wrist, then sprang away from it.

Therain realized the Loremaster was still alive in the defile somewhere, controlling the bodies the way Tolsadri had at Gedsengard. His uncle had described this very thing.

"Cut them to pieces!" he said. Captain Rundgar and two other soldiers moved to take protective positions around him. "There's at least one man alive in that defile," he said. "He's the one animating these bodies. We need to kill him."

"I'll take care of him," said Rundgar. "You two, protect the prince with your lives." The hulking captain ran across the clearing at an amazingly fast pace for a man of his size. The two soldiers closed ranks and placed themselves between Therain and the clearing.

The flesh of the animated corpses was black and desiccated, as if they had lain dead for a decade rather than a few minutes. But they moved with the speed of the living, puppets dancing on invisible strings of power held by a Loremaster hiding somewhere in the defile. Therain counted fifteen corpses that had risen and were now engaged in combat with his own men. Balandrick had cut the arms and one leg from the headless corpse that attacked him; its various body parts lay twitching on the ground, groping blindly for some means of fulfilling the commands given to it by its unseen master. Balandrick had moved on to one of the other corpses and narrowly avoided a sword thrust through the belly for his trouble.

There were so many bodies in the defile that Rundgar had no choice but to step on them to go forward. He almost reached the entrance to the bottleneck—where the bodies were piled atop one another two or three deep—when the corpses in the clearing collapsed to the ground, their false life vanishing as quickly as it had come. "What happened?" said Balandrick. "Is that bloody sorcerer of theirs dead?"

As Rundgar climbed onto the bodies, Therain saw the answer. The corpses beneath and ahead of the captain began to squirm with life, sitting upright with an awkward, shambling motion. Therain realized that the Loremaster was shifting his power to stop Rundgar. He could only control so many at one time and needed to protect himself.

Captain Rundgar chopped the arm off the corpse standing directly in front of him, then kicked it in the chest. It flew backward as if it weighed no more than a scarecrow. Therain noticed that the severed limbs did not bleed, or even appear wet. It seemed that Hollin's spell had burned away the blood and other bodily fluids of whatever it touched.

Balandrick and others had by now rushed to help Rundgar. They cut down three of the corpses coming at him from behind, hacking them apart with axes they had recovered from the fallen Havalqa. Meanwhile, Donael Rundgar disappeared in the darkness of the bottleneck, with two or three corpses giving chase.

Balandrick had shot past three of the dead warriors and was clambering over corpses that had not been revived when the animated bodies slumped to the ground. A moment later Rundgar appeared, holding his sword in one hand and something else in the other that Therain could not at first make out. Then Rundgar cleared the bottleneck and made his way to the clearing, and Therain saw that he was carrying a man's severed head.

"The sorcerer was alive, but just barely," Rundgar said as he tossed the head among the bodies littering the dead grass. "Hollin's power had cooked him good. He didn't put up much of a fight."

They buried their own dead while Elaysen tended to the wounded, then moved into the hills a short distance before stopping for the rest of the night. They were exhausted, their horses jittery and nervous, having sensed the powerful magic that had been surging all around them. Hollin was so weakened that he could not stand. He was helped onto Balandrick's horse, and Balan rode with the wizard in front of him to keep him from falling to the ground.

They found a sharp cleft in the hillside with several cave entrances in the rock face. Therain ordered soldiers to stand watch, then commanded everyone else to get some rest.

They slept late into the day. Therain consulted his maps, trying to deduce where in the Belkan Hills they might be in relation to the southern stair. He cursed silently. *I need better maps,* he thought. *These are no help.*

"Stand slowly, all of you, and keep your hands from your weapons," said a voice from one of the caves. Balandrick, Rundgar, and three other soldiers wheeled around, drawing their weapons. Arrows thudded into the ground between their legs, freezing them all in place.

"The next ones kill," said the voice. "The only reason you're not dead already is I'm curious what brings Khedeshian soldiers into these hills. Sheath your weapons or my curiosity will have to remain unsatisfied."

Therain peered into the blackness of the cave mouths but could make out no figures, and the echoes in the cleft made it hard for him to determine from which cave the voice came. "If you are a friend of Khedesh, then we mean you no harm."

"I would know why soldiers are *here* when the enemy is elsewhere," said the voice. "I will not ask again. Sheath your weapons or blood will be spilled."

"Do as he says," said Therain. He took his hand from the hilt of Baleringol and glanced around the camp to make sure his order was obeyed. Balandrick and Rundgar were the last to comply, and did so with obvious reluctance.

"We've done as you ask. Now show yourself and tell us who you are."

A short, slender man of middle years emerged from the leftmost cave. He had the ruddy skin, slender features, and curly hair of the Pashti. He held a nocked bow in his hand, though the arrow was pointed at the ground. A score of other men and women came out of the cave mouths behind him. All Pashti, by the looks of them, and all thin and scrawny, as if they had not eaten well for weeks. They were armed with swords, bows, or knives. *Pashti with weapons!* Therain thought. They remained on the upper part of the slope, where they could easily retreat into the caves if the situation turned violent.

"I am Vensi Leitren," said the man. "And that is all I will reveal until I have heard your tale."

"You are Pashti," said Therain. "How did you escape the invaders?"

Leitren tightened his grip on his bow but did not raise it. "I said I would hear *your* tale, not relay my own. Why are soldiers of Khedesh in the hills rather than defending the villages of the Hurion?"

"We are making for Castle Pelleron and Baron Thoreal," said Therain. "We entered the hills to avoid enemy troops, but were pursued from an abandoned village southwest of here. We made a pitched battle at the northern end of a defile back there, where we defeated our foes." He turned and gestured down the hills behind him. "There is a stair somewhere in these hills that leads to the castle. Can you take us to it, or give us news of Pelleron? Does it still stand? Are the invaders attempting to take it?"

Vensi Leitren relaxed a bit. "And why would you be going to Pelleron?" he asked. "If he's under siege your company will make little difference, even if you could enter. From what we've seen and heard, the invaders are massing their forces to march on Almaris. Aren't you headed in the wrong direction?"

That was too much for Balandrick and Rundgar. "Lower your weapons, all of you!" shouted Balan at the people on the slope. "How *dare* you question us!" He drew his weapon and pointed it at Leitren's heart. "Lower your weapons *now*—which the law forbids you to have—or Telros help me, you'll all find out what trained Khedeshian soldiers can do in battle!"

Some of the Pashti faltered and looked to Leitren for guidance. He stood still, regarding Balandrick warily.

Therain decided to put an end to the standoff. He took a step forward. "Vensi Leitren, order your followers to disarm at once. I am Prince Therain Atreyano, son of the king. My need is great, and I have neither the time nor the desire to explain myself to you. If you *can* help us you *will* help us, or else you will find yourself arrested for treason and destined for Nyvene's Wall, along with any who disobey me further. I will forgive your impertinence—and the fact that you are all armed—since you did not know who I was, and with invaders in our lands it is not unreasonable for you to defend yourselves. I commend you for being cautious. But my need is great and my patience is at an end." He looked around at Leitren's followers, who had gone pale. "Lower your weapons and you will not be harmed. To defy me further is to defy the will of the king, and the punishment will be suitably swift and harsh."

All but Leitren quickly put their weapons on the ground. He stared at Therain with a cold, appraising glare, then released the tension on his bow and deftly placed the arrow in the quiver slung across his shoulders.

He bowed his head. "I beg your pardon, my prince. I

thought we had come across deserters from the army."

"As I said, your are forgiven your assumptions. Now, join us here, all of you. I would hear *your* story."

Cautiously, and with obvious trepidation, the Pashti maneuvered their way down the rocky slope to the small shelf of land where the Khedeshians had made their camp. Leitren came last, watching Therain as he walked, as if expecting a deception or trap of some kind. He approached the prince and knelt before him. "I apologize again, my prince. If I have offended you in any way—"

"You have not. Sit, and tell me how you came to be here."

Leitren told them that they lived in the village of Tuelon's Vale, the abandoned community Therain and the rest had been searching when the Havalqa began their pursuit. The invaders had first appeared about two weeks earlier, he said, several hundred infantrymen and a sizable number of cavalry, and swept through the village before any kind of defense could be mustered.

"We live outside the Vale, behind its western rim," said Leitren. "Those of us in the fields or in the village itself were taken by the invaders. Those who were in our homes escaped into the Belkans before they knew we were there. We hid in the hills, and after they left we returned for whatever food and weapons we could find."

"Did you know these caves existed beforehand?" asked Hollin. There were dark circles beneath his eyes, and his cheeks were still sunken and gaunt.

"Of course," said Leitren with a trace of pride. "We have known about them since before your ancestors came to these lands. They were once shelters we used when raiders harried us."

"Can you lead us to Pelleron's stairs?" asked Therain. "Or tell us of the castle's fate?"

"I know nothing of the castle's situation, my prince. I can lead you to the stairs, but we will have to enter the caves. There is no overland way to reach them from here without going back almost to Tuelon's Vale."

Therain swore. "We can't afford the time to double back.

Besides, we might very well run into more enemy soldiers." He was silent for a few moments. "You will lead us through the caves. How long is the journey?"

"A little more than a day, I would think. We have not gone that way since coming here. We've remained in this area of the hills, wondering when we might return home."

"Soon, I pray. But not yet."

Unable to take their horses any farther, they stripped off their packs and bedrolls, then left the horses with the Pashti. "They will be well cared for," said Leitren to Therain as he led them into the mouth of the largest cave. "If you return this way, they will be waiting for you."

"I will hold you to your word," said Balandrick.

They lit torches once inside the cave. The passage continued in a more or less straight path for a hundred feet or so before beginning a gentle, downward slope. The ceiling rose to ten or eleven feet in some places, but in others dropped so low they had to crouch in order to pass. The idea of becoming trapped in here through a ceiling collapse or some other accident grew in Therain's mind. *A day or more beneath these hills,* he thought grimly as they rounded a sharp turn, beyond which the passage widened considerably. *You had best appreciate this, brother.*

The passage widened dramatically at one point, the ceiling stretching to more than fifteen feet in height. The walls and floor were more regular here, as if they'd been smoothed and polished. Hollin paused and ran his fingers along the stone. "Power has been used here," he said quietly. "Of a kind I do not recognize, but there are definite patterns, though they are old, very old." He looked at Leitren. "How were these passages made? Do you know?"

"They are ancient beyond reckoning. They were old when the Pashti first came here. It is said that long ago, before the coming of men to Osseria, beings of great power and dread lived here, walking the hills like giants before vanishing forever. Parts of these caves were fashioned by them, though for what purpose no one can say."

Therain soon lost all measure of time. They could have been traveling for minutes or hours for all that he could tell. The disconcerting thought of the oppressive weight of the hills above him did not lessen, as he hoped it would; if anything, it got worse as they wound their way deeper into the stone, deeper into the dark. He felt short of breath, as if all the air had been sucked from the caves, and at one black moment feared that his panic would overwhelm him. But he paused, closed his eyes, pictured the open skies above Agdenor, and the moment passed.

The air grew damp and cool and smelled faintly of rot. In places the walls and floor were wet and slick in the light of their torches. A few times they splashed across ankle-deep pools of fetid water bordered by patches of muddy earth that made their footing even more treacherous than it had been. Loose rocks were scattered across the floor, some as large as a man's torso.

"What is that stench?" said Balandrick, covering his nose and mouth.

"There are bats in the caves," said Leitren. "Their droppings are—"

Elaysen screamed as hundreds of bats exploded from the passage ahead and flew toward them. Therain covered his head with his arms just before two bats crashed into him, making his skin crawl with revulsion. One flopped to the floor, stunned for a moment, before taking flight and rejoining its brethren.

He crouched low as the bats flew all around him like a leathery column of smoke twisting its way through a horizontal chimney. The sound of their wings was deafening.

Then they were gone. Elaysen gasped for breath, her eyes wide with panic.

"Let's hope *that* doesn't happen again," said Balandrick.

Fortunately, they did not have to pass through the dank, reeking chamber from which the bats had just flown. The stench from the opening when they passed it was strong enough to make their eyes water.

They came to a wide circular room into which four passageways spilled. The black openings in the wall reminded Therain of upright coffins. Leitren directed them to the passage second from the right. "Be careful," he warned as he stepped through. "The descent is steep."

Therain followed him down a stairway carved into the rock. It reminded him of the secret passage that spiraled down beneath the Thorn, the great keep of Agdenor, which led to a cave where boats were hidden that could be used to cross either the Samaro or Azren rivers in the event of a catastrophe. He'd been forced to use that escape route to flee Agdenor when the Storm King overran the castle in his search for Gerin and the Horn of Tireon.

After what seemed an interminable descent, they reached a massive chamber at the stairway's end. He could see nothing but absolute blackness beyond the short reach of the torchlight, but nevertheless sensed they had come into an immense space. "Where are we?" He spoke quietly, as if he were in a temple and feared to incur the wrath of its unfriendly god.

"There is a restless air here," said Hollin in the same hushed tone. "As if half-wakened spirits were all around us, watching. It is an unsettling feeling."

"You may be old and wise, Hollin," said Balandrick, "but you still don't know when it's proper to leave something unsaid."

The wizard laughed quietly. "An old fault of mine. One it seems I will never be rid of. My apologies, Captain."

"Just keep the restless spirits off our backs and all is forgiven."

Leitren led them along the right wall for several hundred feet. Strange and eerie images loomed at them in the torchlight, carved into the walls and freestanding pillars that formed a kind of colonnade. Therain could make no sense of them; there was no writing that he could recognize, and the few carvings that had not been obliterated by time were of abstract forms, which nonetheless instilled in him a sense of unease.

"I don't like these carvings," said Elaysen. "They remind me of something from a nightmare."

"Are you taking lessons from Hollin?" asked Balan. "Telros save us, it's troubling enough in here as it is without the two of you pointing out every disturbing thing you see."

"The old stories tell us that this cavern was once a place of worship for the Nameless who ruled Osseria before the coming of men," said Leitren. "What they worshipped, we do not know, and do not ask."

"Will everyone just shut up already?" said Balan.

They reached another stairway, whose ascent was not quite as steep as the first. By the time they had climbed its long length to the chamber where it emptied, Therain's legs felt like weights of lead. He leaned back against the wall and slumped to the floor, exhausted.

"We rest for now," said Leitren.

The second half of their journey passed in a dreamlike blur for Therain. Weary, his legs burning from fatigue, the stump of his arm throbbing with a bone-deep ache, he felt as if he'd sleepwalked through winding passages and tortuous climbs up two tunnels that ran so near to vertical they had to use ropes to make the ascent. Leitren, with a rope tied about his waist, went first, bracing himself against the close walls with his knees and elbows, then anchored the rope at the top for the rest of them to use. Therain had a difficult time of it with just one hand and was trembling with exhaustion when he reached the top.

When he saw a pinprick of daylight at the end of a long upward slope, it was like waking from a dream. The cave opened onto a funnel-shaped hollow high up on the side of a jagged peak.

"More climbing," said Balandrick as he eyed the steep walls of the stony hollow. "But Shayphim take me, it's good to be out of those tunnels and breathe some fresh air."

At the rim of the hollow, Leitren pointed to a split crag to the east. "The stair to Pelleron passes through that crag. Pelleron itself lies behind those peaks." He faced Therain. "With your permission, I will leave you now, my prince."

"You have my gratitude. Fare well, and protect your kin. The king will not let the crimes committed against you go unanswered."

"Thank you, my prince."

"How did you know your way through those caves?" asked Elaysen. "You could not have learned such paths in the short time since you fled there."

"These were once our lands," Leitrin told her, "before they were taken from us by the Raimen in ages past. Much of what we had was lost or destroyed, but we retained much as well, lore and knowledge passed down from fathers to sons and from mothers to daughters. We have not forgotten all that we were. Even as we lived among the Khedeshians, we still ventured into the Belkans to walk the ancient paths. There are places here that are holy to us. Some lie upon the hills, but others lie below. We know them all."

"It is to our benefit that you've kept the faith of your fathers."

Therain regarded Leitren in a new light. Indeed, he wondered about all the Pashti, what secrets they kept from those they served. *Gerin understood something of this,* he thought. *The revelation granted to him upon the Sundering. He spoke of it but I didn't comprehend his meaning. The Pashti have their place in the world and have always seemed content to me. They serve, and receive our protection and guidance in return.*

But the revelation that they held on to the knowledge of their past, keeping their culture alive beneath the very noses of the descendants of their conquerors, startled him and made him wonder how much else he thought about them was wrong.

"I want to reach the crag by nightfall," Therain said. "Let's get moving."

35

As he followed Algariq through the streets of Palendrell, Gerin took note of everything he saw, hoping he would discern some crucial detail that would help him defeat his enemies once he had freed himself.

He was stunned by the number of ships in and around the harbor, and was told by Algariq that it was but a fraction of the fleet that had been sent. "More still will come, I have been told. Yours is a large country, and it will take a great effort to subdue it."

You will never subdue us, he thought. She had not granted him permission to speak, and so his defiance was silent.

But what he saw in Palendrell chilled him. Though there were obvious signs of battle in the town—burned buildings, shattered windows and walls, scaffolding from which dangled bloated corpses like overripe fruit in the orchards of Velyol, and a subtle but ever-present stench of smoke and death, mingled with the salty smells of the sea—it remained largely intact. Castle Cressan itself looked mostly undamaged save for some broken doors and smashed windows, though strange pennons fluttered atop the walls and spires. He had expected to find the town and castle largely in ruins, and wondered how the defenders were so completely overwhelmed. Did the Havalqa possess powers he had not yet seen, some ability to subdue an entire populace?

He passed Gedsengarders dressed in the attire of the

Havalqa, who went about their business under the watchful eyes of enemy soldiers, both humans and the grotesque murdrendi. They looked like beaten dogs, moving with heads bowed, shoulders hunched, shuffling quickly from place to place, glancing furtively at the clusters of soldiers with naked fear. He saw children dressed in gray rags carrying buckets of water to the soldiers; after setting down their burdens, the children bowed to the foreigners and said, "Praise to the Powers and Holvareh the All Father."

They reached the castle after a long climb past a series of guard stations where Algariq was questioned. Despite the obvious scorn heaped upon her by the soldiers, she explained politely, if somewhat coolly, that her captive was wanted by the Voice of the Exalted himself, and that she had been charged with his capture by no less than the Dreamer who accompanied the fleet. At the mention of the Voice and the Dreamer the soldiers sobered a little and, if they did not exactly show her respect, at least no longer openly displayed their contempt.

They were taken to a sitting room in one of the upper floors of the castle. The single window in its western wall offered a dramatic view of the town and harbor below.

Seated at the table in the center was Vethiq aril Tolsadri, the man who had done the impossible by escaping from the dungeons of the Tirthaig unassisted. Gerin wanted to lash out at him with his sword, his fist, his magic, anything that would hurt Tolsadri and wipe the smug, arrogant smirk from his face.

Tolsadri leaned back in his chair and laughed, then regarded them with a withering, contemptuous look. Gerin sensed Algariq stiffen beneath his gaze and lower her eyes.

"So, you have fulfilled your duty," he said. "I thought the Dreamer's plan to set you loose in the wild was madness— who can trust one such as you?—but it apparently saw something in you that I did not."

He rose from the table and walked a circle around Gerin. "He is in your complete control?"

"Yes, Honored Voice." She spoke without looking up from the floor.

"If I ask him a question, can he lie?"

"No, Honored Voice. He will speak the truth if I command it."

"Then do so."

Algariq regarded Gerin. "You will utter only the truth in answer to whatever question the Voice of the Exalted asks."

Gerin felt the slightest breath of her power blow through him, releasing his voice, though by her command he could only reply to questions.

"Where are the Words of Making?" hissed Tolsadri in his ear. "Tell me the nature of their power and where they may be found. Speak."

"I know nothing of them. I never heard of them until you said their name to me in the dungeon."

"Lies!" Tolsadri punched Gerin, snapping his head backward. Pain flared in his jaw and teeth. "I saw your face in the vision of the Dreamer. I know it is you!"

He stepped away from Gerin and backhanded Algariq across the face. His rings lacerated her cheek in three places, painting her flesh with dark lines of welling blood. When she straightened, he struck her again with his other hand, knocking her to the floor. She'd bitten her lip or tongue, and blood flowed freely from her mouth and down her chin.

"You said he would speak only the truth!"

"That is so, Honored Voice. He cannot lie while under my power if I forbid it."

"Are you saying the Dreamer is in *error*? That a being of such power has made a *mistake*?"

"No, Honored Voice, I am not. But it is not possible for him to lie. I have commanded that he not. He has powers of his own, it is true, but I do not think he can use them to thwart my will. If he could, he would have broken free of me long ago."

"Then how do you explain this contradiction? You and the Dreamer cannot both be right."

She got to her feet, wiping away blood with the back of her hand. "I cannot explain it, Master. But I have fulfilled my duty. I have brought him to you. I was promised as a reward that I would be elevated from the Harridan's caste. I—"

Tolsadri lashed out with his fist, connecting solidly with the side of her face. She reeled and staggered, but did not fall.

"How *dare* you demand anything from me! You are the garbage of the Harridan. It soils my spirit to be in the same room with you, but I must endure it for now since you are the one who holds him captive. But know that if I choose to kill you, I will, and once you are dead, I will revive your corpse and have it dance for my amusement. Never forget that your life is mine, wretch. And never demand anything of me again."

Eyes downcast, she said, "Yes, Honored Voice. Forgive me."

Tolsadri turned to Gerin. "We must solve this mystery. You will come with me to the Dreamer. I do not doubt that it has the power to unravel this contradiction, if one truly exists. If you are lying, it will see through it, and I promise you that your punishment will be so severe you will beg for death."

Gerin was taken through the narrow corridors of Cressan to a set of mahogany doors guarded by soldiers in black armor that bristled with spikes and blades. The chamber within was dimly lit by candles; the windows were shuttered and had been draped with black cloth. A large gauzy curtain divided one half of the room from the other. Gerin sensed a presence on the other side of the curtain, something alien and ethereal, saturated with power that leaked from it like cold from a block of ice.

Blood crusted Algariq's face and hand. Tolsadri had not allowed her the dignity of cleaning her wounds before ushering them to this chamber. Her presence was required to maintain control over Gerin. Until such time as Tolsadri released her from her duty, she would be with him, a jailer whose invisible bonds could not be undone.

The Voice of the Exalted spread his arms and bowed his head. "Great Dreamer, I have brought the man seen in your visions, the one you said will lead us to the Words of Making and our salvation against the Great Enemy who is to come. He is enslaved in the bonds of the soul stealer you sent to hunt him, and she claims he cannot lie while under her power. Yet when questioned, he claims to know nothing of the Words, neither their location nor their nature. How can this be? Is he truly the one?"

Gerin felt as well as heard a deep, sonorous exhalation from the thing called a Dreamer. There was power in the exhalation, an expelling of energy that caused reality itself to tremble like a plucked harp string. It was a profoundly disturbing sensation, and left him weak and nauseous.

He saw a bright light emanate from behind the curtain, a piercing beam directed at his face. Closing his eyes could not shut it out, nor could he turn his head away. He felt a coolness in his mind, as if a sudden frost had just settled there. This was no ordinary light—it was power of some kind, penetrating the surface of his thoughts.

Looking for something.

He felt the power skim through his mind, though only its upper reaches. The strength of the light was limited. He could not fight it, but there were things beyond its ability to see or understand.

"Dreamer?" asked Tolsadri. "Is this the man we sought?"

"Yes, Voice of the Exalted, he is indeed the one. He is the path to the Words of Making, but I also sense that he speaks the truth."

"How can that be?"

"I do not know. It is a mystery I must ponder."

"How can you not know? It was your visions that set the voyage to these lands in motion! What of the Great Enemy? How can we battle it without the Words? The Exalted will be *enraged* when she learns of this."

There was another exhalation from the Dreamer, though different from the first. This emanation contained whispers of malice and death, and carried with it the stench of rotted flesh, as if they had suddenly found themselves upon a field of battle where untold thousands lay dead beneath a scorching sun.

Then it was gone, but they were all shaken. *So that is what a threat from it feels like,* thought Gerin, trying to force the lingering, ghostly smell of dead meat from his nose. *Tolsadri has succeeded in making it angry.*

"You forget your place, Voice. Do not presume to lecture me over matters beyond your ken. Your powers as an Adept are great for one of your kind, but they are nothing compared to my own. Ponder that before you think to speak to me in such a manner again."

Tolsadri paled and bowed his head. "Forgive me, Great Dreamer."

Gerin could see Tolsadri bristle at the Dreamer's chiding, and though he held his tongue there was still a flash of hatred in his eyes at the creature that lurked behind the curtain. He realized that Tolsadri hated and feared the Dreamer because it was a reminder that there were beings in the world stronger than he, creatures to whom he had to bow.

"Do not delude yourself that you understand our powers, Voice. The visions of my kind pierce the boundaries that separate this world from an infinite number of others. Some are like this world, while others are strange beyond your ken, whose very air is poison. Others are utterly barren, destroyed by catastrophes so thorough that life will never return. Some are separated from our own world by unimaginably small distances—they exist *here*, with us, but in a plane of existence that is slightly skewed from our own. These things we have seen. It is the nature of our power, and not something you can understand."

Gerin thought of his creation of Nimnahal and how he had seen the vision of the king receiving the sword—the same weapon, yet somehow different—and he recalled Hollin's explanation that the sheer amount of magic saturating the sword had seeped across the boundaries separating this world from others.

These things we have seen. An idea occurred to him suddenly, a flash of intuition about the nature of the Dreamer he felt instinctively to be true. *It sees across worlds, and speaks as if it has visited some of them. Perhaps it has.*

"I would hear him speak," said the Dreamer. "Allow your prey his voice, soul stealer."

Algariq bent low. "Your will is done, Great Dreamer."

Gerin felt a shift in the power that held him and sensed that he could now speak of his own volition.

"Prince Gerin Atreyano, what say you?" said the Dreamer. "Do you have questions of your own?"

"Many, but I will start with this one: you are not originally from this world, are you? That's how you know of other worlds, because you came from one of them. Your exhalations . . . I felt reality itself tremble and weaken. You can break down the barriers between the worlds to pass between them."

The room shook with a harsh, metal-scraping sound, and Gerin realized they were hearing its laughter. "Such a perceptive mind! You have discerned what no other before you has guessed, because none thought even to consider such a thing. The Steadfast have always known us; therefore they believe we have always been here. It did not occur to them to think otherwise, any more than they would question where the Tumhaddi Desert came from, or the stones of Ja'lensi; they simply have always been."

"Where it is you came from?" he asked, ignoring the look of shock on both Tolsadri and Algariq. "Don't you want to get back to your homeland? *Can* you get back?"

"Our home is lost to us. Our ancestors came to the lands of the Steadfast ages ago, fleeing a catastrophe that laid waste to our world. Even if we could return—and we cannot, as the means of traveling between worlds has been lost—it would be only to die, as our world was reduced to a boneyard of ash and dust.

"And now *this* world is threatened by a power of darkness that is slowly gaining strength. It is as yet diffuse, little more than a whisper of malevolence, yet in time it will grow into the enemy of all life."

He remembered Zaephos's words about the Adversary: *He is everywhere and nowhere. The Adversary has no physical form as yet. He is a spirit of illness and malice, a black wind in the night.*

Were the Adversary and the Great Enemy of the Havalqa the same being?

"How do you know of this Great Enemy?" he asked. "Another vision?"

"Yes. All of the Dreamers have seen it."

"So you can see the future?"

"At times."

"How can you be sure that this vision will come to pass? Why have you vested so much in the rise of this Great Enemy? The future is not a fixed thing."

"Because all roads to the future, no matter how varied, lead to a point where the Great Enemy will arise. It *will* happen. The manner and timing of his coming is unclear, but we saw that he would manifest himself here, in these lands far across the sea from the home of the Steadfast. And while the nature of the battle against the Great Enemy was also unclear, we all saw that the Words of Making must be found and used against it if there is to be any hope of his defeat. Without them, all will be lost."

"What *are* the Words of Making?" asked Gerin.

He caught a gleam of excitement in Tolsadri. He realized the Voice did not know what they were any more than he did.

"The Words are the power of Creation itself, spoken by Holvareh the All Father to fashion the world and all things in it," said the Dreamer. "They are the only power capable of defeating the Great Enemy."

It seemed an almost absurd idea. How could such a power exist in the world? Did they think their god just wrote down the words and then left them under a rock somewhere? But that was a question for another time.

"If this Enemy truly will rise in Osseria, then instead of invading our lands you should become our allies. We should work together to defeat our common foe."

"Bah," scoffed Tolsadri. "The Havalqa do not become allies with infidels. All must acknowledge the might and righteousness of our true gods over false ones and be shown their proper place in the world. Ours is the pinnacle of civilization. We would not sully ourselves by forming alliances with imperfection. It must be a world united beneath the Havalqa that faces the Great Enemy when he arises."

"This audience is ended," said the Dreamer. Gerin was about to say something else, but apparently Algariq took the Dreamer's announcement as a command to silence Gerin once again, and he found he could no longer speak. *Damn her power!*

"Take him to the dungeons," Tolsadri said to Algariq. "The guards will show you the way."

"As you say, Honored Voice."

Bound once more in silence, Gerin followed her out of the chamber.

36

"Halt in the name of Baron Thorael!"

The shout came from somewhere in front of Therain. They had reached the stair less than an hour earlier and begun the long climb up the high-walled pass toward the castle, which was still hidden behind the sharp peaks of the hills.

"Make no sudden moves," Therain cautioned them quietly. Then, in a louder voice, he said, "We are Khedeshians on our way to Pelleron. Will you escort us to the baron?"

"Stay where you are, and if you value your lives do not raise your weapons," said the voice. This section of the stair was in truth a gently rising stone path, with no treads cut into the ground, as there had been on the steeper parts behind them. It followed a long curve between two sheer walls of stone. Therain felt as if he'd been trudging along the bottom of a trench.

He could hear scrabbling noises atop the walls. A few seconds later armed men appeared on the path both ahead of and behind them. A helmeted soldier bearing the insignia of a lieutenant stepped forward. "Who are you, and what is your business with the baron?"

Before Therain could speak, Donael Rundgar stepped forward. Though his weapon was lowered, his size alone conveyed a sense of menace, and Therain saw the baron's men tense.

"Prince Therain Atreyano comes before you," he said, gesturing to Therain without taking his eyes from the men in front of him. "He has urgent business with the baron. You will provide an escort to take us to him and issue no further challenges and threats to his person."

"The prince is among you?" said the helmeted lieutenant.

"Yes," said Therain, stepping forward. "It is as my captain says. I would speak with your lord as soon as possible."

The lieutenant gave Therain an appraising glance, then bowed his head, as did the men behind him. "Yes, my prince. I offer my apologies for—"

"We're at war, Lieutenant. If you hadn't challenged us, you would be offering not only an apology but perhaps your head."

"Yes, my prince." He saw Therain's arm, and his eyes widened. "My prince, your *hand* . . ."

"A gift from the invaders I intend to repay."

The lieutenant—a sandy-haired man named Duren Kelimaris—and one other soldier escorted Therain and the rest of the company. "Why have you come to Pelleron, my prince?" he asked. "It seems strange that you should struggle northward while our enemy marshals his forces to the south, and seems intent on striking Almaris."

"My brother has been captured by the enemy and taken to Gedsengard Isle. We mean to get him back, and have come for the baron's help."

"Paérendras save us! May the gods watch over you and your brother both, my prince, and see that he is returned safely to you."

"How does Pelleron fare?" asked Therain. "Have the invaders tried to siege you yet?"

"No, my prince. The castle stands unmolested, though they have blocked the southern exit to the valley. I would ask how you made it past them. Our scouts have reported that they have the end of Selwaen's Stair completely closed off."

"That's an interesting story, Lieutenant. We didn't come through the valley or even over the hills, but rather under them. With the help of some Pashti from a village that the invaders have otherwise destroyed."

Kelimaris nodded his head knowingly. "Ah, the old caves. I had no idea they extended so far, or that Pashti would be aware of them."

The path had become true stairs again as the trail cork-screwed its way up the side of a spire of rock shaped like an upright pinecone. There was no rail or curb on the outer edge, and at its peak, where the stair spilled at last onto a wide paved path that stretched to the gates of Pelleron itself, the drop off the side was nearly two hundred feet deep. Therain felt dizzy from the height and kept as close to the inner wall of the stair as he could. He remembered Gerin's story of Dian's Stair and could not imagine climbing something so much higher.

Kelimaris left them with the castle guard at Pelleron's main gate. "I need to return to my post, my prince. I wish you well in your quest."

"Thank you, Lieutenant. I feel better knowing that Sel-waen's Stair is guarded by such capable men."

Pelleron was seated on a tall bluff whose eastern side fell away in a sheer drop of nearly a thousand feet into a shadow-filled valley that was itself encircled by jagged peaks. The high walls encased three close-set hills: the highest was in the center, and upon its summit the castle's keep had been built. It looked like nothing so much as three stacked circles of black stone with a single needlelike spire rising from its crenellated roof.

They were taken up a ramplike road to the iron-banded doors of the keep. News of their arrival was sent ahead to the baron, who was at that moment conferring with his advisors. The castellan showed them to a large dining hall where they could rest and eat. "The baron will be here soon," said the castellan, a slight man who wore a leather skullcap and whose long fingers never seemed to cease moving, like the legs of a spider dancing on the ends of his hands.

They had been eating only a short while when the baron entered the room, followed by two men whom Therain took to be his counselors. Ommen Thorael was a short, stocky man with a thick tangle of black hair upon his head and a heavy beard to match. He and his men bowed to Therain, who had risen at the baron's entrance.

"My lord, it is an honor to have you in my castle and at my table, but I fear I do not understand your visit," said Thorael. He stared at Therain's arm. "Norles said you had been maimed, but I thought he must have been mistaken."

"He was not. I was wounded on the road home from my sister's wedding."

"A terrible thing, my lord."

"I have come seeking aid, Baron Thorael. The invaders succeeded in taking my brother captive. We followed and learned they've taken him to Gedsengard. I intend to go there to fetch him, but it's a rather long swim, so I need a ship to get there. I'm hopeful you can provide one."

The baron was aghast at Therain's news. "Prince Gerin in the hands of these foul invaders!"

"Baron, can you help us? I know there is a fishing village to the north of here. Is it still accessible? Do you have ships there?"

Thorael drummed his fingers upon the table. "Yes, my lord, Haldrensi remains unknown to the invaders. So far they have focused their attentions to the south, and have sought only to bottle us up here. Their first few raids up the stairs ended in the wholesale slaughter of their men, so they have abandoned the idea of taking Pelleron." He leaned forward, his expression growing even more grave. "But, my lord, why would you throw your life away on a mission that must end in failure? Gedsengard is where their fleet first landed. The entire island is theirs. If your brother has been taken there, then he is either dead—I hate to even utter such a thought, but it must be said—or beyond our reach."

"He is not dead, Baron. His capture was not random. The invaders believe he has information that is vital to their cause."

"Then, my lord, when they have taken the information from him, will they not ransom him back to us? Would it not be better to pay the ransom rather than risk the life of the next in line to the throne? I do not mean to argue, but it seems that the course you have chosen is the most dangerous and least likely to succeed."

"They cannot get the information from him, no matter what enticements they might employ to make him talk, because he does not have what they want."

"If he cannot give them what they want, my lord, does that not put us back to them ransoming him back to us? I'm sure the king would find paying a ransom preferable to risking you—"

"I appreciate your concern for my safety, Baron, but this is not a debate. Time is of the essence. If you have a ship, then you will provide it, along with a crew that can take us to Gedsengard and return us safely once our task is complete."

He could see Thorael bristle at the command, but did not doubt that in the end he would be obeyed. *He thinks me a callow and reckless youth. He sees my maimed arm and probably believes I am looking for vengeance as well. Or perhaps he feels I'm a glory-seeker hoping to prove myself with a daring rescue of a kidnapped prince.*

Let him think what he wills. I don't care, as long as he gives me the damn ship.

Thorael conferred quietly with his advisors for a few moments, then faced Therain and cleared his throat. "My lord, I will see to it that *Cregar's Glory* takes you to Gedsengard. Please rest here tonight, and in the morning I will send men to take you to it."

"I thank you, Baron. Neither I nor my father will forget your aid."

Later that night, in her chamber high up in the windswept keep, Elaysen prepared herself for bed. She felt ill at ease, and mixed herself a hot draught of melka leaves and honey to help her sleep. She worried about her father and Gerin in equal measure, her heart torn between them. Would her father's enemies use the arrival of the invaders to move against him? Would he perish in the eventual siege of Almaris, his death blamed upon the Havalqa but in truth caused by those who longed to see him eliminated? The priests of the Temple would like nothing more. Even the king . . . *The One God preserve me, what if Gerin's father harms mine?*

She tried to push the thought aside. She could not trouble herself with events so far beyond her control. She had more pressing matters at hand. In the morning they would head for the fishing village, where they would board a ship and sail for Gedsengard. For the first time, she feared that their journey would end in ruin. The baron's words had removed a veil from her eyes, allowing her to see their predicament clearly. Did they truly have any hope of rescuing Gerin? He was in the heart of the enemy's domain, their most valuable prisoner. Would it not be prudent to do as the baron had suggested and wait to see if the enemy offered to return him for a ransom?

She clenched her teeth and shook her head. *I will not give in to fear. I will not consider defeat. Therain does not. Balandrick does not. If they believe it is possible, so will I. Prince Gerin deserves no less from me.*

37

Gerin's head snapped back against the stone wall of the cell, striking it with a dull thud. Pain flared in his jaw where Tolsadri had punched him with a fist encased in a metal-studded glove. "Do not fear for your life, infidel prince of an infidel kingdom," he said. "I will not kill you. Indeed, I *cannot* kill you if the world is to have its salvation. It sickens me to know that you are the key to finding what we need, but never let it be said that the Powers do not have a sense of irony. I'm sure this pleases them in some way. But *I* am not pleased. The keys to the Words of Making are somewhere within you. I feel it in my bones." He stepped closer to Gerin and pulled up his head by the hair. "No, you will not die here. But you will become one of the Steadfast in heart, mind, and spirit."

Gerin had been shackled to the ceiling of the cell, the length of chain ratcheted to the point where the toes of his boots just grazed the stone floor. His shoulders burned with a deep fire; his forearms had gone numb except for his wrists, where the manacles bit into his flesh. Warm blood trickled down his arms.

Tolsadri produced a small knife and pressed its tip about an inch deep into the tender flesh of his armpit. The pain was excruciating; sweat covered his entire body. Tolsadri then twisted the blade in the wound. Gerin could not so much as grimace. Tolsadri continued to make small incisions in his arms, chest, and thighs. Blood flowed freely down his body and pooled on the floor beneath his boots.

"I will take great pleasure when you swear your obedience to the Powers," said Tolsadri. "Not because you are threatened and fear for your life, or the life of a loved one, or because you feel it is what we want you to say. You will swear it because in your heart it will be what you believe. More than anything else, you will want to please the Powers and serve them in every moment of your life."

One day I will kill you, thought Gerin. *One day I will be free and I will kill you. The last thing you will see in this life is me taking yours from you, and knowing I've beaten you. I will never swear to your false gods. Never. I will bite out my own tongue and spit it in your face before I utter such blasphemy.*

He kept his mind occupied with thoughts of vengeance, trying to distance himself in some way from the horrors being inflicted on his body. He began to lapse in and out of consciousness, but was always roused by Tolsadri.

A guard appeared at the cell door, carrying an oddly shaped ceramic container. "Ah, good, they are here," said Tolsadri when he saw the guard. Another guard opened the door to the cell; the soldier with the container placed it on a stool near where Algariq sat.

The Voice reached into the container with his gloved hand and withdrew a wriggling, leechlike creature about the length of Gerin's index finger. Its glistening body was covered with long, bristling legs.

"This is a pelonqua," said Tolsadri. "They are rare creatures, difficult to keep alive when captured—you have no idea the trouble I had with them in the sea crossing—but they have uses that make the difficulty worthwhile. You see"—he took the pelonqua and placed it over the bleeding wound in Gerin's armpit—"they are drawn to blood, which they drink, but not in quantities that will kill. Yet they are not ungenerous creatures. They give something in return for what they take. Do you feel it there, slurping the blood that flows from you? Its legs have hooked themselves into your flesh, and within their small barbs—and in the tiny teeth within their mouths—is a secretion that will numb the wound.

"But, their secretion has another property as well, one discovered by Loremasters centuries ago." He reached into the container and withdrew another wriggling pelonqua. "When enough of them have been applied to a human, the secretion acts to make a mind more—what is the word for this? Ah, yes—*compliant*. Open to suggestion. It numbs the mind as well as the body. Quite a feat for such a small creature, is it not?" He placed the second pelonqua on a wound on Gerin's other arm.

Gerin felt nothing where the creatures had been applied to his flesh, but his already tortured mind became groggy, as if he'd drunk too much wine. Tolsadri's voice took on a hollow, distant quality.

"It will take time for you to fully embrace the ways of the Steadfast, even with the help of the pelonqua." He removed another creature and pressed it against a wound on Gerin's thigh. "But it will happen, infidel prince. You will deliver the secret to the Words of Making to my hand—*my* hand, and no other—at which point your usefulness will come to an end, and I will gladly give you the death you so richly deserve."

The northern coast of Gedsengard Isle was a forbidding wall of low cliffs surmounted by windswept heaths. The waters beneath the cliffs were a treacherous stretch of half-submerged shoals and jutting shards of rock, as if gargantuan pottery had been broken and the refuse dumped unceremoniously into the sea.

"How can we possibly land here?" said Therain. The sea churned and foamed as waves rolled through the shoals. "A ship would be dashed to bits on those rocks."

"The answer is we don't land here, my lord," said Belrus Gethelaine, the captain of *Cregar's Glory*. He was a short, ruddy-faced man with a prodigious stomach that he threw before him like a herald announcing his arrival. "You're right, any craft trying to pierce Marwen's Sorrow would soon find herself in Paérendras's cold embrace. But there's an inlet just beyond that promontory there"—he pointed with a long-nailed finger toward a jutting headland coming into view ahead of them—"where you can make landfall. It'll still be dangerous—there's not a foot of coast along these northern shores that's completely clear of rocks—and there's more'n half a chance your boat'll get punched full of holes and sink fast beneath you, but there's nothing to be done for it. There ain't no other places to land on this forsaken crust of dirt that ain't guarded by the invaders. And damn me if there ain't a lot of them."

"You mean there's a chance our landing boat will not survive the crossing?" said Donael Rundgar, glaring at the captain crossly.

"That's exactly what I said. Wasn't you listening? I can't do naught 'bout the lay of the land, good sir. If you want to land without sailing into the waiting arms of the enemy, this is where you've got to go." He glanced up and down Rundgar's imposing form. "I wouldn't wear your armor for the crossing if I was you. If the boat sinks or you fall overboard, you'll drown 'fore you can get it off. Stow it in the boat and put it back on once your feet are firmly on dry land, I say."

"I'll be able to help guide the craft safely," said Hollin.

They were quiet as they sailed toward the promontory. Balandrick and Rundgar oversaw the preparations of the provisions and gear they would take to the island. Therain wandered up to the forecastle of the ship and stood at the railing, letting the wind blow across his face. He wondered where Gerin was and how he was being treated. Did he wonder if anyone was coming for him? *Hold on, brother. Help is on the way.*

Their journey from Haldrensi had been mercifully uneventful. Twice they'd spied Havalqa ships on the horizon, but they were sailing south and had not given pursuit.

He worried about his father and Almaris. It was evident the enemy was going to lay siege to the city in addition to its naval blockade. The city's walls were strong, and defended by the Taeratens as well as Khedeshian men-at-arms. They had stores to last at least a year, even with the city's numbers swollen with refugees. But still his heart was filled with doubt. The murdrendi, the creatures who wounded him, their Loremasters' power to animate the dead . . . What else did the Havalqa have that they had not yet seen? How safe was his father, even within the heart of the Tirthaig?

They rounded the promontory and saw a wide stretch of white sand nestled between sloping hillsides of crumbling stone and scree. A half mile behind the beach the land swept up in a long crease toward the highland heaths. They saw no settlements and no signs of enemy soldiers.

"Ah, here we are, my lord," said Captain Gethelaine. "Time for you to head ashore. I'll keep the *Glory* here as long as I can, but we're not a fighting ship. She's built for speed. If some of those enemy ships appear, I'll have to run."

The crewmen of *Cregar's Glory* helped the Khedeshian soldiers haul their gear and provisions into the two longboats they would use to reach the coast. They lowered the boats into the water, and then Therain and the rest—having taken the captain's advice and earlier removed their armor—climbed down hemp ladders. Captain Gethelaine wished them a swift success as they rowed toward shore.

Hollin was in the lead boat with Therain. The wizard stared intently at the sea ahead of them. "Row that way," he said, pointing a little to the left. "That way is clear. I'll do what I can to keep the boats on course, but I don't think we'll have any trouble."

Therain's boat scraped across submerged rocks five times. He held his breath when he heard the sharp sound of the wood against rock, but the boat's bottom held firm.

When they reached the shore they dragged the boats onto the sand and down the beach a quarter of a mile so they could be hidden beneath nets they'd brought with them among the boulders and detritus at the bottom of the hill. When the boats were concealed and they'd put their armor back on, they set out for the gentle, creased slope behind the beach and made their way inland. Therain looked back once at *Cregar's Glory* as they left the beach, wondering if he would ever set foot upon her again. *I won't unless I have*

Gerin with me, he told himself. *I leave here with him, or not at all.*

Their journey across Gedsengard toward Castle Cressan took a little more than a day. They traveled as quickly as possible across the uplands, keeping off the few roads they happened across but shadowing one of hard-packed dirt that likely led to the castle. They passed three small villages that had been occupied by the Havalqa. The Gedsengarders seemed to go about their lives much as they had, under the eye of foreign soldiers stationed at key points throughout the thatch-roofed buildings. The sight lit a deep fire of anger within Therain, but he could do nothing. They did not have nearly enough men to consider a liberation of the villages, and even if they could, what then?

Four patrols of enemy soldiers passed down the road, heading away from the castle. Therain and the others concealed themselves behind low folds of land or within small copses and waited until the soldiers were completely out of sight before moving again.

At last they saw the spire of the Seilheth Tower rising hazily in the distance. They halved the distance to the tower, then halted in an overgrown gully to wait for night to fall. Hollin created a Farseeing that showed two guards stationed at the door at the tower's base.

Therain managed to nap a little as the day grew long. Captain Rundgar roused him as twilight was settling over the island.

The prince stood. "Come. It's time to get my brother."

38

For three days Tolsadri continued to apply pelon-quas to Gerin's suppurating wounds. The effect of the creatures' secretions built up in him until his mind shifted between two conditions: unconsciousness and a groggy, semilucid state of awareness in which the world around him seemed little more than dream, something so fragile and precarious that he imagined the sound of a hand clap could shatter it. Tolsadri spoke to him of the might and majesty of Holvareh the All Father and the Powers that ruled the world in His Name in such a way that Gerin sometimes thought he saw fleeting images of the Powers within his cell, divine beings wreathed in silvery light watching him solemnly, their bodies somehow larger than the cell itself yet still contained within it, waiting for him to acknowledge their existence and his place in their grand design. But in those moments, when he stood on the brink of a precipice from which he dared not fall, he drew back and told himself that Tolsadri's words were lies and blasphemy.

On the second day, Tolsadri had forced him to drink a harsh, biting liquid that set a fire in his belly. He vomited the substance the first few times the Voice forced it into him, leaving him nauseous and feverish. "This will help your conversion," said Tolsadri as he poured the liquid down Gerin's mouth, opened at a command from Algariq. "It will open your eyes to the error of your ways."

After he'd drunk the liquid four or five times, a dull pain awakened in his joints, as if the tendons and ligaments were being heated over a slow fire. The pain did not diminish. Indeed, each time he drank the liquid the pain increased, until he reached a level of agony he did not think he could endure. The pain consumed him, left him unable to consider anything but a hope for its end.

The beatings continued. Tolsadri was careful never to injure him in any permanent or lasting way. He was skilled at finding points on Gerin's body where the application of pressure set his muscles and nerves quivering uncontrollably. And the Voice continued to use his knife to inflict small but agonizing wounds all over his body. "You will recover from all your hurts, I assure you," he whispered to Gerin after withdrawing his knife from the prince's lower back. "Oh, you will have some interesting scars, but your body will suffer no lasting damage. It would not do to make you lame or a cripple." He asked again and again where Gerin had hidden the Words of Making, but Gerin's answer was always the same: "I don't know where they are." His answer always brought him more pain.

When Tolsadri left the cell on this day, he gave the guards orders that Gerin be given some small measure of water and food. From time to time he was lowered from the chains and placed on a stone bench, his hands manacled to a heavy iron ring bolted to the wall. He barely noticed the relief granted to his shoulders and arms because of the agonizing burning of the elixir and the half-wakeful state in which the secretions of the pelonquas left him. He tried to remember the faces of his family and friends—Reshel and Therain, Balandrick, Elaysen, his father, his mother, Hollin, even Claressa—but their features shifted and blurred into one another as if they were images made in oil drifting upon water. He begged Telros to give him strength to endure, and to the One God to have mercy and send Zaephos to free him, but his prayers were answered only with silence. He felt no surge of strength is his burning limbs, no lessening of Algariq's hold on his body, no relief from his delirium; and Zaephos did not appear.

Algariq remained with him throughout the torture. She needed to remain close to maintain her control, and in effect was as imprisoned as he. But if this displeased or bothered her in any way, she did not show it. She sat impassively while Tolsadri administered his techniques to convert him to the belief of the Havalqa. She took her meals in the cell, brought to her by the guards, and left only to relieve her bladder or bowels. She did not permit him to speak unless the Voice commanded her to allow it.

Her elevation out of the caste of the Harridan was scornfully denied by Tolsadri, even though it had apparently been her promised reward for delivering Gerin. Did she believe Tolsadri would acquiesce when he was done with him, that by her quiet acceptance of Tolsadri's abuse she would ultimately get what she wanted? He knew that Tolsadri would never grant her wish. He hated her—no, he hated her *kind*—too much to ever allow it to happen. Was she so blind that she could not see that?

She hoped for her son. It was one of the few coherent thoughts Gerin was able to hold. She would believe anything for him, delude herself until death took her. She could do nothing else. She could never give up on her hope because it meant her son was doomed to her fate. He wanted nothing more than to convince her that the Voice of the Exalted would never keep his word, that she should take her vengeance on him by using her power upon the Loremaster and commanding him to plunge his cursed knife into his own eye. But he could not even speak, let alone formulate an argument to convince her to murder Tolsadri.

He did not know how much time passed before the Loremaster returned. His body and mind both burned, lost in a constant agony that seemed close to obliterating everything he was. He was hauled to his feet and hung once more from the ceiling. He tried to focus all of his hate on Tolsadri, all of the pain he felt that he wanted to return tenfold upon the man who so afflicted him. It helped him clear his mind, but only a little.

"I have it within my power to end your suffering," said

Tolsadri in a silken voice. "I have been granted the ability to heal both your body and mind by Holvareh's grace and the generosity of Bariq the Wise. This elixir"—he brandished a flask filled with a milky substance that gave off a strong citrus odor—"is called *wassan*. It is quite potent. Two sips and you will pass into a dreamless sleep. When you awaken, your mind will be clear and the burning you feel deep in your bones will be gone. Two more sips and you will sleep again while the wounds of your body are mended. When you awaken they will be little more than pale scars upon your flesh. This was a gift made to the Loremasters long ago from Bariq the Wise, the Power in whose name I serve. It is difficult to make, and never given lightly.

"To receive this gift, you have but to call upon Holvareh and promise to serve Him, and to thank Bariq the Wise for blessing the world with his generosity. That is all. Swear it, even though I know your words will not reflect what is in your heart, and I will give you a respite from your agony. All journeys, as they say, begin with one small step. Wretch, allow him to speak."

Algariq opened her eyes and said, "His voice has been freed, Honored Voice."

Gerin raised his head. "I will never serve your false gods. I follow Telros, the god of my fathers, and the One God who is above all others. Kill me if you will, but I will never utter your lies."

Hollin caused a heavy mist to rise from the ground that blanketed the land from the gully to the Seilheth Tower. It was so thick that they could scarcely see one another. "How are we going to find our way to the tower in this?" hissed Balandrick.

"I can see through it," said the wizard. "I will lead. Follow me, and stay close. I would suggest that you keep your hand on the back of the man in front of you."

They set off across the barren landscape. A steady wind had blown across them earlier, but the mist's power appeared to thwart or nullify it, so that the air hung still and heavy.

Hollin drew up short; Therain nearly walked into Rundgar's back, as did Balandrick behind him. Hollin said something to Rundgar that Therain could not hear; the captain turned and whispered, "Wait here." Then the two of them disappeared, swallowed at once by the mist.

Therain tightened his grip on Baleringol and tried not to worry. It seemed an age passed before Rundgar and Hollin returned to lead them to the tower's door.

The wizard waved his hand and the mist shrank away from the tower as if pushed back by an unseen wall. Therain stared at a single door deeply sunken into the tower's dark bulk. On the ground in front of the door lay two dead guards.

They found keys on one of the dead men and used them to open the door. Hollin created a small spark of magefire to light their way and said he would warn them if anyone approached. Then they followed the long spiraling stairway down into the castle.

Gerin stared defiantly into Tolsadri's eyes after he refused to swear his loyalty to the Loremaster's gods. He felt invigorated by his own words, and part of him wondered if this were not the strength for which he'd prayed to Telros. *Fickle are the ways of the gods, and their works among us are often subtle,* he thought, recalling an old westland saying. Then, aloud, he said, "Shayphim take you, Tolsadri, and may his Hounds feast on your soul."

The Loremaster was still a moment, as if Gerin's words had cast a spell upon him; then he put the flask of *wassan* on the small table next to the lamp. "You will bow to me yet, and pledge your everlasting devotion to the Powers. This *I* swear." Tolsadri could barely contain his rage.

Gerin felt a loosening of Algariq's control over him. She rose from her stool, her face suddenly ashen in the light of the cell's single lamp. "Honored Voice, the elixirs you have given him have weakened my hold on him. I need—"

"Silence, whore!" shrieked Tolsadri. The rage that had been building toward Gerin found its outlet in the soul stealer. The Loremaster wheeled about and punched her in the face.

Algariq reeled backward and crashed into the wall. Tolsadri was on her in an instant, pummeling her with his fists. Gerin heard her cry out and raise her hands to ward off the blows, but she did not fight back in any way. Gerin tried to will her to use her power on Tolsadri, to capture the Loremaster as he himself had been captured, but she would not.

Tolsadri had his hands around her neck and slammed her head into the stone wall three times. He released her and she slumped to the floor, unconscious or dead, Gerin could not tell which. Tolsadri straightened and kicked her once in the ribs, then muttered something in his native tongue that sounded like a curse.

The iron vice of Algariq's power that had gripped Gerin for weeks fell away. It was such a shocking sensation to have control of his body back that he gasped aloud. Both body and mind had been released.

The Loremaster faced him again, unaware that he was no longer under the power of the soul stealer. Gerin lashed out with his feet and knocked Tolsadri's legs from beneath him. He fell to the floor hard, then scrabbled for his knife, his face twisted with hate.

Gerin yanked down hard on the chain and tore it free from the ceiling. Chunks of rock and a cloud of dust fell upon him, but he ignored it. He was filled with his own rage, and it fueled his strength.

Before Tolsadri could rise or call for help, Gerin kicked him in the throat and crushed it beneath the toe of his boot. . Blood spurted from the his mouth as he clutched at his neck and sank back to the floor, unable to breath. Gerin picked up Tolsadri's knife and held it up for the Loremaster to see. His eyes widened.

"You lose, Tolsadri."

He drove the knife between Tolsadri's ribs and into his heart. The Loremaster stiffened, his eyes widening in shock, and then his life left him.

Hollin told them that he could sense a single man at the foot of the stairway in the Seilheth Tower. Rundgar went down alone, the cloak from one of the dead soldiers thrown over his shoulders.

The large captain appeared less than a minute later with a bloody knife in his hand and gestured for them to come down. A guard lay at the foot of the stairs, his throat cut. Rundgar dragged the body into a nearby storage room.

They continued to work their way downward and reached the central section of the castle. They were passing down a corridor with a sharp turn a short distance ahead when Hollin whispered that there were two men coming toward them. There was no place for them to hide and they were too far down the corridor to retreat. Balandrick and Rundgar rushed ahead and waited at the corner while the corridor around the bend brightened with approaching lamplight. Hollin made a gesture and his spark of magefire winked out.

As soon as the men rounded the turn, the two Khedeshians drove short knives up through their jaws. The guards died instantly without a sound. They hid the bodies in an empty room around the corner, then continued on.

They followed a stairway that emptied into a gallery above the Twilight Hall. There were five men in the room below, drinking and chatting quietly, but they did not notice Therain and the others, who crept along the inner wall of the gallery until they reached another passageway.

Once they were all in the corridor, Hollin placed his hand on Therain's arm. The wizard closed his eyes and drew several deep breaths.

"I'm sensing something familiar. Magic . . ."

"Is it Gerin?"

"No . . ." He grinned. "It's his sword, Nimnahal."

"Can you tell where it is?"

"Somewhere below us. I can take us to it. We can hope that Gerin is close by."

"You're better than a bloodhound, Hollin. Lead the way."

Tolsadri did not have the keys to Gerin's manacles on his body. Gerin opened himself to magic and was stunned when what should have been a raging river of power flowing through him appeared as the merest trickle. He panicked, then forced himself to grow calm so he could determine what had happened. He decided that the combination of Tolsadri's elixir and the poison from the pelonquas was preventing him from drawing on his full power. Part of him feared that his magic might never return to what it was, but he forced that thought aside.

He used what little magic he could muster to unlock the manacles, then flung the pelonquas from him in disgust, crushing them beneath his boots. He was weakening rapidly. He'd lost a great deal of blood, and the elixir the Loremaster had forced into him still clouded his mind and burned in his joints. The vial containing the *wassan* was broken on the floor, the liquid soaked into Tolsadri's pant leg. Gerin considered smearing some on his fingers and sucking on them to see if it relieved any of his pains, but feared it would make him sleep, so he worked two minor healing spells on himself instead.

He pulled on Tolsadri's cloak and raised its hood, then knelt beside Algariq. He did not touch her, and held the knife he'd just pulled from the Loremaster's chest at her throat, which he would slit if she so much as twitched. He would not allow himself to be taken by her again.

She was alive. He knew he should kill her, but he hesitated. She'd done what she had to him for the love of her son. That did not excuse her actions, but they made her less evil. He'd seen how she was treated by her countrymen, and could understand her desperate desire to raise herself up by whatever means she could.

Still, she was incredibly dangerous. He leaned toward her with the knife, poised to drive it into her heart.

He could not do it. His mind filled with the image of a little boy speared through the chest by an Atalari soldier, and the boy's sister, who jumped screaming to her death rather than face the warrior intent on her slaughter. An unspeakable crime forgotten for thousands upon thousands of years, revealed to him in a powerful vision precisely so it would no longer be forgotten, the victims remembered at least in some small way.

He did not—*would* not—forget. His memory was a grim reminder of what happened when the dark passions of the heart grew all-consuming, overpowering reason and compassion. He resolved to never fall into that trap, and to do all he could to prevent such an abomination from happening again. Because what he'd witnessed had been no mere battle, nor even the conclusion of a war, but the end of a race, the extermination of a people from the face of the world.

Gerin stood and looked down on Algariq's unconscious form. "I hope you remember the mercy I showed to you today. Don't make me regret that I spared your life."

He carried the lamp and concealed Tolsadri's knife in his other hand. As he climbed the stairs to the guard door he pulled the hood lower to hide as much of his face as he could.

He banged twice on the door. He heard the lock turn, then the door was pulled open. Two men waited in a small round room on the other side. They spoke to him in the native tongue of the Havalqa; it sounded to Gerin like a question.

He killed one soldier with a death spell that drained what was left of his magical strength, then stabbed the other just above his collarbone, driving Tolsadri's knife in to the hilt. He took the second soldier's sword and left the room.

He killed three more soldiers as he ascended through narrow, winding flights of stairs on his way out of the dungeons. The sight of Tolsadri's cloak made each of them hesitate, which proved to be a fatal mistake, but the last soldier opened a deep wound on Gerin's side that bled profusely. He was too weary, his magic still too weakened, for him to perform even a basic healing spell, so he tore off part of the cloak to bandage the wound as best as he could.

In a small room at the top of the stairs, he paused. He felt the presence of magical power nearby. It was diffuse, unfocused, and at first he could not be sure it was not merely a product of his weary and poisoned mind. But when he concentrated on it, he was sure it was real. There was magic—wizard's magic—somewhere very close.

A grin spread across his face. It was not just any magic. *Nimnahal*.

He took a step toward the stairway, then collapsed, unconscious before his head struck the floor.

"How far to the sword?" Therain asked the wizard.

"Not far. One or two levels down, I think. But—"

Five enemy soldiers appeared ahead of them. As they charged the Khedeshians, Hollin killed two with fleeting lines of golden fire that shot from his hands. The other three, startled by the display of magic, faltered. Balandrick, Captain Rundgar, and one of the Khedeshian soldiers—the hardened veteran Kamis Teldren—were on them in an instant and quickly cut them down.

They descended another stairway, then followed a long corridor. Hollin stopped before a closed door. "It's in here." He tried the handle, but it was locked. He broke the lock with a spell, then pushed it open to reveal a small storage room. Nimnahal was inside, resting on a shelf.

They took it and set off for the dungeons. Therain wondered how much longer their luck would hold.

At the base of a spiral stair they saw a figure crumpled against a wall. Rundgar approached the motionless form with his sword out, prepared to run the man through, when he lowered his weapon and crouched down.

"My lord, it is your brother."

Therain knelt by the unmoving form. His breath caught. It was indeed Gerin: thin and bloody and battered, but it was him, and he was alive.

The wizard performed a quick examination. "He's been poisoned. It's not deadly, but it's clouded his mind and made him weak. He's also been badly beaten. I should work some healing spells on him, but that will only push him into a deeper sleep."

"Do it," said Therain. "We'll carry him out of here."

"Wait," said Elaysen. "I can give him something to clear his mind and give him enough strength to get out of the castle. Then Hollin can work his spells."

She quickly mixed several powders in a flask, which she

filled with water from the skin she carried. Gerin spluttered when she poured some in his mouth, then began to swallow on his own. After the entire mixture was in him, he took several long deep breaths before opening his eyes, though to Therain he still appeared only half awake.

"Therain? Elaysen?" said Gerin, his voice weak and rough. "Is that really you?"

Therain hugged his brother. "What a bloody chase you've led us on! We've come to rescue you. But how did you get out here? I thought you'd be locked in the dungeon."

"I escaped, but then I guess I collapsed. My sword is right around here . . ." He got shakily to his feet.

"We already have it." With a grin, Hollin handed the sheathed weapon to Gerin.

"Gods above us, you look terrible," said Balandrick. "But it's wonderful to have you back."

"My lord, it is good to see you," said Elaysen.

Gerin's face brightened. "You are a sight for my weary eyes. All of you."

"Can you manage on your own?" asked Therain.

"Yes, for now."

"Then let's get out of here before this whole place comes awake."

They killed five more soldiers on their way back to the Seil-heth Tower. Gerin's strength gave out on the long tower stair. Balandrick threw the prince's arm across his shoulder and helped him up the rest of the way. Gerin's face was ashen and covered with sweat, grime, and blood.

Hollin's magical fog had not completely dispersed. As soon as they were clear of the tower the wizard created a spark of magefire in the air beside him, then faced the door to the tower and spoke a long spell in Osirin. The surface of the tower darkened and became blurry and indistinct. The darkening effect began at the base of the tower and rose upward, like a glass filling with murky water, until it was lost in the mist, beyond the reach of Hollin's magefire light.

"I've placed a powerful Closing upon the tower, all the way to its summit," said the wizard. "No one will be able to follow us for some time. It will take most of a day before it dissipates. Even if they battered a hole in the wall, the spell would still prevent them from leaving."

Therain could still scarcely believe they'd recovered Gerin. He realized now that despite his words to the others, he'd never had much hope that they would rescue him. It seemed almost a miracle that they had accomplished it.

Hollin made another gesture with his hands, and a kind of tunnel opened in the mist ahead of them. "Follow that," he said. "It will take us out of this mist."

Gerin and the others were beyond the tower before it was discovered that he had escaped. Algariq was found slumped in the cell, near to the Voice of the Exalted's cold body. A search began at once, and all of the exits to the castle were sealed. The Sai'fen guards around the Dreamer were doubled in case the intruders attempted to capture or kill it.

They quickly discovered that the ground-level door to the castle's uppermost tower would not open. When the door was forced from its hinges, the soldiers were startled to find their way still blocked, this time by a shroud of darkling power. They summoned an Adept of Bariq, who probed the barrier with the Mysteries, uttering several powerful Commands, but he could neither penetrate nor break it.

Algariq had been taken roughly from the cell and kept in the guardroom until it could be determined what had happened and what role she'd played in the prisoner's escape. She heard the men whispering about the strange power sealing the tower door and how the Voice of the Exalted himself was killed beneath their very noses.

It did not matter to her. She knew that her life was forfeit. Because of Tolsadri's arrogance, she felt certain she would soon be executed. When she was summoned to the presence of the Dreamer, she resigned herself to her fate, though she wished deeply and bitterly that she had not failed her son.

Tolsadri's body was in the Dreamer's chamber when she arrived. "Tell me what happened, soul stealer," said the Dreamer from behind its curtains. It sounded neither angry nor reproachful.

She bowed her head. "Great Dreamer, the elixirs the Voice of the Exalted gave to Prince Gerin weakened my hold on him. I tried to tell him that I needed to replenish and strengthen my powers, but the prince had just defied him and the Voice beat me senseless in his anger. My hold on the prince failed. I do not know what happened after that."

"You saw no one else?"

"No, Great Dreamer. I have heard that his countrymen slipped into the castle and escaped with him, but I saw no one. I apologize for my failing and for the death of the Exalted's Voice."

"Do not concern yourself with the Voice of the Exalted. He will return. He is dead now, but a Loremaster of his might can return from death several times if the wounds to his body are not too severe. See how he does not decay? Even now his powers strive to return him to life. But his anger will be great, and it would be best if you were not here when he rises."

"Yes, Great Dreamer. Do you have a command for me? Shall I hunt the prince once again?"

"In time. I must think on why he does not appear to possess knowledge of the Words of Making. Until then, go and reflect on why *you* are still alive, since he had it within his power to slay you but chose to let you live."

She had wondered that herself. He could not have known how long she would be unconscious. She might have raised the alarm before he left the dungeons. Why hadn't he killed her? She certainly would have killed him if their positions had been reversed.

She wondered where he was, her prey who had not held her in the contempt that her countrymen did even though she had taken him as a slave. Why had he spared her? It was incomprehensible to her, an irrational act. She would do as the Dreamer asked and reflect upon it until understanding came to her.

39

Gerin drifted in and out of consciousness as they made their way across the bleak uplands of Gedsengard. Balandrick supported much of his weight, but somehow Gerin managed to keep his feet moving beneath him, as if they had assumed a fierce desire of their own to escape the island.

From time to time he glanced over to make sure it was truly Balandrick supporting him, fearful that this was some malign trick of Tolsadri's to further break his mind. *Tolsadri's dead,* he told himself. *I slid his own knife into his heart. That was no trick.* The image of the Loremaster's corpse gave him no small measure of satisfaction.

At some point he felt sand beneath his feet, and a short while later was lifted into a rocking boat. He sat between Balandrick and Elaysen, too weary to even open his eyes. He heard Hollin speaking in Osirin and realized the wizard was working healing spells. Elaysen's voice came to him distantly, asking him to swallow the elixir she was holding up to his mouth. He did as she asked. It had a bitter taste, like burned cedar, but he drank it all. Hollin's spells worked their way through his body. He felt dozens of spots of warmth come to life as the spells focused their powers on his many wounds.

Then he slept, and felt nothing more.

* * *

Gerin found himself in the grip of several strange and fever-ish dreams. He saw the Dreamer's curtains billowing within its chamber and heard its voice echoing from the stones, con-firming his guess that it had indeed come to this world from another. He saw Nimnahal blazing with amber fire, spinning among the stars, its form shifting within its cloak of flame, though he also knew that all of the swords were still the *same* sword, connected by the immense power he'd infused into the weapon. He saw once more the vision of the nameless king from another world accepting that world's version of Nimnahal from a sorceress on the shore of a tree-shrouded lake. He saw the clearing where he'd summoned Naragenth's spirit—a location which itself was no longer fully in Osseria, the very reality of the place transformed by the power of the Baryashins' spells and the Horn of Tireon—and once again heard the dead wizard's shade tell him, *The Chamber of the Moon was a great secret, and one of my greatest creations. It is not in Osseria.*

He saw Nimnahal once more, its flaming blade spinning in the darkness faster and faster until it was a circle of fire as bright as the sun. His dream ended abruptly when he felt himself being lifted from the longboat onto a much larger ship. He forced his eyes open and saw stars wheel-ing over his head, but there was no fire-drenched sword spinning across the heavens. Closing his eyes again, Gerin lapsed back into sleep, but this time did not remember his dreams.

He slept for most of the journey back to the coast. Hollin's healing spells and Elaysen's elixirs kept him in a state of half wakefulness much of the time, while they mended his sorely wounded body. As Tolsadri had promised, none of his wounds threatened his life, but the cumulative effect of so many injuries, as well as that of the elixirs the Loremaster had given him, took a long time to heal.

"How are you feeling, my lord?" asked Elaysen on the morning the Belkan Hills came into view on the horizon. She held up a stoppered flask of whitish liquid.

He propped himself up on his elbows. "Better. I suppose I have you and Hollin to thank for that."

"I wish I had his powers. Or yours. Magic is so much more precise in its healing than my medicines."

"In some things, yes. But one day wizards will be gone, and the skills of healers like you will be all that remains. What you know is precious, and needs to be preserved and passed on."

"I make notes of everything I learn. My knowledge will not die with me."

"Why did you come for me? I know Almaris is besieged. I thought you would go to your father."

She smiled at him. "I made a promise to you, my lord. I do not make such promises lightly."

He studied her face in the cabin's dim light. *Such a strong woman,* he thought. Yet she was wounded as well, scarred by the horrible manner of her mother's death.

He knew that Claressa would hate Elaysen because she would see her as a threat, a woman she could not cow or intimidate. She would fear her as well, because Elaysen would see right through to Claressa's heart, something his sister guarded more closely than the kingdom's crown and scepter.

He frowned. Wheels began to turn in his mind. The Scepter of the King . . .

"My lord? You have a faraway look in your eyes."

"It's nothing. Just thinking. I had some odd dreams while I slept." *The scepter, other worlds, the Chamber of the Moon . . . There was something in all of this—*

The door swung open. "You're awake at last, my lord," said Balandrick. "About time." He gave Elaysen a sly wink. "Hollin said you're just faking it now to get sympathy. Do you think you can walk off the ship by yourself when we dock, or shall I wheel you off the deck in a barrow? I'm sure Captain Gethelaine could find one for me somewhere."

"Perhaps I should test my strength by thumping you soundly on the head," Gerin replied. "Elaysen can listen for the hollow sound it makes to determine exactly how empty your skull is."

"I'll leave you two to bicker without the benefit of an audience." She rose and inclined her head. "My lord."

They reached the coast without incident. They saw no
Havalqa ships during their return, for which Captain Gethelaine profusely thanked Paérendras. He burned so much
incense that it seemed his cabin had caught fire, with blue
smoke coughing from the windows. Three dockhands at the
waterfront, unaware that the smoke was there by design and
not because of an out-of-control blaze that would consume
Haldrensi if not quickly doused, rushed onto the deck with
buckets of water and hurled them through the windows. The
sight of Gethelaine charging from his cabin with a cutlass in
each hand sent them fleeing for their lives.

Gerin managed to make the long climb to Castle Pelleron without help, though he did stop frequently to catch
his breath. *At least that bastard Tolsadri's dead,* he thought
each time he leaned against the rough stone while he drew
deep breaths. *He won't torture me or anyone else ever again.
But Telros save me, I wish I had my strength back!*

He ate and slept for a few hours once they reached the
castle, then roused himself and met the rest of his company
and the baron in the keep's council chamber. Three iron
chandeliers hung low over a table. A number of maps of the
lands between the castle and Almaris had been spread out
upon it.

"My lord, I am grateful to the gods for their mercy in de-
livery you to us from the clutches of the enemy," said the
baron. "I admit, I had little hope that your brother's rescue
attempt would succeed. While you rested, Prince Therain
told me the tale of your escape. Remarkable. I'm glad to be
proven wrong."

"Tell me what our enemy has been doing," said Gerin.
"What of Almaris?"

Baron Thorael cleared his throat. "The enemy staging area
south of here has close to thirty thousand men at last count.
We expect them to march on Almaris any day. They've sent
several smaller forces ahead of the main army. Four coastal

fortresses—Melchen, Fargave, Runlos, and Highspire— have been captured and occupied by the Havalqa, which they are using to land more ships with supplies and matériel for the larger force when it moves. Almaris itself has been blockaded and is completely cut off from the sea. We've received word that your uncle is in Tan Orech, where the fleet is gathering. An army is also massing in the plains south of the Samaro River under the leadership of Duke Andrel Reilmen, with the goal of driving the invaders back, but I don't have any idea how large the force is or when it's expected to march. The Taeratens and City Watch hold the capital, and even swollen with refugees from the countryside they should have provisions to last a lengthy siege. We will break this enemy, my lord. I have no doubt of that."

"We need to get to the city," said Therain. "We're the princes of the kingdom and the capital is about to come under siege."

One of the baron's counselor's let out a deep breath that fluttered the long gray whiskers of his moustache. "The path out of the hills is guarded, my lord. The enemy has fenced us in. You would have to break through that, then ride as if Shayphim's Hounds were on your heels if you expect to reach the city before the siege begins."

"Then that is exactly what we'll do," said Therain with a trace of irritation. "We will not sit here on our hands while the capital—and the king—are besieged."

The counselor lowered his eyes. "Yes, my lord. Forgive me, I meant only to explain what trials we will face."

"There's another reason to get to Almaris," said Gerin. He felt ready now to tell them what he'd pondering since his dreams on *Cregar's Glory*. "I think I know where Naragenth's library is hidden, but I need the Scepter of the King to reach it."

40

A heavy silence fell across the room after Gerin's abrupt pronouncement.

"Before I say more, let me explain to the baron what it is we're talking about." He gave an abbreviated account of Naragenth's conclave of wizards, the creation of the Varsae Estrikavis, and its loss during the Wars of Unification.

"So you now believe you know where to find this lost library, my lord?" asked the baron.

"Yes."

"Hollin, you should check him for a fever," said Therain. "I think he's delusional."

"Indeed," said the wizard. "I admit to being skeptical, Gerin."

"Just hear me out."

Balandrick and Therain stared at him as if he'd lost his mind. Donael Rundgar's expression, as usual, was impenetrable. Elaysen watched him curiously, apparently the only one willing to trust him.

"I've already told you that the Dreamers come from another world, a plane of existence different from our own. Now, when I refashioned my sword into a weapon of magic, I had a vision of another version of the same sword being given to a king. Hollin believes I saw a real event that was taking place in a world different from our own."

"What does this have to do with Naragenth's library?" asked Therain.

"We know that the Dreamers come from another world, and that Nimnahal's magic flows out of Osseria into other realms as well. This tells me that these other worlds are accessible from our own. That not only can magic flow between them, as with the sword, but that living beings can pass from one to another, as the Dreamers did."

He leaned forward, growing more animated as he spoke. "I remembered what Naragenth's spirit told me when I summoned him on Maratheon's Hill. He said that the Varsae Estrikavis was hidden in the Chamber of the Moon, a name no one had ever heard before. And he said that the Chamber was not in Osseria. I took that to mean that he might have hidden it on an island in the Gulf of Gedsuel, or out in the Maurelian Sea. Almaris, after all, is a seaport. Or perhaps somewhere to the south, beyond Khedesh's borders.

"But he also said that the Chamber of the Moon was one of his greatest creations. I never gave it much thought before, but now I think it might be the key to understanding where the library is hidden. If the Chamber of the Moon was one of his greatest creations, it doesn't make sense that it was simply hidden away on an island, or beyond the border of Osseria. After all, anyone could accomplish that. It doesn't take the power of an amber wizard to hide a library in that manner. Any competent builder could do it.

"What if Naragenth meant that the Varsae Estrikavis was hidden in another world? That he had somehow found a way to penetrate another plane of existence as the perfect hiding place for the knowledge gathered in his conclave? That's why no trace of it has ever been located—because there's nothing in Osseria to find."

"Is such a thing possible?" Elaysen said to Hollin.

"Not long ago I would have thought the idea ridiculous. But I've felt Nimnahal's power myself, and have no reason to doubt the tale of these Dreamers. And this . . . theory . . . does make sense of Naragenth's words to Gerin. It is incongruous that he should call the hiding of his library one of his greatest achievements if the hiding itself were a mundane matter. It seems to indicate that unique magic was involved in its concealment."

"And you already believe the Scepter of the King contains the key spells for the Varsae Estrikavis," Therain said to his brother.

"Even if you learn to activate the spells, where will you use it?" asked Elaysen. "Don't you have to know where the door to the library is before you can unlock it?"

"She's got you there," said Therain.

"I haven't completely figured that out yet," said Gerin. In truth, he hadn't thought about it at all, and now felt his enthusiasm evaporate a little.

"If this library is truly hidden in another world," said Balandrick, "couldn't the door to it be anywhere you want it to be?"

"Interesting," said Hollin. "You may be on to something."

"I agree," said Gerin. "That's a brilliant idea."

"All this guesswork is wonderful and interesting," said Therain, "but we're never going to find out one way or the other unless we actually *get* to Almaris."

As the discussion turned to more practical matters of breaking past the enemy soldiers blocking Selwaen's Stair and then managing, somehow, to slip past an invasion force thirty thousand strong, Gerin's thoughts kept returning to what Balandrick had said about the location of the entrance to the Varsae Estrikavis. The more he considered it, the more sense it made.

There were a lot of assumptions, to be sure—the most notable being his conjecture that the library was indeed hidden in some other realm of existence—but if *that* were true, then it did seem pointless to fix a door to a physical location. Maybe any door could work. As long as Naragenth had the scepter, maybe he could have just wandered the halls of his royal palace and entered the library at will, making his closet door, or the door to his gardens, the entrance to the Varsae Estrikavis by directing the scepter's key spells into them. It was always possible that the door had to be anchored in a specific physical location for reasons they had yet to understand. All of this was, after all, wild conjecture. He would have to speak to Hollin later about what, if anything, was known of such doors. But it still felt right to him, and made the most sense of Naragenth's cryptic and unfinished comments to him on Maratheon's Hill.

A question from the baron brought Gerin back to the conversation at hand. The others were concerned that a journey overland was too risky; the chance of being captured, or simply not reaching the city before the siege began, was very high. They were contemplating a sea voyage, though that too was not without its dangers. "The enemy holds the coastal fortresses between here and the capital, with supply ships traveling between them and Gedsengard," said Baron Thorael.

"So the waters between us and Almaris are crawling with enemy vessels," said Therain. "It seems little different than a journey over land. And the city itself is blockaded, in case you'd all forgotten."

"We have not forgotten, my lord," said the baron as he leaned over one of the maps spread on the table. "You're right, the city itself cannot be reached directly by sea, but a ship can still set down a longboat south of the Blackwater Marsh. The city can be reached within a day from there." He tapped his finger against the thick vellum, at a small sheltered inlet just below the marsh.

They decided that a sea voyage was their only choice to reach Almaris. "We leave tonight, as soon as a ship can be made ready," said Gerin. "Baron, I leave the arrangements of a vessel to you. Everyone, get your things and meet in the great hall in an hour. We'll worry about sleep once we're on board."

Gerin's exhaustion returned as they descended the northern stairs toward Haldrensi. Balandrick placed a steadying hand on his shoulder a number of times during the descent. Gerin wanted to shrug him off, but his captain was having none of it. "You're still recovering your strength, my lord. These stairs are treacherous, and if you fall you could easily break your neck, amber wizard or not."

Once more they would be voyaging on *Cregar's Glory.* Captain Gethelaine greeted them at the end of the gangplank, his hands resting comfortably on his bulging stomach. "The baron's men tell me we'll be sailing south through that tangle of unholy bastards who've dared to set foot on our sovereign soil," he said as they filed past him. "Don't you worry 'bout anything, my lord. *Glory*'s a fast ship, faster than those lumbering behemoths they got, laden with men and beasts and Paérendras knows what else. We'll spit in their eyes as we sail past 'em and then drop our trousers and fart at 'em for good measure."

A half-moon partially hidden by a thin veil of clouds cast a frosty light across the ship as sailors clambered through the rigging and finished stowing supplies below deck. The waters of the inlet were calm, and sloshed gently against the sides of the ship and the algae-crusted pylons supporting the piers. Behind them the small town was dark and quiet. The baron and his men, lanterns in hand, had taken their leave on the pier and watched Gerin and the rest file onto the ship.

A deckhand led Gerin to the captain's low-ceilinged cabin, which would be his for the duration of the voyage. He slumped onto a bench built into one wall and closed his eyes, listening to the sounds of sailors moving above and below him, cursing and muttering to one another, and the creaks of planks as they flexed with the shifting weight of men and supplies.

He'd almost drifted off to sleep when he was roused by a knock at the door. He forced his eyes opened and called for the person to enter.

Hollin stepped into the cabin. "We'll be under way shortly," the wizard said quietly. He stepped closer. "Venegreh preserve me, Gerin, you need to rest."

"That's what I was doing when you knocked."

"My apologies, then. I'll come back later—"

"You're here now. Tell me what you've come to say and then I'll get some sleep."

"I wanted to explain to you that we may have . . . difficulties . . . using our magic out at sea. Deep water does strange things to a wizard's powers."

Gerin straightened and almost cracked his head against the sloping wall. "What do you mean? You never told me anything about this before."

Hollin shrugged, and a sheepish expression came over his face. "There was no need. No one has ever learned why a wizard's magic is corrupted over the sea, only that it is. In shallow water there's no problem, but in the open sea . . ." The wizard shook his head. "Even simple spells can become wildly unpredictable."

"Hollin, I was hoping that you and I would be able to drive off any enemy ships that threatened us. This isn't a warship. There are no oarsmen to propel it if the winds fail. Are you saying we're defenseless?"

"Not entirely: I've never attempted magic on the sea before. I'm only telling you what I've read and learned from others. I don't know what will happen if we attempt magic. Our spells *may* work fine, at least some of them. Others may not work at all, and some may have unintended consequences. I read an account of a wizard who attempted a spell to calm rough seas and somehow tore his ship in half."

"This isn't instilling me with confidence."

"I don't think we should attempt magic unless our hand is forced by the enemy. Let Captain Gethelaine do what he can to get us to our landing area. If the Havalqa threaten to board or sink us, then we'll act, but not before."

"Are there any other places where magic doesn't work that you neglected to tell me about? A latrine under a full moon? A bathtub before the ten o'clock bells?"

"I'm sorry, Gerin. I wasn't withholding anything from you. It simply hadn't come up yet as a topic in your studies. It's not as if we have to worry about sea voyages at Ailethon."

"This is between you and me for now. I don't want to alarm anyone else. If we need to use our magic and it blows up in our faces, then we'll have a chat with everyone about this quaint but little known fact that magic doesn't work right over water."

"That's why I came to you privately."

"Is there anything else?"

"No."

"Good night, then. I need to sleep." Gerin closed his eyes as Hollin left the cabin. Outside, he could hear the deck-hands casting off the ropes holding *Cregar's Glory* to the pier, and Captain Gethelaine bellowing orders. They were under way.

The wind picked up once they cleared the sheltered inlet around which Haldrensi had been built, blowing steadily from the east. Sailors scurried up the masts and across spars and rigging to unfurl the rest of the gray canvas sails. Captain Gethelaine prowled back and forth across the forecastle, watching both his men and the sea with seemingly equal attentiveness.

"He looks ready to bellow orders at the waves," said Therain to Hollin. "And expect to have them obeyed."

The wizard smiled, but it seemed tight and forced to Therain.

"Is something bothering you?" asked the prince.

Hollin shook his head. "I'm just distracted. Your brother's ideas about the Varsae Estrikavis took me by surprise."

"You and me both." He couldn't fathom the convolutions of logic that Gerin's mind had followed to arrive at his bizarre conclusions. *Then again, I wasn't captured and tortured, and I didn't see this Dreamer firsthand or hear its tale for myself. Maybe it would seem more plausible if I had.*

Or maybe the torture scarred him more deeply than we realize. "Do you really think he's on to something?"

"I don't know. I truly don't."

"It seems like he made quite an improbable leap."

"It does, but I've learned that your brother's mind works in very reasoned, rational ways. I think some of the mental exercises he's done in his training have helped him hone those particular skills. He's very smart. You all are, in fact. Reshel was especially bright."

"It's too bad Claressa wastes her brainpower worrying

about men and trying to see how disagreeable she can be to everyone around her."

"Well, now that she's married she may turn to more productive pastimes."

"Oh, I'm sure she will. Like setting herself up as the absolute ruler of Tolthean. Mark my words, Hollin, Baris will become her total puppet, like Ponce the Dunce at a mummer's show. I can see him dangling from strings, with my dear sister laughing as she yanks him along." He mimicked a puppet's off-kilter movements for a few steps across the deck.

Hollin laughed aloud. "You have a gift for interesting descriptions, Therain."

"It's easy when they're true."

"Paérendras has blessed us so far, my lord," said Captain Gethelaine the next morning when Gerin stepped onto the deck. "We've had calm waters, a steady wind, and no sign of those buggerin' bastards despoiling our fair seas, may Shayphim take their screaming souls."

The captain was on the forecastle, exactly where Gerin had last seen him the night before. *Gods above me, does the man sleep at all?* He held a seeing-glass in one hand, tapping its brass-capped end against his thigh as if keeping some secret inner time.

"Let's pray the sea god's mood remains favorable," said Gerin. "Unless he wants to whip up a storm and send a few of the Havalqa ships to the depths."

"Aye, my lord. I'll say a prayer to Niélas to beseech her husband to drag a score or so of the bastards' warships down to a watery grave. 'Course, I've been saying that prayer for weeks with no luck, but you never know . . ."

There was little for them to do other than keep out of the sailors' way. Gerin and Hollin talked a little more about what spells they should attempt should the need arise. Gerin wanted to know if simpler spells had less of a chance of being disrupted by the effect of the sea than complex ones.

"From what I've read, *any* spell can be corrupted," said

the wizard. "There is no way to predict which spells will work and which will not. If we need to use our magic, then we should use the proper spells for the situation and hope for the best."

Gerin and Elaysen spent some time talking about the One God. He learned more of what was required of the *taekrim* who followed the Holy Path of the Prophet, and what steps he could take to encourage others to follow his example. "We want people to follow us willingly, not out of fear," she said.

"You've already told me that Aidrel Entraly doesn't agree with the Prophet about this. That he wants as many converts as possible, no matter how he gets them. Even if he has to use force."

"He does not speak with the Prophet's voice."

"But why does your father keep such a dangerous man around? Why make him a member of the Inner Circle if he's going to argue against everything your father wants to do?"

It was good to be in her presence again. He felt revitalized simply being around her.

"Because if Aidrel wasn't among the Inner Circle he might very well go off and create his own version of the One God's religion, and my father desperately does not want that. He does not want his faith splintered, especially now, when it is still so young. He believes it is inevitable that factions will rise—they always do. People will form their own ideas about different aspects of the faith, and some will become so convinced of the rightness of their position that they will brook no argument from anyone, even their religion's founder."

"Fanatics. And lunatics. They seem closely related. At least second cousins."

She smiled. "You're teasing, my lord, but yes, every religion spawns fanatics. It's inevitable. There are people who spend their lives waiting for something to give them a purpose, to fill the emptiness at the center of their existence, and when they find it, whatever it is, they latch on to it with a fierce resolve that consumes them like a fire. I've seen it happen before, with priests of the Temple, or different ascetics with their vows of silence or poverty, or the men and women of the various religious orders in Almaris, like those who follow Laonn or Thureen."

"Or the Daughters of Reshel," he said. "Some of the girls who swore to serve the needs of the dead have killed themselves on the anniversary of my sister's death. They slit their throats, as she did." He spoke matter-of-factly, but speaking of Reshel's death caused a cold hand to clutch at his heart.

Elaysen nodded. "Yes, and in doing so completely misunderstood your sister's sacrifice. Those girls were ending their own pain, and by copying the Lady Reshel's noble and selfless act, they felt they were somehow also acting nobly. But they were not. They were acting selfishly, though I'm sure none of them thought of it that way. They were looking for a *purpose* to their lives, and since they had none of their own, they took your sister's, hoping to redeem the hollowness in their hearts and the empty spaces in their souls."

"So your father keeps those potential fanatics close so he can control them, or at least counter them should they decide to betray his teachings."

"Yes, exactly. Though they never see their actions as betrayals. When Aidrel was asked to join the Inner Circle he was humbled and moved by my father's request, and for years has worked tirelessly to spread the word of the One God's return. But he's become frustrated by what he sees as the slow progress of the faith—though in truth it is spreading beyond my father's wildest dreams—and that has led him to question my father's ways more and more. But he was not always so disagreeable."

"How does your father control what happens in other countries? How does he know what is being taught in Threndellen, for example, or Ellohar? That his emissaries are truly following his word?"

She flashed him one of her smiles that made his breath catch. "He does not, my lord. And they will no doubt form their own unique forms of the faith, imbuing it with whatever they need to make it work for them, to make it speak to their souls and help them with their lives." She shifted on the bench and leaned closer to him. The creaks of the ship and the muffled voices of sailors moving above them vanished from Gerin's perception as he lost himself in the fierceness of her eyes. "Faith is a living thing. It must be in order to have meaning. That is not to say that the rules and tenets of a particular religion can be ignored or overlooked—they cannot be, not without losing the very essence of the faith itself. The rules and rituals and tenets of a faith are what bind its adherents together, making them a community, a family of the faithful. Without that, there *is* no religion, only a person's particular set of ideas, isolated and alone. But within the rules and rituals there must also be room for the faithful to practice and understand them in their own way; it must be flexible enough to accommodate everyone, else it is of little use, and in the end will wither and be forgotten."

Gerin frowned. It seemed to him that Elaysen contradicted herself—that faith must be both monolithic and absolute in order to thwart those who would twist it for their own extreme and fanatical ends, yet also malleable so it could speak to the widest possible group of people and still have meaning for them.

He was about to ask her about this, but upon further reflection realized it was not the contradiction it first appeared to be. Rules guarded against fanaticism but could never completely dispel it, since there would always be those whose notions of the way things *should* be would conquer their longing to follow the rules set down before them, and they would twist and distort the meaning of what they'd been taught to suit their own goals, no matter how far removed from what they professed as their faith.

But he also understood her point that a religion had to live and breathe and adapt to the situations of its adherents, or else be threatened with irrelevancy. Would a mercenary from Ellohar have the same needs as a tanner from Armenos? Aunphar claimed his religion was for all people, of all classes and stations, both highborn and low. How could it *not* be flexible and hope to succeed?

It must succeed. It seems the Havalqa have corroborated one of the key underpinnings of the Prophet's religion: that the Adversary of the One God is going to arise in the world. The Great Enemy the Dreamer spoke of and the Adversary must be the same being. It's incomprehensible to think otherwise.

"My lord? Are you well?"

"Yes, Elaysen. You are not only a gifted healer but an orator as well. Your father would do well to make you one of his emissaries."

"I do what I can in that regard, my lord, but healing is my first love and the passion of my life. I don't think there is room to do both with equal measure."

41

Gerin and Hollin attempted several spells in the privacy of his cabin to see what effect the sea might have on them. They first created sparks of magefire, five each. Gerin's appeared and vanished as he willed, but Hollin's third spark flared suddenly, as if a bucket of oil had somehow been splashed upon the suspended bit of magical fire; both men threw themselves down as the flames darted across the room and licked the ceiling before disappearing.

Hollin cursed. Gerin rolled to a sitting position and said, "I'm guessing you weren't trying to do that."

"No, the gods damn this sea, I wasn't trying that!" He stood and straightened his tunic. Gerin saw that some of Hollin's hair had been singed, the ends of his pale blond hair curled and blackened along his left temple and ear.

"Did it draw more magic from you?"

"No."

"Then how did it flare up like that? It would take more magic to make it—"

"I don't know! I *hate* this," said Hollin. "I hate that our powers have been neutralized by nothing more than water. It's absurd. It *offends* me, by the gods."

"And no one's ever learned why water has this effect? I mean, how big does the body of water have to be before this starts to happen? Does it happen on a lake? A river?"

"As I told you, no one knows why. Many wizards have

studied this over the centuries, and I'm certain most of your questions have been answered, but at the moment I can't recall—"

The door banged open and Balandrick barged into the room. He opened his mouth to speak, then shut it and sniffed, wrinkling his nose. "Are you burning something in here?"

"It's nothing, Balan," said Gerin. "A little spell got away from Hollin, that's all." He winked at his captain as Hollin gritted his teeth.

"I'm sorry to break up you're your little . . . whatever . . . my lord, but you need to come on deck. We've been spotted by an enemy ship, and Captain Gethelaine says it's going to catch us before nightfall."

On the deck, sailors were running everywhere—hauling rope, lashing down barrels, climbing up the masts and rigging, and shouting to the captain, who stood on the port side of the ship, his seeing-glass pressed against his right eye.

Gerin followed his line of sight and saw a black ship on the horizon. It was little more than a dark dot against the hazy blue-white sky; obviously a ship, but he could make out no detail. He created a Farseeing and saw the ship as if he were about a hundred yards from it. It was a massive vessel, at least three times the size of *Cregar's Glory*, with four masts of blue and red sails and trim painted crimson and gold. The wood of the hull was dark, almost black, though whether from paint or the weathering of the wood he could not say. He could see bare-chested and barefoot men moving along the spars like ants crawling across a stick.

Gods above, it's big! Larger even than his uncle's flagship, the jewel of the Khedeshian fleet.

His Farseeing stretched sideways into a long oval, its edges rippling like shreds of paper being blown by a fierce wind. The next moment it vanished completely. "What the . . . ?" he muttered. He was still sending magic into the spell—he'd felt no disruption of any kind in the flow of his power. *So where is my magic going if the Farseeing is no longer there?*

He cancelled the spell and saw Hollin watching him. The wizard shrugged. It did not appear that anyone else had noted the odd disappearance of his Farseeing; they were all staring hard at the ship bearing down on them from the northwest.

Captain Gethelaine pulled the seeing-glass from his eye and tapped its brass end against his thigh. "By Niélas's honeyed tits, we're in a bit of a spot."

"A bit of a spot?" said Balandrick. "*A bit of a spot?* Is that all you can say?"

Gethelaine glowered at him. A less formidable man might have cowered beneath that withering gaze. "No, but it seems it's all that *you* can say, Master Balandrick. Now shut up so I can think, if you will. And fear not—I've been in worse spots before."

"How could it be worse than this? Were there two princes on your ship when you were in one of your other 'spots'? Tell me, how did you get out of the other ones?"

"Why, I gave the bloody pirates what they bloody well wanted. What did you think? Are you an imbecile, man? Can you not use your brain?" He thumped one of his fingers against his temple.

Gerin thought Balan might actually draw his sword and go after the rotund captain, but after several deep breaths he wheeled about and stalked away from Gethelaine. "Excitable, ain't he?" said the captain.

"What *is* your plan?" asked Hollin. "Your previous means of escape from pirates—while possessing a certain admirable practicality—won't work with the Havalqa, I'm afraid. Their goal is to take everyone on this ship and convert them to their caste system, as the prince saw in their encampment and on Gedsengard. They're not after cargo, Captain Gethelaine. Or rather, the only cargo they care about is *us*."

Gethelaine looked at Hollin as if he'd sprouted a second head. "Are you daft, too?" he said after a lengthy pause. "Did you knock yourself on the head coming up from below? Of course I've got a plan. By the sea god's weedy beard, I've got two wizards on board! Can you not do something to make *us* go faster or *them* go slower? I'll say your magic isn't worth a bit of spit in a hurricane if it can't do something like that."

He glanced at Gerin. "Begging your pardon, my lord. But I say as I think."

"Your honesty is admirable, Captain. No need to beg my pardon for it. So there's nothing you can do to outrun or evade the ship pursuing us?"

"No, my lord, there's not. That ship's bigger, faster, and she's seen us. The wind favors us both, which means she'll keep closing the distance until she can grapple us and pull us alongside her hull, like two lovers in a bosomy embrace. And if the winds fail, she's got two banks of oars to our none."

Gerin and Hollin exchanged knowing looks. *I guess we'll see just how badly our magic can go wrong when we unleash the kind of power we'll need to take them on. Maybe we'll split* Cregar's Glory *in half by mistake. Wouldn't that be something?* He laughed despite the direness of the situation. Then he saw Elaysen standing to one side, her hands clenched with worry, and the smile vanished from his face.

"We'll do everything we can, Captain. Come on, Hollin. Time to plan a strategy."

Back in the captain's cabin, Gerin said, "I think we should try to knock them out fast. Something really powerful and just hope it works the way we want. If we try lots of smaller spells it just increases our chances that one of them will go wrong on us."

Hollin paced the small space, tapping his index finger against his lip. "I think we should first try to use our magic to help us outrun the other ship. If that fails, then we can worry about a battle."

"Are you sure we should be directing our power at our own ship? After what happened with your bit of magefire—and how my Farseeing just evaporated in front of my eyes—I'd be more comfortable directing our power as far from us as possible."

"I understand your sentiment, but there are other things to consider. There is very little we can do to that ship from afar. We'd have to let it close the distance substantially before we could attack, and then if our spells failed or damaged us instead . . ." He shrugged.

The prince considered what Hollin said. Even if they attempted something as simple as firing raw magic at the vessel to pierce its hull and set its sails ablaze, it would have to be much closer than it now was. Hollin was right. If it came to a fight, they would have to let the Havalqa ship get close.

"What do you think we should try?" he asked.

When they emerged on deck a few minutes later, they proceeded to Captain Gethelaine and told him their plan. The captain nodded, and muttered something every few seconds that sounded to Gerin like "Hrumpha."

The plan was a simple one. Gerin would use his magic to intensify the wind propelling *Cregar's Glory*; at the same time, Hollin would use several spells to make the prow of the ship move more smoothly through the water. "The Wardings should reduce the friction between the hull and the sea. I've never attempted such a thing before, so I don't know how effective it will be. If it doesn't seem to be helping, I'll stop and help Gerin with the wind."

"Aye, well, you're the wizards," said the captain. "Far be it for me to tell you how to conduct your magical affairs. But if you can boost our tailwind I'll give you a hug and kiss like I usually hold for my favorite whores."

Hollin stiffened. "That won't be necessary, Captain."

"I suppose not. But the look on your face was worth it, Master Wizard." He clapped Hollin on the shoulder, laughed, then waddled off toward the forecastle. He was halfway up the ladder when he paused and turned toward them. "You'll be starting now, yes? Otherwise there won't be much point to it." He glanced toward the enemy ship.

"Right away, Captain."

Gerin moved to the stern of the ship, while Hollin followed the captain onto the forecastle. Balandrick, who was lurking near the base of the main mast with Therain, accompanied the prince.

Gerin summoned magic into himself and began the incantation. He decided he would start with a minimal amount of magic and increase it slowly. He did not want to create a sudden gale that might have enough force to rip through the sails or break spars. Once he had the feel of the power and how he was affecting the ship's speed, he would increase the magic flowing into the spells.

He created two different and distinct kinds of magic, one for the starboard side of the ship and the other to port. They were both weather spells, designed to generate wind by creating imbalances in pressure. Though the end results were the same, the incantations and the underlying principles were very different. He decided to use both to see which might work best for his needs.

He was not sure how the spells would interact with the wind already blowing—the spells were made to work in still air, not air already in motion. Hollin had not known what might happen either. He could only hope they would increase the wind's force enough to help them outrun their pursuer.

Gerin fashioned the starboard tailwind first, and then the one to port. The incantations were difficult, and once created, he had trouble keeping them not only stable but blowing at approximately the same strength, so that one did not overpower the other. Sweat broke out on his forehead as he struggled to maintain control of the spells while he slowly fed them more magic. Wind blew across the ship in fits and starts, but after a few minutes he managed to keep his magical wind—still using both spells, since neither seemed more efficient than the other and he feared to stop one abruptly, unsure of what effect it might have—moving at a strong, steady rate.

Sweat dripped down into his eyes, but he was concentrating so intensely on the spells that he did not dare move to wipe his face. His breath came in ragged gasps as the power flowing through him intensified—he needed to draw more now merely to maintain the wind he'd already created. If the spells continued to drink so much magic from him, he did not think he would be able to increase the wind's speed any more than it now was.

"How are we doing, Balan?" he managed to say.

"I'm not sure, my lord. We seem to be moving faster, but I'm no sailor. I'll check with that annoying dog of a captain." He rushed off toward the forecastle, where Gethelaine stood with Hollin.

Elaysen approached him. "I can see the strain this is taking on you, my lord. Is there anything I can do to help?"

"No, but thank you for the offer."

Balandrick returned. "The fat old goat said that we're starting to pull away from the other ship and to keep doing whatever it is you're doing, my lord."

"I think you . . . and the captain . . . should bunk together tonight . . . assuming we're still in one piece," said Gerin between deep breaths.

Balan laughed. "Not if you want both of us to be alive in the morning."

The magic flowing through him was growing at an astounding rate. It was all he could do now to keep the spells from collapsing into—

He saw a flash of golden magic from the prow of the ship. A moment later a shimmering translucent curtain of golden light rolled down the deck. It was very weak, so that its touch did little more than leave the crewmen with tingling and itchy skin and a dim afterglow in their eyes.

But the wave was enough to disrupt Gerin's already tenuous hold on his own spells. The shock and distraction of what had happened on the forecastle collapsed the weather spells with a final heaving gust of salt-tinged air. He sagged to his knees, exhausted, and tried to catch his breath. He felt hands on his shoulders and knew before he raised his head that they were Elaysen's.

"My lord, are you hurt?"

"I'm fine. Just . . . tired." He looked up, wondering what had happened to Hollin. The wizard was no longer visible on the forecastle. Captain Gethelaine was shouting something Gerin could not hear and gesturing to a spot on the deck blocked from Gerin's view.

He stood and saw that Hollin had crumpled to the planks,

where he lay in a heap. Gerin's heart lurched in his chest.

Hollin was being examined by a wisp of a man who'd been introduced to Gerin as the ship's cutter, adept at stitching wounds and sawing off crushed limbs but good for little else.

"Is he alive?" asked the prince as he knelt.

"Aye, my lord, 'e's still breathin'," said the cutter. "Can't really say what 'appened to 'im—'e ain't got no 'urt to 'isself that I kin see. I seen a flash o' light, like the settin' sun glintin' off the sea, and then 'e just fell like someone clobbered 'im on the 'ead with a big ol' stick."

The prince gently nudged him aside. "Thank you for your help, but I'll look after him now."

Elaysen crouched on Hollin's other side and felt for his pulse in his neck. "His heartbeat's strong; so is his breathing. What happened with his magic? What went wrong?"

"You'll have to be asking him that," said Captain Gethelaine. "One minute he's standing there right as rain, telling me his spells look to be working the way he hoped—and I'll be buggered if we ain't picking up more speed than I would have thought possible—and the next . . ." The captain smacked the fist of his right hand into the open palm of his left. "He falls down just like old Gibs said. If I didn't know better I'd say he was drunk out of his skull."

"Did he say anything at all before he collapsed?" asked Gerin.

"Not a damned thing, my lord."

He shook Hollin's shoulder and called his name several times, but the wizard did not respond. "I think he'll be fine," Elaysen said. "He seems stunned more than anything. What do you think happened?"

"He told me that a wizard's magic can be corrupted over water. We kept it quiet because we didn't want anyone to worry needlessly. It's a random thing—sometimes spells work, sometimes they don't."

"Gah," said the captain. "That's a fine thing to be learning now."

"I only found out about it when we set off on this journey." He gave Hollin's shoulder a reassuring squeeze, then straightened. "Have your men take him to his cabin. Elaysen, if you have anything that might rouse him—"

"I'll get my things."

"So how are we faring against our pursuers?" Gerin asked the captain. The dark ship did not seem any closer to him, but he did not trust himself to accurately judge distances and speeds at sea.

Gethelaine extended his seeing-glass and peered through it at the Havalqa vessel. After a long silence he lowered it. "We pulled away somewhat, my lord—your magic-made wind helped us for sure, there's no denying that. But it's not enough. We'd need a few more hours of it to lose them completely."

There's no way I can work even one of the wind spells for hours, especially as drained as I am. "That's not an option, Captain. I can't work those spells again, at least not for a while." He thought for a moment. "What if I raised a fog? Could you use that to change course, maybe go out to sea farther, where they wouldn't expect?"

"A fog would help, my lord. At this point I'll take anything you can give."

"I need to rest a while before making the fog. I'll create it at dusk, Captain. Will that suffice?"

Gethelaine grinned. "Aye, my lord. That'll be fine."

＊ 42

Elaysen's pungent salve did little more than cause Hollin to moan and thrash about in his sleep. "That should wake him," she said, frowning. Gerin had just entered the room, ducking his head low to keep from banging it on the ceiling. "Is his sleep somehow being induced by magic, my lord?"

Gerin sensed no magic at all in Hollin, but created a Seeing spell to be certain. No sooner had the spell formed in front of him than it folded onto itself like a piece of parchment and faded from the air. "*Damn* this ocean," he muttered.

Elaysen raised Hollin's eyelids. Both pupils were rolled up toward the top of his skull. "He should have awakened unless he was seriously injured, but I see no sign of that."

"I don't detect any magic active in him. The Seeing spell collapsed before I could be certain, but if any magic is there, it must be very weak."

Elaysen folded her arms and stared at Hollin with a look of deep contemplation. "I'm going to try the salve again." She removed the cork from a small pouch of what looked to be oiled leather; instantly a powerful medicinal smell filled the air. She stuck her finger in, then smeared a dab of whitish paste beneath Hollin's nose and around his nostrils.

The wizard thrashed once, then opened his eyes and gasped for air. "Kamor's hairy balls, what in the—"

Gerin laughed out loud, and Elaysen turned her head to hide a sudden grin behind her hand.

"Who is Kamor?" said Gerin, still laughing. "Gods above, Hollin, I've never heard you swear like that before."

The wizard propped himself up on one elbow and wiped furiously at his nose with his free hand. "Kamor is a minor god in the lands where I grew up. And of course I'll swear when someone smears this foul-smelling paste on my—" He stopped and looked at Elaysen. "Oh. Is this something of yours?"

"Yes." She used a cloth to wipe the remainder from his nose. "We needed to waken you. Do you remember what happened?"

He took the cloth from her and rubbed his face several more times for good measure. "I remember working the Wardings, and then . . ." He glowered and sat up in the bed, locking his hands around his knees. "They shattered. They just . . . broke, and there was a sudden release of magic that struck me. That's all. How long have I been unconscious?"

"Not long," said Elaysen. "Perhaps half an hour."

"How is the ship? Did I damage it?"

"No, it's fine," said the prince. "But we didn't gain enough to escape the Havalqa." He told Hollin about his idea of using a fog to mask their movements to evade the enemy.

An hour later the enemy ship looked alarmingly large to Gerin, but the captain was nonplussed. "Until they get close enough to piss on us, my lord, there's little to worry about." His expression suddenly darkened. "Unless they have sorcerers of their own who can snare us with their powers. Do they have such men? I've heard about these Loremasters . . . I didn't consider that one of *them* might be aboard. Maybe that's why their ship's so bloody fast."

"I don't know, Captain. Even if there is a Loremaster aboard that ship, I have no idea of the extent of his powers."

The eastern sky purpled and the western sky turned a bloody red as the sun vanished beneath the horizon like the head of a drowning man. Gerin and Hollin set to work. They stood at opposite ends of the ship, hoping that if one of the spells collapsed, it would not interfere with the other. Gerin remained on the forecastle this time, while Hollin retreated to the stern.

He wished Hollin luck and watched him as he walked the length of *Cregar's Glory* before turning to face the enemy ship, now a black silhouette against the darkening sky. It looked almost like a hole in the world, a tunnel into which one could leap and emerge . . . where? The world of the Dreamers? The realm of the gods?

He closed his eyes and cleared his mind, then drew a deep breath and began the spell.

Gerin had recovered most of his strength since his earlier invocations of the weather spells. The fog spell Hollin had taught him was almost child's play in comparison—a straightforward bit of magic that could be as small or as large as one wanted. It needed only more magic to grow, but it did not draw vast amounts of power from a wizard the way the treacherous weather spells had.

He wanted as much fog as possible, and so opened himself to a river of magic, as much as he could stand.

In the span of several heartbeats, a thick wall of fog sprang from the sea between *Cregar's Glory* and the Havalqa ship.

The fog rose straight from the waters like a curtain being hauled skyward. Though it was impossible to tell from this vantage point how thick the mist was, Gerin was pouring enough magic into the spell to create a fog bank at least several hundred feet deep. Their goal was to confuse and confound the enemy ship—after all, if they simply wrapped *Cregar's Glory* in an envelope of mist, the Havalqa needed only to follow the moving bank of fog to intercept them.

From the corner of his eye Gerin saw Hollin stretch out his hands. A few moments later tendrils of mist rose from the sea around their ship like the tentacles of some ghostly sea serpent.

The fog grew and spread as darkness fell across the waters.

* * *

Gerin and Hollin worked the spells continuously for more than an hour before fatigue forced them to stop. The captain had ordered that no lanterns or torches be lit, and that everyone keep as quiet as possible. He wanted no errant noise or light to give away their position. They had no idea how far the fog extended, but Gerin could not help but be pleased that the ill luck plaguing their earlier attempts with magic had not returned. He and Hollin went below to get something to eat and rest for a time. They planned to work the spells again later in the night to ensure that the winds did not disperse what they had already created.

Gerin slept for a few hours before Balandrick roused him near midnight. He splashed water on his face, then left the cabin.

He emerged on the deck of a ghost ship. The tops of the masts were swallowed by the mist-shrouded darkness. Even Gerin's sensitive eyes could only make out vague shapes of sailors moving around him. The creaking of the ship's hull, the slap of water against the prow, the sound of bare feet on the deck planks, the rasp of billowing sails, and the groaning of taut ropes filled the foggy air. Beyond a dozen feet or so, the world was swallowed by the mist.

At his side, Balandrick whispered, "Kind of spooky, isn't it, my lord? I feel like we're on Denorian's Ship of the Dead."

"Yes, it is. Where's Hollin?"

"Beside you," said the wizard, who had appeared on his right, little more than a murky shadow.

Therain joined them. A little later Captain Gethelaine appeared. "Thought I heard something out there," he said to them quietly.

"Maybe it was a fish," said Balandrick. "I've heard they live out here. In the water. You know, down there, where it's wet."

"We're ready to create more fog whenever you feel we need to, Captain," said Hollin.

"I think we're fine for now, Master Wizard. We'll see come dawn how things fare.

Gerin decided to sleep for a few more hours, and soon

drifted off into a dreamless slumber. When he woke, the cabin was so utterly dark that at first he wasn't sure he'd opened his eyes. He created a small spark of magefire to illuminate the room, then quickly cut off the spell before it could flame out of control the way Hollin's had. The ship was rocking more than it had earlier, rising at the prow before crashing back down into the sea. He could hear a strong wind blowing the sails. He rose and went up onto the deck.

The ship was still shrouded in fog, though the wind had indeed strengthened while he slept. He heard thunder grumble somewhere in the distance but saw no lightning.

"Do we need to worry about the storm?" he asked Captain Gethelaine.

The captain made a dismissive gesture. "Bah, I've shat turds into the sea that made bigger waves than this, my lord. Might get a bit bumpy, but nothing to worry about."

As if on cue, the prow of the ship shot into the air so suddenly that Gerin would have been knocked from his feet if he hadn't managed to grip the forecastle's railing in time. As it was, he nearly lost his footing when the ship slammed down into the waves, sending a spray of cold, salty water over them. Gethelaine only leaned forward, his knees bent, one hand on the rail to help his balance, as if the thrashing of his ship did not warrant his attention.

The captain chuckled as Gerin straightened, his hands still firmly holding the wale. "Not used to sea voyages, are you, my lord?"

"No. As Hollin reminded me, my home at Ailethon is rather far from the ocean."

"Ah, that's too bad. There's nothing like a—" Gethelaine wheeled about, his expression one of sudden alarm.

"What is it?" asked the prince. Gethelaine held up his hand and cocked his head, obviously listening for something. Gerin listened as well, trying to blot out the howl of the wind and the many creaks and groans of the ship. He could hear nothing but the slap of the waves against the hull and the continuous background noise of the sea itself.

But then . . .

"Ship, ship!" shrieked the sailor manning the crow's nest. "Ship to port!"

The captain swore loudly and scrambled to the starboard railing. Sailors had abruptly appeared all across the lower deck, as if they'd coalesced from the fog itself, many with short knives and cutlasses in their hands.

Then Gerin saw it. The Havalqa vessel loomed out of the fog, a massive black shape less than a hundred feet away, sailing almost parallel to their course but angled slightly toward them so they could close the distance between the ships without actually ramming *Cregar's Glory* broadside.

Gerin saw small flames spark to life on the other ship and at first thought they were lanterns or torches. But then they arced high in the night air toward them and he realized they were arrows dipped in pitch and set alight. Some dropped short of the *Glory* and fizzled in the waves, and a few overshot the deck. But others found their mark, ripping through the sails and starting small fires in the canvas.

"Damn them buggers, they've found us," said the captain.

43

The flaming arrows continued to rain down on
them with increasing accuracy. Fires had blossomed
across most of the sails, and a few unfortunate sailors had
been struck and killed. One was pinned to the mainmast by
an arrow that pierced his left eye.

Gethelaine was bellowing orders to his men, but Gerin
wasn't listening. He scrabbled down the ladder to the main
deck and called for Hollin, Therain, and Balandrick. He
saw Elaysen first and told her to go back to her cabin. "The
Havalqa ship is almost on us," he said. "There's going to be
fighting. Stay below until it's over, and then you can tend to
the injured."

"But, my lord—"

"I mean it, Elaysen. I don't have time to argue."

Her eyes flashed with anger. "You may be a lord and
prince, but you are not my master. I am no servant that you
may command on a whim. I'll prepare my medicines and
will help those who need me, whether you wish it or not."
She wheeled about and disappeared into her cabin.

He was shocked by the depth of her anger, and for an instant considered banging on her cabin door and demanding
that she explain herself and follow his wishes. After all, he
only wanted to keep her from harm.

But he had no more time for this. He let out an exasperated
breath and stalked away.

The sailors had managed to put out some of the flames in the sails, but two of the billowing canvas sheets were engulfed in fire and would soon be completely gone. Men were cutting ropes to keep the flames from spreading across them to other parts of the ship.

The enemy vessel was less than fifty feet away. Gerin saw three grappling hooks arc through the air in an attempt to snare *Cregar's Glory*. Two fell short. The one that reached the deck was tossed over the side by a sailor before it could find purchase.

"Gods above, that's a bloody big ship," said Balandrick. The main deck of the Havalqa vessel was at least a dozen feet higher than the *Glory*'s deck. He forced his gaze from the ship and faced Gerin. "My lord, we can't let them get aboard. We'll never win a close-quarters fight. Once they grapple us and pull us close, they'll have the high ground. They'll be able to rain arrows down on us from their deck until there's—"

"Yes, I get the point."

Another grapple sailed through the darkness. This one hooked itself and held fast.

"I think it's time I found out just what Ninmahal can do."

They rushed to the starboard side of the ship. Hollin created a Warding in front of them to shield them from the incoming arrows. Three flaming missiles slammed into the magical barrier and ricocheted off, spinning down into the sea. Two more grappling hooks had been secured to *Cregar's Glory*, though the rope attached to one of them had been hacked through by a sailor with a machete.

Gerin drew Nimnahal. The sword's blade shimmered with a cool silvery glow, as if it had been dipped in a pool of liquid starlight. "Balan, if the fight goes poorly, I want you to get Elaysen to a longboat and get her off this ship." Despite her earlier obstinance, he still wanted her to be safe.

"My lord, my duty is by your side."

"Your duty is to obey me. I can take care of myself. I'm very serious about this command, Captain Vaules."

Balandrick straightened a little. "Yes, my lord."

"Hollin . . ."

"For now I'll keep these Wardings in place to protect us. If I need to enter the fray I will, but let's see what you can do first."

"I'm going to the stern," said Therain. "We need to cut as many grappling lines as we can." Donael Rundgar followed him like an immense, hulking shadow.

Gerin wrapped both hands around the leather-bound hilt of the sword and raised the shimmering blade. He could feel the immense power imbued in the weapon's metal thrumming beneath his hands—though if Hollin were correct, the sword was now fashioned as much from magic itself as from ordinary steel. An astounding thought, one he still did not fully understand. A blade that existed in many worlds at once, whose power bled across the barriers that separated a multitude of dimensions. And he had made it. What would happen in those other worlds when he released Nimnahal's power? Were the other wielders of Nimnahal's echoed blades about to unleash some power of their own? Were they locked in battles, or would their blades ignore the vast outpouring of magic that was about to take place here?

He didn't know, and at the moment did not have time to further ponder the question.

It was time to fight.

With a shout of *"Lonach!"*—the ancient battle cry of the Atreyanos—he opened himself to magic and directed the raging torrent of power flowing through him into the blade.

Nimnahal erupted with brilliant amber fire. A silent shock wave rippled from the weapon that knocked Hollin, Balandrick, and three nearby sailors back several steps.

The enemy ship was now firmly latched to *Cregar's Glory* by at least a dozen grappling lines. The side of the Havalqa vessel was bristling with armed men ready to leap onto the deck of their quarry the moment they were close enough. Archers still fired flame-tipped arrows into the sails, which continued to burn despite the best efforts of Gethelaine's men to douse the fires; it was simply too difficult to get buckets of water high enough, and fast enough to fight the flames.

Gerin did not unlock any of the dozens of spells he'd imprinted in the blade, keyed to his commands alone. Instead he channeled raw, unshaped magic through the sword in a quantity he never could have achieved otherwise. Without Nimnahal, so much magic would bleed off of him through his aura, or he would have had to shape it into powerful spells. He could not have released so much unshaped magic through himself without burning out his *paru'enthred* and ending his life as a wizard, but the sword could, drawing power itself in addition to the magic Gerin directed into it.

The blazing bolt of amber fire that shot from the tip of the blade was as thick around as Gerin's wrist. He'd never before seen such a massive amount of unshaped magic. Before now the most powerful blasts he'd been able to create were no thicker than a finger. But this . . .

With a single downward thrust of the blade, the amber fire sliced through every grappling line connecting the two ships, releasing the tension on the ropes. Both vessels rocked back hard in the opposite direction, sending men flying across the decks. Gerin dropped one hand from the hilt, grabbed the rail in front of him, and managed to stay on his feet.

Before the Havalqa soldiers could react, he directed the scything blade of amber fire along the enemy vessel's hull, cutting a burning line through the wood that penetrated deep into the ship's interior. Furniture, clothing, rations, barrels, bunks, hammocks, and men all burst into flame when touched by Gerin's power.

Gerin felt his strength weaken. He knew he couldn't maintain this much longer. His arms began to tremble with fatigue.

He aimed the blade across the length of the deck and cut through anyone standing there. Havalqa soldiers caught fire and fell screaming into the sea; others were cut in half, or had limbs burned off as they tried and failed to flee from his attack.

He sheared through two of the Havalqa ship's masts and surrounding rigging. The masts toppled and crashed into one another with a tremendous roar. The spars of the largest mast broke suddenly. Much of the rigging was now crawling with fire—it looked to Gerin like a spiderweb set aflame—and began to collapse, dropping Havalqa sailors to their deaths on the deck or into the sea. The sails too were burning, as were the standards that had flown atop the masts.

Knowing he had almost reached his limits, Gerin paused to catch his breath before making his final attempt to seal the doom of the enemy ship.

Balandrick watched as the Havalqa archers who were still alive fired frantic volleys of arrows at this nightmare figure wielding a flame-drenched sword, but their missiles bounced harmlessly off Hollin's invisible Wardings. A score of Havalqa soldiers tried to leap to the deck of *Cregar's Glory,* some to avoid the collapsing masts of their own ship, others in an attempt to salvage their mission and take control of this troublesome Khedeshian vessel. A few succeeded, but most fell flailing into the black sea and vanished beneath waves reflecting the hellish fires of the burning ships. Those who made the jump were immediately set upon by Gethelaine's men, but the Havalqa soldiers were superbly trained and mercilessly cut their way through the sailors who attacked them. Four of the Havalqa went down beneath the sheer weight of Khedeshians falling on them, but two more fought their way clear, leaving a trail of blood-soaked bodies in their wake, and advanced toward Gerin, who was too focused on the enemy ship to notice them. Hollin was also preoccupied protecting Gerin. Two others made their way clear of the knot of sailors and headed for the rear of the ship, toward Therain, but there was nothing Balan could do about that.

He stepped in front of the advancing Havalqa soldiers, his sword raised. "Pray now to whatever foul and false gods you worship," he snarled. "Because I'm going to send your souls to Shayphim if you take another step."

The soldiers, if they even understood him, did not reply. They spread apart as far as they were able, then rushed him.

Balan dropped his left hand from his sword's hilt and

pulled a long knife from his belt. The Havalqa soldiers attacked in unison, one coming high from his right side, the other low on his left. They were strong and fast, but he was able to parry their strikes, leap forward and spin around to face them again as they came at him a second time.

Balan knew he would have to dispatch one of them quickly or he was going to die. He was tall, strong, and fast, but could only remain on the defensive so long against two trained attackers before he would lose.

Balan fell back against the gunwale when they charged at him, and lunged to his right with his sword, forcing that soldier to block his strike with a downward swing of his blade. The man did not halt and slammed hard into Balan, but his weapon was pointed toward the deck, momentarily caught between the two men. Before the soldier could react, Balandrick smashed his forehead into the bridge of the other man's nose. The Havalqa grunted and fell back, blood gushing from his nostrils.

The deck lurched beneath them as the ship crested another wave, then crashed down into the sea, its prow parting the waters like a knife blade.

The second soldier, attempting to stab Balandrick on his left side, was thwarted by the sudden motion of the ship and Balan's deft twisting that put the first Havalqa between him and the other soldier. When that soldier fell away, nose broken and bloodied, the second soldier lunged. Balan was only able to partially deflect him with his knife, and felt the weapon's keen edge bite into his thigh below his mail shirt. Hot blood poured down his leg.

The man drew back to strike again, but before he could, Balan rushed toward him, bringing his sword up across his body and knocking his weapon aside. The soldier tried to back away, but Balan pressed the attack, and in a swift single motion swung his knife up beneath his own outstretched right arm and drove it into the man's chin and into his brain. The Havalqa died instantly. Balandrick yanked his knife free and whirled about as the lifeless body collapsed to the deck.

He barely managed to deflect a downward blow from the

other soldier that would have cut through the soft tissue where his neck and shoulder met, just above the collar of his mail shirt. As it was, the blow was powerful enough that the flat of the blade still smashed into his left shoulder, driving the mail rings into his skin and sending a shock down his arm that left it numb.

The Havalqa said something in his native tongue—it sounded to Balan like a taunt—as he brought his sword up with both hands and swung it down with lightning speed. Balandrick's one-handed parry kept the blow from killing him, but the blade bit into his scalp and sent a gush of blood running down his forehead into his left eye.

The soldier pressed his attack, hammering blows at Balan that he only barely managed to ward off. His wounded leg was growing weak beneath him, and he knew that if it gave out or he stumbled he was finished.

The Havalqa attacked from Balan's right, then feinted and whirled his sword around his head, hoping Balan would move to parry the feint and leave his left side open. It almost worked; the Havalqa had skill, Balan gave him that, and his feint had been convincing. It was hard to believe the soldier could change the direction of his heavy blade so quickly, but he had.

Balan attempted his own feint, expecting the Havalqa to recognize it for what it was, and the soldier did indeed swing his sword around to block where he anticipated the real attack would come from. Balan did press him from that direction, but as he lunged forward, his sword extended to block the other's weapon rather than to attempt a kill, he dropped to one knee and scooped up his knife without taking his eyes from his opponent. His fingers closed around the wire-wrapped hilt, and then he swung it viciously across the man's abdomen, just above his pelvis. He felt his knife sink into soft flesh and saw the man's guts slide from the long wound a second later.

The soldier covered his mortal wound with his left hand and attempted to raise his weapon in his rapidly weakening right, but before he could, Balandrick drove the point of his sword through the man's heart and twisted. The Havalqa's weapon fell atop the steaming pile of guts, followed by the man himself.

Balandrick stood slowly, put his foot on the dead man's chest and pulled out his sword. He pressed his hand on the bloody gash in his thigh and said, "I told you not to take another step."

Gerin was so focused on maintaining control of the magic flowing through him and into Nimnahal that he had taken no note at all of Balan's bloody battle, raging so close behind him. Exhaustion dragged at his limbs. He knew he had only a few minutes—perhaps less—before he would have to stop.

He intended to make every moment count. Most of the sails were either shredded by the collapsing spars or had caught fire in the growing conflagration on the deck. The Havalqa vessel was drifting away from *Cregar's Glory* despite the efforts of a score of oars to maintain its proximity to its intended quarry. But Gerin's magic had turned more than half of one of the rowing decks into an inferno of swirling orange flame that licked out of the oar ports. The larger mast had partially snapped where it struck the port gunwale and now dipped in the waves beside the vessel like a broken arm. Soldiers and sailors leaped into the sea to escape the growing fires. Some floundered for a while, trying to keep their heads above the churning waves; others found bits of debris to cling to precariously; and still more sank almost at once beneath the fire-washed sea. Gerin had destroyed every longboat he could see, using his amber magic to blast them to splinters.

He tightened his grip on Nimnahal and tried to open himself to even more power. The spear of magic shooting from the sword pulsed and brightened, but his exhaustion increased as well.

He aimed the lance of fire at the center of the upper deck, where it began blasting through the planks. Smoke and fire belched up into the night.

Then he brought the sword down, hoping to cut the ship in two.

He could not move the weapon quickly, or the magic would not cut all the way through. His arms were trembling so badly he thought he might drop Nimnahal, but he managed to hold on. His lips pulled back, baring his teeth in a rictus as he strained against his weakening limbs.

He'd cut down through about half the ship when it groaned like a wounded animal as the stress on the remaining parts of the hull grew too great for the timbers to bear. Wood snapped violently with loud retorts that echoed across the water. The ship began to bend in the middle as if it were slowly being folded in half, collapsing away from the rent Gerin was cutting through it, the groans of the overstressed wood growing louder with each passing second.

Suddenly, the core of the ship exploded in an immense ball of orange flame that rolled up into the still foggy sky. Gerin could feel the heat of the blast against his face. He wondered what could have happened, then remembered Therain's tale of the small explosive spheres the Havalqa carried and wondered if he'd set off a supply of them in the ship's hold. He would never know for sure, and it didn't matter. The only thing that mattered was that he'd destroyed the vessel.

The burning ship emitted a thunderous groan as fire washed over it, then split completely in two, the separate halves falling away from one another before beginning to sink. The forward half listed on its starboard side. The prow tilted high into the air until it was nearly vertical; then, in a matter of moments, it slid under the water as if it had been swallowed whole.

Gerin dispelled the magic flowing through him and lowered Nimnahal until its point rested on the deck. It felt too heavy to lift, even to return to its scabbard, so he simply let it remain there. Drenched in sweat and panting heavily, he watched as the rear half of the Havalqa ship capsized in the frothing waves, smoke and steam belching from the doomed vessel as the inferno in its hold struck the water. Within minutes, the ship was gone beneath the sea.

The night was suddenly much quieter than it had been. The wind had lessened, and Gerin could only guess that they were clearing the storm's edge. The Havalqa who swam in the sea or clung to debris did not call out to the Khedeshians; they would not surrender, and would be shown no mercy even if they'd tried. Gerin would not take prisoners who might turn against them. *Let Paérendras have them,* he thought. *Drown them, god of the sea, and send their souls to Bellon.*

There was a noise behind them. Both wizards turned to see Balandrick sag toward the deck. Only then did Gerin notice the two dead Havalqa soldiers. He managed to slide Nimnahal into its scabbard as Hollin knelt by Balan.

"I'll stop the bleeding and work some healing spells to close up this wound," the wizard said.

"I'd appreciate that," said Balandrick. His face was soaked with sweat and blood, his hair clinging to his forehead in wet strands.

"I see you've finally earned your pay, Captain," said Gerin, sitting down next to Balan on the deck, too weary to stand.

"Someone has to watch your back, my lord."

On the forecastle, Captain Gethelaine shouted orders for his men to put out the remaining fires and work on replacing the burned sails. He stood at the edge of the higher deck and stared down at the wizards and Balandrick, his hands on his large waist. "Remind me never to throw dice with you, my lord. I'd not want that temper of yours aimed my way."

"Don't cheat, Captain, and all would be well."

· Therain and Captain Rundgar approached from the stern. The prince's sword was covered in blood. Rundgar's blade was equally bloody, and there was a shallow cut on his forearm. "The bastards fought hard, but we swarmed them and cut them to bits," said Therain.

Elaysen appeared, her hands slick with blood. Her expression was grim as she knelt by Gerin's side.

"Are you injured, my lord?"

He shook his head. "Just exhausted."

"I am sick of war and death," she snarled. "The world is

hard enough. There is no need for men to create even more suffering."

Gerin did not know what to say to her, and so simply closed his eyes.

Bits of wood still burned upon the sea, like campfires bobbing on the waves, falling behind them as *Cregar's Glory* continued its journey. Soon the fires vanished from sight, swallowed by either the fog or the sea.

Hollin and Elaysen tended to Balandrick's wounds. Therain went below to wash the blood from him and get some sleep. The dead Havalqa were unceremoniously dumped over the side. The fallen Khedeshians were taken to the stern, where their bodies would be cleaned, wrapped in linens and weighted down, then given to Paérendras's watery embrace.

"Let's pray we have clear sailing till we reach land, my lord," said Gethelaine.

Gerin nodded and went to his cabin, where he collapsed on the bunk.

His dreams were haunted by exploding ships and fire-flecked seas filled with burned, bloated corpses. He did not awaken until late in the morning, when Therain banged on his door and told him it was time to go.

44

They gathered their belongings and met on the main deck. Captain Gethelaine said farewell to them and wished them a safe journey. "And I'd like a dozen of them swords you have if you're planning on making any more, my lord. Come in handy in a fight."

"Even if I could make more, you wouldn't be able to use them, Captain. Only a wizard can release that kind of power, I'm afraid."

"Ah, that's what I thought. But still had to ask, my lord. I wouldn't have to fear pirates and brigands with one of those aboard. Maybe you'd like to sign on as my second? Forget all that courtly intrigue and politics that comes with the crown. The high seas are beckoning!"

Sailors lowered the longboat into the water, then Gerin and the rest climbed down a wooden ladder that hung from the ship's gunwale on heavy hooks. Balandrick, his leg bandaged, had a hard time climbing down and nearly fell when he slipped on a wet rung. Hollin and Gerin helped steady him when he got near the boat and ushered him to a bench.

The sailors in the longboat with them pushed them away from *Cregar's Glory* as other men on the deck hauled up the ladder. Gethelaine waved to them and once more wished them a safe and uneventful journey to Almaris before turning away and vanishing from view.

* * *

They came ashore at a curve of beach sheltered on its northern side by long grass-capped dunes. Before leaving *Cregar's Glory*, both Hollin and Gerin had used Farseeings—which worked without incident, much to their relief—to look for enemy troops or encampments on the mainland. They saw nothing, but also could not see very far inland, and knew that even if the lands here were relatively clear of the invaders, that would not last long. The army gathered to the north would soon begin its march on Almaris, if it hadn't already.

Despite his wounded leg, Balandrick kept the pace Gerin set. He was resolute in his determination that he not slow them down. Captain Rundgar helped him along for part of the day, allowing him to keep most of his weight off his injured leg, which throbbed and itched in a maddening way.

Hollin asked Gerin what he meant to do with the scepter that they hadn't done in their earlier examinations. "We know that the spells are Warded with their own protections," he said. "We couldn't get through them before. We couldn't even discover the nature of the spells. It seems we are really no better off than we were."

Balan watched Gerin in the growing darkness, wondering how the prince would respond.

Gerin paused to consider Hollin's question. Balandrick knew the expression on his face well and was sure that he had been pondering the very problem Hollin just voiced ever since he arrived at the conclusion that the Scepter of the King contained the spells that would allow him to find Naragenth's library. No doubt there were wheels turning in Gerin's mind, sorting through bits of knowledge and things he had been chewing over for days if not weeks, trying to find answers to questions whose resolutions had proved elusive.

"I've been thinking about that since we left Pelleron," Gerin finally said.

Balan could not help but grin. *I knew it. Always chewing over problems.*

"I still don't know about the door itself. Naragenth told me that he wasn't concerned that the palace of his day had burned because he hadn't hidden it there. He also said that it was where no man could find it."

"That's pretty vague," said Therain. "That could mean your other-world idea, but it could just as easily mean he hid it beneath a mossy stone in Blackwater Marsh."

Gerin nodded. "I know. It's not much to go on. I have an idea about what might release the spells, but I don't want to talk about it yet. I'm still mulling it over, and it's such a crazy idea you'd probably think I've lost my mind. Until I'm more certain that it will work or decide it's complete lunacy and give it up, I'm not going to say anything else about it."

Balandrick could see a look of annoyance flash across Hollin's face. "If you tell me—even if you'd prefer to do so in private—I may be able to offer some guidance."

"Not yet, Hollin. Maybe later."

Hollin doesn't like Gerin's coy little games, thought Balandrick. He didn't either, for that matter. It was one thing to keep an idea to yourself; it was something altogether different—and far more irritating—to announce you had an idea but then not say what it was. *I guess that's one of the prerogatives of being a prince. You can annoy and irritate pretty much anyone you want.*

They were following a hunting track that wound through a tangle of woods when the trees suddenly yielded to a long downward slope at whose foot stretched an open, grassy plain. On the far side of the plain—called the Varga—perhaps a mile distant, were the walls of Almaris, high upon the Almarean Plateau. A palpable sense of relief filled Gerin as he gazed at the city of his fathers. The plateau and eastern half of the city were sunk in a shadowy gloom, but the setting sun lit the tallest of the city's towers so they shone with a golden glow, like beacons to light their way home.

They descended the slope and hurried across the Varga toward the Okoro Gate. Gerin could see that the walls were manned with soldiers watching them crossing the field. He hoped they didn't think they were the enemy and lob a boulder at them with a trebuchet.

They were perhaps three-quarters of the way across when a company of soldiers appeared on the higher ground ahead of them. They were Taeratens, marked with distinctive gold armor glinting in the dying light. They made no move toward Gerin and the others, waiting for the travelers to come to them.

"Halt in the name of the king!" called one of the Taeratens when the distance between the two groups had closed to about one hundred feet.

"I'm the son of the king," Gerin shouted back. "My brother is with me. You will escort us to my father at once."

There was a murmur through the soldiers, then the man who'd spoken spurred his horse forward to meet them. Gerin noted that three of the others nocked their bows, though they kept them pointed toward the ground.

Gerin did not stop marching as the soldier arrived and turned his horse about to fall into step with them. The man studied Gerin's face for a moment, then said, "I recognize you, my lord. Forgive us, we did not know—"

"Our arrival was not announced, Captain," said Gerin, who'd seen his insignia rank. "Send one of your men ahead to inform my father that my brother and I are here."

"Yes, my lord." He bowed his head and galloped toward his men, where he barked several orders. One of the men wheeled his horse around and raced back toward the city's gates.

The captain ordered his men to dismount and give the princes and their men their horses. Gerin helped Elaysen onto her horse, then swung up onto the saddle of the captain's black charger. The Taeratens fell in around them in a protective cordon as they started for the city.

Gerin had known that Almaris would be swollen with refugees, but he was still startled by the sheer number of men, women, children, donkeys, mules, carts, wagons, tents, lean-tos, soldiers, and mercenaries choking the Nathrad Road and every square inch of space they could cram themselves or their belongings into. Masses of people were huddled around small cookfires or trying to keep out of each other's way, an entirely futile endeavor. Even the flat-topped roofs had tents and other makeshift shelters perched atop them, like a field that had sprouted mushrooms after a hard rain.

"This is quite the sight," said Therain.

The Taeratens cleared a path for them down the road, forcing people aside so their horses could get through, but even so their progress was maddeningly slow. Now that he was actually within the city's walls—it felt almost unreal to be here after his captivity; he realized that part of him had never believed he would leave Gedsengard alive—he was impatient to get to the Tirthaig and test the scepter. There were still so many unanswered questions, and he would never find the answers until he could hold the damn thing in his hands and try out his ideas.

The Old City was not quite as crowded as the rest, but it still held more people by far than Gerin had ever seen in it. At least the Needle was relatively clear. He relaxed a little now that the pressing throng had lessened.

There were no refugees within the twin walls encircling Vesparin's Hill, and the open spaces between the buildings felt like prairies after the crush they'd just passed through.

They reached the Tirthaig and were escorted to a private meeting chamber on one of the upper floors. Gerin's father and Jaros Waklan were already there. When they entered, Abran pointedly ignored Gerin and embraced Therain. He held up the stump of Therain's left arm and gingerly touched the bandages that still encased it, though Hollin's healing spells had long since forced the skin to close over the wound. Therain, for some reason, felt more comfortable with it bandaged, and had Elaysen help him change the wrappings every few days.

"Oh, my son," said the king as he stared at Therain's arm, as if he could scarcely believe what he was seeing. "I'd heard that you'd been grievously wounded, but to see it with my own eyes . . ."

"I'll be fine, Father," said Therain, a little embarrassed by

Abran's show of emotion. "If you'd seen the bloody damned creature who bit it off you'd realize I'm lucky to be alive. Truly a thing from nightmares."

Abran glowered at Gerin with such naked hostility that it struck him almost like a physical blow. He felt himself redden but refused to look away.

The entire room fell silent, all of them sensing the deep rift between father and son. Finally Jaros Waklan interceded. "How did you escape your captors?" he asked Gerin. "The last we had heard, you'd been taken from your very bed in Ailethon."

"Yes, tell us how you escaped," said Abran, a disapproving tone to his voice. "I thought your magic would have served to protect you better."

Gerin swallowed the anger that rose in his throat and tried to keep his voice steady. "We'll tell you the whole story, Father. But would you please have some food brought in? We're all hungry and thirsty."

Abran commanded a servant to do as Gerin had asked, then turned to Elaysen. His gaze was steady and unflinching, and more than a little stern.

"And who is this?"

"Elaysen el'Turya, Father," said Gerin. "She is a gifted healer who has helped all of us recover from injuries."

"Indeed. El'Turya, you said. Are you related to the so-called Prophet of the One God?"

Elaysen bowed her head. "He is my father, Your Majesty."

"Curious that you would be traveling with my sons." He strode to the head of the long table. "Sit, all of you. I would hear this story."

They spent nearly two hours talking and answering questions from the king and Minister of the Realm. They recounted everything, from the attack by the creatures near Ailethon to the sea battle with the Havalqa ship. Gerin did not speak of his humiliating sexual bondage at the hands of the soul stealer. He was not sure he would ever confess that to anyone. The memory of it made shame burn hotly in him.

"An incredible tale, my lords," said Jaros Waklan, shaking his head with astonishment when they finished relating it.

"We came for something else as well, Father," said Gerin. "I need to examine the Scepter of the King again. I've had some insights about the Varsae Estrikavis that—"

"This kingdom has had enough of magic," said the king. "It is *dying* of it."

"That's nonsense!" said Gerin.

The king slapped his hand against the table. "Twice we have been invaded because of your magic! Thousands have died because of it! An army is marching upon this very city because of it! *My* city! And your sister is dead because of it. Your magic is a pestilence, and I would burn every last bit of it from you if I could."

Gerin was speechless. The hatred in his father's face and voice stunned him.

"Your Majesty, if I may—" began Hollin.

"You may not. I have had enough of your pernicious influence upon my family, and I assure you that it is soon to come to an end."

"Father, I think you're being unreasonable," said Therain.

Abran's fury shifted toward his younger son like a sudden storm gust. "Unreasonable? Look at your arm, Therain! You're a cripple because of your brother's magic! I am not being *unreasonable*. I am correcting an error that should have been addressed a long time ago." He swung back toward Gerin. "And make no mistake. A wizard will never sit upon the throne. If you do not divest yourself of your magic, I will name Therain crown prince."

Gerin could not believe what he was hearing. Had his father lost his mind? Really and truly gone mad? "You can't do that, Father. There are laws governing the succession—"

"You do not tell the king what he can and cannot do! Now leave me, all of you."

"He's out of his bloody mind," said Gerin in the hallway. He paced back and forth, filled with anger that left him trembling.

Jaros Waklan stepped in front of him, a look of alarm on

his face. "Please do not say that, my lord! Your father's behavior has been . . . erratic of late, and much of it stems from
his feelings about your magic. Do not do anything to aggra-
vate him further."

Gerin studied the minister's expression. "You're afraid of
him, aren't you? You think he really *has* lost his mind."

"My lord, I would never say such a thing about the king!"

"You don't have to."

"Father's not going to stop me," said Gerin. They had all
retired to Gerin's rooms except Elaysen, who had left to go
to her father, escorted by palace guards. "This is too important." He was still furious with the king's treatment of him
and stood stiffly, his arms folded.

"So what are you going to do?" asked Therain again.
"Steal the scepter?"

"If he's not going to give it to me, yes."

There was a long silence, which Balandrick finally broke.
"My lord, shouldn't you first try to reason with him again?"

"No. I'm done with him. If this is how he wants it to be
between us, then it's on his head."

"What will he do when he finds out, my lord?"

"I don't care. If I'm right it won't matter at all."

"And if you're wrong?" said Hollin. "I agree your father's
behavior is irrational and disturbing, but to flaunt the king's
will . . ."

"I'll do it alone so none of you will have to bear his wrath.
But I am going to take it, one way or the other."

"Not me," said Therain. "I'll help you in any way I can."

"Count me in, too, my lord," said Balan. "If the choice is
you or the king, I choose you."

"And me," said Hollin.

Gerin smiled despite the grimness of the situation. He was
pleased they had chosen to stand by him, even though such a
choice might come with a cost.

It was a simple thing for him to obtain the Scepter of the
King. The storeroom where it was kept was not guarded; ap-

parently his father had not considered that he would disobey his commands.

He opened the door as he had before and retrieved the scepter. He returned to his rooms as calmly as he could, but his insides were shaking with nervousness and fear. He had crossed a very dangerous line, and he worried that the price for crossing it would be high indeed. For him and everyone else.

"I'm still stunned by the size of that bloody fleet out in the gulf," said Therain as he came in from Gerin's balcony.

"The resources the Havalqa have brought to bear on us—and across such a distance as the Maurelian Sea—are considerable," said Hollin.

"Where is Nellemar?" asked Gerin. "Why aren't we doing anything about that blockade?" On their slow climb up Vesparin's Hill they had all seen the cluster of enemy vessels lurking a mile or so from shore, their numbers so great that in areas they seemed almost a solid mass of spars, masts, and sails. Gerin wondered how the people of the city went about their lives with such a deadly threat visible to anyone with a clear view of the sea.

"He's assembling our fleet at Tan Orech," said Therain. "Now that I've seen this blockade, I can understand why it's taking so long. And what's out there doesn't include the ships these bastards have back at Gedsengard and along the coast. It's like they're conjuring the bloody things out of the air."

"Where do we start?" asked Hollin. He was staring at the case containing the scepter, obviously impatient to begin.

Gerin sighed heavily. It was time for him to tell Hollin his ideas about the scepter, but he was reluctant to do so. They seemed ridiculous, almost crazy. And considering what was at stake . . .

But he knew he had no choice. He either confided in Hollin or gave up.

"I need to tell you my ideas, but I want to do it my way. Let me lead you through what I was thinking and see if you come to the same conclusion. Or at least don't think it's completely crazy." He took a deep breath, aware of the wizard's attention, and of Therain and Balandrick quietly listening. "Naragenth wanted a way to keep the Varsae Estrikavis safe from those wizards who didn't take part in its making."

"Of course."

"Yes, but what about the wizards who *did* take part? The ones who placed their own knowledge in the library? Why didn't they know how to find it? Did he betray them? Or did the outbreak of Helca's wars throw everyone's plans into disarray? This wasn't something Naragenth did alone. I know that Helca's wars broke out soon after the library was completed, but how could it be that not a single other wizard knew where it was or how to get to it? That no one else wrote anything down?"

"They may not have been able to reach it with Helca's armies marching across borders, and would not write it down for fear of it falling into the wrong hands."

"That's possible, I suppose, but it seems unlikely. I think that a few of them would have wanted to leave *some* record of its location. But nothing has ever been found. Even the words 'Chamber of the Moon' had to wait until I could speak to Naragenth's ghost."

"Which only seems to prove that the other wizards took great care not to write down what they knew."

"Or that Naragenth was the only one who knew where it was and how it had been hidden." Gerin grew excited as the words poured out of him, his father's fury with him forgotten for a moment. "No one knows the exact date of the completion of the Varsae Estrikavis. Everyone seems to think it was completed just before the Wars of Unification began. But what exactly does 'completed' mean? That the building or structure or whatever was used to store everything was finished? That all the magical knowledge was put in it? No one knows."

"What do *you* think it means?"

"I don't know any more than anyone else. But the way Naragenth spoke to me—the way he said that the Chamber of the Moon, where the library was hidden, was *his* greatest creation, and *not* the work of a group of wizards—leads me to believe that he alone was responsible for concealing it. Whether that was always the plan or whether the outbreak of war forced his hand is impossible to know. I think the reason no other wizards ever spoke of or wrote down the words 'Chamber of the Moon' was because *they didn't know about it*. They knew about the Varsae Estrikavis, the library itself, which some of them *did* write about, because those records have been recovered. But the Chamber of the Moon was something different, something they *didn't* know about. It was how it was *concealed*."

Hollin nodded, his face pinched with concentration. "Let's say for the sake of argument that Naragenth alone was responsible for concealing the library, and let's go a step further and assume that he managed to conceal it in another world, as you have supposed. I still don't see how that helps us find out where it is."

"If Naragenth alone was responsible for hiding it, and if he placed the key spells in the Scepter of the King, then it is something only an amber wizard can open, because any other kind of wizard can't even sense the spells. That means he wanted to be the only one who had access to it. Maybe he did that to keep it safe for the duration of the war—he certainly didn't intend to die so early in the siege of Almaris—or maybe he was double-crossing the other wizards who had contributed to it."

"A lot of ifs, Gerin."

"Let me ask you a question, and then I'll tell you what I'm thinking. Would the wizards of Naragenth's day have had better luck penetrating the defenses in the scepter than us? The contributors to the Varsae Estrikavis were the most brilliant wizards of their time, or so we've been told. If one of them had obtained the scepter, could he have figured out how to use it?"

"I don't know. We only know a few names of those who contributed content to the Varsae Estrikavis. But I think they would have a better idea than we do how to pierce the spells. They *can* be undone, even by a wizard whose flame is not amber. But we don't know enough about them to even have an idea of where to start, and the defenses he's placed around them could easily kill us in the attempt or destroy the scepter itself. Or both."

"So Naragenth might have believed that some of his contemporaries had the ability to gain entrance if they had the scepter, despite all the precautions he took."

"We're so far in the realm of speculation at this point that almost anything is possible. How *likely* these things are is another matter entirely." Annoyance crept into Hollins's voice. "And I *still* don't see what you're getting at."

"There's only one way I can think of for Naragenth to be absolutely sure that no one other than himself could enter the Varsae Estrikavis."

And he told Hollin his idea.

The older wizard was quiet for a long time, a faraway look on his face as he pondered what Gerin had said. *He thinks I'm out of my mind,* thought the prince as he waited for Hollin to say something. *He's trying to figure out the best way to tell me that I'm crazy, that my idea is sheer lunacy—*

"That's nuts, Gerin," said Therain. "But it's so crazy I almost think it must be true. Maybe it's a thing with amber wizards."

"I'm withholding comment, my lord," said Balandrick.

Hollin straightened a little in his chair. "I follow your line of reasoning, but there are so many guesses, so many unsupported suppositions—"

"Yes, but it's the only explanation that makes sense."

"It makes sense if Naragenth was thinking the way you believe he was, if he feared that other wizards would try to take control of the library from him. It is just as likely that all the wizards would have had equal access since that was part of the original agreement for the library's creation. All who contributed would have full rights to the knowledge it contained."

Gerin would not be deterred. "But that doesn't take into account the outbreak of Helca's wars. Forget about Naragenth trying to double-cross the other wizards who helped him. Maybe he wanted to secure it from Helca. The emperor had wizards of his own, and Naragenth would not have wanted it to fall into their hands."

"But if you're wrong . . ."

"Do you have any other ideas?"

The wizard shook his head. "No. Even with what you've told me, I can't think of anything we can try that we haven't already done."

Gerin stared hard at the scepter. Should he dare it? It was such an audacious idea, and if he was wrong . . . His father was already furious with him. Had threatened to disavow him of his birthright if he did not somehow undo his wizardry! He could not do that, any more than he could divest himself of his arm.

If this did not work he could not even imagine how angry the king would be. The scepter would be destroyed.

But if he was right . . .

He would have it at last. The Varsae Estrikavis. The prize he'd been searching for when he released Asankaru. Which led directly to Reshel's death. He'd vowed long ago that he would find Naragenth's lost library, not for himself, not for his own glory, but for her, in memory of her sacrifice.

But he knew that was a lie. Or at least not the complete truth. He would do it for her, of course—how could he not?— but the old hunger he had for doing such a great thing by himself, finding something that other wizards had sought for more than eighteen hundred years without success, yawned opened within him once more. He could blame it on some kind of residual effect of the Neddari compulsion, but that too would be a lie. The desire was from his own heart, his own yearning to achieve something as great as the founders of his family's line. Even to best them.

And it was so close now. So very close.

He could not turn away. Not when they had no other course of action to try. It was either this or face defeat.

He stood and grasped the scepter. "Brace yourself, everyone, in case this goes wrong."

"Gerin, I don't think you should—"

It was too late. He was not listening.

Gerin opened himself to magic. His aura burst to life around him. Balandrick took a step back and covered his eyes. Therain gasped in surprise.

He let his magic fill him, then poured every bit of amber power flowing into him down into the scepter.

A silent concussion of power shook the room as the scepter took, and contained, all of the magic Gerin sent into it. Glasses trembled on the table; he felt the floor vibrate like a plucked string beneath his boots.

The ivory should have burned to ash in an instant; the gold and silver should have melted and dripped to the table like syrup or hot wax, or puffed into vapor—but they did not. A faint amber radiance shimmered around the golden gull at the head of the scepter, but other than that there was no visible sign of the tremendous energies surging through the ivory rod.

But what he could *feel* . . .

The spells within the scepter were using the vast influx of magic to unfold themselves and perform the tasks they'd been designed for. He felt layer after layer of defenses—most of them designed to unleash lethal magic if they were improperly activated—fall away, the spells discharging harmlessly upon sensing Gerin's amber magic.

More and more protective spells rendered themselves inert as his magic continued inward to whatever it was that waited beneath Naragenth's impressive array of defenses. The only way through them was to use amber magic. More power than any other wizard could create, even in Naragenth's day. *That* was Naragenth's ultimate defense: no one but an amber wizard could give the spells what they needed—only an amber wizard could send enough magic into the scepter to activate the spells. Even several wizards acting in concert could not duplicate the properties of amber power; that was an inviolable rule of magic. And since there were no other amber wizards in Naragenth's time, the Varsae Estrikavis was safe. Even if the scepter had fallen into Helca's hands, none of his wizards would have been able to penetrate it. They would have destroyed it, and probably died while doing so.

He'd been right, but what an awful risk he'd taken. Not only with the safety of the scepter itself, but with his own life.

The last of the defenses fell away and the magic contained in the heart of the scepter drank Gerin's power. The final spell—the one beneath all of Naragenth's protections—was so strange that Gerin could not recognize it. It felt almost like a knife of some kind, invisible yet more keen than any physical knife could ever hope to be. *But what is it designed to cut?* he wondered.

A rectangular door appeared in the air in front of him, floating a few inches above the floor. The others gasped at the sight.

Then he realized: it was for cutting a hole between worlds.

On the door was the sigil of Naragenth, an upright staff bisecting a rayed sun.

Below that was a silver crescent.

"The Chamber of the Moon," he whispered.

45

"Venegreh preserve us, you've done it," said Hollin. "You've found the Varsae Estrikavis."

"I've got to say, even I'm impressed," said Therain. "What in Shayphim's name are we looking at?"

"The entrance to the Varsae Estrikavis," said Gerin. "But we're not in yet." He put the scepter down, his eyes locked on the strange door, but the opening did not vanish when he released his grip on the ivory as he feared it might. He wondered how they would conceal it again. Would it just remain here, hanging in the air for anyone to enter, if they could not figure out the correct spells?

"Congratulations, Balan," he said. "Your idea about where the door would open was right." He made no pretense that he'd coincidentally stumbled onto the exact location where Naragenth had placed his door. That kind of coincidence was too large to be believed. The door would open anywhere. Here, Ailethon, Agdenor, Gedsengard . . . wherever the spells within the scepter were activated.

A door to another world.

Gerin stepped toward the door and looked at it more closely. It was made of some dark, finely grained wood, highly polished, with an ornate gold handle on the left. He could sense preservation spells in the wood, keeping at bay the decaying forces of time.

He and Hollin both examined it with Seeings and other

spells in case there were defenses on this door as well, but they found none. "It doesn't even have a lock," commented Gerin.

"I think the scepter is lock enough."

Gerin reached for the handle. Balan placed his hand on the prince's forearm to stop him. "My lord, please, let me. If there are unseen dangers—"

"I thank you for your concern, Captain, but I want to be the one to open this door."

Gerin grasped the handle and pushed the door open.

There was a slight exhalation of stale air from the room beyond, but other than that, no sign whatsoever that the door marked a boundary from their world to another. He stretched his hand forward and tentatively broke the threshold, prepared to draw it back quickly should something untoward occur. But he felt nothing at all. The transition between worlds was completely transparent.

He stepped up and into the room beyond the door.

"Is everything still all right?" asked Hollin. "Can you hear me? Can you come out again?"

Gerin stepped back into his study. "It's fine. It behaves just like any other opening."

"Go in again and close the door," said Hollin. "Count to five, then open it."

Gerin did as he was asked. He opened it and returned to the room. "Well?"

Hollin's eyes were wide. "When you closed the door it vanished. I admit, my heart gave a shudder. I thought you might be lost."

Balandrick was white. "You're not the only one."

"Interesting," said Gerin. "I guess Naragenth didn't want to risk the possibility of getting trapped in whatever other world this place exists." That also answered his question about how to hide the door again once they were finished. Apparently, once it was opened, closing it activated the concealing spells. Simple and elegant.

"One more test," said Hollin. "Take the scepter in with you, and then close the door. I want to see if it still vanishes."

Gerin saw what Hollin was getting at and did as he was asked. He waited a few moments behind the closed door, scepter in hand, and then opened it again. "Well? Did it vanish?"

"No. I was hoping it wouldn't. I didn't think Naragenth would be foolish enough to overlook the possibility of leaving his key behind the door by accident."

"Wouldn't it be ironic if the true reason the library had never been found was because Naragenth locked the key in it?"

"Yes, well, I'm glad he had enough foresight to take simple precautions. Sometimes one can overlook the basics."

"I can't believe you did it," whispered Therain, absently rubbing the newly fashioned leather cap over the stump of his arm. "Reshel would be proud of you."

Gerin nodded and swallowed. Tears stung his eyes, but he blinked them away. He imagined the look of joy that would come across her face if she could step into the Varsae Estrikavis and behold its wonders.

The glory and pride he'd felt at his accomplishment dimmed a little as he realized what he'd lost to get here. But what had been done could not be undone. She was lost to them until they too died and joined her in the Mansions of Velyol beneath the silent stare of Bellon.

He stepped up again, then gestured for the others to follow.

The room beyond the door was a small antechamber, a rectangular space paneled in the same dark wood from which the door was made. The floor was cut stone, polished to a high luster. In the center was a larger diamond-shaped tile inlaid with an amber flame. Gerin smiled. *He marked this place as his own. Other wizards may have contributed to it, but it was the amber wizard's idea, his creation, and he would not let anyone who entered here forget it.*

Magefire sconces were set opposite each other in the longer walls. They were lit, glowing with a warm half-light. Neither he nor Hollin had lit them. Had they been burning for eighteen hundred years, or were they activated when the door was opened?

Opposite the door through which they had entered they saw another door, identical to the first, with both seals upon it and the same golden handle.

Gerin opened it. They paused on the other side to take in what they were seeing.

They stood on the threshold of a circular room five stories tall with galleries leading off in many directions from each level. The walls were lined with shelves, cases, niches, doors, paintings, tables, chairs, curving staircases, and magefire lamps, all of which were lit at the same half-light as the ones in the antechamber. The floor of the chamber was blue-gray stone covered with an assortment of rich rugs. The ceiling high above them was a dome painted to resemble a twilight sky, with a bright crescent moon at the apex. The shelves were packed with books, scrolls, parchments, boxes, crates, busts, statues, reliquaries, and other items lost in the gloom. In many ways, it reminded Gerin of the Varsae Sandrova at Hethnost.

There was a black stone pedestal in the center of the chamber. Upon it was a rod or staff about five and a half feet tall. As soon as his eyes fell on it, Gerin could sense the power of the thing, though it was a strange, enclosed kind of magic. The power of the scepter felt like heat from a fire, but that of the staff was altogether different. The magic within it seemed bent back around itself. Instead of radiating from it in all directions, it was enveloped in a cocoon of power.

"Do you see that?" he said to Hollin.

Hollin nodded, his mouth hanging open. "Can it be? Is that the Staff of Naragenth?" His voice was little more than a whisper.

"You mean the one that he was said to have fashioned from magic itself? The one the legends say is actually *made* of magic and not any physical substance?"

Hollin could only nod again.

They went to the pedestal, a knee-high disc of black marble shot through with veins of silver and crimson. The staff rising from it was as black as midnight and seemed to swallow any light that fell upon it, so that they could see no details at all of its surface. The ferrules at each end were fashioned from silver intricately etched with arcane symbols.

"It's hard to look at," said Therain.

Gerin understood what his brother meant. He was having a hard time focusing on the staff; his eyes kept sliding away from it, as if it were a spot in his vision caused by staring at the sun or a bright light. The sense of immense power within it was also much stronger now.

"Hollin, is this even *real*?" Gerin asked.

"It's making me dizzy just looking at it." The wizard rubbed his forehead, then invoked a Seeing. Gerin did the same, and saw only pulsing power where the body of the staff should have been. There was no wood, and no metal except for the ferrules.

"I've never seen anything like it," said Hollin. "The legends are true. Somehow Naragenth was able to force magic itself to assume and hold a physical form."

"What are these symbols on the ferrules? I don't recognize them. Are they helping the staff to hold its shape?"

"I've never seen those symbols before either. I would guess that they were created by Naragenth just for the staff. There is power in it both subtle and grand. We can only hope he left some writings here about how he created this."

"Can you feel the magic in it?" He wondered if Hollin was blind to the power of the staff the way he was to the magic in the scepter.

"Yes, but it's strange. It's contained somehow, held very close to the staff itself."

Gerin forced his fingers to pass through the cocoonlike layer enveloping the staff like a barrier of thickened air. His hand tingled as the dense web of magic danced across the surface of his skin.

He staggered and cried out when his fingers touched the black surface. Tides of immense power flowed up his arm and around his body. The protective cocoon swelled outward to envelop him as well, and within its embrace truly unimaginable forces swirled in a chaotic maelstrom.

He released his grip and stepped back from the pedestal, trembling. He felt Balandrick's hand on his shoulder to steady him. "Are you all right, my lord?"

"What happened?" asked Hollin.

Gerin did his best to describe what he'd felt, then gestured toward the staff. "Try it for yourself."

Hollin was strangely reluctant to do so.

"I don't think it will hurt you," said Gerin. "But the amount of power is almost overwhelming."

The wizard rubbed his hands together. "I'm not afraid of being hurt. It's the idea that this staff actually exists. I admit, I've always thought it nothing more than a fanciful legend. But now, to be standing here facing it, and actually able to touch it . . ." He drew a long breath. "I almost feel I should apologize to Naragenth's spirit for my lack of faith."

Gerin laughed. "I wouldn't have thought you were so superstitious. So you were wrong about the staff. Lots of other wizards were too. What does that matter now? Apologize to Naragenth if you feel you must, *but touch the damn thing.* I want to know what you think."

Hollin laughed as well. He reached out and gripped the staff firmly in his right hand.

The wizard's knees buckled beneath the onslaught of magic. Gerin could see a faint aura flickering around the other wizard's body.

Hollin released the staff and stared at it, wide-eyed and shaking. "Venegreh's hand, I've never felt anything like that before!"

"I was hoping for something a little more colorful from you, along the lines of 'Kamor's hairy balls,' now that I know you have it in you."

The older wizard gave him a sharp glance. "Now's not the time to be making jokes, Gerin."

"Now's the *perfect* time for them. If I don't, I'm liable to burst." He regarded the staff again. "How could Naragenth use such a thing? There's so much power there it's difficult to hold."

"One might become used to it over time, but I think that the staff did not feel so strong to Naragenth when he made it. When I touched it I could feel magic bleeding *into* it from the vast reservoir of power all wizards draw upon. Did you feel that as well?"

"Yes, but it was all confused with the rest of the power flowing around the staff."

"I think it has been accruing magic around itself for nearly two thousand years. It's been absorbing magic like a sponge, but with no outlet—no wizard to dispel the magic—it's increased to this immense, almost unspeakable level of power."

They left the staff and spent some time exploring other areas of the Varsae Estrikavis, trying to determine the cataloging scheme. After a while Hollin said, "I think it's time we let others know what we've found."

"I'm not ready to tell my father yet."

"Gerin, the longer you keep it from him the worse it will be."

"It doesn't get much worse than it is now." He knew Hollin was right, but he did not want to provoke another fight with the king. And a part of him did not want to share this with his father. His father had been cruel beyond words, and Gerin did not think he'd earned the right to share in this discovery. It was the king's decree that had forced him to steal the scepter. His father would have denied him this achievement, and he would not appreciate its value. After all, the library was filled with magical knowledge and devices of magic, things the king now despised.

"No. We're going to wait until we have something that will help us face the siege. We need to find war magic. And until we do, this is our secret."

Therain only knew a little Osirin from his days as Master Aslon's pupil, and Balandrick none at all. Hollin told them what words or symbols to look for. Therain started down a gallery to the left, Balandrick took the gallery next to that one, and Hollin began a slow circuit of the ground floor hall.

Gerin returned to the staff, drawn to it as if it were whis-

pering a wordless, seductive song that spoke only in the un-
derbelly of his thoughts. At certain moments when he saw it
from the corner of his eye it seemed the utterly black form
was somehow *moving*, as if particles smaller than flecks of
sand were blazing up and down its length with incredible
speed, prevented only by the silver ferrules from blasting out
of both ends in twin fountains of tangible night. But when
he tried to fix his eyes on it directly, the sense of motion
ceased. Then it seemed more like a hole in the air, not so
much a thing but the absence of it, a puncture in reality that
merely held the illusion of the staff for his benefit, so that his
mind—and hands—had something to grasp.

Unable to contain himself, he reached out and took hold
of it again.

The titanic forces swirling about it struck him as they had
before, a maelstrom of magic stronger by far than anything
he'd ever encountered. But to his surprise, he acclimated to it
quickly, as if the sheath that slipped over his body like a cool
whisper of wind had adjusted itself to help him better cope
with the tremendous power the staff contained. He marveled
at this almost intelligent manipulation of magic; that it could
adapt itself to its user seemed—

He shuddered and nearly dropped the staff. The bottom
ferrule clanged on the floor before he recovered.

"Gods above me . . ." he whispered.

Hollin ran to his side. "What is it? What happened?"

Gerin held the staff at arm's length and stared at it as if
seeing it for the first time. "I think the staff is alive."

46

"What do you mean alive?" said Hollin.

"That it's . . . conscious somehow. Aware of things. Aware of *me*."

Now that he had sensed a presence in the staff—and there was no other way to think of it now other than some kind of living thing—he could not ignore it. He was certain it had revealed itself to him deliberately, like a face rising out of black waters that he thought had been lifeless and empty. He wondered how Naragenth could have done such a thing. He recalled that when he'd fashioned Nimnahal he'd desired to make it aware of him at some level so it would respond to his touch and presence by actively recognizing him. He'd gotten nowhere with that—had not even known where to begin. But Naragenth had done it. There was a mind of some kind within the staff.

He handed it to Hollin, who reacted with surprise when the protective envelope adjusted itself to him. "Do you feel it?" asked Gerin. "That there's something *in* the staff itself, aware of you?"

Hollin did not answer at once. Gerin could see the faraway look come across his face, the telltale sign that the wizard had slipped into a mild trance to better concentrate and block out distractions. He placed his other hand upon the black rod and held it firmly.

Hollin's gaze resettled back into the room. "It's disturbing, but I think you're right. There is an awareness locked within this object." He handed it back to Gerin as if he no longer wanted to touch it.

"How could Naragenth do something like that?"

"I don't know. I pray we can find any notes he made about the creation of the staff. But for now we must put this aside."

He suspects something and is afraid to say what it is, Gerin thought as Hollin resumed his search of the lower floor. There was no mistaking the troubled look on the wizard's face.

Gerin tried to reach out to it with his mind. *Can you hear me?* He projected his thoughts as forcefully as he could and felt a little foolish doing so, but at least no one else knew. *Are you able to communicate? Are you aware of what you are?* Then he realized that if Naragenth had been able to impart the ability of speech to the entity within the staff, he would have almost certainly used Osirin. Gerin repeated his questions in the language of wizards.

But there was nothing. He heard no words, sensed no attempt by the presence to change or alter itself in response to his questions. It simply lingered there in the fabric of the staff, a part of it yet somehow separate from it at the same time.

He sighed. This mystery would have to wait. He returned the staff to the pedestal and joined the older wizard in his search.

They slept very little over the next few days while seeking spells and objects of war. Gerin kept the scepter carefully hidden and prayed no one noticed it was missing from its proper place.

The evening of the first day they discovered that an entire gallery on the third floor was devoted to the conduct of war and exhausted themselves scrutinizing the contents of the shelves. Hollin was astounded at much of what they found. He held up a large bronze amulet dangling from a silver chain. "The devastation this can unleash is incredible," he said as he read the runic characters inscribed in it.

"Then why wasn't it used against Helca's armies when they invaded?" asked Balandrick.

"Maybe it was. You have to remember that there were thousands of wizards in Naragenth's time, so while this amulet can quite literally kill hundreds of soldiers in the blink of an eye, there were wizards on the opposing sides who had spells to counteract just these kinds of powers. But today . . ."

"There are no other wizards to block its magic," said Therain. "We can use it against the Havalqa and they can't do a damn thing to stop us. We can rip them to shreds."

Gerin wondered what had become of Katel yalez Algariq. Strange that he should think of her now, after what she had done to him, the utter shame she had inflicted. And yet he could not bring himself to blame her completely or truly hate her. She had been forged in the harsh society of the Havalqa, cast into a role she had no power to change. She loved her son, and had wanted a better life for him. That was something he could understand.

She is probably dead, executed for her failure to keep me captive. He tried to push the thought of her from his mind, but could not completely do so. He wondered what would become of her son. She'd told him his name once. What had it been? It came to him in a moment: Huma. Was he still alive? What chance did he have in that unfeeling world without his mother?

That's not my concern, he told himself. *There's nothing I can do.* Still, he hoped that she had somehow survived and would find her way back to young Huma.

"Yes, exactly," said Hollin in answer to Therain's statement. "There was more or less a balance in Naragenth's day, with kingdoms able to keep each other in check, at least until Helca came along and shattered all of that. But these weapons were probably the strongest of the strong, which is why they were placed here."

Balandrick stood and stretched his back. "All of this stuff and I can't find so much as a Shayphim-cursed knife. Where are the *real* weapons? I can't use a magic amulet."

"Wizards don't make those kinds of weapons, Balan," said Gerin. "They never have. That's why I had to make Nimnahal myself."

"Well, if all of these so-called weapons in here need wizards to use them, we're going to be sorely pressed to beat back a thirty-thousand-man army."

"We've had word that Nellemar's fleet has finally sailed," said Therain. "They'll still be outnumbered, but it's long past time we started fighting back. The smug bastards have been sitting out there for weeks controlling the waters with barely a bowshot from us to contest it."

Balandrick left to get them some food. He came back a short time later, empty-handed, and called out, "My lord!"

"What is it, Balan?"

"The enemy has been sighted to the north, heading toward the Varga. The siege will soon begin."

Mellam yun avki Drugal, Sword of the Exalted, halted his war horse atop the wooded ridge when he first caught sight of the city. *Too damn long at sea,* he thought. *I'm a soldier, not a sailor. I belong on land.* He raised the visor and called out for the march to halt.

The city looked little different here than it had from the sea. Its walls were tall and strong, but he had faced other cities and other walls—some much taller and much stronger than these—and they had all eventually fallen to the righteousness of the Steadfast. Herol would watch over his soldiers as they bent these unbelievers to their will.

Drugal surveyed the empty field that lay between his army and the stony promontory upon which the city had been built. "Make camp and establish pickets," he said to Gaiun Pizan. "We'll be too vulnerable if we try to cross that open plain, and there is no gate on this side of the city for us to drive through. In the morning, we'll swing around to the west and concentrate our forces there."

"At once, sir," growled Pizan.

Tomorrow the trial begins in earnest, he thought. *And we will see just what these heathens are made of.*

* * *

"I should have you thrown in the dungeons for what you've done," said the king. He sat at his council table with a look of barely controlled rage on his face. Gerin had just admitted to his father that he'd used the Scepter of the King to find the Varsae Estrikavis.

"Go ahead then," said Gerin defiantly. "Be a fool. Throw away the best weapons you have to fight the Havalqa."

Balan and Jaros Waklan each took a sharp breath. Therain's eyes widened at his brother's words and harsh tone. Hollin stood to the side, arms folded across his chest, watching the exchange intently.

"How *dare* you speak to me that way!"

"It's nothing less than you deserve for how you've treated me! I am not the enemy, but you treat me as if I am!"

"You defied my will—"

"You forced my hand! If you hadn't tried to deprive me of—"

Therain stepped forward and held up his hands. "The two of you need to calm down. This is worse than when Claressa and Reshel would go at it. And that's saying something."

"I agree with Prince Therain," said Jaros Waklan. "These accusations are pointless. We need to be united against our enemy, not bickering among ourselves."

Abran sat back in his chair, his jaw tight. "What is it you've found in this library of yours that can help us?"

Gerin, his heart still thumping in his chest, took a deep breath. He realized that he and the king had just passed some crucial point of no return. There would be no forgiveness from his father for what he had done. Their relationship had been irrevocably broken, and he wondered—and feared— what dark thing would arise to take its place.

But he could not worry about that now. What was done was done. Let his father hate him if he must. He would try to mend things later, though his heart told him it was a hopeless task.

He and Hollin explained the weapons of war they had collected from the Varsae Estrikavis. The king listened in silence, his expression harsh. He asked no questions, gave no indication that he cared about what he was hearing.

When Gerin was done speaking, the king swung his gaze toward Hollin. "Will you fight for us, wizard?"

Hollin looked offended by the question. "I have already fought them, Your Majesty. They are as much my enemy as they are yours."

To Gerin, he said, "You will do whatever you can with your magic to hurt our enemies."

"Yes, Father." He bowed his head, then turned to go.

"Gerin."

He turned back toward the king.

"This is not over. I will not forget your defiance."

Gerin held his father's eyes for a moment, then left the room without another word.

The wizards spent all night in the Varsae Estrikavis, deciding which war spells they would use against the Havalqa and in what order. Some were designed for relatively close-quarters fighting, or for duels against other wizards, and so were not considered; they needed magic that would work against as many soldiers and from as great a distance as possible, as neither wizard saw themselves wading into the ranks of clashing armies. Many of the spells and devices were so powerful they would exhaust both of them after a single attempt; others required more magic than Hollin could create, so they were set aside for Gerin.

After a brief discussion, they decided it would be better to use some of the more devastating spells first, even if it meant draining them so heavily that they could not work other spells for hours, if not days. "I'd rather hit them early and hard," said Gerin. "Make them afraid of what else we might have at our disposal. *They* don't know there are only two of us here."

After midnight, Gerin fell asleep at one of the tables in the Varsae Estrikavis for a few hours, his head resting on his forearms. Hollin woke him with a gentle shake of his shoulder. "Come, Gerin. We should prepare for the day."

Throughout the night Gerin's gaze had been continually drawn to the staff, and now, as he rubbed his eyes, he found himself staring at it again. They had given it no consideration as an implement of war because that was not its intended use; they'd been busy enough with the spells and devices they found in what they had named the "war gallery" to even think about the mystery of the staff. But now he thought that ignoring it was a mistake. There was a literal ocean of magic contained within it, just waiting for him to use.

The problem was, there was actually *too much* magic to power an ordinary spell. If he wanted to create death spells to use against the Havalqa, for example, he could only use the barest fraction of the magic the staff contained to make them; too much magic and the spell itself would be overwhelmed and fail to work. That was a basic principle of magic: use the correct amount of magic for a spell—no more, no less. There were many different kinds of death spells because some were designed to be stronger than others. Such a fracturing of magic had come about when the old powers of the Atalari—who did not use spells at all—had become diluted in the blood of the Gendalos. The various colored flames of wizards had begun to manifest themselves in the second millennium of the Dawn Age, with the result that some wizards were not strong enough to work more powerful spells, so new ones had to be devised for them.

No more, no less. That was why he and Hollin had decided early on that there was little point in using the staff to meet their immediate goals. Better to use the spells and devices designed specifically for war rather than attempt to adapt the staff to their needs, especially when they had no spells that could make use of its vast power.

But what if he didn't use spells? He rose from the table. No one had ever had this much magic at his disposal before. Who knew what could be done? The Atalari had not used spells. They simply directed their power with their thoughts, and it was done. Maybe he could get the staff to work the same way. Maybe he didn't need spells.

"Gerin, where are you going?" asked Hollin as the prince

made his way to the marble pedestal. The older wizard held several magical devices in his hands. A padded box was on the table beside him, partially filled with other objects.

Gerin grasped the staff and grinned as it once again adapted itself to his touch, shielding him from the overwhelming effects of so much magic even more efficiently than it had the last time. It was learning, he realized. It was taking measures to protect him. He concentrated on the black void of the rod, trying to detect the consciousness he'd felt in it before.

It was there, lurking silently in the background of the staff's magic, waiting.

It *wanted* to be used, he realized. It had been dormant for centuries, and after all this time it was hungry to unleash its power.

"What are you doing?" asked Hollin.

Gerin called for one of the soldiers standing guard by the door to come and carry the box of magical devices for Hollin. "I'm going to put this to the test," he said as he marched from the chamber.

He did not tell anyone what he was planning. He sent word to his father that he was going to the northern wall of the city to survey the Havalqa army, then set off with Hollin, Balandrick, and a company of Kotireon Guards who rapidly ushered them through the still-dark streets. The guards forced a path through clusters of sleeping refugees who shouted and cursed at the disturbance until they saw the mounted figures and a cordon of heavily armed soldiers surrounding them, then they quieted and melted away into whatever shadowy niches they could find.

"I think this is ill-advised," said Hollin. "We should not be experimenting with the staff. I don't think it's wise to even remove it from the Varsae Estrikavis. We don't know enough about it. Venegreh preserve us, Gerin. Stop for a moment to consider what you're doing."

"I *have* considered it."

Hollin let out an exasperated sigh. "Will you just *please*

tell me what it is you're planning? Your infatuation with secrecy is incredibly trying."

"I want to see if I can get the staff to work for me without using spells." He'd fastened the staff to his saddle, but even without touching it directly he could feel its power, flowing around the rod like the ebb and flow of the sea.

The eastern sky was beginning to brighten with a translucent rosy light when they left their horses and climbed the steep stone stairs to the battlements. Far below them the Varga was shrouded in darkness, like a lake of night evaporating with the rising of the sun to reveal a bed of dried brown grass.

Gerin created a Farseeing and studied the distant ridge. The enemy camp was preparing to move.

The staff pulsed faintly in his right hand, its power lapping warmly against his skin. He tried to tap into it. At once he felt a surge of magic flow around and into him. It was a decidedly strange sensation. When he unleashed his own power, the magic was focused outward through his *paru'enthred*, but this was the opposite: the magic of the staff was pouring *into* him, filling him with its potency. There was something oddly familiar about it, and then he remembered: it was like the Ritual of Discovery. The power of that spell had filled him as it searched for the color of his flame.

He tried to bend his thoughts toward the presence within the staff, hoping that somehow it would help him manipulate the magic without using Osirin invocations. He envisioned the ridge erupting with fire, the woods and men and horses there consumed by a conflagration of magical flame. He willed it with all of his might, trying to force the immense energies within the staff to rush out toward the enemy and do his bidding.

Nothing happened.

He cursed to himself and tried again, this time envisioning a different attack on the Havalqa. Again, nothing happened.

"We're wasting time," Hollin whispered, so that the guards would not hear. "Whatever you're doing, it's not working. I understand your desire to use it—the gods know there's enough magic in there to level a mountain—but until we understand it better, it's not a weapon we can use. Please, Gerin. We need to go to the gate to prepare the weapons we *do* have."

Gerin made one last attempt to hurl the power of the staff at the Havalqa army. When that failed he lowered the staff, angry and humiliated by his failure. *How did Naragenth use the damned thing?* he wondered. Then he remembered that at the time of its creation the staff did not have even a fraction of power it now contained, having accrued magic for the eighteen hundred years it had been locked away. He wondered if he would somehow have to bleed off the magic around it before putting it to use. Discarding so much power would be an almost obscene waste, but at the moment he was at a loss as to what else to do. Certainly there were no ordinary spells that could make use of so much magic.

His knees buckled as an image flashed in his mind with a searing, knifelike pain. He saw himself far beyond the city's walls, standing in the open lands nearer to the Havalqa, holding the staff high in his hands. It blazed with amber fire.

"Are you all right?" asked Hollin.

He nodded, trying to understand what he had just seen. He shook his head to clear it. "You're right, this isn't working. Let's go to the—"

The image flashed in his mind once more. The pain was so intense that a muffled cry escaped his lips. If Hollin had not grasped his shoulders he might have fallen to his knees.

"Gerin, what is wrong?" said the wizard. "Are you using your magic? I felt a sudden surge of power."

"Shayphim take me, my lord, you're bleeding," said Balandrick.

Gerin could feel a hot stream of blood running from his nose. He wiped it with the back of his hand as he straightened.

"I don't know." He described what he had seen. "It was like a vision, something from outside of me. It wasn't a memory, or something I was thinking about."

He looked at the staff in his hand.

It was trying to tell him something. The presence within the staff was conscious enough to not only understand his desires but also communicate with him. He was stunned by this revelation. How had Naragenth accomplished such a thing? Not only had he placed an awareness within the staff, but he'd somehow contrived to make it conscious and intelligent.

"Let's get to the gate. I have something to tell you along the way."

Gerin spoke as they hurried along the battlements. The wall provided the fastest route to the Okoro Gate. Though well-manned with Taeratens and men of the City Watch, the twenty-foot-wide wall-walk was practically empty compared to the jammed city streets and allowed them to move swiftly and unimpeded.

Hollin was unsure what to think. "The power of the staff is so unique that I have no gauge to tell whether this is possible or just some headache of yours gone terribly awry."

Gerin stopped and held the staff toward Hollin. "Take it. See if it shows you what it showed me."

Hollin took the staff and regarded it with a piercing, unblinking stare. "I don't see or feel anything."

"Could it be that it can only communicate with an amber wizard?" asked Balan.

"It's impossible to know," said Hollin. He handed the staff back.

Gerin took it and continued walking. "You need to trust me."

"I do, which is why I've agreed to do this with you. But until I see proof that you're right I will harbor doubts."

"Fair enough."

They hurried along the wall-walk in silence as dawn broke over the sea. On the far ridge the Havalqa army was making an orderly march along the northern rim of the Varga.

Gerin wondered how Elaysen was faring. He'd not seen her since she went to check on her father. He realized he should have sent word to her and the Prophet. He wondered what Aunphar thought of the mission of the Havalqa and their belief in a coming Great Enemy.

He was silent for the rest of their journey along the wall-walk, wondering about the One God and his own confused relationship with Him and the Prophet's nascent religion. The messenger of the One God, Zaephos, had appeared to him twice to deliver cryptic messages about the relationship of the divine and mortals. He still did not know what to make of it. On the road to Hethnost, Zaephos had warned him of the coming of the Adversary, a being who opposed the Maker—the messenger's name for what Aunphar called the One God; that at the beginning of all things the Adversary had suffered a defeat, yet was now entering the mortal world. The One God needed willing mortals to fight against the Adversary when he arose, since, in the words of Zaephos, "The Maker cannot strike him without undoing all that He has built."

A long time ago Gerin had vowed that he would not be used by a god, no matter the reason. The Neddari compulsion that had rendered him the unwitting instrument of Asankaru's release only reinforced his desire to follow only his own path and not some destiny or divine plan laid out for him by unknown and unseen powers. *I will not be a tool, to be used and discarded,* he thought as he marched along the wall-walk. The bloody Havalqa were trying to use him to find the mysterious Words of Making, a power whose very existence he still questioned. How could the words that powered the act of Creation itself be somewhere in the mortal realm? It was a ludicrous idea.

And yet . . .

He felt deep in his heart that all of this was true. The One God, the Adversary, even the Words of Making—there was something about them that felt right to him. He could not say why, because another part of him wanted to reject them utterly and his implied role as finder of the Words, since that seemed to reduce him once more to little more than an implement in some grand design not of his own making.

But if the Adversary is real, we will have to fight him. I can't refuse to battle him when the time comes because it goes against my lofty principle of refusing to be used. Not if he threatens my family and country. If a god declares war on the mortal world, I have a duty to fight.

And it will be my choice, no one else's. It doesn't matter what the Foretellings of Bainora Estreg say about the remainder of my life. I will make my own choices for what I want to do and how I want to live. If it conforms to some moldering Foretelling or the beliefs of the Dreamers, so be it. And if it doesn't, I don't care. Shayphim take them all. I will do as I see fit.

He realized now that struggling against an unknown— whether the desires of the One God or the wishes of the Dreamers—was the wrong way to live. He should not spend his life fighting *against* what he perceived others wanted him to do; he should instead simply live as he saw fit, and do what he felt was right for himself and his kingdom. If doing what was right happened to conform to what others wanted from him, well, he could live with that, because the choice was his. Or at least it felt as if it was, and if he could not tell the difference, then it did not truly matter.

Gerin felt a burdensome weight lift from him as the full force of this realization sank in. He'd not understood just how oppressive and wearying his struggle against being used had been until now, when he finally shrugged it off. Foretellings and visions didn't matter. The only thing that mattered was that he did what was right for him. He would do his duty to the kingdom and those he loved, and that would be enough. The rest would take care of itself.

Which meant he should do whatever he could to find the Words of Making. If they existed, then they were a weapon to be used against the Adversary.

He decided then, quite easily and naturally, to follow the One God. Not only had he met the Maker's messenger, but felt that the *idea* of a god of gods was right and true. He had learned a great deal of what was required of the *taekrim* who followed *dalar-aelom,* but had not completely given himself to it: he'd listened to what Elaysen had taught so he would be better able to decide what path he would follow, but until now had held back on completely committing himself. That would end when he next spoke to Aunphar. It was what he wanted in his heart. He didn't care that it would make his relationship with his father worse or cause problems with both the Temple and the noble houses. Nothing mattered except that he did what he felt was right.

"You're grinning like a cat that's just eaten a particularly delectable mouse," said Hollin. "Have you just had another one of your crazy ideas?"

"Not at all." Gerin picked up his already quick pace. "I've just realized how I should be living my life."

Hollin laughed, then realized Gerin was serious. "You are at times the most befuddling man I've ever met."

"I try, Hollin. I try."

47

The Presence—as Gerin now thought of the consciousness within the staff—sent him no more visions, for which he was grateful. But it was still there, lurking on the edge of his awareness like someone hidden in a forest watching him from behind the trees, trying to remain out of sight.

They found the gate towers teeming with Taeratens. Lord Commander Levkorail was in the north tower issuing orders to his captains to clear the streets behind the gates for two additional blocks. "I don't care if you have to jam the people down the sewers or onto the roofs, I want those streets cleared for our men."

"Lord Commander, a word with you, if I may," said Gerin.

Levkorail looked up, the lamplight gleaming on his shaved skull. "Yes, my lord." His tone was cordial enough, but the tightness around his eyes made it clear that he considered Gerin's presence a distraction from the task at hand.

"I need a company of your men to escort me outside the city. Hollin and I have weapons of magic we wish to use against the enemy, but to do so we need to be closer."

Levkorail straightened. "Then I feel you should wait to use your weapons until the enemy has come within range rather than venturing out to meet them, my lord."

"I understand your reluctance, Lord Commander. Nevertheless, I insist."

"My lord, I don't believe—"

"This is not a debate, Lord Commander. I expect a mounted company to be waiting in the courtyard within ten minutes. I have my reasons, which I have neither the time nor inclination to share." He wheeled about and left the room.

"Are you sure you know what you're doing, my lord?" asked Balandrick as they made their way down the tower stairs past Taeratens climbing to the castle wall. "I don't mean to question your abilities, but you weren't able to get the staff to work for you before. And even if you're right about the . . . whatever is in the staff telling you to move closer, *how* much closer do you need to be? Are you just going to keep closing the gap and trying to make it work until something happens? Because they're not going to let us advance on them without trying to do something in return."

Gerin bit back a stinging retort. Balandrick irritated him because he was right; he didn't have any idea how close he needed to be. His plan could become a fiasco witnessed by every soldier upon the walls, with everyone compelled to make a hasty retreat if he could not get the staff to release its magic.

They still had the war devices taken from the Varsae Estrikavis. He would simply have to decide when to abandon the staff as a lost cause and turn to the other sources of magic at their disposal.

"My lord?"

"I don't know, Balan. But we're going to try. I feel I'm this close"—he held his thumb and forefinger about an inch apart—"to bending the power of the staff to my will. If I'm right, I think I can end this siege before it begins."

While they waited for the company to gather in the courtyard, Hollin strapped vambraces formed of gold and black steel to his forearms. Devices of magic, not intended to be used as defensive armor in battle, they were inscribed with arcane symbols and Osirin spells that would allow the wizard wearing them to use and control far more power than would ordinarily be possible. "They contain their own source of magic, similar to what you did with Nimnahal," said Hollin as he buckled the straps.

"Just so they work," said Balandrick. "We'll need you to distract the Havalqa while Gerin's shouting at his stick to make it do something."

One of Levkorail's adjutants appeared and told them the company would be there momentarily. Stablehands brought horses for the three men. Hollin stuffed his saddlebags with as many devices as they would hold.

A hundred mounted Taeratens on armored war horses clopped across the cobblestones from a stable hidden behind a customs house. The captain spurred his mount forward and bowed his head to Gerin. "My prince, I am Leso Baldrin. We await your command."

Gerin introduced Hollin and Balandrick. "If all goes as planned, Hollin and I will unleash a magical assault on the enemy forces. Your duty is to protect us from any enemy counterattack."

"As you will, my prince. We will not fail you."

With Gerin in the lead, they headed for the gate.

Once outside the city, they swung to the right onto a path that followed the contour of the wall. Ahead of them to the left lay the huddled mass of shacks, barns, and houses that comprised Terimon, a town of criminals, orphans, the lost, the destitute, and outcasts. It had begun its existence two centuries ago as a temporary tent town of marketplaces and bazaars for those who could not afford the vendor fees for the city's markets, but over the years became a permanent settlement, though one rife with lawlessness. The City Watch did not patrol there. When orphans and urchins became too troublesome within Almaris itself, they were rounded up and taken to Terimon, forbidden to return to the city.

The town was now almost completely deserted because of the threat of siege. Gerin supposed that a few hardy souls remained there, well hidden in cellars dug into the bedrock or other places of concealment. He did not hold out much hope that anyone remaining there, no matter how well hidden, would last long if the town were to be occupied.

Gerin kept them at a swift pace. Soldiers upon the wall cheered them as they passed.

The path continued through the stretch of hard-packed earth that lay between Terimon and a westward-jutting section of the city's wall that housed the poor and crime-ridden district of Kazain. Gerin spurred them into a gallop, charging across the final length of flat ground before they reached the long slope of the Almarean Plateau. They did not venture down into the Varga; instead, they continued on a northward path, across the Nellin Fields toward the end of the ridge the Havalqa had occupied.

Gerin placed his hand tentatively on the staff, bracing for another pain-drenched vision. But there was nothing. He took that as a sign that he was close enough to use the staff's power.

He asked Hollin if the war devices he carried would work from this distance. "I have no idea," said the older wizard. "But we can certainly try."

Gerin halted and got down from his horse. Hollin unbuckled the saddlebag containing the devices of magic from the Varsae Estrikavis.

"Captain Baldrin, form up your men beside and behind us. I don't want our view obstructed."

"My prince, I don't feel we can adequately provide protection if you are exposed to the front."

"If you get in the way of our magic, you won't be able to provide anything except being dead. If things go badly you have my permission to close ranks and get us all out of here."

"Yes, my prince."

The forward lines of the Havalqa were just clearing the edge of the woods that covered the ridgeline.

"Hollin, are you ready?"

"Yes."

"Then let's get started before those bastards get any closer."

* * *

"What are they doing?" muttered Drugal as he spotted a mounted company of soldiers appear from behind the city's high walls. They were riding fast toward the approaching Steadfast army. He reined his horse to a halt and raised his seeing-glass. What he saw did nothing to clarify matters. They carried no standards or banners.

"Have they come to parley?" asked Gaiun Pizan.

"I don't think so." The riders could have been an envoy of some kind—there was no outward sign to belie that thought—but in his gut Drugal believed otherwise, and over the years he'd learned to trust what his gut told him.

Then he saw that one of them was the man from the Dreamer's vision, Gerin Atreyano.

"Get the Adepts up here," he said to Pizan.

Gerin couldn't decide whether to use Nimnahal to begin the attack or wade in with the unknown—and untested—power of the staff. He decided to start with the staff and use his sword only if the staff remained unresponsive.

He tightened his grip on the staff and opened himself to the tremendous energies it contained. The strange sensation of magic flowing into him occurred once more, filling him with a kind of giddy elation.

"I'll wait for you to begin your attack, then I will follow," said Hollin. "I don't want to do something that will interfere with your magic or have us waste our strength attacking the same targets."

"I'm going to take out as much of their forward lines as I can. At least that's my plan."

"When I see how far your magic extends, I'll aim my own spells beyond them." Hollin touched the vambraces on his arms in an almost ritualistic manner, then summoned magic into himself, which he held in check, waiting for Gerin to begin his work.

Gerin fixed his gaze on the wedge of murdrendi moving down the treeless ridgeline like a living arrowhead aimed directly at him. He knew they had seen them by now and must be wondering at their purpose.

It was time to show them.

He thrust the staff forward and told it in Osirin what he wanted it to do, at the same time visualizing the event in his mind. It was not a spell, not an incantation, but a simple command: *Break the ground beneath them. Swallow them up.*

The staff erupted with amber fire. The startled Khedeshian war horses snorted and stamped their feet until their riders brought them under control.

With a wordless shout, Gerin slammed the heel of the staff down against the ground. He felt the sea of magic contained in and around the staff bend to his will and flow out of the ferrule and into the thin soil beneath his feet. But he also realized that the Presence was exerting its own control over the magic, ensuring that it did indeed do as he wished.

The Presence was performing the same task as an incantation. His command was too vague to control magic directly—Osirin incantations were by their very nature precise. The Presence, he realized, understood his generalized command and was causing the magic to do what he desired.

Then he had no more time for thought as the earth itself heaved and groaned beneath him. Even he was not prepared for the staggering might unleashed through the staff. The ground under the ferrule rippled like a rug flung violently to clear it of dust, the ripple racing ahead of him at incredible speed, the wave spreading wider and growing higher as it charged toward the forward lines of the Havalqa. The dirt and rock within the wave seemed to liquefy, changing into something akin to thickened mud, the wave leaving a visible scar in the earth as it passed, a widening wedge-shape, its apex centered on the bottom ferrule of the staff, where the ground had sunk a foot or more from where it had been moments before. In some places the ground was churned so hard it had completely turned over, burying grass beneath dark clumps of soil that marred the newly made depression like wounds or open sores. The few trees dotting the landscape in the affected area toppled; three or four were heaved into the air by the violence of the wave's passage like javelins inexpertly thrown, spiraling through the air with clots of dirt flying from their pinwheeling roots.

Telros save me, the power I've unleashed . . . The amount of magic flowing through the staff was truly beyond his ability to comprehend. The onslaught he'd waged with Nimnahal aboard *Cregar's Glory* was nothing in comparison. He wondered if the world had ever seen such a release of magical power, outside of perhaps the Unmaking that ended the Doomwar many thousands of years ago.

Then the wave reached the point of the murdrendi wedge and changed its nature to comply with Gerin's command.

Break the ground beneath them. Swallow them up.

As the half-mile-wide wave whose crest was by now nearly twenty feet high began to fling the murdrendi into the air, the wave crest suddenly collapsed and inverted itself, becoming a fissure yawning beneath the enemy's feet. It continued to deepen, completely obliterating the ridge. Murdrendi fell screaming into the fissure, whose sides collapsed as the bottom deepened, leaving no means for them to climb out. Dirt flowed down upon them, burying them alive; boulders became exposed in the collapse, then tumbled down, crushing anything beneath them before being buried once more in the churning mass of earth at the fissure's bottom.

The fissure slowed its momentum as it chewed deeper into the ridge, but as yet showed no signs of abating. The entire contingent of murdrendi had been erased by his power. The human soldiers behind them were scrambling to get out of the fissure's path, but it was now so wide that only those on the flanks of the army had any chance of escape. Men dashed madly down the southern face of the ridge toward the Varga, but only a handful managed to outrace the devouring force of Gerin's magic.

The woods atop the ridge crushed hundreds of men and horses as the ground fell away. Trees snapped as they tumbled down. Falling boulders smashed the trees and the bodies of men and horses caught within them before vanishing beneath the line of churning earth.

Swallow them up indeed, thought Gerin. The effectiveness of his command was beyond his wildest expectations. He had not known what to expect, but it had not been this.

More than half the ridge had been demolished by the time the fissure halted. There was no sign that anyone who fell into the chasm was still alive. All had been completely buried and crushed beneath tons of earth and stone. A brown and gray cloud of smoke billowed out of the ground and was now settling over the remains of the ridge, obscuring much of their view.

He had just killed thousands of men in only a few minutes. He felt no guilt—they were enemies of Khedesh, after all, and he would kill them all if he could—only a deep sense of awe that he had been able to accomplish such a thing single-handedly.

And he'd only used a tiny part of the reservoir of power that had accrued around the staff.

But it was not without cost. Blood poured again from his nose, and his skull throbbed with sharp pain. Even though the barest fraction of the total power expended had flowed through his own *paru'enthred,* he felt weak, and sensed that he could easily burn out his own power if he were not careful.

Still, there was nothing to do but continue.

"I would not believe this had I not seen it for myself," said Hollin, staring wide-eyed at the devastation. He tore his gaze from the ruined ridge and looked at Gerin. "How did you do such a thing?"

"I told it what I wanted and it obeyed."

Hollin drew a long breath to calm himself, then pointed toward what was now the leading edge of the Havalqa troops and shouted the incantation that released the magic in the vambraces.

48

Drugal watched in mute horror as the ridge ahead of him vanished in a display of power the likes of which he had never before seen, or had even conceived possible. How could they battle this kind of might? But he dismissed the thought as a moment of weakness, unworthy of him. He was the Exalted's Sword. He would not waver, he would not bend. He served Holvareh and the Powers, and Their desires would not be denied.

The collapse of the ridge had mercifully halted several hundred yards from his position. Pizan and his fellow Kantu tribesmen had encircled Drugal and moved him back across the heaving ridge until the Sword had screamed for them to stop when he realized the gaping maw devouring earth and trees and men alike had halted.

"Where are the Harridan-damned Adepts?" he'd shrieked at Pizan as a cloud of dust and smoke billowed across them. Their horses were nearly mad with terror. Men began to cough and retch from the choking cloud that had settled over them like a curse.

"We have come," said a voice from above him. Drugal looked up the slope of the ridge to see Farso Laghil and five other Loremasters, their dark-skinned faces and pointed beards covered with gray dust. They stared at him dispassionately, as if the devastation the army had just suffered were somehow beneath their threshold of awareness.

"Can the power of your *tendrashis* counter what we have just seen?"

"No." The certainly of Laghil's reply startled Drugal, but the Sword showed no outward sign of the alarm that had gripped him. "The source of the power is far different from our own. It is not something we can block."

"Then what *can* you do?" Drugal had no patience for the kinds of formal pleasantries and verbal sparring the Loremasters found so desirable. *It is a fault of their training. All of them are the same—proud, disdainful, and craving to show their superiority at every chance.*

Laghil raised an eyebrow at the Sword's tone. "From this distance there is nothing we can do directly. I admit to a certain surprise and admiration at the display of power we have just witnessed. I did not think these infidels were capable of commanding such might, and I must wonder why it was not directed at the blockade fleet. It is possible that—"

Drugal restrained the sudden, overwhelming urge to choke the life from Laghil. "If there's nothing you can do directly, then do something *indirectly*, before they attack again!"

As soon as Hollin finished the incantation, the symbols etched on the vambraces began to radiate a bright golden light. Magic erupted from the older wizard's arms and raced toward the edge of the demolished ridge, now hidden from their view by the thick cloud of smoke and dust. It was a kind of magic, Gerin realized, that was invisible to nonwizards. The Khedeshian soldiers would see nothing, not even the glow from the vambraces.

But the magic was there, and it was potent. He could see and feel the concentrated power of the death spells. They were bound with Wardings, Shields, Reflections, and other countermeasures designed to ensure that the death spells penetrated whatever magical defenses would be surrounding the intended targets. When the vambraces were made there had been wizards defending the enemy, but now there were none.

The death spells reached the Havalqa and unfolded as designed, slaying only animal life—men, horses, livestock. The trees atop the ridge would not be affected, and might even afford some scant protection to those soldiers deeper in the woods.

After a few moments Hollin halted the spells and lowered his arms. "We're too far away now for this to be effective," he said quietly to Gerin. "You destroyed so much of their forward lines that what's left is now on the very edge of how far these spells can reach. I'm killing some of them, but too much is being wasted, dissipated by the distance."

"Keep your guard up, Captain," said Gerin to Balandrick. "We need to move closer now to make Hollin's weapons useful."

"I need them stopped," Drugal said to Laghil. "If they continue their attack as before, this entire army will be obliterated by the end of the day."

"Sword, I have no answer for you. We are too far—"

"Then you'll have to get closer."

Laghil first looked aghast, then offended. "You mean to send us into battle like common soldiers?"

"I mean to send you into battle as Loremasters who may be the only hope of saving this campaign from utter ruin. You are attached to this army to *fight*, Laghil. If you cannot fight from a distance, then you will move closer."

"Sword Drugal, you cannot possibly think—"

"You would be surprised what I can think, Loremaster. I will send the Brathkars to escort and protect you. This is not a request, Laghil. If you defy me, I will have you arrested and sent home in chains, assuming we live until sunset."

Laghil swallowed thickly, then bowed his head. "We obey the Exalted and her Sword."

Gerin and the rest rode swiftly along the edge of the sunken land where the staff's power had passed. The air was filled with the cloying smell of fresh dirt and smoke.

"They must be planning something," said Balandrick. "They can't just let us come to them unchallenged. Not after what we've already done."

"I've kept Wardings in front of us," said Hollin, "but so far there have been no attacks against them."

They reached the point where Gerin's power had created

the trench and veered to the right to skirt around its southern edge.

There was a raw, clifflike face across the spine of the ridge where Gerin's power had torn away the ground, revealing dark earth, the tangled roots of trees, and dirty clumps of stone. Bits of loose dirt tumbled down the nearly vertical slope as the devastated ridge continued to shift and settle. He wondered what his father would think of his renovation of the landscape.

"I think our challenge has just appeared," said Captain Baldrin, pointing through the thinning smoke that lay ahead of them.

A group of horsemen had appeared along the southern side of the ridge, heading straight for them. Armed soldiers surrounded a smaller group of men. Gerin fashioned a Farseeing and guessed that the protected men were Loremasters like Tolsadri.

Hollin touched a rayed amulet hanging from a slender chain around his neck, another of the treasures taken from the Varsae Estrikavis. "Allow me."

Still weakened, Gerin nodded, wiping at the slowing trickle of blood from his nose. He'd worked a healing spell on it, but it was proving stubborn.

Gerin sensed a flare of magic from the amulet, then Hollin staggered back a step as invisible power surged away from him. Gerin was uncertain what kind of magic Hollin had released. It had the flavor of a death spell, but there was something odd about it, something different—bits of magic wholly new to him, something he'd never before experienced but that felt very, very deadly.

In the three or four heartbeats it took for Hollin's magic to reach the riders, Gerin opened his senses further in an attempt to see some of the power at work. He caught glimpses of shimmering, translucent waves emerging from the amulet, flashes like reflections of sunlight on a wind-rippled lake, shot through with writhing tendrils of a darker, more ominous power.

Then the widening waves of magic slammed into the Havalqa horsemen.

Even Gerin gasped as the flesh of the men and horses simply exploded in a bloody spray of meat and bone. In moments there was nothing left but chunks of scattered, blood-soaked bodies lying on the grass. If the Loremasters had attempted to defend themselves against Hollin's power, they had failed miserably.

"Shayphim take me," muttered Captain Baldrin. "How can anyone stand against your magic? Why did those who created your devices not conquer the very world?"

Hollin choked off the amulet's power. He looked shaken by the viciousness of what he had done.

"When these devices were made, there were many other wizards in the world with the power to counter them," said the older wizard.

"Who would create such an awful power?" Baldrin asked him. "I mean no offense, but it is one thing to fight a man sword-to-sword, but to rend his body to bits from afar . . ."

"They are our enemies, Captain," said Balandrick, "and it doesn't matter *how* we win, only that we do."

Baldrin looked admonished. "You are of course right. I was imagining if the tables were turned and that power was directed at *me*."

"Be thankful it's not," said Balan.

"All that matters is that we kill our enemies," said Gerin. "And there are a great deal more of them out there. They brought their deaths upon themselves, no matter how gruesome. They deserve no pity, no mercy, and shall get none from us."

The Sword of the Exalted felt his heart flutter beneath his armor when the Loremasters and their Brathkar protectors . . . exploded. There was no other way to describe it. Nothing had touched them. The enemy horsemen were still hundreds of yards distant. He saw no power strike them. One moment Laghil and his fellow Adepts were riding swiftly with the intent of countering the power they faced, and the next . . .

Through his glass, Drugal had clearly seen the head of one of his commanders disintegrate. And the others . . . their flesh had been flayed from their bones as if invisible hooks yanked them apart.

How do I answer this? He did not fear death; he feared *failure.* He had lost battles before, but never one so large, or so important to the future of the Steadfast. The world itself required that they find the Words of Making to defeat the Great Enemy. And to do that, they needed—*he* needed—to conquer these lands.

"What is your command, Sword?" asked Gaiun Pizan. Even he had blanched at the sudden, violent deaths of the Loremasters. "They are not yet within range of our archers."

"Send a company of bowmen out to challenge them," said Drugal. "Have them shoot the moment they're in range. Maybe we'll get lucky and an arrow will take one of them."

He did not expect the archers to do anything but die horribly, but knew he had to do something. He could not let these infidels approach his army unchallenged.

Herol guide me, he prayed. *I am in a dark place, unsure of the action I must take. I fear I do not have the weapons to counter what I face. I am your faithful servant, Mellam yun avki Drugal. If it is your will that I die here I will do so, but spare my army that they may fight for you another day. Show me what I must do.*

But Herol was silent, and Drugal was left alone.

The archers launched their volley. Fifty red-fletched arrows arced high through the smoky sky. Hollin adjusted his Wardings to intercept the missiles, which bounced harmlessly from the invisible barriers.

Gerin whispered another command to the staff, and the Havalqa archers simply fell over dead, slain by the death spells he'd directed at them. He had hoped that a less dramatic use of power would lessen the harm he was doing to himself. Pain still throbbed in his head, but the bloody nose had mercifully stopped, and the death spells did not start the flow anew.

"That's far less messy than my last attempt," said Hollin.

"I don't know what the staff will be capable of once the reservoir of magic that's accrued around it is gone," Gerin told him, "but I'm going to make the most of it while I can."

Gerin dismounted and handed his reins to a soldier with a reddish beard and an old scar beneath his right eye. He held out the staff and surveyed the Havalqa army. They were arrayed within the forest that covered the ridge like a skein of tangled hair. Hollin began to unleash death spells from the vambraces and a foot-long rod of leather-wrapped iron with a copper-plated sphere at one end. The spells slaughtered dozens along the army's flanks, but the trees were proving to be an impediment. Hollin's magic could only extend a short distance into the forest before the sheer density of the woods disrupted the spells.

"We need to get those trees out of the way," said Gerin. He pondered for a moment how to proceed, then issued another command and braced himself for the pain that would accompany it.

Burn the woods.

Invisible power surged from the staff. Blood burst from both of his nostrils, and he felt a liquid warmth in his ear. He squeezed his eyes shut at the searing pain that ripped through his head while leaning hard on the staff to keep himself upright.

A wide section of the leading edge of the woods exploded with flame, as if the trees had been doused with oil and torched. Fire and smoke shot into the air as the flames raced up the trunks and out onto the branches. Men and horses screamed as the conflagrations engulfed them before they had a chance to escape. The blaze pushed deeper into the woods and eastward along its southern edge.

The Havalqa army was in a panicked rout. Soldiers surged away from the flames as fast as they could. An acrid stench reached Gerin and the others as the pall of smoke upon the ridge grew thicker.

Hollin lowered his arms and ceased his spellcasting. "There's not much else I can add to that. Best not to waste the power we have." He was so focused on the devastation that he did not notice Gerin's distress.

The prince did not respond. He was busy directing the staff's power deeper into the woods. Flames now reached thirty and forty feet into the air and rushed along faster than soldiers could outrun them. He could feel waves of heat rippling across him and could not imagine how much hotter it must be within the conflagration itself.

Burn, you bastards. Every one of you. Burn for what you did to me and my homeland. I want you all dead and gone. If the Words of Making are to be found, I'll find them without you. Shayphim take you all.

The Sword was running for his life from the approaching flames. How could they keep flinging such sorcery at them? A hundred Adepts—a thousand—working together could not conjure such devastating might.

Pizan and his fellow Kantu tribesmen had encircled Drugal and were keeping him from falling as he stumbled through the tangle of underbrush beneath the trees. Small animals fled ahead of him, insane with fear, unseen except for the wakes they left through the undergrowth. Thousands of his men were burning behind him, and he knew that thousands more would perish before this Harridan-cursed fire ended. The air was so hot that each breath scorched his lungs, and his armor had grown hot to the touch. Pizan, several dozen yards ahead of him when the fire erupted in front of their position, had lost his eyebrows and some of the hair on the left side of his head to the flames. His face was scorched and raw, and smeared with soot and ash.

They ran on as fast as they could, away from the flames, which roared behind them like an enraged, ravenous beast. Other soldiers were running beside them, unaware that the Sword himself was among them. All sense of military order had been lost, the chain of command collapsing as frantic soldiers of every rank raced to escape.

They came to a break in the trees, and Drugal realized they'd reached the northern edge of the woods. But he did not stop running. He continued down the folded slope until he had placed considerable distance between himself and the trees and only then turned around, panting hard. He began to cough uncontrollably. It felt as if hot coals had been lodged in his lungs. He bent over, his hands on his knees, and coughed until he retched. The Kantu and other soldiers around him fared little better.

When he finally managed to look up he saw a vast black cloud billowing upward from the woods, churning and twisting into the darkening sky as the flames consumed more and more of the trees. *And my men,* he thought bitterly. Soldiers were emerging from the red-lit trees atop the slope, but he knew that many thousands more would be burned to ash within that immense fire.

I cannot win here. I have failed the Exalted and Herol. I have no answer to the powers arrayed against us. All I can do is save as many of my men as I can and speak to the Dreamer. Perhaps it has a solution that I cannot see.

A company commander appeared beside him. "Sword, what is your command?"

Through a mouth that tasted of smoke and ash—of defeat and bitter failure—Drugal said, "Sound the retreat. We will make with all haste to the staging area, and from there return to the island to regroup."

The man blanched at the order but did not question it. "Yes, Sword. I will relay your orders." Then he dashed off.

A few breaths later a soldier approached him from behind and gripped his shoulders to help him straighten. It was an outrageous breach of etiquette to be touched so, and Drugal bristled with sudden anger.

A knife slid beneath his breastplate and between his ribs. "A gift from your enemy," the soldier whispered in his ear as he twisted the blade. Then he withdrew it and was gone.

Drugal slumped to his knees. He dimly noticed that his Kantu guards were dead around him, their throats slit. *Tolsadri has done this,* he thought as he toppled to the earth.

The last thing he heard before his life fled him were the horns calling for retreat.

49

Gerin heard horns blowing faintly over the monstrous roar of the fire and knew that the Havalqa were sounding the retreat. He lowered the staff and halted its power. The fire was large enough now that it would feed on itself, perhaps for days. He wondered if he had made a mistake in using fire. What if it threatened the city? He told himself he would worry about that if and when the time came. For now, he'd watch with grim satisfaction as the fire ravaged the ridge.

"Gerin, what have you done to yourself?" said Hollin, taking note of the blood covering him.

"There's apparently a downside to using so much power."

Hollin created a Seeing. He was about to create a healing spell, but Gerin stopped him. "It can wait," he said. "You'll make me sleep."

He swung his gaze toward the sea. He could just barely make out the black flecks upon the water that marked the ships of the Havalqa blockade. "I'm not done with them yet."

As they rode outside the northern wall of Almaris they were cheered by the soldiers upon the battlements. Men shouted and clapped and waved banners and flags; some had managed to find rose petals and tossed them as the riders passed below.

Gerin fought his exhaustion, but every so often had to

close his eyes. He even dozed off for a few moments in the saddle.

To their left across the Varga the woods continued to burn. He could see no more living enemy soldiers. Those who escaped down the southern face of the ridge were killed by Hollin's death spells before they'd gone fifty paces. Two or three hundred bodies littered the ridge slope. A few continued to burn where they lay.

"What will you do to the ships, my lord?" asked Balandrick.

"I don't know yet. Now be quiet and let me think."

They passed the section of the city's wall behind which lay Arghest and the Prophet's house. He wondered about Elaysen. Had she seen what he'd done? No one in the city could miss the smoke-filled sky to the north, but how many knew what had caused it?

He felt strangely distant from himself, as if suffering from a fever, though he did not feel ill. It seemed a veil had fallen over his mind, occluding some of his perceptions. Having bound the staff to his saddle again, he was constantly aware when he lacked its touch.

They continued around the northeast corner of the city wall, following its curve back to the southwest before it turned eastward once again, down the long arm of Eigrend. In this place, the edge of the Almarean Plateau was a narrow shelf that ranged between fifty and a hundred paces from the base of the wall before sloping down toward the bright white beach.

The cheering followed them along their entire route—word of their deeds spread among the soldiers atop the wall far faster than their horses cantered. Gerin was elated by the sound, though he kept a stern, almost grim look upon his face. They were cheering for him. They'd seen his power and knew that he'd used it to defend their homes. *They will want a wizard-king upon the throne after this,* he thought. The nobles and their objections be damned. And his father's. He wondered if the king realized the full import of what he had done here today.

He had made himself a hero to the people of Almaris.

They stopped at the first closed gate they reached on the inner arm of Eigrend. The docks and piers were choked with ships rocking gently in their berths, unable to leave the Cleave because of the blockade.

The throng that waited inside the gate cheered madly when they entered. The press of people was so intense that they could not move forward for several minutes, until the cheering slackened and the overwhelmed City Watch and Taeratens who had come down from the wall were able to make their way to them. "We are in awe of your power, my prince," said a young man of the City Watch who looked close to weeping as he regarded Gerin.

The prince was startled and somewhat alarmed to see that many people in the crowd had tears upon their faces as they shouted his name and asked the gods to bless him. "What is your desire? Command us, and it will be done."

Gerin's unease increased. *This is not right. I don't want bloody worshippers!*

"I need to get to the Vartheme," he said to the City Watch man, gesturing toward the light tower built just inside the city's wall. Behind him, Balandrick swore as his horse was slammed into by a sudden surge of the crowd. "Get us out of here now," he added. "Before this mad throng crushes us."

The man bowed his head low. "At once, my prince." He turned and shouted orders to his men, who began to push the crowd back with sheathed swords. Gerin hoped the situation didn't turn into a riot. The last thing he wanted was Khedeshians killing each other in a frenzied stampede.

There was a gated courtyard around the tower, which was mercifully empty except for the tower's two attendants. The taller of the two men bowed after Balandrick growled that they were standing in the presence of the crown prince and informed them of the proper form of address; the second, a young man with close-set eyes and an unruly shock of dark hair, bowed a moment later.

"Are you the one what ripped up the land over yonder and set the enemy to runnin' for their lives?" asked the taller man. "Uh, my lord."

"I am, and have no time to discuss it," said Gerin. "Take me to the top of the tower. I have business with the blockade."

"Yes, um, my lord."

Captain Baldrin and his men remained in the cobbled yard while Gerin, Hollin, and Balandrick entered the tower behind the attendants and climbed the spiral stair that wound about its core, with a pulley through its center used to lift firewood. There was a trapdoor in the ceiling at the top that the younger attendant threw open, revealing a stone fire pit that was lit each night to mark the northern boundary of the harbor. The wall behind the pit was lined with polished steel that directed the light out toward the sea. A chimney above the pit would relieve the smoke from the circular room, whose eastern face was completely open. An iron-railed balcony circled the turret.

A steady, salt-tanged wind blew across them. "Have you figured out what you're going to do yet, my lord?" asked Balan.

"I have an idea. Whether it will work or not is something else." His strange sense of disassociation had grown more pronounced, but he brushed it aside and tightened his grip on the staff. A sudden spell of dizziness struck him, and he placed his hand on the railing to steady himself.

The Havalqa fleet lay anchored beyond the range of the city's trebuchets, an impenetrable cordon of ships that had severed the shipping lanes for weeks. Gerin could see three Havalqa ships on the horizon heading toward the larger mass of vessels.

"Is there anything I can do to assist you?" asked Hollin.

"Not with this."

He angled the staff forward and called out to the Presence. *Sink them. Drag them down to the bottom of the sea.*

The staff erupted with amber fire. Power surged beneath Gerin's fingers, a flow of energy so vast it seemed he gripped a bolt of black lightning. The magic was directed at the waters in the heart of the blockade fleet. As much magic as had been used to destroy the ridge, more by far was now flowing through the staff.

Hollin staggered and put a hand to his temple. "Venegreh save us . . ."

"There's a tingling all over my skin," said Balandrick.

"You're sensing some small measure of the power Gerin is using," said Hollin. "It is *immense*."

The sea where the Presence was directing the power of the staff was now churning and roiling as if heated from below. Frothy white waves spread outward from the turbulence, lapping against the hulls of the closer ships. As the churning grew stronger, the nearer ships began to rock back and forth.

But the vast energy pouring through the staff was still not sufficient to carry out his command, Gerin realized. There was a . . . hesitation from the staff, a sense of uncertainty. The magic flowing through him and the staff faltered for a moment.

Then he felt a strong sense of resolve coming from it.

Unexpectedly, Gerin's *hronu* exploded around him, amber flame engulfing him and the staff. Hollin and Balandrick cried out in surprise and jumped back, and the two tower attendants fell to their knees and began to pray.

The swirling amber fire rose higher and higher as the Presence used Gerin's own magic as well as the power that had accrued around the staff to fulfill the prince's command. Soldiers on the city wall below him shouted and pointed up at the sudden blaze of magical fire.

The frothing water shot a geyser fifty feet into the air. The Havalqa sailors rushed to the sides of their ships to see what was happening in the water beneath them. It must have looked as if the sea had gone mad since they could see nothing of Gerin's power except the result. If any had seeing-glasses, they might have spotted the flaming figure atop the city's northern light tower, but he doubted that they were looking in his direction.

The geyser collapsed suddenly. The churning water had expanded to encompass half the fleet, though the currents were still weak at the periphery. Gerin sensed from the Presence that even the vast amount of magic at his command had its limits, which he had just reached.

He hoped it would be enough.

The waters at the center of the turbulence began to spin. At the same time, the pain in his head grew white-hot, as if a needle freshly drawn from a forge had been thrust into his temple. His vision blurred; his back went rigid with the sudden agony. But he remained upright, leaning hard on the staff and locking his knees to keep them from buckling.

The rotation of the water started slowly, mostly hidden beneath the choppy waves. But as it increased in strength and speed, the spinning sea drew the waves into it, smoothing the waters around the small depression that had formed in its center. Waters farther from the center began to spin as well, succumbing to the growing power of the vortex.

Gerin's body shook uncontrollably. There was so much magic pouring through both him and the staff that he was in danger of losing consciousness. He felt hollowed out, as if everything within him save his power had been burned away, leaving only the raging torrent flowing out of him. The disassociation he'd felt earlier had grown stronger, to the point where it now seemed that his soul was in danger of fleeing his body altogether.

Gerin wavered on the edge of consciousness. His aura scorched the stone beneath his feet and heated the iron railing in front of him to a cherry red. But he would not stop. He was determined to finish what he'd begun. He would break this blockade, even if it cost him his life. He hoped fervently it would not come to that, but if that were the price to be paid, so be it. He lived to protect his kingdom, his people.

At the notion of his possible death, he wondered what that would do to the plans of the Dreamers and the One God, and managed a wan smile. At least he knew that this decision was entirely his own. They would certainly never countenance it.

The depression at the center of the vortex was now at least a hundred feet across and half that in depth. The nearer ships were being dragged into its current, and all of the ships in the fleet had extended their oars and were rowing frantically to get away from the expanding whirlpool. But those caught in its grip were unable to escape.

A two-masted warship closest to the center suddenly cap-

sized into the vortex's throat. Men were flung screaming
from the decks and disappeared into the spinning water—
none resurfaced. The masts snapped as they dipped into the
powerful current. Then the keel appeared as the ship rolled
completely over. It made two revolutions around the whirlpool before it vanished, drawn inexorably down toward the
sea floor.

Three other ships near the vortex's funnel crashed together
violently, their oars splintering as the hulls ground together.
The smallest of the three was struck broadside by the prow
of the largest and broke in half. The forward section rolled
over and sank immediately. The rear half of the ship fought
for life a little longer, but after a single revolution around the
vortex it turned sharply downward and plunged out of sight.

The two remaining ships were listing dangerously. The inner ship could no longer remain upright and rolled onto its
side. The second ship slammed against the exposed keel of
the first, which punched a long gash along the length of its
hull.

Still tangled, the two vessels were swallowed by the sea.

Those ships outside the reach of the vortex were turning
frantically toward the northeast. Gerin noted that the three
ships that had been approaching were turning about, fleeing
back to Gedsengard.

But the ships caught within the grasp of the whirlpool
could not escape. Oars snapped as banks of rowers fought a
losing battle against the powerful currents. The vortex continued to widen and its throat to deepen as it drank every last
bit of magic directed into it by the staff.

Gerin's vision darkened then, as if a deep twilight had fallen
across him. He thought he heard Hollin speaking to him, but
the older wizard sounded far away, his words unintelligible.
His connection with the staff had grown so strong there almost seemed no distinction between them anymore. There
was the staff and its power, with no room left for him.

The immense amount of magic that had accrued around
the staff was being depleted at an incredible rate to maintain
the vortex. He could not comprehend how it could channel
and control such power. But it did.

Gerin felt completely detached from his body, his mind sluggish and fevered. Dimly, he realized he could not longer hear anything. And his vision had darkened until he could see nothing but faint smears of blurry light. *I wonder if Reshel will be waiting to greet me at the gates of Velyol?* he thought. *It would be wonderful to see her again.*

Then a sudden surge of magic violently snuffed out his aura. He knew there should have been a great deal of pain at such an occurrence, but he felt nothing as he toppled to the side and everything went black.

$\ast$

50

I think he's waking up."

Gerin recognized Hollin's voice and struggled to open his eyes. They fluttered, stubbornly resisting his will, and refused to open to more than slits that let in dark blurry shapes hovering over him. He was lying on a bed—he realized he could feel his body again—and could vaguely make out a large window in one wall, a bright rectangle of hazy light in an otherwise dark room.

He tried to speak but his voice worked only a little better than his eyes. "What . . . happened . . . ?"

He felt a reassuring squeeze on his shoulder. "You're in the Tirthaig," said Hollin. "You collapsed on the Vartheme two days ago."

"Ships . . . ?"

"They're gone. Those that weren't destroyed by your whirlpool have fled back to Gedsengard. Your uncle Nellemar arrived with his fleet yesterday evening and was utterly dismayed to find the blockade already broken."

A man Gerin did not recognize swam into view, holding a slender glass in his hand. "He needs more rest," said the man in a gruff voice. "He has hovered on the edge of death and is not yet recovered. He should not speak further." He slipped a hand beneath Gerin's head and lifted it from the pillow. The man's scarlet tunic and tattooed arms marked him as a vendri physician. "Here, my lord, drink this. It will speed your healing."

Gerin wondered where Elaysen was as the physician poured a bitter liquid into his mouth. He coughed and spluttered but managed to swallow most of it.

"We'll talk more after you've rested," said Hollin.

Gerin felt much better the next time he awoke. He was able to open his eyes and prop himself up on his elbows, though doing so caused a dizzy spell so intense he had to close them again and drop his head back on the pillow until it passed.

When he opened his eyes again, he did not move for several minutes. There was no one else present—his only companion an unlit lamp upon a small corner table. The window was open and a faint breeze blew into the room. The clouds he saw outside were streaked with crimson, but he had no sense of whether it was morning or evening.

He raised his arms and was stunned by how weak he was. He did not think he had the strength to dress himself, and wondered if he could even stand. *So I was on the edge of death. At least I stayed on the right side of it.*

Sometime later he'd managed to get himself into a sitting position when the door opened and Hollin entered. The older wizard helped him shuffle to a high-backed chair, where he slouched, already fatigued.

"It's good to see you up and about," said Hollin. "I thought you had died when you collapsed on the Vartheme. Your pulse and breathing were so shallow that I had to use my powers to make sure you were still alive."

"Water?"

"Oh, of course." Hollin stepped out of the room and asked a servant to bring them water and food. "You must be famished," he said, returning.

"Starving." His throat was parched, his voice hoarse from a lack of use. "The staff?"

"It's safely locked away for now. Don't concern yourself with it. You need to regain your strength first."

The vendri physician entered while they were eating and

was pleased with Gerin's progress. "Your wizard friend is an adept healer, my lord, but not all ailments can be cured with spells." The man set another glass upon the table and admonished the prince to drink it to aid in his recovery.

Hollin handed him the glass. "I think you should drink this and rest some more. In the morning, if you're strong enough, we can talk again, and maybe get you out of this room for a while." He straightened, and folded his arms as he looked down at Gerin. "You've become quite the legend. The people haven't stopped talking about what you did."

Gerin drank the elixir, then climbed back into bed with Hollin's help and fell asleep.

"Finally got yourself out of bed, I see," Therain said to him the next day. Gerin was sitting in the chair, rocking gently. "About time. I always knew you were a roustabout."

Nellemar entered and clapped him on the shoulder. "If you're gong to take care of my work for me, nephew, you should at least let me know before I go to the bother of assembling a war fleet. I just wish I could have seen what you did. I have a hard time believing what I've heard. Out in the streets you'd think a new god has come among us from the way people are talking about you. I've heard there are even shrines to you in the markets and in the Temple district."

Hollin brought the staff to Gerin near noon. When the prince grasped it, he felt nothing. He was still too weak to call magic of his own, but the vast reservoir of magic that had accrued around the staff was gone, depleted to create the vortex in the Gulf of Gedsuel. Gerin felt an odd sense of loss that so much power had been spent before they even understood the staff.

That evening, he was summoned to his father's council chamber. He was still very weak and the walk to the chamber left him exhausted. But his father did not ask him to sit, so he remained standing on the far side of the candlelit table.

The king made a point of ignoring him and asked his councilors to speak.

Arilek Levkorail told them of the progress the Taeratens

were making in hunting down the remaining pockets of Havalqa still within Khedesh's borders. He estimated, based on the number of empty villages and towns discovered, that several thousand Khedeshians had been taken captive by the enemy and transported to Gedsengard before the empty staging area was destroyed by his men.

Nellemar then relayed how the fleet he'd assembled to break the blockade had been redeployed to protect the coast and intercept any Havalqa ships that attempted to land. "So far none have done so. They've remained grouped around Gedsengard."

"What are your plans for retaking the island?" asked Abran.

"Ships are on their way to scout it, but if all their forces have withdrawn from the mainland, that means there are tens of thousands of Havalqa soldiers to contend with, as well as what's left of their fleet."

"Surely Gedsengard can't sustain so many for very long?" asked Gerin. The king gave him a sharp look but said nothing.

"No, it can't," said Nellemar. "They will likely attempt to establish footholds on other areas of the coast to keep them supplied. If they try, we'll break their supply lines and starve them out."

The king turned to Levkorail. "What will it take to drive them from the island?"

"With your son and his staff, I would need little else, Your Majesty," said Levkorail.

"I won't be putting on a repeat performance, unfortunately," said Gerin. The king reluctantly gestured for him to speak, and he continued, explaining about the depletion of the staff's reservoir of magic that had made his defeat of the Havalqa possible.

"The fact that the power of the staff has been expended should not be made known outside of this room," said Levkorail. "As long as the enemy believes we have such power, it will deter them."

"Can this reservoir of magic that you said was around the staff not be refilled?" asked Jaros Waklan.

"Not without locking up the staff for another two millennia," said Gerin.

"A shame," said Waklan with a heavy sigh.

"Then what of retaking Gedsengard *without* my son or his staff?" said the king.

"Certainly it can be done, Your Majesty, but the cost will be high," said Levkorail. "We will need to assault them with overwhelming numbers if we're to have hope of success. We are ready to begin preparations at once, but I humbly suggest that we follow Admiral Nellemar's advice and intercept any shipments the enemy makes from the mainland. A starving enemy will be much easier to defeat, and if we can choke them tightly enough, they may even abandon the island without an attack."

Abran reluctantly agreed to the proposal, though it was clear to Gerin that he would rather smash them off the island than allow them a moment's more peace there.

Finally, the king regarded him with an icy stare. "You have done a remarkable thing for this city and the kingdom, but do not think it absolves you of your crime against me and defiance of my will."

"Then throw me in the dungeons and be done with it," said Gerin. "I'm too tired to argue with you."

There were a number of gasps from around the room. Abran did not flinch. If anything, his gaze became even colder.

"Before I decide on a suitable punishment, I would hear about your plans for the Varsae Estrikavis and Naragenth's staff."

"We haven't had time to think about that, Father."

"You do plan to examine the library, don't you? And get a better understanding of the staff's power?"

"Of course."

"And how do you plan to do that? The library is here. You will be needed in Ailethon, unless you plan to designate a steward to take—"

Gerin held up his hand. "No, Father. We can study the library anywhere. It is *not* here. It's located in another plane of existence. The doorway is here because that's where I opened it, but it will work just as well if I open it in my study at Ailethon. The Varsae Estrikavis is not physically bound to any one spot in this world."

The king folded his arms. "Very well. But you *will* need the Scepter of the King to open the door?"

"Yes. Unless you plan to lock it away from me again. Then the knowledge contained in the library is once more lost."

Abran was silent for a while. "I have misjudged several things about your magic. I admit I did not truly realize the magnitude of your power, or how it could be used as a weapon of war."

"I've already explained that I can't do what I did again—"

"Do not interrupt me. I understand that the . . . *immensity* of what you accomplished cannot be repeated, but you most certainly remain a potent weapon to be used against our enemies. They have no means of countering you. That is something I had not considered, but your display of strength made it readily apparent.

"That said, you may take the scepter to Ailethon, conditionally."

"And what are those conditions, Father?"

"First, that I be kept apprised of everything you discover. It was a mistake for me to take no interest in your training as a wizard, though the gods know I had my reasons. But that comes to an end. I will know of the things you find so that I can determine their proper uses."

Gerin saw Hollin's eyes narrow at this, but the older wizard said nothing. "I will certainly keep you informed of what we find."

"My second condition is that no wizard from Hethnost be permitted to examine the Varsae Estrikavis or the staff."

"What?" said Gerin. Hollin stiffened visibly and his expression darkened. "Why would you place such a condition on its use?"

"Your Majesty, with all due respect," said Hollin, "there may be things we can learn from the wizards—"

"Be quiet, both of you," said the king. "I realize that the

wizards of Hethnost have done us a grave disservice by remaining aloof in their fortress, uninterested in the needs of
their neighbors. If they wish to partake of the riches to be
found in the Varsae Estrikavis, that policy must end."

"Your Majesty," said Hollin, "with all due respect, it is not
for you to dictate the policies of Hethnost. You already know
that I disagree with their isolationist views, but coercion is
not the way to effect the change you desire."

"I said nothing about coercion. In exchange for access
to the Varsae Estrikavis, I want the wizards of Hethnost to
make themselves available to help defend this kingdom in
the event of further invasions."

"And what if you decide to wage war upon Threndellen,
or Armenos, Your Majesty? Would you demand that wizards
fight in your armies?"

"That, of course, is a point I expect would be negotiated
between us. We would fashion a binding treaty between one
sovereign and another. I have no illusions that they would
fight for Khedesh upon my whim, but in the past few years
we have suffered two invasions that both involved magic in
some fashion. Having wizards available to help counter those
threats is my goal. And in return for their agreement to help
us in times of great need, they may study the contents of the
Varsae Estrikavis, or some other remuneration agreed upon
between us. Monetary or other compensation is certainly not
out of the question.

"I will draft a formal request to the Archmage detailing
my terms. You might also wish to contact her to explain
about the library's discovery. Do either of you have any more
questions?"

"No, Father," said Gerin. Hollin shook his head but still
did not look pleased.

There was shouting from the hallway. Gerin heard
the snick of guards drawing swords from sheaths. More
shouts . . .

Then silence.

Before anyone in the room could move, the heavy twin
doors were violently flung open. There was something im-

mense on the other side, a figure of some kind, taller than the doors themselves. When it lowered its head to enter the room, its footfalls made the floor tremble.

In the moment before disaster struck, time seemed to slow as Gerin tried to make sense of the being before them. Its head reached almost to the chamber's high ceiling. Straight ebony hair fell from its broad head to its shoulders. Its skin was like burnished bronze; its body was sheathed in a black sleeveless tunic. It carried no weapon but was roped with muscles. The being looked strong enough to smash through the stone walls with its bare hands. Beneath a heavy brow, venomous yellow eyes regarded them coldly.

Levkorail was the first to react. He rose and in a single deft motion hurled a knife at the creature's head. The being did not even turn toward the Lord Commander as it swatted the knife from the air.

Levkorail leapt across the table as Hollin unleashed a death spell. The creature backhanded the Taeraten with such force that he flew back across the table and smashed into the wall behind the king, then slid to the floor in a heap. Balandrick moved between the creature and Gerin, his sword held ready. Therain held a long knife of his own but made no move either toward or away from it.

Hollin's death spell might as well have been a wish for all the harm it did. The spell should have pulverized the being's heart and lungs and shattered its ribs, but it did no damage at all that Gerin could see.

The thing turned to Gerin and spoke. Its voice was deep, cavernous. A pale red light appeared within its mouth when its lips parted. He sensed that the being was asking him a question but he did not recognize the language.

"Hollin, do you have any idea what it's saying?"

The wizard shook his head.

"Do you have any idea what it *is*?"

"No."

The creature spoke again, more insistently this time. It pointed at Gerin with its thickly muscled arm. Balan lunged at it, his sword arcing through the air toward the thing's wrist.

The creature whipped its arm about with incredible speed, avoiding Balandrick's weapon and smashing its fist into his shoulder. Gerin heard bones break as his captain was completely lifted off the floor. Balandrick flew six or seven feet through the air and collapsed behind Gerin, either unconscious or dead.

Gerin's fury ignited. He drew Nimnahal and opened himself to magic.

Nothing happened.

He could sense his *paru'enthred* in the core of his being but could not open it. He willed with all of his might for his inner eye to open, but it remained closed, immune to his commands.

The creature's gaze shifted to Nimnahal. It spoke again and pointed at the weapon. It seemed to be waiting for something.

Abran had been on his feet since the creature entered the room. He shook off whatever paralysis had gripped him and began to shout, his face red with rage.

"Guards! Guards! Defend your king from this abomination! *Guards!*"

The creature looked at the king for the first time, then reached out and gripped the king's wrist with its hand before Abran could pull it away.

It spoke a single word, and Abran collapsed upon the table, dead.

Gerin knew with absolute certainty that his father was dead. He had *felt* his father's life flee his body like a chill wind whipping through the room. And he sensed, somehow, his father's essence become *part of* the creature that had killed him. His spirit would not journey to Velyol to be with his ancestors beneath the silent gaze of Bellon. This thing had robbed the king of that right.

Shrieking, Gerin drove the point of Nimnahal toward the creature's heart, praying that the thing's death would release the spirit it had stolen.

The creature grabbed the blade with its fist and held it immobile. Gerin could not move it at all, as if it were sunken deep into the bedrock of a mountain. He felt tears streaming down his cheeks and heard himself screaming at the thing.

The being spoke again and released the blade. Gerin had been pushing it so hard he nearly fell over with the sword's sudden release.

Then the creature knelt to him, sinking its massive frame down to one knee before bowing its head. Somewhere in the room, Gerin heard Jaros Waklan gasp.

The creature stood, turned, and vanished into a shimmer of air.

Only then did Gerin realize that Therain was weeping over their father's body.

"My lord," said the servant boy, "the lady Elaysen is here to see you."

Gerin looked up from the table as she entered the room. He stood and gestured toward the chair across from him. "Please, sit."

"Thank you, my lord. It's good to see you, though I am grieved for the passing of your father the king."

He nodded, his expression dark. "And what are they saying in the city of the manner of his death?"

She paused to contemplate her words. "I've heard many stories and rumors, my lord. I've heard whispers that the city has been infiltrated by the Havalqa who took revenge for their humiliation at your hand by killing your father. There are stories of a demon coming upon the king and killing him. Some say the demon was conjured by the Havalqa; others say it was conjured by you or Hollin to do your bidding so you could seize the throne. And there are some who say there was no demon, that the king was killed by your own hand, or by the power of your magic." She leaned closer to him. "I of course believe none of those tales, and would hear from you what happened, if you will tell me."

Gerin's jaw had clenched so tightly that his teeth hurt. "There was a demon, for want of a better word for it. We still have no idea what it was." He described what had transpired. His stomach cramped with pain as he spoke, and he had difficulty drawing breath. No sign of the creature had been seen since.

"I do not know what to say, my lord. You have no idea why it knelt to you?"

"None. I'm partial to the idea that this is all a Havalqa plot. We know they've brought foreign creatures to our shores. It's hard to believe this is a coincidence."

He closed his eyes and saw his father's lifeless body upon the table. He still did not know how he felt about his death. Part of him could not believe his father was dead, vanished forever from the world. It seemed impossible. Their relationship had been so strained recently, so filled with mistrust, he could not accept that they had parted with nothing resolved between them. It was too unfair, too unjust.

Yet it was true. His father was gone, as dead as Reshel. And many believed the king had died by his hand, or at least at his command.

He had not yet mourned. He'd cried once, in bed in the dead of night, with no one around to see or hear; but it had been brief, a thing born more from exhaustion than sorrow. But true grief, the kind that had torn his heart when his mother died, and later Reshel, had not yet placed its cold hands upon him.

Nor had he visited the king's body in state. He did not know how he would react when he did. Would he weep for his father and king? What if he did not? How would either course be interpreted by the nobles already scheming against him, prodded by the machinations of Sedifren Houday? He knew they would view anything he did as an admission of guilt and try to turn it against him in the Assembly of Lords. But he would be king. He would not allow them to take his birthright from him.

"I came to visit you after your collapse when you broke the blockade," said Elaysen.

"I heard. Thank you."

"I offered my help, but Althanos, your physician, would have none of it."

"I'm sorry for that. I would have preferred your ministrations to his. How is your father?"

"He's well, and in awe of the powers at your command. We saw what you did to the ridge, and the vortex you brought about in the sea. My father sees it as a sign that you are indeed a chosen instrument of the One God."

"I don't know if I am or not, Elaysen. I only do what seems right to me."

"That is all anyone can do."

She went to the balcony overlooking the Cleave, where he joined her.

"Do you think the Havalqa will return to their homeland?" she asked.

"No. If anything, they will redouble their efforts. They truly believe they need the Words of Making to battle the Great Enemy."

She faced him. "Do you think the Words exist?"

He paused before answering. "Yes. I saw enough of the Dreamer's powers to believe that even if it got some of the details wrong, the Words themselves are real."

"Will you look for them yourself?"

He nodded. "If the Adversary and the Great Enemy are the same being—which I think is likely—then they're a weapon we'll need. I'm hoping to find a clue about the Words in the Varsae Estrikavis. I won't give up looking. I don't want the Havalqa to find them first." He still did not understand why they thought he already had them, but that was a question he did not think he would ever solve.

He cleared his throat. "Will you remain as my teacher? I do not know what will happen in the coming days. Even as my father lies in state in the Temple of Telros the nobles are devouring the rumors surrounding his death, and many are refusing to support my claim to the throne."

"I do not care what the nobility thinks or does. I made a promise and I will keep it. Though if the One God is working His will through you, I wonder which of us will be the real teacher?"

He wanted to ask here then about the sudden anger that had gripped her on *Cregar's Glory* just before the Havalqa attack. He was still startled when he recalled the viciousness of her response when he'd asked her to remain in her cabin.

But he felt, for some reason he could not articulate even to himself, that to do so would serve only to provoke an argument with her, that she would heatedly deny that her reply was improper in any way. He was in no mood to argue; he'd had enough of that with his father to last him several lifetimes. And so he let it go.

Standing side by side, they looked out over the sea.

Epilogue

The door to the Dreamer's chamber opened and Tolsadri entered. He walked with the careful, shuffling gait of the very old, and there was a palsied trembling in his hands and neck. He was very thin, and his beard and the hair at his temples were shot through with thick streaks of white that had not been there before his recent death.

He would recover his strength and vitality, he knew. His present condition was the result of *fet-attan*, the secret means by which an Adept of Bariq could return from the dead if the wounds to the body were not beyond repair.

So much had gone wrong! The man they had sailed half a world to discover had slipped from their grasp—*his* grasp. He burned with shame and humiliation at his failure. He would have slain the wretched soul stealer in a most painful and horrific manner, but the Dreamer had denied him that pleasure.

Ah, well. At least the troublesome Sword was dead. Apparently slain in the disastrous rout from the city before the siege could even begin—a monumental failure that in itself would have sealed the Sword's doom—but Tolsadri felt certain his agent had been the one to finish Drugal. He would never know for certain, since the agent was now dead as well. It was too dangerous to leave such loose ends lying about. But still, he could derive some small satisfaction from the pious bastard's death.

"Voice of the Exalted," boomed the Dreamer from behind its gauzy curtains. The exhalation of its power made the dark room swim in Tolsadri's eyes.

"Yes, Great Dreamer," said Tolsadri, bowing his head. "I have come as you asked."

"We have suffered a grievous loss. Yet our mission remains unchanged. We must take this continent in the name of the Exalted so that we are prepared to face the Great Enemy when he arises."

"I agree, Great Dreamer. And we must retake Gerin Atreyano."

"See that you do not lose him a second time. If you do, even your status as the Exalted's Voice will not be sufficient to protect you from my wrath."

Tolsadri blanched and swallowed. "I apologize for my . . . failure, Great Dreamer."

"We cannot remain on this island," said the Dreamer. "If Gerin Atreyano unleashes his powers against us here, all might be lost. We must abandon this place in favor of a more secure location on the mainland, beyond the borders of this kingdom. This continent is larger than we had anticipated. We will need unprecedented resources to convert them to the ways of the Steadfast. I must think on this as well, but I feel I will have no choice but to attempt to open the Path of Ashes."

Tolsadri was startled by the Dreamer's words. The road outside the world. He'd heard rumors of the path, but had never considered them to be more than fanciful imaginings. Certainly it was far beyond the power of any Adept or Loremaster.

The Voice of the Exalted bowed his head. "I will see that your will is done, Great Dreamer."

Glossary and Pronunciation Guide

The pronunciation guide included in this glossary is in no way intended to be absolute, especially where Kelarin is concerned, which was a language of diverse regional dialects, accents, and vocabulary. The pronunciations of Kelarin words given here reflect the speech of central Khedesh, where in later years these accounts were compiled. For reasons of clarity and brevity, alternative pronunciations, even when they are known, are not included.

Osirin poses less of a difficulty since by Gerin's time it had long been a "dead" language and therefore mostly immune to the kinds of changes in vocabulary and pronunciation that affect a language used in everyday speech. The forms of Osirin had been fixed for centuries and had changed little since the time of the Empire, when its widespread use ceased. Osirin became a largely ceremonial language, used by wizards in their rituals and spellmaking but for little else, not even record-keeping—at least not consistently—and even in Hethnost centuries had passed since it had been used for daily intercourse.

An apostrophe *after* a syllable indicates stress (*af'ter*).

Ademel Caranis (*Ad'-eh-mel Ka'-ran-is*): The Lord Captain of the City Watch of Almaris.

Aidrel Entraly (*Ay'-drel En'-trah-lee*): Member of Aunphar's Inner Circle.

Aleith'aqtar (*Ah-layth' Ak' -tar*): "Land of the Obedient," homeland of the Havalqa.

Al-fet: The "second life" of a Loremaster, who is able to resurrect his own dead body if the injury is not too grievous.

Almaris (*Al-mare'-is*): Capital city of Khedesh.

Archmage: The elected ruler of the wizards of Hethnost.

Arilek Levkorail (*air'-ih-lek lev'-kor-ail*): The Lord Commander and Governor-General of the Taeratens of the Naege.

Aron Toresh (*Air'-on Tor'-esh*): Earl of Tolthean, Knight-Lieutenant of the Realm.

Baelish Aslon (*bay'-il-ish as'-lon*): A Master of the Order of Laonn and member of the Atreyano household, charged with teaching the princes and princesses.

Balandrick Vaules (*bah-lan'-drick vole'-es*): Youngest of the four sons of Earl Herenne Vaules of Carengil, and the captain of Gerin's personal guard.

Bariq the Wise (*Bar-eek'*): One of the Havalqa Powers, god of those who study the Mysteries.

Baris Toresh (*Bare'-is Tor'-esh*): Claressa's betrothed, son of Aron and Vaina Toresh.

Baryashin Order (*bar'-yah-sheen*): A secret order of wizards who committed murders in an attempt to grant themselves eternal life. They originated within Hethnost but fled when they were discovered and were later destroyed.

Bellon (*bel'-on*): The Khedeshian god of the dead, who dwells in the mansions of Velyol.

Black Willem: Common folk name for the executioner of Almaris.

Brathkars: Elite cavalry unit in the Havalqa army.

Brothers of Twilight: An order of the Temple of Telros, who prepare bodies for burial.

Burquai (*Bur'-kway*): A power in which an Adept of Bariq determines the caste assignment of one recently brought among the Steadfast.

Chamber of the Moon: The secret location of the Varsae Estrikavis.

City Watch: Military order charged with enforcing the king's law in Almaris.

Cleave: Deepwater harbor bisecting part of Almaris.

Dalar-aelom (*da-lahr' ay'-lom*): Name of the religion of the One God, an ancient Khedeshian phrase that means "holy path."

Dera: One of the coins of the realm of Khedesh.

Donael Rundgar (*don-ay'-il rund'-gar*):captain of Therain's personal guard.

Dreamers: Non-human entities with many mystical powers. Their exact numbers are not known; even their appearance is kept secret, under pain of death. They are the advisors of the Exalted of the Havalqa and wield enormous power.

Drufar (*Droo'-far*): "Silent servants," Loremasters of Bariq chosen to serve the Dreamers.

Elqos the Worker (*El'-kohs*): One of the Havalqa Powers, god of workers, laborers and servants.

Fet-attan: "Life rekindled." The unique power that enables an Adept of Bariq to recover from death.

Fetwa'pesh: "Secret heart." The will and volition of a person that Soul Stealers are able to acquire with their power. Once taken, the Soul Stealer has absolute control over the person until the *fetwa'pesh* is relinquished.

Gadjil (*Gad'-jeel*): A power of blindness used by Loremasters of Bariq that blocks the ability of those around them to perceive them. They are not truly invisible, but their presence is not registered in the mind. Similar to a wizard's Unseeing.

Gaiun Pizan (*Guy'-oon Pee'-zahn*): A Kantu tribesman and the Second Sword, behind Mellam yun Drugal.

Gleso in'Palurq (*Gles'-oh in Pa-lurk'*) Founder of the Havalqa more than five-and-a-half thousand years ago.

Haldrensi (*Hal-dren'-see*): Fishing village that lies to the north of Castle Pelleron.

Havalqa (*Ha-val'-ka*): "The Steadfast," name of a people from beyond the Maurelian Sea who follow a multi-god pantheon and whose society is organized into a rigid caste system.

Havalos (*Hav'-ah-lohs*): Language of the Havalqa.

Hellam Ostreng (*Hel'-am Os'-treng*): Member of Aunphar's Inner Circle.

Herol the Soldier (*Hair'-ol*): One of the Havalqa Powers, god of warriors and mercenaries.

Hethnost (*heth'-nost*): Fortress-city in the Redhorn Hills, home of most of the remaining wizards in Osseria.

Holvareh (*Hohl-var'-eh*): God above the Havalqa Powers, the Father of All.

Hronu (*hron'-oo*): "Aura" in Osirin, describing the radiance of fire that engulfs a wizard if enough magic flows through his body.

Huma endi Algariq (*Hyoo'-mah en-dee Al-gahr'-eek*): Katel's son.

Jaros Waklan (*jar'-ohs wahk'-lan*): Minister of the Realm of Khedesh and one of King Abran's counselors.

Jeril Horthremiden (*Jair'-il Hor-threm'-ih-den*): Balandrick's second in command.

Kalmanyikul (*Kal-man'-yih-kool*): capital city of the Havalqa.

Kamor (*Ka-moor'*): Minor god known to Hollin in his youth.

Katel yalez Algariq (*Ka-tel' yah-leez' Al-gahr'-eek*): A Soul Stealer, hunter and follower of the Harridan.

Kirin Zaeset (*keer'-in zay'ih-set*): A wizard of Hethnost and Warden of Healing.

Kotireon Guards (*koh-teer'-ee-on*): Elite soldiers charged with protecting the royal family.

Kurein Esdrech (*Kur-ay'-in Ez'-drek*): A member of Aunphar's Inner Circle.

Kursil Rulhámad (*Kur'-seel Rool-ha'-mahd*): A maegosi, hunter and follower of the Harridan.

Lonach (*Lon'-ahk*): Ancient battle cry of the Atreyanos. There is confusion as to the meaning of the word. Some have thought it simply means *victory*, while others believe (with some justification) that it refers to a now unknown minor "house god" of the Atreyanos.

Maegosi (*May-goh'-see*): A Kelanim sorcerer able to control *quatans*.

Mandril's Milk: Potion for relieving pain.

Matren Swendes (*mat´ren swen´-des*): The castellan of Ailethon.

Mauro-root (*Mahr´-oh*): A plant that when ground and dried to a powder helps staunch wounds.

Meitha the Maiden (*May´-ih-tha*): One of the Powers of the Havalqa, goddess of young women and virgins.

Melka leaves: A plant with medicinal properties, often used to help someone sleep.

Mellam yun avki Drugal (*Mel´-am yun av´-kee Droo´-gal*): the Sword of the Exalted, supreme military commander of the Havalqa invasion fleet.

Metharog the Father (*Meh-thar´-og*): One of the Havalqa Powers, god of the ruling class.

Methlenel (*meth´-leh-nel*): Magical device used by wizards in the Ritual of Discovery to locate potential wizards.

Mori Genro (*Mor´-ee Gen´ro*): A soldier of Ailethon.

Mountain-and-gull: Sigil of the kingdom of Khedesh.

Mulai ibel Algariq (*Moo´-lie ib´-el Al-gahr´-eek*): Katel's mother.

Naege (*Nayg*): Immense double-ringed fortress within Almaris where the elite Taeraten fighting force is trained.

Naragenth ul-Darhel (*Nare´ah-genth Ool-dar´-hel*): The first amber wizard. He was a king of Khedesh and creator of the Varsae Estrikavis.

Neddari (*ned-dar´-ee*): Warrior society ruled by various clan chieftains.

Neddari War: Conflict caused by Asankaru, the undead Eletheros Storm King, who posed as a Neddari god in order to acquire the Horn of Tireon in an attempt to regain true life for himself and his people.

Needle: Local name for the Nathrad Road from the Azure Gate in the Old City wall to the road's end at the lower level of the Tirthaig.

Nellemar Atreyano (*nel´-eh-mar At-ray-ahn´-oh*): Brother of Abran, Gerin's uncle, Grand Admiral of the Khedeshian naval fleet and ruler of Gedsengard Isle.

Nellin Fields: region of land northwest of Almaris.

Nimnahal (*Nim´-na-hal*): Gerin's sword, originally called

Glaros, rechristened as Nimnahal ("Starfire" in Osirin) after he infused it with magic.

Norles (*Nor'-les*): The castellan of Castle Pelleron.

Niélas (*Ny'-ih-las*): Khedeshian godden of the sea, wife of Paérendras.

Nyvene's Wall (*Ny'-veen*): A series of scaffolds outside the walls of Almaris upon which the bodies of executed traitors are hung. Also called Traitor's Fence.

Odnir Helgrim (*Ohd'-neer Hel'-grim*): Taeraten Swordmaster of the Ailethon who instructed Gerin and his brother in the ways of combat.

Omara Atreyano (*Oh-mar'-ah At-ray-ahn'-oh*): Nellemar's wife.

Ommen Thorael (*Oh'-men Thor-ail'*): Coastal baron, lord of Castle Pelleron and its holdings.

Padesh (*pah'-desh*): Walled town near Ailethon.

Paérendras (*pay-air'-en-dras*): Khedeshian god of the sea. Niélas is his wife.

Pahjuleh Palace (*Pah'-joo-leh*): Imperial palace in the center of Kalmanyikul, home to the Exalted and the Dreamers.

Palendrell (*Pal'en-drel*): Town at the foot of Castle Cressan, at Barresh Harbor.

Parel (*Pah'-rel*): One of the Havalqa Powers, the god of Dreams who alone of the Powers touches all the castes when he so desires.

paru'enthred (*par'-oo en'-thred*): "Inner eye" in Osirin, describing the ability of wizards to focus and shape the flow of magic through their bodies.

Pashti (*pash'-tee*): Indigenous people of southern Osseria, conquered by Khedesh and his Raimen when they came to the southlands. They are now mostly a servant-class in the kingdom.

Pelleron (*Pel'-er-on*): Coastal castle that lies to the north of Almaris, home of Baron Ommen Thorael.

Pelonqua (*Pel-on'-kwa*): A leech-like creature from Aleith'aqtar that secretes a substance that can render a mind compliant and open to suggestion.

Ponce the Dunce: One of several characters used in puppets shows throughout Osseria.

Pranal-iveistu (*Pran'-al eev-ee-ihs'-too*): An Illumination, a single word of magic invested with tremendous power.

Putan (*Pyoo'-tan*): Any object into which a Soul Stealer places the "souls" she has taken from her victims.

Raimen (*Ray'-ih-men*): The original followers of Khedesh, a nomadic warrior society from the distant south, beyond the borders of Osseria.

Rendo Pallan (*Ren'-doh Pal'-an*): Harbormaster of Barresh Harbor.

Rhega (*Reg'-ah*): The orange-and-blue spiral symbol of the Dreamers.

Rullo Astis (*Roo'-loh As'-tis*): Soldier of Castle Cressan.

Ruren the Silent (*Rur'en*): One of the Havalqa Powers, god of the Underworld and Master of the Dead.

Sai'fen (*Sigh'-fen*): Elite, black-armored soldiers of the Steadfast entrusted with the physical safety of the Dreamers.

Scepter of the King: Ivory rod inlaid with gold, silver, and pearl filigrees that is the official symbol of the King of Khedesh. Its upper end is formed of gold in the shape of a gull, its sleek wings thrown forward so that their tips nearly touch beyond the bird's beak.

Selwaen's Stair (*Sel-way'-en*): Long stair through the Belkan Hills that leads from Castle Pelleron down to the Epalauril Valley.

Shayphim (*shay'-fim*): Demonic figure of evil who is said to roam the southlands of Osseria with his Hounds Venga and Molok. He searches for wayward men and women whose spirits he captures and deposits in the Cauldron of Souls, where they are trapped forever, cut off from the light of the gods and unable to enter Velyol. The saying, "To Shayphim with him!" or "Shayphim take him!" is a curse that the dead will be denied the afterlife with the gods.

Street of Poplars: Road on which the Prophet lives.

Taekrim (*Tay'-krim*): "Vigilant," name of those who follow *dalar-aelom*.

Taeratens (*tare´-ah-ten*): Elite fighter of Khedesh, marked with a circle-within-a-circle tattoos on the backs of their hands. They are trained in the fortress of the Naege in Almaris.

Tar-fet: The "new life" that can be granted to the recent dead. Part of the Mysteries of Bariq the Wise.

Tel'fan: A power in which an Adept of Bariq determines the caste assignment of one recently brought among the Steadfast.

Telros: The chief god of the Khedeshian pantheon.

Tendrashi of Bariq (*Ten-drash´-ee*): Mystical voids within a Loremaster of Bariq that are sources of power.

Tirel Hurent (*Teer´-el Hyur´-ent*): Interrogator and torturer in the royal palace of Almaris.

Tomares Rill (*Toh-mahr´-es Rill*): Advisor to Nellemar.

Tronus Foskail (*Troh´-nus Fos-Kayl*): The castellan of Cressan.

Tulqan the Harridan (*Tool´-kwan*): One of the Powers of the Havalqa, goddess of the outcast. She at times opposed to the wishes of the other gods, and her followers are often wicked for its own sake.

Uthna'tarel (*Ooth´-na ta-rel´*): The flagship of the Havalqa invasion fleet.

Vaina Toresh (*Vay´-na Tor´-esh*): Wife of Aron Toresh, the Earl of Tolthean.

Vanil (*Van´-ihl*): Mysterious beings who inhabited Osseria before the coming of the Atalari.

Varsae Estrikavis (*var´-say es-tri-kah´-vis*): Library of magical knowledge assembled by Naragenth and the great wizards of his age. The library was hidden due to the outbreak of the Wars of Unification and its location lost when Naragenth was killed in the siege of Almaris.

Velyol (*Vel´-yol*): The mansions of the dead where the god Bellon reins.

Vensi Leitren (*Ven´-see Lay´-ih-tren*): A Pashti from a village in the Belkan Hills of Khedesh.

Vesparin's Hill (*Ves-par´-in*): Rocky mound on which the Tirthaig is built, named for the eldest son of Khedesh.

Vethiq aril Tolsadri (*Veh-theek' air'-il Tol-sah'-dree*): Voice of the Exalted, Adept of Bariq the Wise, Loremaster of the Mysteries, and First of the sailing vessel *Kaashal*.

Viros Tennor (*Veer'-ohs Ten'or*): Emissary of the Prophet in Padesh.

Wassan (*wah-sahn'*): A powerful healing potion, reportedly given to the Loremasters by Bariq the Wise.

Words of Radiance: A very powerful and dangerous kind of magic designed to pierce shields, Wardings, Forbiddings, and other protective barriers.

Yendis the Mother (*Yen'-dis*): One of the Powers of the Havalqa, Spouse of Metharog; also called the Nurturer. Yendis is the goddess of older women and women who have given birth.

Zaephos (*Zay'-fohs*): Name of the messenger of the Maker.